HELL'S GATE

Also by Richard E. Crabbe

Suspension
The Empire of Shadows

HELL'S GATE

Richard E. Crabbe

THOMAS DUNNE BOOKS
ST. MARTIN'S MINOTAUR NEW YORK

THOMAS DUNNE BOOKS.
An imprint of St. Martin's Press.

HELL'S GATE. Copyright © 2008 by Richard E. Crabbe. All rights reserved. Printed in the United States of America. For information, address St. Martin's Press, 175 Fifth Avenue, New York, N.Y. 10010.

www.thomasdunnebooks.com
www.minotaurbooks.com

Library of Congress Cataloging-in-Publication Data

Crabbe, Richard E.
    Hell's gate : a novel / Richard E. Crabbe.—1st ed.
        p.   cm.
    "Thomas Dunne Books."
    ISBN-13: 978-0-312-34159-6
    ISBN-10: 0-312-34159-8
    1. Police—New York (State)—New York—Fiction.   2. Street life—New York (State)—New York—Fiction.   3. Gangs—New York (State)—New York—Fiction. 4. New York (N.Y.)—Fiction.   I. Title.
    PS3553.R18H45   2008
    813'.54—dc22

                                                                        2008012280

First Edition: June 2008

10   9   8   7   6   5   4   3   2   1

For Chelsea

Acknowledgments

WITH GRATITUDE TO Peter Joseph, my editor, whose judgment and insight I have come to rely on. His emphasis on economy and pacing have shown me the error of my ways and made this a better book.

Thanks go to Richard Barber, my agent and friend. His unstinting generosity of time and effort have kept me from sudden death on publishing's minefield.

And to Kim, my wife, the anchor of my life and the sirocco of my dreams, I give my love.

I will not doubt, though sorrows fall like rain,
*   And troubles swarm like bees about a hive;*
*   I shall believe the heights for which I strive*
Are only reached by anguish and by pain;
*   And though I groan and tremble with my crosses*
*   I yet shall see, through my severest losses,*
*   The greater gain . . .*

—ELLA WHEELER WILCOX, *Faith*

HELL'S GATE

1

THE FLOATING BETHEL rolled on the oily, black waters of the East River, riding the swells of a passing steam tug. Its steeple sketched lazy arcs against the moonless sky like the needle of a compass, searching for true north. There was no sound save for the restless slap and swish of the river against barnacled hulls and pilings. The church windows were dark. The organ was silent. Any souls in need of saving would have to wait for the light of day.

Detective Mike Braddock wondered whose idea it had been to build a church on a barge in the East River. New York had no lack of churches and wouldn't seem to need another, especially not the floating sort. Still, the little church had bobbed on the river for many years now. The notion had been to bring a church to the seamen of the port, who notoriously shunned those inland, where finery trumped soul-saving most Sundays.

Mike glanced at the other officers in the steam launch, all men from the harbor police, the steamboat squad as it was called. All five of them were armed to the teeth. They were hard men, used to the cutthroat brand of criminals that worked the waterfront. Mike had insisted they be handpicked by their captain for this job. They were the best the squad had and they knew what they were about.

The police dock was watched, they'd told him. On moonless nights, when the gangs did their best work, there was always a watcher, ready to signal the comings and goings of the water cops. So tonight they'd headed upriver to throw any scouts off and had ducked in behind the Floating Bethel at the foot of Pike Street.

"We'll sit tight here for a time," the sergeant in charge of the squad said. "Stay outa sight an' be sure we weren't spotted."

Mike nodded. Though it had been his informant who'd tipped them, it was the steamboat squad who'd be running the show. Mike checked his watch. It was nearly one. Almost time. He watched as a big gray rat ran across the barge and up a hawser to the dock, where it disappeared behind a barrel. He could hear the squeak and scuttle of others. Where there was one to see, there were always at least three more hidden in the shadows. That was the way with rats regardless of how many legs they walked on.

The gang Mike was after was a last remnant of the Hookers, so-called for their territory around Corlears Hook, just up the river. They were getting more ambitious from what he'd been told and tonight they'd planned on looting a ship anchored just south of Governor's Island. Though Mike didn't usually concern himself with waterfront crime, this was a special case, a chance to grab the whole gang in the act, the kind of case that made a career.

Being the son of the legendary Thomas Braddock, captain of the Third Precinct, a man as appreciated for his facility at cracking skulls as cracking cases, did not provide a sure ticket to the top. In fact, the pressure had always been a notch higher, the expectations greater. He accepted that. He'd never asked for special treatment or plum assignments. Tom wouldn't have helped if he had and he definitely wouldn't have approved. Mike had wanted to earn his stripes on his own merit. He'd done well enough, rising through the ranks to detective sergeant in solid if unspectacular fashion. Still, he wanted more.

"Let's get moving," Mike said. The sergeant looked about one more time and nodded. They'd lain hidden for more than half an hour, enough time to throw off anyone who'd seen them leave the dock. The patrolman at the wheel threw a long, brass lever and the launch started to back out into the current. The propeller churned up the black waters. The stink of salt water and sewage rose off the river like a choking hand. The shoreline was dotted with open drains for miles upstream. Human waste, horseshit, brewery dregs, slaughterhouse effluence, and industrial wastes of every description drained in sluggish streams under the city. The river was the biggest sewer of all.

As they cleared the cover of the Floating Bethel, the men scanned the shoreline, searching for signal lamps in darkened windows. Once out in the river, the engine was reversed and the bow turned toward the harbor. They gathered speed, the heavy waters whispering behind, so that in minutes the steeple's outline was lost in the tangle of masts and hulls moored on the waterfront. One of the patrolmen threw a small shovel of coal into the boiler, lighting his face briefly. It was their only show of light, still, Mike wished they'd had one of the new naphtha-powered launches, which needed no stoking.

In a few minutes they were closing on Governor's Island, heading for Buttermilk Channel between the island and the Brooklyn waterfront. One by one the men checked their weapons. Rounds were chambered and safeties thumbed. Once they cleared the channel, they'd be exposed. There'd be no time to check weapons then.

The plan was to make a dash from the cover of the island and surprise the Hookers while still on the ship. Mike knew how often plans went wrong. Everyone aboard did. The Hookers had been close to impossible to catch in the past and even harder to hold. They'd fight if given the chance. With men in their ranks like Smilin' Jack O'Banion, Joey Bones, and a one-eyed thug known as the Oysterman, the Hookers were as hardened and vicious a collection of butchers as the city had ever seen. Mike's men were ready though. Two of them had model '97 Winchester pump shotguns. The short-barreled riot guns had six loads of buckshot, carrying nine .32 caliber balls to a load. The others were armed with standard-issue revolvers, but they all had at least one backup tucked in a waistband or pocket. Mike had his service revolver, but preferred a new Colt .38 auto. He kept the revolver as a backup. Though the automatic wasn't much good for anything beyond fifty feet, it could fire as fast as he could pull the trigger. He carried it in a holster under his left arm. Its bulk felt hot against his side, the leather holster damp with sweat.

They could see the ship, a big sidewheeler called the *Warrior Prince*. It swung at anchor, its bow pointing off toward the Statue of Liberty. The tide had turned an hour before and she was turning with it. They couldn't see anything, no activity, no other boats near. The cop at the helm throttled up for the dash across the open water. They'd decided to run flat-out, then cut the engine, and drift to the ship's side in silence. The wind picked up and the bow skipped through the water. They all crouched low as a mist of salt spray dashed over them. The engine thumped like a galloping horse. Mike found himself remembering another night fifteen years before, an age ago it seemed, when he was just sixteen and barely shaving. He, his father, and Mitchell Sabattis, the legendary Adirondack guide, had pursued a murderer for more than a hundred miles through lakes, rivers, and forest in the wildest reaches of upstate New York. On a moonless night, they'd rowed after him for miles up Long Lake, sweat and spray soaking them. That had been a chase for the ages. This little dash was nothing by comparison.

A hundred yards off and the engine went silent. Their momentum and the tide carried them in toward the hulking form of the steamer. The twin masts cut across the stars and the massive, rounded sidewheel housing loomed above their heads as they closed in.

"There," one of the men said in a hoarse whisper, pointing to a darkened space behind the sidewheel. A launch just slightly bigger than theirs lay in the shadows. They couldn't see if anyone was aboard. The sergeant tapped the patrolmen with the shotguns, pointing where he wanted their weapons trained; one on the launch, one on the ship's rail. They bumped against the side of the launch a few moments later. Mike held his .38 on it as two men clambered over the side. A few seconds later, the men waved an all clear.

"Up," the sergeant said and they began to rise. But at almost the same instant there was a commotion from above, muffled shouts and stamping feet. They all looked, turning their eyes toward the starry sky as a body came hurtling over the side. There was no cry, no sound at all except a laugh like the barking of a dog. There was no time to react, no place to go. The body crashed into them, a leg landing square across one man's back, the rest of the body striking with splintering force, then careening overboard, arms and legs at impossible angles. It splashed into the harbor and disappeared.

The patrolman was down, moaning in the bottom of the launch. A voice from up on the steamer said, "What da fuck? Hit our goddamn boat!"

Two heads appeared over the rail, black balls on hunched shoulders. The sergeant and another patrolman didn't see them. They were bent over their fallen man. Mike and the rest saw well enough, heard one of them curse, and for a moment they disappeared. "Up!" Mike shouted, but it was too late. In a burst of sound and light a hail of bullets rained down on them. Splinters flew off the deck and rails, lead pinged off the iron boiler. There was the unmistakable sound of bullets on flesh. Men dove and ducked for whatever cover they could find. Mike hid behind the boiler. An officer fell on him. Someone stomped on his hand and he almost lost his pistol. It seemed as though nobody was returning fire. The boat rocked. Curses and cries rang out. A shotgun

5

boomed. Mike got himself untangled as it fired again. He was looking up and saw a chunk of the ship's rail disintegrate in splinters. The firing stopped from above, though it was hard to tell as the steamboat squad fired blindly, those that were able.

"Now! Move!" Mike bellowed. He stood on the stern and grasped the sidewheel housing, pulling himself up, and setting his feet on the footholds built into it. One officer followed, two others climbed up the side. One man lay motionless in the launch. The sergeant groaned on his knees, trying to tie off a wound in his thigh. A pistol cracked from somewhere behind Mike as his head cleared the big ship's rail, throwing up splinters from the housing as he climbed. He turned and saw a dark form about twenty feet away on deck, saw a flash, felt a tug at his jacket. He brought the .38 around and snapped off three shots. He didn't know if he hit anything. He didn't stop climbing. A moment later, he dropped on the deck in a crouch. The officer hopped down at his side. There was a form sprawled on the deck just feet away, a black mass on the gray boards. Mike checked him. The top of the man's head was gone, from the eyes back to the ears.

"One of them," Mike said to the cop. "Shotgun."

The other patrolmen came over the rail. There was no more firing, just a ringing, black silence. There was no light aboard save for the distant glow from the city, which cast a tangled net of shadow from the masts, smokestack, rigging, lifeboats, and dozens of objects Mike couldn't identify. Mike signaled the men to go aft toward where he'd last seen the man who'd shot at him. With a twist of his head and a nod in the other direction, he went forward, the third officer close behind. They crept toward the bow, going from shadow to shadow. They were beside the massive structure of the walking beam engine when Mike kicked something soft and fell to one knee over a body. He put the Colt to the man's side as he pushed away. There was a groan.

"Who's that?" the officer said.

"Dunno." Mike looked closer. "One o' the crew maybe." He felt for the pulse at the man's neck, then went over the body, feeling for wounds, starting with the hands, wary that it might be one of the Hookers playing possum. "Blood," he said. "Don't think he's shot though." He shook the body and slapped the man's cheek. The eyes fluttered. "We're gonna get you some help," Mike whispered. "Can you hear me?" He got a nod and a grunt in reply. "How many of them? Where are they?"

"Fi-six," the man managed. "Fo'c'sle."

Mike didn't know a fo'c'sle from a main yard. He exchanged a look with the officer, who nodded toward the bow.

"Okay," he said. "We'll be back for you."

The ship had a raised forecastle, or fo'c'sle as the seamen called it. A companionway door led down into a deeper darkness. The door hung open. They crept to opposite sides, careful of the noise their hard shoes made on the wooden deck. Mike took a quick look down the stairs. Only the top three steps could be seen. The rest was too black to make out.

"Lemme go first," the officer whispered. "You don't know these ships like I do."

"What's down there?"

"Crew's quarters, mostly. Should be another door not far from the bottom. Careful. Steps're steep." The officer stepped into the door with Mike turning in just behind him. From the stern pistol shots cracked, followed by the booming of shotguns, coming so fast they were hard to separate. Mike turned and ducked. From somewhere in the blackness of the fo'c'sle companionway there came a rattling series of explosions. Mike could not tell how many shots there were or even if the patrolman had the chance to fire back. The deafening sound of the firing and the impact of the patrolman's body as it toppled back on him were almost indistinguishable events. He was knocked flat, his head hitting the deck. He thought at first that he must have been hit. A sickening panic swept over him as he felt a trickle of

7

blood on his face and his head went fuzzy. He tried to sort out what had happened, but things were moving far too fast for rational thought. There were shouts and feet pounding up the stairs, then more shots, throwing up splinters from the deck and jerking the body of the patrolman sprawled atop him. Twisting, Mike brought the Colt around, saw shadows appear in the doorway. He fired until there were no more bullets. The shadows disappeared with a tumbling crash down the companionway. Mike rolled from under the body, found his service revolver, and emptied it down the companionway, firing blindly.

Mike reloaded the Colt, dropping as many bullets as he managed to load into the magazine. The sound of running feet brought him around, but he held fire.

"It's us," one of the cops said. "We got the other one. Oh, Christ! Dickey! They shot Dickey!" the cop cried when he saw the body. The officer bent over his friend's corpse, which now had a spreading, black stain surrounding it, leaking into the joints of the teak and running in straight lines down the deck.

"Get outa there!" Mike shouted. "They're down there."

Without a word, the other officer fired into the companionway while the first dragged the body back. The patrolman reloaded while the other checked on the body.

"Oh, shit," Mike groaned. "Shit, shit, shit!"

"Two kids," the patrolman said. "Fuckin' . . ." He took up the shotgun he'd dropped when he moved the body, stepped to the companionway and started firing, letting loose three blasts before he stopped. "Body at the bottom o' the stairs," he said. "Saw it in the muzzle flash."

"There were two," Mike said. "Certain of it. You see anything else?"

"Nah."

Mike tried calling into the companionway. "Give it up! The rest're dead. Give up now an' we won't shoot." He didn't get a reply. "Any way a man could get outa here, through the ship?"

"Not sure," one of the patrolmen said. "Probably. These ships are all different. Coulda . . . got in the hold, engine room maybe. Big ship."

"We need light; some lanterns. I'm not going down there without one," Mike said. "None of us are." The shock was beginning to set in. This was only the second time he had used his pistol in the line of duty and his first experience with carnage like this. He had thought he'd be ready when it came. He did his best to keep his voice from trembling. "I'll find a lamp," he said.

"There's lamps in the boat," one reminded him. Mike didn't want to take the time to climb back down to the boat, but at the same time he knew that someone should check on the sergeant and the wounded patrolman. The thought of searching the ship alone wasn't very appealing either. He just grunted a reply and walked back down the deck. He found the seaman he'd stumbled over minutes before. The man was sitting up, propped against the rail, his head in his hands.

"Hey. Doin' better?" Mike said. He got a groan in reply. "We'll get you some help soon. Listen, I need a lamp. Where can I find a lamp?"

Without looking up, the man raised a hand, pointed toward the stern, mumbling something. The only words Mike caught were *aft hatch*. He went quickly, taking a detour to the rail and calling down to the sergeant.

"I'm shot in the leg," the sergeant called back. "Can't climb up. Purdy's pretty bad, too. Don't know. He's unconscious."

"Hang on," Mike called back. I think maybe we got 'em." He turned back to the deck with its maze of shadows and went where he thought an aft hatch should be. He saw a lantern hanging on a mast. He saw the hatch half open, its cover slid to one side. Mike crouched as a flash erupted from the hatch with the crack of a pistol. From somewhere to his left another barked. He felt a bullet pass his face as he rolled for cover. More shots followed and he saw a shadow emerging from the hatch, firing as it rose. Mike brought the Colt up. The Colt cracked three or four times, so fast he couldn't be sure. A shotgun boomed behind him, another pistol too. Hard shoes pounded the deck. The man in the hatch was down, hands hanging, motionless. More shots from the running patrolmen. Return fire from behind the mast. The Colt came 'round, banging and bucking so he wasn't sure where the shots were going. The slide clanged open when the last bullet left the muzzle. He reached for his revolver, but it was over.

Mike got up and approached the man in the hatch. With one foot he pushed at the body, keeping the revolver ready. He bent and grabbed a handful of hair, pulling the head back. It was the Oysterman, with a black hole where his left eye had been.

"This one's still alive," one of the patrolmen called, standing over the other body. Mike let the Oysterman's head bounce on the hatch. He straightened up quickly and as he did it seemed as if all the blood had run out of his head. His knees buckled and the deck started to spin. He took a step, but stumbled and fell to his knees. He didn't think he'd been shot, but now he wasn't so sure.

"You all right?" one cop called.

"Yeah," Mike heard himself say. "Tripped on somethin'." He shook his head and felt himself for any wounds. He took a couple of deep breaths and his head seemed to clear a little, enough so he set one foot on the deck and, after another pause, hauled himself to his feet. Tom had warned him that no amount of training could make this go away entirely. Though Mike had learned everything he could teach, Tom could never train away the shock of being shot at, or of taking a life.

Mike took another breath and made his way to where the cops stood. They both looked pale gray in the darkness and their eyes were as big as saucers. They were breathing hard and one grasped a length of rigging for support. Mike looked down at the man on the deck.

"Smilin' Jack," Mike grunted. Jack O'Banion had earned the nickname when he got fish-hooked in a brawl at a rat pit many years before. The scar curved up his cheek, pulling his lips into a ghastly semblance of a smile. Nobody ever called him Smilin' Jack to his face, nobody who wanted to live, but he was leaking all over the deck now and in no condition to do anything about it. Mike knelt beside him. He could hear the sucking chest wound bubble.

"You ain't got long, Jack," he said.

"Fuck you," Jack wheezed back, his hand coming up, darting toward Mike's side. Mike slapped it away, sending a knife skittering across the deck.

"You miserable shit!" Mike pulled his hand back and stood, looking at a stinging cut near the wrist. He shook the hand, flicking blood. "I'd fucking kill you for that if you weren't dead already, you piece o' shit!"

"Must be dead, I can't gut a half-cent pig like you."

Mike wrapped his hand in a kerchief, feeling the lightness return to his head as he did. He stepped back beside Smilin' Jack and stood on his hand.

"Agh, me hand! Get off, goddamn you!"

"Oh, is that your hand, Jack," Mike said without lifting his foot. "You won't need it where you're goin'." He ground down with his heel and O'Banion let out a gasp. He tried to punch at Mike's leg with the other arm, but he only flailed weakly. "Now, do yourself a favor before I cut you up so bad your own mother wouldn't know you. Where's that knife?" he said to one of the patrolmen.

"But—"

"But nothin'," Mike said with an icy look. "Get the fuckin' knife."

The man fetched it for him. Mike bent low over Jack, his face only a foot away. He put the tip of the blade under O'Banion's left eye. "Tell me who set this up? Who's getting a percentage?

11

I know this wasn't just you. One o' the fuckin' bosses are in on it, Jack. This ain't your style."

Jack said nothing. He closed that eye and tried to turn his head away. Mike poked the blade, drawing a small stream of blood from the lower lid. "This can be as painful as you like, Jack," he said.

"Don' cut," was all Jack managed. He was weakening as they watched, the eyelids beginning to flutter.

"Then who was it? Goddamn it, one fuckin' good deed before you die!" Smilin' Jack coughed, spraying blood, but Mike hardly flinched.

"Tell me an' you'll get a proper funeral, a big hearse an' everything, flowers, the works." He'd heard how vain Jack was and thought a good send-off might appeal to him. Apparently it did because O'Banion said one word before he passed. Half gasped, it was a word for sure, but Mike didn't get to ask its meaning. He stood, the knife loose in his bloodied hand, his hair wild, and his skin pasty white. The two patrolmen looked at each other. Mike almost told them that he hadn't been about to cut O'Banion's eye out, but he stopped himself. "Did he say *bottle* or was it *bottler*? Could have been boodle too, now that I think about it. Don't make sense, but that's what it sounded like to me."

"Bottler," one patrolman cut in. "Definite it was bottler, whatever the fuck that means."

"Bottle," the other patrolman said. "I heard bottle for sure. The rest was just him gurglin'."

Mike looked down on Smilin' Jack. "Never said a straight word in his life from what I hear. Why start now?" He looked around the shadowed deck. "C'mon, we've got work to do."

2

"THAT WAS WONDERFUL, Harry," Ginny said in her best dreamy voice. "You were so strong tonight. Have you been taking one of those tonics?"

Harry smiled as he put on his shoes, quite pleased with himself.

"Well, whatever it was, you just wore me out." She rolled over and got up on her knees, hugging Harry, if that was his true name, as he tied his laces. It was close to six A.M. and Ginny Caldwell wanted nothing more than to push this paunchy, pale banker out of her bed. But she knew her trade and what the house required. Harry turned and kissed her with an apprecia-tive, "Mmm."

"You'll be back next week, won't you?" she asked as if she'd be counting the days.

"Oh, I'll be back," he said. "Don't I always?"

He did. Ginny could have set a clock by him. She stroked his neck where it bulged over his collar. "You do," Ginny said with a forced, but convincing smile.

Harry left her a generous tip, though Ginny didn't count it till the door was closed. She smiled for real as she pushed the bills into a high-topped boot under her bed. It was getting full again. She'd have to stop at the bank this week and make an-other deposit. Ginny was one of the more popular girls in the house and the money was starting to add up. If she'd been work-ing for a pimp, or in one of the hundreds of low-class houses, she'd never have seen a tenth of the money she earned, but Miss Gertie was different, allowing her girls a healthier cut. Ginny figured she'd have nearly six hundred now and she'd only started saving a couple of months before. That was one thing she had Harry to thank for. The banker had given her some prudent ad-vice along with his greenbacks. For all of the year before that, ever since her family threw her out, she'd spent every dime, but not anymore. Clothes, hats, shoes, and a bowl of opium now and then had left her flamboyantly dressed, forgetful when she needed to be, and broke most of the time. Now she had some-thing put by, and maybe in another year or so, enough to open her own shop, not a whorehouse, but a proper shop.

She poured some water into a washbasin, soaped her hands clean, and splashed some water on her face, which she rubbed dry with a washcloth. She listened to Rachel in the next room, moaning like it was the best fuck of her life, which of course it was. Here every time was.

Ginny got dressed and went down the back stairs to the kitchen, where the two cooks worked constantly, supplying meals for the girls and their clients whenever they wanted. The smell of pancakes and maple syrup put her in mind of home. For a moment she imagined she was still a child and it was her mother who was clattering pans and plates, filling the house with wonderful smells. She was the last one up as always and her father and brothers were hunched over their plates already, eat-ing as if the cakes might walk off if they didn't hurry.

"Have a good fuck, Ginny? It was the banker, wasn't it? He likes the screamers."

Ginny blinked at the three girls around the big, plain table in the kitchen, all in various states of undress. Tousled hair, cig-arettes, and smudged makeup were the look of the morning. Ginny knew she didn't look much better.

"If he gave you the money he gives me you'd be screaming, too," she said. She grabbed a plate from a stack near the sink.

"Hard to get excited about that little thing of his," a girl named Eunice said. The other two agreed, laughing and slurping coffee.

"I've seen bigger pizzles on Chinamen," a girl said as she laughed.

"You haven't really, have you?" the third girl said with a look on her face like she'd swallowed something sour. Fucking a Chinaman was worse even than working in a black-and-tan or walking the streets. Only the shanty Irish seemed willing to marry them, and damned few at that.

"Figure of speakin'," the other replied with a dismissive wave of her cigarette.

There was a long moment of silence, punctuated by clattering plates in the sink. Ginny couldn't contain herself and finally burst out laughing, nearly spilling the coffee she was pouring. "It's true," she said. "I saw it in *The Farmer's Almanac*," which set off gales of laughter, and for a moment Ginny forgot her mother's kitchen.

"Where's that cop o' yours?" one of the girls asked when they had run down to giggles. "Haven't seen him 'round the last few days."

"Yeah. He was a real regular, too," Eunice said with a sideways glance at the others. "I've heard you with him. You sing a different tune when he's in your bed." She looked at Ginny with a narrowed eye. "Those're the worst, the good ones. Rip your heart out, you let 'em." The others went silent. Ginny shrugged as she buttered her pancakes.

"He's a sporting man," she said as the butter ran in little rivers off her pancake mountain. "A regular subscriber to the *Weekly Rake*, that one. He's like a dog that has to pee on every hydrant." She nodded toward one of the other girls. "He took you to the masked ball last year, right? And you've had him

15

more than once yourself, Eunice," Ginny pointed out. "We all have."

This was true, but for months now it had been only Ginny he'd asked for. He'd either wait for her or leave if she was otherwise engaged. They all knew it.

Rachel came down then, rubbing her ass, which was by popular consent the finest in the house. Nobody filled a bustle like her, a talent she'd made pay handsomely.

"Good God, I thought he'd never spend."

"I thought you sounded a bit off," Ginny said, happy to have a distraction from their uncomfortable topic.

Eunice got up with a concerned look. "Come have a rest. I'll get you some coffee," she said. She held a chair as Rachel eased into it then went about getting her coffee and a cinnamon roll. The girls watched her as they chatted. Eunice and Rachel were the only "real" Sapphos of the house. Though most of them had put on sapphic shows for private parties at one time or another, they were the only ones who seemed to enjoy it.

"He didn't hurt you, did he?" Eunice asked when she set the coffee and roll on the table. "I'll have him dusted up for you if you want." Eunice's brother was the bouncer and all-round insurer of the girls' well-being. He was as adept at splitting lips as he was at escorting the girls on the Ladies' Mile.

"Hell, no! Don't do that. Sonofabitch is my best customer," Rachel said, looking alarmed. "Don't you even say anything to Kevin, either. That gorilla would break his legs just for exercise."

Eunice calmed Rachel as Ginny's mind wandered. Her mother's kitchen had never been like this, though her brothers would have liked it a sight better than she did. To her it was now just business, not much different than swapping gossip over the counter at Wolke's General Store back home. The gossip had been very different, it was true. Sex was never mentioned except in whispers, winks, and giggles. Innocence and purity were the words she and her girlfriends had been supposed to live by. Sex

16

was something the beasts did in the barnyard and impure thoughts were rounded up every Sunday and drowned in a flood of "Hail Marys."

There were no Hail Marys in this house. The brothel was two houses really, adjoining brownstones on West Forty-fourth. They were run by a porcelain-skinned German woman that the girls all called Miss Gertie, though Ginny didn't think that was her real name. The story was that she'd come up in the trade in the 'eighties, working for the famous Mary Braddock in her houses in the West Twenties. They said that Gertie ran the house, but Mary still collected rent, an ultimately more profitable and far safer form of income, and not uncommon for the very few who'd managed to get out of the business with a whole skin. Miss Gertie, prosperous, full-figured, and respectably middle aged, ran the place as if she were its queen. She was solicitous of the girls, keeping them well fed and healthy. A doctor visited weekly and anyone who didn't care for herself or for her room was warned once, then shown the door if it continued. It was perhaps the finest house in the city, the girls elegant downstairs and wanton upstairs.

Ginny stopped her daydreaming when Kevin ambled into the kitchen, a copy of the *Trib* under one arm.

"Mornin,' ladies," he said on his way to the coffeepot. Some mornings Kevin looked even worse than the girls. Dealing with the sports could be a rough business, not that he had much trouble with the swells that made up most of their clientele. It was keeping the riffraff away from the door that could be a problem. Still, this morning he seemed almost fresh.

"No troubles, eh, Kev?" Eunice said.

"Nah. Easy night," he replied as he sat, slapping the paper down in front of him. He smiled at Ginny. He'd been sweet on her for months. Ginny smiled back absently. She'd always made him pay, not because he wasn't easy on the eye, but because there was no spark. He was good enough company though, and a man who knew how to work a woman's body for all that was in it.

17

She stared, suddenly riveted, not by Kevin, but by the *Trib*. She grabbed at it from across the table, spinning it around before her and snapping it open. TERRIBLE SHOOT-OUT IN THE HARBOR, the headline ran. HERO DETECTIVE THWARTS HOOKERS. ONE HARBOR PATROLMAN DEAD, TWO BADLY INJURED. Under the headline, which ran three columns, was a picture of the steamer *Warrior Prince*. Beside that was a photo of Mike Braddock.

"Hey," Eunice said, looking over her shoulder, "ain't that your cop?"

3

IT WAS LATE in the afternoon when Ginny heard that Mike Braddock was downstairs asking for her. She'd been asleep. She put on the white corset that she knew he liked, pushing up her breasts while checking herself in the mirror. Her best black stockings were snapped to the white garters and she threw a Chinese silk robe over her shoulders as she left her room, tying it loosely as she went down. It showed her legs almost up to the thigh. She didn't bother with panties.

As she went down the front stairs she imagined all sorts of things to say, but when she saw him and how he looked she abandoned them all.

"I read what happened," she said, putting her arm through his. "I want to know everything."

Mike just smiled and nodded. He'd told the story all night long and into the afternoon, to his captain, to reporters, to other detectives, and to the captain of the harbor patrol, who had wanted to hear it over and over again. This was the one place he knew he wouldn't be judged. It was Ginny's true talent, though she didn't seem to realize it. Hers was the ear of a priest without the moralizing, the worldliness of a bartender without the advice. She drew her robe closed as Mike followed her to her room.

"Do you want anything," she asked, "a drink or something?"

"No, thanks," Mike said as she closed her door behind them. "I can't stay too long," he added, not taking off his jacket as he usually did. He felt her arms come around him from behind, felt her breasts on his back and breath in his ear. She hugged him and kissed his neck.

"You stay as long as you like. I'm just glad you're here."

Mike turned around in her arms and buried his face in her hair, breathing in her scent. His hands didn't go to her ass as they always did. They encircled her, lingering at the small of her back. "Do you think I'm a hero?" he asked, pulling back so he could look into her eyes.

"The papers say so."

"The papers don't know shit," he said, breaking their embrace. He took off his jacket then and hung it on the back of the door. Ginny noticed for the first time that it was stained a deep red-brown on the sleeves and back. He unbuckled the shoulder holster and hung it too, the heavy Colt banging against the door. Mike shuffled to the bed and bounced on the edge, his legs seeming to give out. He started to take off his shoes, but couldn't seem to untie the laces, so Ginny took them off for him.

"It was a damn bloodbath. One patrolman dead, two more wounded. One's got a broken back. They don't know if he'll walk again."

"Did you break his back?" Ginny asked.

"No, of course not. A body came over the side. They were throwing it overboard. Landed right on us."

Ginny nodded. "The one who was killed, the other cop, what happened?" Mike told her about the shoot-out at the fo'c'sle, that he should have gone first down the dark gangway.

"But then you'd be dead," Ginny said without inflection.

"I should be dead," Mike answered. "I would be except for him. He wanted to go first. Said he knew those ships better than me."

"Did he?"

20

"Sure, I suppose. He was harbor police . . ."

"But heroes go first?"

"Yeah, damn it! They do," Mike almost shouted, standing in his socks, his hands in fists at his side. "And I'm no damn hero. Half the time I didn't know what the hell was going on. Fuckin' papers can say what they want, but they don't know."

Ginny walked over and sat down, patting the mattress for him to sit beside her.

"Who shot the man on the stairs?" she asked.

"Me, I guess. Didn't know what I was shooting at really. Too fast an' too dark."

"You shot them. And the others?"

"The Oysterman, I'm sure," Mike said, easing back on the bed, looking up at the ceiling as if the scenes were playing out up there. "Right in the eye. Smilin' Jack too, but him I'm not so sure. Maybe."

"They shot at you, right?"

"They missed, yeah. Don't know how, but they missed."

"You didn't miss," Ginny said, putting his feet in her lap. She massaged his toes and arches, kneading with practiced fingers.

"That's nice," Mike said. He closed his eyes and breathed deep. "Nice." She didn't say anything more, just watched his face as his eyes fluttered. He was asleep in minutes. Ginny set his feet on the bed and lay down beside him. She pulled close, ignoring the dirt and blood on his clothes and the stink of sweat from the night before. She lay on her side so she could watch his face while he slept.

Mike woke with a start, waking Ginny, too. "Damn. How long've I been asleep?"

Ginny looked at the clock. "Four hours, more or less. You needed it. I could see right away."

Mike grunted. "That's the first I've slept in near two days."

21

He sat up and rubbed his face, knuckling the sleep from his eyes. "All the questions, reports . . . everything. And the shoot-out playing over an' over in my head like one of those picture shows." He turned and kissed her cheek. "Thanks. How'd you do that, with the feet I mean? Like somebody switched off a light."

Ginny smiled, half in remembrance. "My mom used to do that for my father sometimes."

Mike nodded. He ran a hand up her thigh, parting her robe and pulling her close. "You never stop surprising me, Gin," he said as his hand cupped her ass. He grinned. "No panties. That's just what I mean." He lifted her robe. "And the white corset too. Mmm. You're too good to me." He bent to nuzzle her breasts where they spilled over the tight satin. Ginny sighed and threw a thigh over his, pulling him closer. She guided his hand just where she wanted it. Mike didn't object.

"I thought you couldn't stay long," Ginny teased in a breathless whisper a few minutes later.

"Mom's for dinner," Mike growled around her left nipple. "When I tell her why I'm late she'll understand."

Ginny landed a playful slap on his head. "You wouldn't!"

Mike grinned but said, "Nah, I guess not, but Dad sure would like to know."

She slapped at his head, harder this time. "You better not." She laughed, slapping at him with both hands now. "What would he think of his good little boy?"

Mike covered his head with a pillow and in a muffled voice said, "He'll think I'm a chip off the old block. My mom was a whore, too. Hell, they met when he arrested her," he said, laughing. The slapping stopped. Mike poked his head out. "I surrender," he said with an unsuspecting grin.

Ginny wasn't smiling. She looked at the clock as she pulled her robe closed. She seemed about to say something, but stopped herself with a visible effort. She slipped her feet into slippers that lay at the side of the bed. "You should get going then," she said after a deep breath. "You really shouldn't be late for your mother's dinner." She'd almost said, "Your whore's dinner," came so close to saying it she could taste the bitter words on her tongue.

Mike frowned but then agreed, "She is gonna be mad, I guess. She married a cop though, so she should be used to it."

Mike put his shoes on in silence as Ginny watched, her arms crossed over her closed robe.

"You all right, Gin?" he said as he got up. "Listen, I'm sorry I have to go, but you know how it is. I'll make it up to you."

Ginny just nodded. There was much she couldn't say. This was the life she'd chosen after all, the shackles that confined her. She had no right to blame Mike for naming her chains.

"Sure you will, Mike. I know," she found herself saying, "I had a mother once, too." She stopped, surprised at what had slipped through her teeth.

"Oh, Gin," Mike said in a guilty whisper. "I'm sorry. I didn't think. I can be so damn stupid sometimes." He stepped toward her. Ginny took a half step back before letting him hold her, her arms at her sides. "I'm sorry, Ginny. I know how you must miss her," he said with sudden feeling. Puzzled that she didn't hold him too, he tried holding her tighter, wishing he could make her pain go away. He knew about loss. He'd lost his whole family by the age of twelve, though not as she had. Hers was a voluntary loss, a casting aside, an abandonment by those she loved. That kind of loss might be even harder to stand, he figured. He'd been fortunate to be adopted by Tom and Mary those many years ago. Ginny, however, had no one. He felt her heart beating against his but this time it was more than just a muscle in a cage of bone. There were emotions now, coursing through them both in electric pathways long unused. Mike suddenly realized that he possessed the power to alter another's heart. There was deep responsibility in that; the weight of another heart. It was a weight he'd long been unwilling to bear.

Ginny let herself be held. She could tell that he cared, that his concern was genuine. Even if it was misdirected, it *was* true emotion. She consoled herself with that and rested her hand on his shoulder. Maybe it was better this way, she thought. Why let the truth come between them when a fiction was so much more palatable. He cared. In his own way he cared and that was enough for now. It had to be.

"We'll go to Tony Pastor's," Mike said. "That'll brighten you up. I told you I'd make it up to you. Tomorrow. We can catch an early show. Okay?"

Ginny nodded and forced a smile.

"It's a date then," Mike said. He hoped this would help, but looking at Ginny he doubted it. "We'll have fun."

"Sure," Ginny said with wary enthusiasm. "Sounds wonderful." She had never gone out with a customer before, though she hadn't thought of Mike precisely as a customer for some time. Mike gave her a kiss and pressed a twenty-dollar gold piece into her hand, at least double her usual rate.

"Tomorrow then," he said. Ginny stood silently as Mike closed the door behind him. The gold in her hand was heavy. It weighed her down. Her shoulders bent and at last the heavy coin dropped to the floor, where it bounced and spun as if it might never stop.

4

I HOPE YOU'VE got a good excuse," Tom said as he opened the front door for Mike. Brooklyn Heights were quiet in the evening. Tom had heard Mike's shoes tapping out a double-time pace from half a block away. Tom closed the oak door behind them. He was half a head taller than Mike, broader across the shoulders, too. Though he was now sixty, he still sported a full head of hair, mostly gray except on top. His mustache was gray too, though his eyebrows were still a shade darker. Mike wasn't fooled by the gray. There was no stoop to Tom's shoulders, no paunch straining his belt. He still lifted weights twice a week at a German *Turnhalle* on the East Side and spent nearly an hour a day practicing the kung fu he'd learned from Master Kwan many years before. He'd taught Mike all he'd learned and they often sparred in the back courtyard or in the basement on rainy days. Though Mike was quicker and more agile, Tom was far more powerful. Despite his age, he could still take everything Mike could throw.

"Had to see that patrolman," Mike said, taking off his jacket. "The doctors say he might not walk. They got him in a cast like an Egyptian mummy or something. Poor bastard never really knew what hit him."

"Pretty good story. I'd stick with it if I was you, but only after

I wiped the lipstick off my neck," Tom said with a frown that had a tinge of mirth in it.

Mike gave a quick swipe. "I get it?" he asked, his color rising a little.

"More to the left," Tom said. "Yeah, that's it."

Mike shrugged and gave his father a guilty grin.

"Glad to see that the other night's activities haven't gotten you down," Tom said. "A good thing taking a couple o' days off. That kind of action can get a man's head all in knots."

Mike didn't really want to get into that with Tom, didn't want to admit that he was anything less than stoic and as strong as he imagined Tom would be. "I guess so," he admitted. "I want to follow up on that lead though and the longer I have to wait, the colder it's likely to get."

Tom was about to reply when Mary called from the back of the house. "You two going to come in or do I have to set up a table in the foyer?"

"Keep your stockings on, Ma! We're coming," Tom called back. Mike had noticed that Tom had started calling Mary Ma from time to time lately. It was cute, he thought. Still he had a hard time matching it to his vision of his parents.

They walked down the wide center hall with its white marble floor and mahogany staircase. They passed the parlor on the left, the library with its pocket doors on the right. The place was almost a mansion and much more than a captain's pay alone could support. The carpets were thick, the wallpaper expensive, the furniture, draperies, lamps, and paintings spoke of money and the taste to spend it well. For the last year Mary had developed an infatuation for the new electric lamps made by Tiffany. There were three in the parlor, one in the library, and more in the bedrooms. They filled the house with splashes of color like little electric gardens.

Mary appeared through the swinging kitchen doors just as

Tom and Mike entered the dining room. She shook her head at Mike as she put down a tureen of soup.

"Mike, I swear I can never decide whether to kick you or hug you. Where have you been?" Mike gave her the official story, which Mary seemed to accept.

"And how *are* you?" she asked, looking at him closely, noticing the dirt and dried blood on his jacket, but holding a scolding tongue. "You look tired," was all she said.

Mike shrugged. "Haven't slept all that well."

"You keep thinking of all the things you should have done differently," Tom broke in. "All the mistakes you think you made. Doesn't matter if you did or not. You always think it could've gone better."

"Yeah. And maybe it could have and maybe not." Mary gave him a hug. "But the reports say it was a success and that's what people will remember. You try and remember that too. Okay?"

Mike smiled at her, appreciative as always of her concern and common sense. It suddenly came to him that Ginny had told him almost the same thing.

Mary was still a beautiful woman. Like Tom she had aged well. Although the wrinkles at the corners of her eyes and around her mouth were deeper now, they took nothing away. In fact, they added a certain gravity to her face. She still had those high cheekbones, full lips, and long, black hair, though that was now streaked with gray. She wore it up in a chignon with a silk ribbon for good measure. She'd always been beautiful, but now Mike thought he'd have to add "dignified" to her description.

"So, what's this lead you were talking about?" Tom asked.

Mike told him about Smilin' Jack's last word.

"Hmm. Bottle Alley's the first thing comes to mind, of course," Tom said. "But I guess it did to you, too."

Mike nodded. "But that's way out of the Hookers' territory."

"Yeah, I know. That's the Five Pointers' stomping ground.

You've considered all the dance halls and bars with *bottle* in their name? There's a few I can think of on the East Side. That's where to start."

"Yeah, I thought so, too. Concentrate on the East Side. Try and poke around a bit, ask a few questions an' see what I can flush out."

"Take somebody to watch your back," Tom said. It was good advice and something Mike hadn't given a lot of thought to. He was considering that when Mary returned with a big platter of ham in a mist of brown sugar and cloves. Although they had a cook, Mary liked to set and serve. She sat and Tom took up a big knife with a stag handle and started to carve.

"How's Becca?" Mike asked. He hadn't seen his sister in weeks. Their schedules had them both working nights.

"She's having the time of her life," Mary said. "She's up for a leading role for the fall season. She says this time she thinks she'll get it."

Rebecca had been acting and dancing for two years professionally and her efforts were starting to bring her some recognition. She'd played in the Bowery theaters early on as most everyone did, working as a chorus girl for about twenty dollars a week. But she'd moved up quickly to places like Pastor's, where the crowd was a bit more refined and less inclined to throw things at performers they didn't like.

"That David Belasco fellow is planning a new production," Mary went on. "If Becca gets the role, she'll actually be on Broadway."

"I've been meaning to catch her show," Mike said, "but it's been tough to break away." She'd been doing *A Midsummer Night's Dream* at the Academy of Arts, next door to Tammany Hall lately, playing two minor roles and about a dozen lines per show. Mike wasn't much of a fan of the Bard. He didn't like to admit that he didn't understand most of it. The language never appealed to him, although he did like the murders. Shakespeare's plays seemed to have plenty of them.

"Well, at least phone her," Mary said. "She tells me you two haven't talked in ages." Mike was about to make excuses, but a glance from Tom shut him up.

"Guilty," Mike said, holding up his hands in surrender. "I'll call." He looked from Tom to Mary. Neither seemed convinced. "Really," he said. "Promise."

"Good," Tom said with finality. "Let's eat." Mary passed the platter of ham, followed by sweet potatoes and corn. Mike and Tom dug in. "Got something to show you later," Tom said around a mouthful of ham.

"Yeah? What is it? A new pistol?" Mike guessed. Tom had bought many over the years.

"Nope," Tom said with a conspiratorial look at Mary, who let just a flicker of a smile play across her mouth before shrugging her shoulders. She wasn't about to spill the secret, which made Mike all the more intrigued.

"Okay, youse got me goin'," Mike said, letting a bit of the Bowery slip across his tongue. It was hard not to. Half the city spoke in "dese, dems', and dose," and it was the half that he had to deal with every day.

"Speaking of pistols," Tom said, "How'd that new Colt work out?"

"Saved my skin. It's damn fast! Gotta do more rapid-fire practice though. Recoil has it jumping all over. Can't hold on target if you're in a hurry."

Tom nodded. "That's what I heard about those automatic pistols. Takes some getting used to. We can go tomorrow if you want, shoot up some targets."

"Sure," Mike said, doing a quick mental calculation of the time he'd have to allow to meet Ginny and get to Pastor's. Tom must have sensed Mike's hesitation. "Got something goin'?"

"Just going to Pastor's," Mike said, knowing as soon as he said it that he shouldn't have. He hadn't intended to tell them about Ginny. He liked to keep that side of his life quiet. It was a lot easier that way. He knew that neither Tom nor Mary approved. They had no right to actively disapprove, considering how Mary had made her fortune all those years. Tom had been no saint either, so mostly they held their tongues when it came to Mike's peccadilloes.

"Who are you taking?" Mary asked, knowing that Mike would never go to Pastor's with any of his male friends.

"Just a girl. You wouldn't know her."

Tom and Mary exchanged looks. "It's Ginny Caldwell, isn't it?" Mary said. Mike's mouth fell open, but he closed it quickly enough. He didn't ask how they knew. It would only extend a discussion he didn't want to have. They'd been over this ground before, had trodden it down until their arguments were packed beneath their feet, solid as bedrock.

"Yeah," was all he said. If anybody was going to say more it wasn't going to be him. Mary smiled, but sighed. "I know a little about her," she said. "From Long Island, right?" He nodded.

"Listen," Tom said. "Nobody knows the, ah . . . temptations of this city better than me. Being a bachelor in New York is like being a kid in a candy shop." This drew a frown from Mary, but she couldn't disagree. Hers had been one of the biggest candy shops in the city. "But to find the woman of your dreams that way, like I did," he admitted with a warm smile to Mary. "Well, that's a rare thing. Very rare."

Mike knew Tom was right, but he'd never admit it. Still, when he spoke it was to say, "People find each other in all sorts of way, Dad. Who's to say a factory girl is better, or a shop girl, or a chorus girl. They're just girls. My way's a lot less complicated. I know what I'm getting and what I'm not. This way I can know a girl better than I probably ever would before we got married. And what if then I didn't like it, or she didn't? Suppose we didn't get along . . . in that way? You know I may be paying for companionship," he almost used the word *whoring* but had always avoided the word in Mary's company, "but when I do stick

30

with one girl, that'll be it." He wondered if he could actually fulfill that pledge if it ever came to it.

Mary smiled, but her eyes still held a tinge of worry. "Good. I'm glad to hear you say that," she said with a nod to Tom. "We just want the best for you."

"Always have," Tom added. He smiled at Mary. This was the first time Mike had expressed interest in a woman in years. Tom felt like he should propose a toast, break out some cigars or something. Instead he grinned into his soup bowl, watching Mike from the corner of his eye.

An hour passed. Dinner was done, dessert served. The three of them sat back while the cook cleared the remains of the meal. Tom poured some port for Mary and himself, but Mike begged off. "It'll put me to sleep," he said.

"Which reminds me," Tom said, putting down his glass. "I've got that surprise. Ought to keep you from nodding off."

Mike glanced at Mary for any clues, but she said nothing. A cryptic smile was all he got.

"Lead on, Captain!" Mike said, hauling himself to his feet. "I'm all on fire to see this, whatever it is. Ma sitting there like the sphinx. Lotta help she is."

Mary put up her hands. "I didn't say a word."

"Exactly," he groused.

Mike followed Tom out the front door. They took a left toward Montague Street. After going half a block Mike said, "Guess it's not a new pistol."

Tom smiled. "Nope. Not a new pistol."

They continued past Montague, angling down the Heights toward the harbor. Another two blocks went by before Tom stopped in front of the large, double doors of a stable.

"Oh. You got that new trap you were talking about, didn't you?"

31

Tom shrugged. "You'll see."

"New horse, too?" Mike said, sensing there was more. Tom said nothing. He went to the office door off to one side of the building and walked in. A stableman sat behind a well-worn desk, his feet propped on top and his chair leaning back at a precarious angle. He roused when he heard the door, but didn't change position. "Evenin', Mista Braddock," the man said. "Come to show her off?" He seemed about to say more, but a warning look from Tom shut him up. "Oh, I get it. A surprise, huh?"

"Right, Nick. She back where I left her?" Tom asked.

"Sure thing, Mista Braddock. I don' let nobody so much as breathe on that baby."

Tom and Mike walked into the semidarkness of the stable. The pungent smells of leather, horseflesh, and manure enveloping them like a fog. There were only two lights in the place, big, bare bulbs hanging on long wires from the ceiling. They walked past carriages parked on the left and horse stalls on the right. There were rigs of all descriptions, tall, open shays, black barouches, gleaming with varnish, a buckboard or two, and finally a little red Oldsmobile. Tom stopped before it. He looked at Mike with a wolfish grin. "Like it?"

"Whoa! I can't believe you got one. When'd you get it?" Mike said as he looked the car over.

"They delivered it yesterday. Man came out from the factory, all the way from Lansing, Michigan, to show me how to drive it, do the maintenance, that sort of thing. Nice fella."

The Olds gleamed. It was bright red with yellow pinstriping. *Oldsmobile* was painted in gold script on the side. The tires were white and the wheels were wire, like a bicycle's, only wider. The seat was high and good for two, three in a real pinch. In front there was a curved dashboard, much like a sleigh's except a bit lower. For steering there was a curved brass tiller, gleaming in the electric light. "Motor's under the seat," Tom said. "Single cylinder, seven horsepower."

"Seven horsepower! For this little car. Must go like the devil."

"Factory says to break it in a bit," Tom replied while climbing up onto the leather bench seat. "I haven't driven it much yet, but they're supposed to do a good thirty miles per hour once you get 'er up to speed."

Ever since the year before when two men in an '03 Marmon had driven across the country, Tom had dreamt about owning an automobile. He couldn't justify spending more than $2,000 for one of the big Packards or Marmons, a sum only a wealthy man or a true spendthrift would consider. But when an Oldsmobile made the trip from San Francisco to New York just a few weeks after the Marmon, Tom figured that was the car for him. Much smaller than the Packards, Marmons, or Stanleys, the Oldsmobile was also only $650 dollars, expensive enough, but not extravagant. It was perfect for him and Mary, as stylish in its way as any coach-and-four and far more modern.

"How d'you start the thing?" Mike asked as he looked over the various levers. "Crank start, right?"

"Yeah," Tom said. "Over on the side. You give it a couple of good turns and it starts right up. Of course, the driver has to set the clutch and spark and activate the speeder. It's a little complicated." Tom showed Mike how the crank was inserted and the starting sequence. "Only takes about twenty seconds once you get the hang of it, leastwise that's what the factory fella said. Takes me more like a minute or so."

"Let's give 'er a go! Whadya say?"

Tom shook his head with a wry twist of his mouth. "Can't start her up in here. Scares the horses. I gotta have them push it out."

"That's okay. We can push it. What's it weigh? Not much I'd guess."

"'Bout seven hundred pounds," Tom said. "But I think we should be getting back anyway. Ma'll start to worry."

"Nah," Mike said, checking his watch. "We've only been gone a half hour." He was dying to get behind the tiller.

"Really?" Tom kicked one of the tires. "Truth is, I'm a little leery of taking her out at night. Don't feel sure enough at the tiller. Hell, I only drove the thing once yesterday. Give me a week to practice, really get the hang of it. Then we'll go for a good long ride, out to Prospect Park or something, race the El up Second Avenue, have some fun."

Mike hesitated. He'd wanted to go roaring off into the night. He looked at his father in the dim light of the overhead bulbs, suddenly noticing how the shadows made his eyes seem hollow, the creases in his face like a road map. His hair in that light looked thin and wispy and entirely gray. There had been a time when Tom wouldn't have given it a second thought either, would have been like a boy with a new puppy. It was as if he'd aged years in the space of an evening.

Tom picked up on Mike's look, but then gave him a wicked grin and the old Tom was back, the man who'd stood his ground at Gettysburg and the Wilderness, and still had a hard reputation on the force.

"I hear the ladies like a man in a sporty automobile," he said.

Mike smiled. "That so?"

"That's what I hear." Tom put his arm around Mike's shoulder. Mike could feel the strength in it as they turned to go. "Maybe I'll give you some lessons, let you take that Ginny Caldwell out for a drive."

Mike had a sudden image of Ginny, the salty breeze of Coney Island pulling bright strands of hair from under her bonnet, the glow of the summer sun on her skin.

"Don't sound bad," Mike said, trying not to sound like a kid on Christmas Eve.

5

THE CABLES OF the Brooklyn Bridge sliced by Mike's window as the train rumbled toward Manhattan. He sat on one of the oversprung wicker seats, staring out at the city. The East River was a black void below, reminding him of what he'd faced two nights before. He'd managed to forget for a while, but now it was back, replaying behind his eyes. The cables framed the images, so they seemed to pass just beyond the glass, suspended, flickering in space. Mike's jaw tightened and the wound on his wrist throbbed. As the images winked by he tried to alter them, tried to bend the bullets' paths, or back up time and relive a decisive moment. Sometimes it worked, mostly not.

"Bottle," Mike said in a whisper. He looked at his watch. It was only nine. As the train crept to a stop in the Manhattan terminal of the bridge, Mike got up and waited anxiously at the door.

He caught the Second Avenue El, running as the doors closed. He only went two stops. Once he was back on the street, he checked his pistol. Turning into a darkened storefront, he jacked a round into the chamber. He eased the hammer down and set the safety, sliding it back into the holster under his arm.

He patted his vest pocket for his extra clip, then set off on Canal Street, toward Corlears Hook.

Mike worked his way through the jumbled sidewalks of Jefferson, Henry, Madison, and Clinton streets, where the gutters were choked with manure and the stink of outhouses, abattoirs, beer halls, and rotting produce. This was the Eastman's territory, Monk Eastman's old gang, ruled now by Kid Twist, who had taken over after Monk went to Sing Sing just a few months before. The gang, nearly a thousand strong, ruled everything from the Bowery east to the river and north to Fourteenth. The Hookers had paid tribute to them, as did a number of other specialized gangs in the area. There was grim satisfaction in the fact that the Hookers wouldn't be paying anymore.

Mike knew it was a chancey thing to go poking about these streets, especially at night. He pulled his bowler low, keeping a wary eye for any who might recognize him. The night was warm and the streets were full. Pianos tinkled through open saloon doors. Prostitutes in twos and threes jostled men off the sidewalks, sometimes pulling them into tenement doorways. Groups of boys prowled for pockets to pick or drunks to overpower. Sailors, oystermen, dockworkers, factory men, and gangsters mixed.

A uniform caught Mike's eye at the corner of East Broadway and Clinton. It took a hearty patrolman to walk these streets alone. The uniform was a target, particularly to gangsters looking to make a name for themselves. More likely the cop was on the Eastmans' payroll and enjoyed some small measure of immunity, so long as he didn't interfere too much in gang affairs. Mike approached him cautiously. He identified himself as the officer looked him up and down.

"You're Braddock's son, eh?"

"Yeah."

"I heard about him," the man said without inflection. "Ain't heard o' you."

Mike looked at the man directly, not sure what to make of that. He shrugged and replied, "Ain't heard o' you either. So what?"

"What you doin' here?" the patrolman asked, not rising to the bait.

"Looking for a saloon, dance hall, or something like that. A place with *bottle* in the name."

"Huh?"

Mike paused and tried a different tack. "Know any places called *bottle*-something, like Brown Bottle, or Broken Bottle, you know, like that?"

"Sure," the patrolman said. "What you want with places like that? The ones 'round here is all dives; rotgut whiskey, watered beer, and used-up women."

"Sounds like fun."

The cop didn't crack a smile. "Listen," he said, stepping closer. "Watch yerself 'round here. The whores'll pick yer pockets or put knockout drops in yer beer. The gangsters'll stick a knife in yer ribs for a couple dollars. Don' make me come mop you up when its over." He waited for some sign of hesitation from Mike, but saw none. He shook his head. "There's a Blue Bottle over on Montgomery, near Cherry, a place everybody calls the Bottleneck, right down here on Clinton, near Water. Them two are okay if you're careful. Then there's Jimmy's Broken Bottle. That one's full o' Eastmans this time o' night. Kind of a saloon with whores upstairs. That place I wouldn't go within a block. Knock yer head in for sport they will. Take my advice an' stay clear."

"What," Mike said. "No tablecloths?"

"Oh, yer a funny one now. Regular laughin' corpse."

"Thanks," Mike said and meant it. "But I've got sand enough." He turned to go but the patrolman said, "Maybe, but don' think even yer father's got that kinda sand."

37

"Tom's got guts enough for both of us," Mike said as he walked away.

Jimmy's Broken Bottle was in the cellar of an old, wooden row house on Cherry, near Jackson. The windows sagged in the upper three floors. The walls bulged and bowed to such a degree that the clapboards were popping off. The building seemed it would tumble into the street except for the tenements on either side propping it up. A bile green coat of peeling paint gave the place a leprous look.

Three thugs leaned against the iron railing beside the front steps. Bowlers pulled low, they watched Mike from across the street. Their rough conversation stopped as he approached.

"Hey, fellas," Mike said, adding just a bit of an alcoholic slur to his voice and a wobble to his gait. "How's da beer?"

"Wet," one of them said. The others laughed. Mike laughed, too.

"Just how I like it," Mike said as he started down the darkened front stairs.

"Watch yer step," one of the men said.

Mike noticed the glass first. The dirt floor seemed to be covered in it, crunching under his shoes as he walked. The near silence was what he noticed second. Despite the fact that the saloon was close to full, it was as quiet as a Protestant wake. The only sound was an odd sort of music coming from the back beside a tiny stage, not much bigger than a couple of tables put together, which was probably what it was. On the stage were two women, stark naked. They danced and intertwined, their movements liquid, flowing in a stream of sexual suggestion. Hips gyrated and hands ran over each other's bodies. Mike stood still, watching. The gaslight flickered over the crowd of men. They seemed to hunch forward, straining. Mike realized, once his eyes became accustomed to the gloom and smoke that the women weren't naked, but wore flesh-colored tights. Neither was handsome or even pretty, yet they cast a powerful spell over the room.

The music was part of it. A clarinet and a single drum played something that was part snake charmer's melody and part funeral dirge. The drummer gradually quickened the pace as Mike watched. The dancers were close. Thighs and hips ground together as hands went to breasts and buttocks. They writhed in a choreographed frenzy that lasted only half a minute or so before the music stopped and the light that had been on them was suddenly extinguished. The place erupted. The men jumped to their feet and bottles were smashed on the floor or against the brick walls, even against the ceiling. The men bellowed and clapped and stomped their feet until the lights went up and the two women, glistening with sweat took a quick bow, and darted into a back room. A door shut behind them and a huge man with a brass-studded cudgel rolled before it like a boulder before a cave.

Mike pushed up to the bar, a couple of rough, wide planks atop a row of barrels. He managed to get a beer amid the crush of suddenly thirsty men. They were an unwashed lot, most of them, except for the occasional gangster dandy in bright colors and pomaded hair. Their finery couldn't disguise the hooded eye, the scars, the back-alley clip of the tongue. One such up-and-comer pushed up beside Mike and ordered a gin.

"Pretty good show," Mike said, nodding toward the empty stage.

"Yeah, dey get da boys all hot to trot," he said as he cast a darting eye over Mike. "Foist time? Ain't seen ya befaw."

"First time here, yeah," Mike said over his beer. "Lookin' fer somebody." He added a slight leavening of the Bowery to his speech, though he never did feel comfortable saying things like *foist*. "Trouble is, I ain't sure who 'e is."

The dandy got his gin and took a long, slow pull at it, as if he hadn't heard Mike. He gave a small shiver as it went down. His hand had an alcoholic tremor.

"Fuckin good, dis stuff!" He tapped the glass on the bar for another, and turned to Mike, saying "Dis guy youse lookin' faw, 'e got a moniker?"

"Don' know it," Mike said. He lowered his voice. "Was talkin' ta Smilin' Jack last week. Had a job we was plannin'. Jack, he gets on the phone, see . . . you know ta check with whoever 'es gotta check wit', an' I hear 'im say somethin' 'bout *bottle*, like a place or a name or somethin'. So I figure now that Jack's gone . . . rest in peace, dat the thing fer me is ta check aroun', see if I can see what's what."

"Hmm," the dandy said. "Shame 'bout Jack. How ya know 'im?"

"From da neighborhood," Mike said, smiling. "Da one wit' dar bars on Blackwell's Island. We were on vacation together." They chuckled over that. "Listen, I wanna make sure I got an okay on dis. Don' wanna do a job an' find out later the Kid or somebody's got a piece. Dat kinda trouble I don' need. Never been one ta step on toes, ya get my meanin'."

The gangster nodded and frowned. "Smart," he said. "I'm Mickey Todt." Mike nodded and stuck out his hand. "Arnie Beanstock," he said, using the first name that came into his head. Arnie ran the soda shop down the block from his apartment. "Mickey Death? Interesting name."

"Know yer German, huh? Da boys call me dat. Stolzenthaler's my real name. Too big fer dem mugs. After I done da big one a coupla times, dey started callin' me Todt 'cause o' me being German. To dem it's more like *Toad*, but what da fuck."

"They jus' call me Beansie," Mike said. "So, you got any ideas on my problem? I gotta get on dis job. It ain't gonna be good a couple weeks from now, ya get me?"

"Yeah, I get it, I get it. Lemme do some askin' around, maybe give da Kid a call, see what he says. See if he knows anything 'bout any job Jack was plannin'." Another gin slid down Mickey's throat. He gave a small sigh as it spread out. "Don' suppose you'd like ta tell me what da job is, huh?"

Mike smiled, but shook his head. "I'll tell ya dis," Mike said, feeling he had to give up a little information to seem credible, "dere's a ship comin' in soon's got a big cargo. Me an' Jack had some inside information on it. You'll know more when you find me da guy. You get me dat an' maybe then we talk gelt, huh?"

"Gelt. A subject neah an' deah to my heart. I guess if Smilin' Jack was good wit' it den it's a sweet job. He always had an eye for that kinda thing, exceptin' fer dat last job.

"You come see me tomorrow night, see. Maybe I got somethin' by den, maybe not."

"Right," Mike said. "Can't ask fer more'n dat. See ya then."

As Mike walked away from Jimmy's Broken Bottle he couldn't shake the feeling that his promising start had come too easily. He put the idea out of his head though, figuring that Smilin' Jack was such a well-known character in the neighborhood that he'd have been able to get something out of most any man in the place. Still, he stopped to loiter once or twice, watching for anyone following.

It was getting late and the street traffic had dwindled to a trickle. The whores outnumbered the pedestrians and he was propositioned five times in two blocks. One group of three, the youngest no more than twelve, the oldest maybe sixteen, blocked his way near the corner of Cherry and Governeur. It was an old hustle. If they couldn't get him to pay for sex, they'd paw at him until they had every dime in his pockets. Mike put his wallet in an inside jacket pocket as they closed in. Gaudy makeup, cheap perfume, and mismatched colors surrounded him. An arm went around his neck and a hand went in his pocket. He didn't realize it wasn't one of the girls until he saw the man in front of him with the length of lead pipe. The girls ran, laughing. The arm tightened from behind as he started to struggle. The pipe flew toward his head. The best he could do

41

was to duck forward. He was hit, but it wasn't as bad as he'd expected and there was a grunt of pain from the man behind him. The arm loosened. Mike kicked at the attacker in front, cracking him solidly in the knee. His hand found the butt of the Colt. He didn't bother to pull it out of the holster. He thumbed the hammer and pulled the trigger as he tipped the muzzle behind him. Muffled by his jacket, the shot wasn't very loud. The arm around his neck disappeared. He whipped the pistol out as the one with the pipe came again, swinging. Mike crouched and fired as the pipe passed above his head. The man cried out and staggered back, then collapsed, holding his leg. Mike spun about, still in a crouch as the man screamed, high-pitched and frantic. "You shot me! You shot me, you fuck!"

The other man was running away, bent over, holding his side. It looked like Mickey Todt, but Mike couldn't be certain. "We wasn't gonna hurt ya," the other screamed. "Oh, Christ, my fuckin' leg. Oh, Christ."

Mike turned back to him. The leg was at an odd angle and deep red blood was pouring from the wound.

"Empty your pockets!" Mike shouted at him.

"I didn' mean it. Wasn't gonna hurt ya, damn it. Why'd ya shoot me?"

"I'll shoot you again, you don't empty your fuckin' pockets now!" He kicked the pipe away as the man did what he was told. "That was Mickey Todt," Mike said more than asked.

"Tol' me you was the cop killed Smilin' Jack. Had yer picture from the papers. Oh, shit my leg hurts, you fuckin' bastard." A knife came out of one pocket, a pair of spiked brass knuckles from another.

"All of it," Mike said. He glanced up and down the street. The whores watched from a distance, shouting something about filthy cops. A scattering of men, gangsters mostly, some in small groups, some alone, lurked at a distance like scavengers at a kill. There were no lights in windows, no crowds of citizens gathering, no police whistles as there might be in other parts of the city. People here were too afraid of the gangs to even be seen watching.

Mike bent over the man, looking closely at the wound. There was a great deal of blood. "Hit the artery," he said. "Gimme your belt. Hurry before you bleed to death!" The man fumbled at the buckle and Mike pulled it off. He went to work fast, wrapping the belt around the upper thigh and cinching it through the buckle. "Hold this tight." The man did what he was told, gritting his teeth behind blue lips. "Quick now. What's yer name and whadya know about the bottle?"

"Youse know about the Bottler?" the man groaned through his teeth.

"The Bottler?" Mike said, glancing again up and down the block. "It's a person, a man?"

"Fuck, I dunno," the gangster said. "My fuckin' leg's broke. I'm fuckin' crippled, you bastard. Crippled, see!" Even in the dark he looked ghastly pale. Though the tourniquet helped, he was still bleeding out. Mike saw he didn't have much time. "Keep that goddamn belt tight," Mike said, "or you'll be a dead cripple. I'm goin' to get help." He surveyed the street again, Colt still in his hand. "Be back in a couple minutes." He spotted the prostitutes in a doorway across the street. "Keep an eye on this man," he called. "There's money in it for you if he's alive when I get back." Mike stood to go, but the man grabbed his leg. "Shit! Don' leave me," he said, his eyes wide with fear. "Don' go!" Mike turned and trotted off in the direction he'd last seen the patrolman. The gangster's shouts followed. "Don' leave you bastard! Wait! Wait!" When Mike didn't stop, his wails changed. "Fuckin' copper! Shoulda bashed yer head in good! Somebody shoot the fuck! Shoot 'im! Kill the fucker!"

He'd only gone a block and a half when he saw the cop near the next corner. He was walking with purpose, but in no great hurry.

"You the cause o' them shots?" he asked when they met in the middle of the block.

"Yeah. Got jumped. C'mon, I need a hand with one o' them." Mike turned to jog back, but the cop did nothing to quicken his pace. Still, it didn't take more than a few minutes to make it back. But as they rounded the corner they were brought up short. Governeur Street was empty. Not a window or doorway showed a light. Not a soul could be seen. In the block beyond, they could see a wagon moving, hookers working the street, people passing. On Governeur Street, the watching windows stood silent and empty. Even the streetlamps seemed dimmed. A chill ran down Mike's sweating back. The feeling of being watched was overpowering. As he and the patrolman worked their way down the street, going doorway to doorway, it became clear that even Mike's attacker had vanished. A pool of blood was all that was left.

"Take a look at this," Mike said as he bent over the scene. There were footprints in the blood. One was his, but there were more, two others at least. They led off a few feet to the center of the street, then vanished. "We'll need help. We gotta search for him."

"You outa your fuckin' mind? You're lucky you ain't dead already. You wanna go poking' 'round here in the dark, you go right on without me." The cop cupped his hands around his mouth and shouted, "Anybody wants can come see me, Patrolman Sanders." The words bounced off the unforgiving buildings, the locked doors, and shuttered windows. "You know anything about the man shot here, there's ten dollars gold in it for ya."

"That's it?" Mike said.

"No, that ain't it. Gimme ten dollars," Sanders said, holding out his hand. "I sure as hell ain't gonna pay for it." Mike handed over the coins and Sanders shouted the same message once more as they walked down the street. "You come back in the daylight, you wanna poke around," he advised Mike.

"Wait," Mike said. He stepped over to a wall covered in

handbills and tore two of them off. He went back to the bloody footprints and pressed the paper over them, getting a fair impression of the shoe prints.

"Detectives!" Sanders huffed. He shook his head and walked away. "Mark my words, Braddock. When we find him, *if* we find him, he'll be no use to anybody."

Mike followed Sanders, watching their backs as they retreated, their footsteps echoing in the empty street.

6

THE PISTOLS WERE incredibly loud in the enclosed space of the range in the basement of police headquarters. Mike and Tom had stuffed cotton in their ears to deaden the impact. The reports were a physical assault, making it difficult to hold on target as the guns of the other officers hammered at their ears.

Mike practiced rapid-firing the Colt, drawing, aiming, and squeezing off three rounds as quickly as he could. He didn't always hit the target with the second and third shots.

"It's the one who's calm under fire who'll be the last one standing," Tom said as they took a break to inspect their targets. "Ninety-nine percent of the time it'll be the other guy spraying bullets all over. Scary, but not real effective. You just need to slow down a half second on each shot, you'll be fine."

"Yeah, well I could hardly miss last night. They were right on me."

"You did good, but you were lucky. No luck this morning, huh?"

Mike shook his head. "Had officers cover everybody on the block, every apartment, business, whore, and beggar they could find. Nobody saw anything. Like a big hole opened up and swallowed him. All of them scared. You could smell it."

"You checked the hospitals?"

"Done, and on alert if anyone comes in."

Tom shook his head slowly. "And when're you gonna listen to what I tell you an' get some goddamn backup?"

"That's what Captain Woodhouse said, too. Of course, he was a little more upset when he said it. Told me I shoot anybody else he'll take my gun away and put me on desk duty." Mike gave Tom a guilty smirk. "He was not a happy man."

"With good reason," Tom said. "You shot more men in three days than most cops do in an entire career. You have anyone in mind for a partner?"

Mike wasn't in the habit of working with anyone. It hadn't been necessary before and the department didn't require it. "Dunno. There's a couple good guys I could team up with, I guess, but they're all working their own cases right now."

Tom nodded as they set up fresh targets. "You hear about that new detective, the Italian fella working that Black Hand business a few blocks south o' here?"

Mike shook his head. "I know a little about the Black Hand; Italian gang, Sicilians. Extortion mostly. Pretty much keep to their own. They leave a black handprint by their victims. The Italians are so scared o' them they won't even admit they exist."

"That's them," Tom said as they walked back to the firing line. "Scary bunch. They don't like you they kill you and your whole damn family. This detective—Alfieri's his name—he's been doing good work. The Italians'll talk to him and he isn't spooked by that Black Hand crap. He's busted a couple gangsters, wounded another in a shoot-out."

"Oh, that guy," Mike said. They waited for the range master to give the all clear. "Yeah, I heard about him. They say he's just lucky."

"Bullshit! No luck about it. You guys should have a cup of that espresso the Italians drink. See if you can work together. He might be interested."

The all clear sounded. Mike brought the Colt up fast, but

47

aimed with care, squeezing off three rounds, putting them all in the black.

"What makes you think he'll want to work with me, especially since he's been making progress like you say?"

Tom didn't answer immediately. He aimed his revolver and fired once, thumbed back the hammer and fired again and then a third time. Mike noticed how he fired as he exhaled, lest his breathing throw off his aim. The target showed just one irregular hole. "He's had death threats," Tom said. "Not just against him, but his family, too. He's got two kids, a boy and a girl. Had to move them out of the city. He doesn't want to quit, but his captain thinks it's time to take a breather, work on something else."

Mike nodded.

"I'll set it up," Tom said. Then, changing the subject, he asked, "So it turns out that *bottle* was actually a man?"

"Not sure entirely, but that guy I shot said he knew about somebody called the Bottler. I'm guessing that's a man. Didn't have time to question him on it. He was dying right in front of me. I had to try to get help."

"Thought I'd heard of every damn alias and nickname in the city but Bottler's a new one. Only thing I can figure is that if Mickey Todt was in with him, then he's got to kick back to Paul Kelly. Todt is one o' Kelly's men. Makes sense."

"So what do you think I oughta do? Kelly's protected. Got at least two gunmen with him at all times."

"Has the Wigwam on his side, too," Tom said. He took three more shots, firing faster, but with the same kind of care. The shots weren't in the same hole, but they could have been covered by a silver dollar. "So, what I think is that you should be careful, oh, son of mine."

There were giggles from the other girls as Ginny left Miss Gertie's front parlor. She tried to appear composed, but she felt almost giddy under the old madam's concerned, but benign frown. Mike stuck his hands in his pockets like a schoolboy, not even aware he'd done so. He could not recall a time when she'd ever looked so beautiful and despite their history, he suddenly felt shy. Ginny wore a stylish, but understated dress in a pale gray with pink stripes, a short jacket over a high-necked, white blouse, kid gloves, and a modest, but very handsome felt hat with a turned-up brim and a delicate veil of white lace. She looked like any of the countless numbers of shop girls in New York, only better. To Mike she had never looked so good. He couldn't stop staring as he accompanied her down the front stairs to their waiting cab. The other girls had stared too, some with delight, some with the narrowed eyes of jealousy.

"God, you look so beautiful," Mike said. It was wrong of him to encourage her, he knew, but she did look wonderful.

Ginny frowned. "Well, you don't have to sound so surprised." Mike fumbled for a response, much to Ginny's delight. She knew she couldn't embarrass a man who didn't care. "Thank you," she said, putting a soft hand on his arm. "I know how you meant it."

Ginny put her arm through his as they rode to Pastor's theater in the back of a cab. The clip-clop of the horse's hooves on cobbles and pavement was the only sound for some minutes as the newness of the situation tied both their tongues. They had been as intimate as a man and woman could be, yet this was beyond their experience; an everyday intimacy, simple yet profound.

Mike smiled at Ginny, but couldn't help wondering about her true feelings as she smiled back. Was he just another client, one she liked a bit more than the rest, but a client all the same? Was he a way out for her, a stirrup on the saddle of respectability? Did she actually love him? Mike hesitated to even think the question, let alone entertain the idea. More likely this was just a lark, a diversion from the drudgeries of the business, he told himself. That thought put him in mind of the others. How many might there have been? Hundreds? He'd never given that a moment's thought before. She had been there for him to use whenever he wanted, whenever he could afford to pay. That had been his only concern. Why was it that here in the cab, in the light of day, with both of them fully clothed, his mind was doing the sexual math; so many months at the house, so many clients per night, six nights a week. . . . He lost count quickly. But why was he counting at all? Mike couldn't answer that question.

Ginny tried not to think of their outing as a charity date, but the feeling kept creeping into the back of her mind. Mike had felt sorry for her when he suggested they go out. There wasn't any doubt on that point. Still, if he hadn't cared he wouldn't have asked. There was some consolation and hope in that at least. It was hope that helped her pick out her smartest clothes, leaving the flashy outfits on the rack. Today she would be like any other girl in the city, out with her beau. No one would know the things she'd done for her fine kid gloves, the tears she'd shed for her high-laced boots. Ginny was determined to put it out of her mind for just these few hours. She would be Mike's girl-friend, innocent and fresh and the day would be perfect. She felt herself a gardener, tending her hope like an orchid, a rare and reluctant bloom.

Pastor's was wonderful. Ginny couldn't recall when she'd had so much fun. The show was a variety, a Bowery b'hoy one-act play, followed by an Italian tenor, singing opera, or what she thought opera sounded like, a pair of comic jugglers, who had the audience howling with laughter, some chorus girls who did a modest variation of the cancan, showing a lot less leg than they did on the Bowery, followed by a strongman named Sandow, who bent nails and steel bars and lifted ten members of the audience on his back. The finale was a series of poems recited by the great

Bowery b'hoy, Chuck Connors, that left the audience cheering and stomping for more.

Ginny was chattering like a schoolgirl when they filed out with the crowd onto Fourteenth Street. Mike was buoyant, too, taking her arm in his and walking her over to Luchow's for coffee and pastries.

"I had a wonderful time, Mike, really," Ginny said once they'd been seated. "Thank you so much for taking me. Did you like the show?" She wanted to ask if they could do it again, to tell him how she loved to be seen with him, his arm around hers on the street like any other couple.

"I did, Gin. I really enjoyed it." He felt her wait for more and a small flash of guilt shot through him that he could not give it. He took her hand across the table and Ginny squeezed it with both of hers, making Mike wince.

"Oh, I'm sorry, Mike. Did I hurt you?"

"It's just that cut on my wrist from the other night, a present from that bastard, Smilin' Jack. It's a little sore is all."

Ginny pulled his sleeve back and looked at the bandage. She considered what a dangerous job he had. She'd read the account of the shoot-out in the harbor, of course, but somehow it hadn't seemed real to her. It was more like a dime novel the way it read in the papers, the product of a reporter's overactive imagination. But the bandage on Mike's wrist and the small stain of blood from the unhealed wound were real. Ginny's breath caught in her throat, frozen by the image of a blade slicing Mike's flesh, the blood running down his hand. On an impulse she picked up his hand, bringing it to her lips. She kissed it.

Mike let her, a warm amazement creeping into his eyes and greater guilt into his heart. It wasn't fair to let her get too close, Mike reminded himself. He was a sporting man, and unlikely to become anything more. Still, he could not help but admit how

51

pretty she looked in that dress and how her eyes seemed deep enough to drown in.

"There. Feel better?" Ginny said with the sunny voice of a mother talking to a child.

"Yeah," Mike whispered. "It does."

7

THE *General Slocum* gleamed at its moorings, all glossy white in the late-afternoon sun. Lionel Saturn walked down the gangplank to the dock without giving the steamer a second look. He knew what a fresh coat of paint could do, and what it couldn't.

As he approached his carriage and his waiting driver, he wondered how much extra that coat of paint had cost the Knickerbocker Steamship Company. He'd already been forced to pad the payroll with one no-show job. The paint had been another unnecessary expense. It had been "suggested" that maybe a coat of paint would be good for business. It had also been suggested that he do business with a particular dealer in paints. Lionel sighed. He knew he'd have to sign off on the bill and dreaded even seeing it. He was the senior vice-president and chief financial officer of the corporation. If he couldn't bury these expenses, no one could.

He checked his watch as he settled into the back of the carriage. It was a beautiful timepiece, with an engraved gold case, his initials in fanciful script, and an enameled lithograph on the back with two steamers breasting the waves. It was a gift from his wife on their twentieth anniversary, a couple of years before. He wondered, not for the first time, what it might be worth. He wished that he could sell it, sure that it might bring a hundred dollars or more. There was a diamond on the fob that had to be worth that alone. He knew he couldn't though. His wife would surely notice. Lately he'd been investing a great deal of time making sure his wife didn't notice things. Adding to that list was a depressing notion.

He sighed and gave his driver an address, then settled back into the tufted, leather seat. He watched the *Slocum* slide out of view. She'd have to wait a bit longer for the maintenance she really needed. She was a sound ship after all and had steamed for years without incident under a captain who'd just been honored for his safety record. For now the paint would have to do.

The carriage bumped along through the usual congestion of the docks. Wagons and their teams jostled for space, maneuvering around shipments loading and unloading, half of which seemed to take place in the street. Lionel thought about the meeting he was going to. Connors could help, he was certain. Whether he would or not was the question. There wasn't a man in the city that didn't know Connors. He was an icon of the Bowery b'hoy made good, and claimed to know most everyone worth knowing in the metropolis.

Connors was well connected, his annual balls at Tammany Hall attended by swells, politicians, businessmen, and bonebreakers. He'd worked his way into an odd sort of celebrity, making a career of being the quintessential "Noo Yawk" character. For many years he'd conducted tours of the Lower East Side and Chinatown, where he was once one of the few whites who knew the Chinese well. He'd been a "lobbygow" for the best of society, and even led visiting royalty on those tours, but he'd also spent his life on the streets and in the saloons of the city. If Chuck Connors couldn't act on his behalf, Lionel wasn't sure who could.

It took some time for Lionel's carriage to make its way to Connors's "office"—Barney Flynn's Old Tree House on Bowery and Pell—just around the corner from Professor O'Reilley's joint with its garish sign: WORLD CHAMPION TATTOOER. Connors held court in Flynn's most days from around three till whenever, drinking, telling tall tales in his exaggerated Bowery accent, and occasionally taking meetings with those like Lionel, who needed guidance in matters of a confidential nature.

Lionel bumped through the front doors and was enveloped in a haze of cigar smoke and the welcoming smell of spilled beer. The lunch crowd was gone, but the regulars clung to the bar like it was a life raft, elbows planted for stability. Lionel squinted into the semidarkness, his eyes watering from the smoke and stink of stale beer. "Chuck Connors," he said finally to the bartender, once he'd given up trying to spot the man. He got a nod toward the rear and a grunted, "Up to his eyeballs in bullshit as usual." Lionel wandered past the bar where a man turned with a fistful of beers, bumping him and spilling some on his pants and shoes. The man just shouldered past after a withering once-over of Lionel's tailored suit. A burst of laughter brought Lionel around, cutting off his protest. A group of men and a woman sat at a table in the rear. They stomped and howled as one man stood. It was Connors. "'Scuse me whilst I attend to nature," he said, heading toward the men's room. Lionel stopped. He didn't favor the idea of conducting a meeting in a toilet, but on consideration, it seemed a good place to start, better than breaking into the convivial atmosphere of the table. Lionel followed. Connors had his back to the door, his front to a big, porcelain urinal when Lionel entered. He sighed as Lionel took the one next to him. Connors glanced over, then concentrated on the business at hand.

"You're Connors?" Not waiting for an answer, he went on, "I'm Lionel Saturn. Tommy Byrnes told me you'd meet me here."

"Winky? Winky Byrnes?" Connors said. Lionel nodded. He'd forgotten Byrnes's street name. Byrnes ran a coal yard where the steamship company had their contract.

"Sure, sure," Connors said, cobwebs visibly clearing, "You're da steamboat mug dat needs help."

"I'm the ah . . . mug, yes," Lionel said as he unbuttoned his pants.

"Pleased ta meetcha," Connors grunted, sticking out a hand. Lionel hesitated. He was afraid of getting off on the wrong foot, but was equally queasy about shaking a hand that had just been "attending to nature." Connors shrugged and wiped his hand on his vest, sticking it out again, a bit more forcefully. Lionel put on a smile and shook with the famous Chuck Connors, whose bladder seemed bottomless and whose fingers were damp.

"Youse got a problem, huh?" Connors said, raising an eyebrow at Lionel. "What I hear's you gotta push back from the gamin' table. Fine gen'leman like yerself oughta know better. Wut is it? Wut's yer game, then?"

"Stuss."

"Stuss! Fer chrissake, stuss's fer dem suckers from outa town. Where's yer sense?"

"I've won my share," Lionel said, "more than my share actually. Just had a run of bad luck of late. It happens to the best of gamblers." He'd been telling himself the same for months and for quite some time he'd actually believed it. But now it seemed as hollow as an empty barrel. Connors clearly heard the echo.

"Youse got it bad," he said as he shook the last drops. "So how much youse owe?"

"I'd say that's my affair. More importantly, what do you think you can do for me, and exactly what is it going to cost?"

Connors ran water on his hands, splashing some on his face. There was a long silence before he answered. "Da answer to dem questions is da same. Dunno. Gotta have maw ta woik wit befaw I know, like who youse owe fer one, an' how much youse owe fer anotha. C'mon, let's sit an' chew da fat."

Lionel and Chuck went back into the bar where he introduced Lionel to the others at the table. "Dis is Chinatown Nellie,

56

my doll." The others were Frank Ward O'Malley of the *Sun* and Roy McCardell of the *World*. Lionel shrank in his suit, suddenly feeling like an ant under a magnifying glass on a hot day. Connors covered for him though, introducing him as, "Jimmy Buttons, from up Boston way," much to Lionel's relief. Connors asked for a little privacy and the reporters and Nellie moved to the bar without complaint. Connors slapped her on the rump as she left, which seemed to amuse her considerably. "So, where ya been playin' stuss? It's one place, right? If it's all ova town, den I dunno I can help ya. You'd be in da soup wit more'n da one I think youse is."

Lionel nodded. This was very hard for him, hard to admit he had a problem at all, and perhaps even harder to have to come to a rough-around-the-edges Bowery character like Connors. He forced himself to say the name of the man who ran the game. It came out like a death rattle. "The Bottler."

"Oh, boy! Youse got yer balls in a twist, you do! Youse know who really runs dat game? Paul Kelly, dats who. Fuckin' king o' the Five Pointers."

Lionel nodded without looking at Connors. Though he'd never had direct contact with Kelly, it had been made clear by the Bottler to whom he ultimately owed his debts. One of the problems with that was that the Bottler had insisted he deal with him and not Kelly. He'd given the Bottler no reason to doubt his compliance, but Saturn wasn't about to be dictated to by the Bottler. He knew that if he managed to satisfy Paul Kelly, then his troubles would melt away. They had to, for the latest of the Bottler's demands would plunge him into waters that were way over his head.

"That's why I came to you," he said, looking around the bar to see if anyone had heard. "I need a way to negotiate a settling of accounts. Their demands are getting out of hand." Lionel lowered his voice and leaned closer to Connors. "They're making demands that involve the steamship line, not just me. If I could just have a bit more time to liquidate some assets, I could easily settle up, but they've got me over a barrel."

"A barrel of yer own makin' seems ta me," Connors observed. "Yer a smart business fella. Once youse let a mug like Kelly get his flippers in yer pocket, youse'll never get 'em out."

"A bit too late for that," Lionel said, his shoulders slumping.

Connors gave him a hard, but not unsympathetic, look. "So, how much is it?"

"About ten now," Lionel said, lifting his head and sticking his jaw out in a transparent show of confidence. "Not quite ten, really."

"Grand? Ten grand!" Connors whistled. "Dem ain't small potatas. Youse shoulda come see me sooner."

"I should have done a lot of things," Lionel said. "I've always come out ahead before. Or nearly so. That's the thing. I've really been quite lucky till now. In fact, given a little more time I'm sure my luck will turn. Certain of it!"

"Sure thing pigs'll fly outa me arse someday, too," Connors said. "Plan on sellin' tickets ta see it. A sure moneymaker."

"I don't need to be mocked, Mister Connors."

"Sure, sure," Connors said, unfazed. " But youse need me all da same, so save yer huffin' an' puffin' fer dem wots impressed by it."

Lionel sighed and reached into his pocket. "So how much do I need to pay you, Mister Connors?"

"Gimme a hun'red fer now," Connors said as easily as he'd ask for a light for his cigar. It was an amount most men would not earn in a month. "An' if I can arrange t'ings, I'll take ten percent. If not, den we's square."

"What will you do?" Lionel asked, swallowing the ten percent like a horse pill with no water. "Will you go to Kelly directly?"

Connors scratched his head. "Nah, Kelly'd gimme an' ear, but it'd likely be my own if ya get my meanin'. But even Kelly's got higher-ups ta keep happy. Dat's where da juice is. Dat's why a bloke like Kelly's where he's at. He kicks upstairs, ya get me? He gets da votes out an' goin' da right way, t'ings like dat. I gotta go where da levers is. Dat's where ta put on da pressure."

"Tammany."

"Lots o' chiefs in da Wigwam," Connors said. "Trick is knowin' which one's got da pull."

"Indeed," said Lionel, cursing himself for not having done a better job of cultivating contacts there. He got up from the table and Connors rose with him. "I'll leave that up to you then, Mister Connors." He gave Connors the money and one of his cards. "I can be reached there during business hours. When might I hear from you?"

"Gimme a couple days," Connors said. "Hard sayin' 'xactly."

"Thank you," Lionel said, putting out his hand. "There'll be something extra in it for you if terms are favorable."

Connors nodded with a wry smile. "Jus what I'd 'spect from a gen'lman like yerself."

Lionel left not sure of how he should feel. Only time would tell if his hundred was good money thrown after bad. He looked back over his shoulder as he got up into his carriage, half wanting to go back in and call the deal off. Instead he sighed and flopped into the back.

Chinatown Nellie had joined Connors where he stood at the end of the bar watching Lionel leave.

"Who wuzzat, Chuckie?"

"A man dat don't know when ta quit," Connors answered.

"Huh," she said, grinding her rear for him.

"Owes Paul Kelly ten grand."

"No kiddin'? Glad I ain't him."

"Me, too, doll. Me, too."

8

MIKE MET PRIMO Alfieri outside a coffeehouse on Prince Street. Tom had arranged it, just as he'd said he would. At first Mike had walked right by him. Tall, blond, and blue-eyed, with a dimple in the middle of his chin, he appeared at first glance to be English or perhaps German. But something about the way he stood, a wariness that was hard to define, the way his eyes scanned the street made Mike take a second look. When he did, Primo smiled and stuck out his hand. The grip was firm and dry and Mike found himself squeezing hard to match it. They held for a long moment, neither wanting to let go first.

"You don't look Italian, but I guess I'm not the first one to tell you that," Mike said as they went in and sat down at a small table near the front window.

"You know lotsa Italians then?"

Mike knew he was being baited and it put him on edge despite Primo's smile. "Nope. Not many on the force," Mike replied with a straight face. "Maybe they ain't smart enough." Primo stopped smiling. He started to say something, but stopped when a waiter came to take their order. Primo spoke to him in Italian. The waiter turned and left. Mike raised a hand, but Primo said, "I order for you. You no so stupid you didn't know that?" He cocked his head at Mike curiously as he crossed his legs and leaned back in his chair.

"My famiglia is from the north, by Lake Como." Primo said, ignoring Mike's angry frown. "In the north we look like this," he said, his hand moving over his face as if he was putting on a mask. "The Italians you see here, they are Siciliano mostly. Things no so good there. No work. All the good land owned by the dons. If you work, you work for the dons and they pay nothing. Very bad."

Primo's hands moved as he spoke, dancing in a sort of sign language, punctuating and embellishing his words. "The Siciliani, they no like the ones from the north like me. They no trust the outsiders, people who speak different."

"So how were you able to work against the Black Hand?" Mike asked, putting aside his annoyance at Primo's taunting. "I hear they're from the south mostly, particularly Sicily. The Italians are so scared of them they won't admit they exist, not to most cops."

"This is true. The Mano Nera or the Black Hand is spoken of only in the whisper. You see, when I was a boy, for many years I go in summer to Sicily. My papa had family there, so we went. I learn how they speak, how they think, about vendetta, all that is to be Siciliano. I even learn about love in Sicily." Primo said with a wistful smile. "So even though I look Inglese, and they no trust me at first, when I speak they know who I am. Capisce?"

Mike nodded. "And your family, here I mean? I heard you had to move them."

Primo tried to hide the worry behind his eyes, but didn't fully succeed. "They are safe. You understand I can say no more." The waiter returned with two espressos and a small plate of biscotti.

"I understand completely," Mike said once he'd left. "I didn't mean to pry."

"Pry," Primo said with a curious frown. "I don't know this word."

"To interfere, you know, to be nosey."

"Ah, nosey, an interesting word," Primo said, putting his

hand to his nose and seeming to pull it. "Like Pinocchio, except he told the lie." Primo looked closely at Mike as he sipped his espresso, making little slurping sounds. "So, what lies do you chase, eh? What dark things are you sticking your nose in?"

Mike filled Primo in on the details of the last few days, particularly about his encounter with Todt and his accomplice.

"You did not get this man's name?" Primo said. There was no judgment in his voice, but the implication was there.

Mike shrugged. "Things were moving a little fast right then. Been searching the neighborhood two days now. Nothing on him or Todt either. Not sure a name would have helped anyway."

"No find them alive, I think," Primo said. Mike sipped his espresso without comment. "Nice work," he added.

"Whadya mean? I lost both of them. That ain't so nice according to my captain."

"Nice work to be alive, I mean. Two men. Surprise. You shoot both. Nice work."

Mike raised his cup. "Nice to be here," he said. "Aside from a bump on the head, I'm none the worse for it."

Primo grinned as if confirming something to himself. "So we work together, no? We find this Bottler, a very strange name, Bottler. Lots of strange names in this city." Primo shook his head. "Anyway we follow the lira, the dollars; see where they go. We put this Bottler in the Tombs maybe, eh? Maybe more?"

"That's about it," Mike agreed, squinting at Primo to be sure he wasn't being mocked. "You're up for all that? Could get rough."

Primo laughed. "What is rough to you, Michael? You shoot five men in two, three days, an' say things they *might* get rough. You joke, eh? So when do we start?"

They agreed to start by finding Mickey Todt, rather than try to develop new leads to the Bottler. Todt clearly knew who the

Bottler was. With the word out on the street about the shootings of Todt and the other, and the newspapers all reporting it too, new leads would be scarce, unless they were lucky enough to come across someone with a beef against Todt or the Bottler. They agreed that would be their next best shot, but Mickey Todt had to come first. "If he's alive," Mike grumbled. "He was running pretty good after I shot him, so maybe he's not too bad off. One thing's sure. He hasn't shown up in any hospitals. I have them all on alert. First thing I did that night."

"The gangsters, they have doctors who take care of things for them. You have a list of doctors in that place, maybe five blocks around. He maybe no go so far with a bullet in him."

"Yeah. We've been checking the doctors. Nothing so far, but we haven't covered them all. There's others too, men who maybe have medical training from the war in Cuba or even the Civil War. They'll be harder to find."

"We ask the women," Primo said. "The women they always know the doctors. They take the little ones."

Mike glanced at Primo. He hated to admit that the idea hadn't occurred to him so he made no comment.

The day waned as Mike and Primo canvassed the neighborhood, working their way from door-to-door, from basement saloons to six-story walk-ups. After a while they stopped asking about Mickey Todt. The answers were all the same. Almost everybody claimed not to know him either by Todt or Stolzenthaler. The few who admitted knowing who he was claimed not to have seen him for weeks. Some just refused to open their doors.

At one point they passed a flower cart among all the vendors of more necessary items parked along the curbs and on the sidewalks. Flowers were a frivolous luxury in this neighborhood and were more often sold by young girls, whose real line was prostitution. The old man beside the cart looked none too prosperous, but the flowers were fresh enough. Mike stopped for a moment and arranged to have a bunch delivered to Ginny. He took out one of his cards and wrote on the back, "Ginny, I had a wonderful time with you yesterday. I hope you like these. I'll see you soon." He looked at it with a frown, then crumpled it and took out another. He stood for almost a minute, his pencil in the corner of his mouth, trying to find the right words.

"Tell the girl you love her," Primo said with an exasperated sigh. "To love is okay, no? You maybe love her, maybe somebody else. It's all okay to love."

"Great advice," Mike said. "That a bit of Italian philosophy?"

"No, Alfieri philosophy," Primo answered with mock pride.

Mike chuckled and shook his head. "What kind of partner did I hook up with?"

"One who knows the woman, eh? So sign the card and we go."

Mike hesitated a moment, then signed, settling for "Warmly, Mike." Primo sighed and shook his head. "Who is this Ginny?"

"Tell you later," Mike said as they opened the door to a basement cobbler's shop, ringing a little bell on a spring. The smell of leather and shoe polish rolled over them. A workbench occupied one side, with an assortment of tools, shiny from wear spread about its top. A single chair sat opposite. The walls were covered with more tools, shoes and boots already repaired or awaiting attention, and sole leather, cut to various sizes and stuck in little cubbyholes. A man emerged from a back room, through a sheet that covered the doorway. Mike could see the foot of a bed and a small stove behind it. The man was perhaps sixty, but appeared much older. Stooped and bowlegged, with fingers that looked like the roots of a tree, he shuffled toward them, adjusting his glasses and tugging at a boot-blacked apron.

"Shoes're in no need o' mendin'," he observed after a quick look down, "so it's somethin' else ye're after."

"Mickey Todt; you know him?" Mike said, forgetting that they'd decided not to mention him. He gave an apologetic smirk to Primo.

"Stolzenthaler, that fuck! See these?" the cobbler said, holding up his hands. "Miserable prick tol' me he'd break a finger a week till I paid 'im 'is protection money. Held out eight weeks," he said proudly. "Couldn't stand 'im breakin' me thumbs though. Can't make a livin' without me thumbs." The cobbler looked at them sharply. "What's that gutter scum done now?"

"Nothing good," Mike said with a look at Primo. "You know where we can find him?"

"You boys're detectives then, huh? Do me a favor an' shoot the sonofabitch when you see 'im."

"Done that already," Mike said.

"Whoa! Ya don't say? Oh, I get it now. This is about that fracas over on Governeur Street the other night. Didn't know Stolzenthaler got himself shot. Wait a minute," the cobbler said with a satisfied gleam in his eye. He rummaged behind his workbench and pulled out a flask. "Real Jamaican rum this is. Good stuff. Have a drink wi' me. Any man shot Stolzenthaler deserves a good drink."

Mike was going to refuse, but relented, not wanting to dampen the man's enthusiasm. He took a good pull at the flask and handed it over to Primo, who took a polite swig and gave it back to the cobbler. The old man held the flask to his mouth with a bent and lumpy hand, emptying it in one long pull. "Damn that's good! Even better to hear the prick's got himself plugged." The cobbler stopped then and squinted at Mike, pursing his lips. "He ain't dead, is he," the cobbler said, his mood turning doubtful and somber, "otherwise what'd you be doin' lookin' for 'im."

Mike shook his head. "Might be dead, might not. Sad to say he was alive when I last saw him."

"But you're sure he's shot?" the old man said, seeming very anxious on the point.

"Sure as I can be."

"There is a doctor in the neighborhood he would go to?"

Primo asked. "Maybe not a doctor, like a dentist, a nurse maybe?"

The cobbler scratched his head and winced, then rubbing one hand against the other. "Well, that's coverin' a lot o' ground, see. But what yer really wantin' ta know is where would a prick like Stolzenthaler go to get stitched up an' nobody be the wiser."

"That's about it," Mike said. "Any ideas?"

"There's two, maybe three, the gangs use. They ain't docs though. One was a medic in the war with Spain. The other's a dentist, sort of. Not sure where he got his trainin'. He's a terrible drunk. Then there's a woman's got lots o' medical know-how. Been midwifin' fer years, but she was a nurse in the big war. She's old now, like me," he said. "She'd stitch the devil himself fer a dollar. Laudanum addict, cocaine too when she can get it."

"You got names and addresses?"

"You bet. Who ya think fixes their shoes?"

The medic proved to be of little use. He was working on a child with what appeared to be a broken leg. The boy was screaming and a crowd of women and children clogged the little tenement office, filling it with a constant babble. The medic, sweating and distracted, shooed Mike and Primo off, saying he hadn't seen a wounded gangster in at least a week.

"Whadya think?" Mike said as they left.

"We try the dentist. This one, he's too busy to lie to us now."

"Probably," Mike agreed. He looked at the addresses the cobbler had given them. "That dentist is right down the block."

The dentist, a man the cobbler had called Lefty Letters because he wrote letters for the illiterates in the neighborhood and happened to be left-handed, lived and worked in a slightly less ramshackle pile than most on the block. It was crowded on one side by a scrap yard, piled high with iron, brass, copper, and lead in almost infinite variety and form. On the other side were another two tenements and a small coal yard on the corner. A huge black dog, caked with mud, barked at them as they passed. It lunged against its chain, foam dripping from its mouth.

"The dog, he is friendly, no?" Primo said with a grin. "Nice doggy. Good doggy." The dog charged so hard the chain nearly yanked himself off his feet. "Maybe he no understan' English."

"Right," Mike said.

"We see." Primo took a step toward the dog and said in a commanding voice, "*Vai! Vai al canile!*" The dog pulled back his lips in a low snarl. He snapped and growled and strained at his chain, the veins bulging on his neck. Primo shrugged indifferently. "Must be an Irish dog."

Mike punched him in the shoulder, laughing. "I think I like you, you wop bastard."

"Yeah. Us wop bastards are the funny guys, eh?"

"So funny you can go first. Maybe Mickey Todt'll laugh so much he'll forget to shoot you."

They went up the staircase in the front of the building, each checking their pistols. It was instinctive, a loosening of the jacket, a feel to see that nothing was hung up on the weapon. A bit of shirtsleeve twisted the wrong way, a suspender too loose, a tear in the lining of a jacket, these could be the difference between getting a pistol out in time or not. Neither planned on dying of a loose suspender.

The apartment where the dentist worked was on the fourth floor. The building stood oddly quiet. Their footsteps echoed up the staircase, mixing with the groans and creaks of the old wood. The dog still barked from the scrap yard, his snarling seemingly right at their heels. They met no one on the stairs. Little of the late-afternoon sun filtered in, keeping the stairs in a perpetual twilight. Although they could hear people in their apartments, even those sounds seemed muted. Mike and Primo moved even slower as they went up. Twice Primo checked the stairs behind them, craning over the balustrade to watch the floors below.

Reaching the fourth-floor landing, they turned into a long hallway running front to back. It had a single window at the other end, the glass so fouled that the world outside appeared fuzzy and brown. Mike nodded toward the rear. This building was an old law tenement, with the improvement of a single toilet on each floor and an air shaft in the middle, four apartments to the floor. Older tenements had no bathroom and no ventilation of any kind, except windows front and back. Rooms were often sublet though, so it wasn't unusual to have fifteen to twenty people for the one toilet. They checked the single bathroom as they went. Mike opened the toilet door. A cascade of foul air engulfed him and he stepped back as if struck. Primo held his nose and hurried down the hall. Mike could have sworn he said something that sounded like "Irish."

"Probably is," Mike said. "From what I hear the Italians just shit in bed and kick it out in the morning."

Primo gave him a hard look and took out his pistol. With a nod toward the last door in the hallway, he moved to one side. Mike listened on the other, grinning. There were footsteps inside and muffled speech, then a gurgle. He glanced at Primo, then pounded his fist on the door. "Letters, open up!"

They heard footsteps and the door was opened a crack. Half a face peered out. The eye was shot with red, the chin sported a dirty stubble. The nose was a ripe-strawberry red. "You Doctor Letters?"

"Who wants to know?"

Mike shoved the door hard, pushing the man back though he tried to hold on.

"The police want to know." Mike's hand had gone to the butt of his pistol. The dentist's eyes followed it like a man watching a snake. He backed up, bumping into his patient.

"Hey, I ain't done nothing. Just drill some teeth is all. I'm a legitimate dentist." He waved at a diploma in an elaborate frame hanging skewed on the wall. "I'm in the middle of a delicate procedure," he added, seeming to regain some of his professional composure. "This man has a seriously infected molar."

Mike and Primo looked around the dentist at the man in a reclining chair, not a proper dentist's chair, but a wooden one with cracked leather upholstery. A tall, mechanical drill stood to one side. It was pedal-operated, like a sewing machine. A small table held a porcelain tray and an assortment of stained steel instruments. The man in the chair looked back at them, wide-eyed.

"Mickey Todt," Mike said. "Where is he? Tell me now and we'll let you get back to your delicate procedure."

Letters shrugged. "Fixed an incisor for him a while back," he said, turning back to his patient, who was just then taking a wad of cotton out of his mouth. "Can't say I've seen him in months. A very intemperate young man. Quick to anger when he's imbibing, which is most of the time."

The patient started to shove himself out of the chair, but Letters put a hand on his shoulder and said, almost pleadingly, "Surely you can't be thinking of leaving in your condition. I haven't finished the extraction."

"Sit down," Primo said. The man settled back.

"Yes, sit. These gentlemen won't be long, I'm sure. The man they're looking for is clearly not here, so . . ."

"Yeah, so where is he? Where could he be, I wonder." Mike started looking about the office, peering into a cabinet full of instruments and looking at medicine bottles in no apparent order, spread about the topmost shelf. Primo started doing the same. "We do not want you," Primo said in a tone designed to put Letters at ease. "You have done no things wrong, as you say, eh? No things you want to hide?"

"Quite right," Letters agreed. "Quite right indeed. I've done nothing, but help those in pain. I ease their sufferings and pull their rotted teeth."

Mike looked at a curtain covering a door to an adjoining back room. "Not back there, is he?" He didn't wait for a response. He swept the curtain aside with one hand, the automatic in his other. Primo stood by the door, his back to the wall.

Mike searched the room, which housed only a bed, a steamer trunk, a washbasin, and a collection of gin bottles, most of them empty. A chimney protruded from one wall. The hearth had been covered over with a cast-iron plate and a stove added, its flue stuck through a hole chopped through the brick. Mike looked through the trunk and under the bed before checking the back room. It possessed the only window in the place and allowed a measure of dirty light to filter in. This room was quite different, with more furniture in varying stages of decay and a quantity of women's clothing hanging from lines strung about the room. Mike guessed from the clothes that the woman worked the streets. There was no other entrance except the way they'd come in. Mike searched the room just as he had the first, finding nothing pointing to Mickey Todt ever having been there. Disappointed, he turned and walked back through the other room. He had a hand on the curtained doorway when he realized there was one place he hadn't looked. He stepped to the little stove and bent to open the door. He stopped with his hand on the latch. A small, bright drop of blood glistened on the floor. Mike went down on one knee for a closer look. It was fresh, or nearly so. Looking up, he noticed for the first time a small smear on the lower edge of the stove door.

"Primo! Nobody in or out."

"Okay. What you got?"

"We'll see," Mike muttered back. He used his sleeve to cover his fingers as he opened the stove door, not wanting to mix his prints with any that might be there.

The door squealed. Behind it, stuffed in a hard ball, was a bundle of clothing. Blood was clearly visible. Mike heard a scuffle from the next room, stamping feet, a cry, and a shuddering thud. He was at the door in an instant.

"I had to! He said he'd shoot me. He will, too. He'll shoot me. I'm a dead man." Letters was lying on the floor, holding his head. Blood was oozing through his fingers. "I had to. You don't know Mickey. He'd have killed me if I hadn't fixed him up. He came in bleeding all over the place, put a gun to my head. My head! I had to!"

Primo lifted an eyebrow at Mike. "He try to run. I stop him."

"You broke my head. I didn't do anything and you broke my head," Letters cried, his shoulders shaking as he wept into the floorboards. He bounced his forehead on the floor and said again, "He's going to kill me."

"Yeah, you mentioned that," Mike said.

The man in the chair hadn't moved. He sat still, gripping the arms as if he was under the drill. "I don' know nothin,'" he ventured, looking from Primo to Mike. "I jus' got a real bad toothache."

Mike went back and pulled the bloody clothes out of the stove, putting them in a paper bag he found in a corner. The dentist quieted down after a few minutes. Primo got him a bandage and some Mercurochrome for his head. Mike questioned the patient first. He clearly was what he said he was, a man with a bad tooth. Mike got his name and address and let him go.

Before they started questioning the dentist, Primo reluctantly told Mike to wait while he used the toilet down the hall. He tried to hold his breath as he opened the door and it worked for maybe twenty seconds. What made him forget about the foul air was actually an insignificant thing, a shifting of the shadow that crossed the window. The window opened on an air shaft, which ran from the basement to the roof. The shaft was only about four-feet-by-five with windows opening to it from the toilets on each floor and the four apartments on every floor. There was just one floor above and the sunlight wasn't bad, the air a little better than the floors below where the sun reached only at high noon if at all. But what Primo realized was that there was no good reason for a shadow to shift, not in that small shaft, no reason he could think of except perhaps for pigeons or maybe laundry on a line. But pigeons made noises and cooing sounds and laundry wouldn't be moving because there was no breeze. There almost never was. Primo pissed and tried to think. The window glass was the kind that you couldn't see through. It had little starburst designs cast into the surface so that it diffused light and color. He buttoned up and was about to open it, had his hands on the sash, ready to push up when he stopped. There was blood on the sill, just a small smear, but still red and wet. The sash was open just a crack. Primo drew his pistol, pointing it at the frosted glass while he peered at the sill and the sliver of light at the bottom. The sill was scuffed and part of a shoe print was clear in the dirt. The shadow didn't move again.

Primo didn't stay long in the toilet. If Mickey Todt was in the air shaft he wasn't going anywhere. And if he was there, then there'd be a pistol on the other side of the glass. Primo backed out and slammed the door, letting it bounce off its hinges so it opened a few inches. He waited, watching the window.

"Primo," Mike called from the dentist's office, "that's the longest piss on record. You flush yourself down the pipe or what?"

Primo didn't respond and when Mike stuck his head into the hallway, Primo waved to him and put a finger to his lips.

Mickey Todt was getting tired. His legs ached and his side was a huge ball of pain, shot through with nails whenever he moved. He was weak and sick from the chloroform and laudanum that Letters had given him. He needed a drink bad, could imagine the gin going down his throat, feel the burn in his belly. His head swam at the thought and he had to catch himself from falling.

At least he had his pistol. He felt good about that. He looked down at the hand that held it. He did his best to make it stop shaking. It had a will of its own and would not listen to him no matter how many times he told it to stop.

He cursed himself for not using the pistol on Braddock. He'd been so surprised at being shot, all he could do was run. He closed his eyes and saw himself pumping bullets into the cop even after he fell to the street. That's the way it should have been, the way it was going to be if he saw Braddock again. He could make his hand stop shaking long enough for that, he thought. He imagined Braddock's back, a big target on it as he rushed up the street to shoot him. Wouldn't he be surprised?

Mickey had almost used the pistol a few minutes before when somebody was at the window. He'd held fire not out of concern for shooting some poor joker taking a piss, but because he didn't want to alert the two detectives, one of which was almost certainly Braddock. Though he wanted to kill Braddock, he wasn't brave enough or stupid enough to try it, not in his state. He still had enough presence of mind to know that. Braddock would have to wait for his killing. Mickey smiled as he leaned against the rough brick of the air shaft. Even if he didn't have the pleasure himself, there'd be others. He'd gotten the word out.

The sash by his left foot flew open. Mickey was startled and shot quickly without aiming, shattering the glass. Before he could see if he'd hit anything, before he could even fire another shot, the window on the fifth floor just above his head opened, too. Hands reached down and grabbed his shoulders. He tried to fire up, but his aim was thrown off by the arms that had popped out of the lower window, pulling at one leg. Another shot went off by itself as his hand tried to clutch something solid. Chips of brick rained down as his bullet ricocheted. But his balance had been lost and he began to fall.

Mike felt Todt go. He didn't have much of a grip on the man's undershirt and Mike was already as far out the fifth-floor window as he could go. The sash was blocked by layers of old paint and hadn't opened all the way. He'd barely been able to get his head and shoulders out. He'd held on as the shots seemed to explode in his ears, but Mickey Todt had still slipped away, tumbling, his shirt ripping in Mike's hand. Primo nearly went with him.

Mickey Todt fell to the bottom of the shaft, arms and legs twisting and thumping off the walls, his head striking a windowsill so hard the glass shattered and rained after him. He landed amid a pile of trash, the detritus of the tenement's families. It threw up a billowing brown plume that was sucked slowly up like smoke from a chimney. Mike and Primo waited while the dust cleared, straining to see.

The body seemed to float up, as if emerging from a great depth. Mickey's face stared up at them. He didn't move. His head rested on his right leg, which was twisted up behind him, almost as if he'd put it there, like a man might put his hands behind his head. Primo looked up at Mike from the window below and shook his head. Mike thumped his fist on the windowsill, but said nothing. There was nothing to say.

9

GINNY COULDN'T GET Mike out of her head. His flowers stood in a pitcher by the bedside, a riot of hope with the hint of curling, brown edges. Their afternoon together had somehow changed everything. She knew it shouldn't be so. No few hours in any day should be so full of promise and yet also dread.

She tried to remember the last time she'd felt things shift in her life. Not even the day her family had cast her out could be counted that way. There hadn't been the sense then that things had changed in some fundamental way, as though the moon no longer rose at night. In truth she had left her family before they left her, had already made her choices in every way but her address. The cutting of that cord had been hard, but not unexpected, not unplanned.

The opening of a door, the extended hand when they'd descended from their cab, the chair held out for her at Luchow's, these were things unexpected. They had a meaning far beyond what they might for an ordinary girl. Mike had seen her not for who she was, but for who she wanted to be. After all the men who'd seen only her sex, she'd begun to lose her faith. That a man might see her as she saw herself was a wonder indeed. He'd treated her like a lady, a woman of grace and refinement, a woman worthy of respect and even love. She knew she had no right to those things, not by society's rules. She had forfeited those rights when she'd chosen her life. But she had not forfeited her dreams.

Mike had given her more than any man had before, a thing that had nothing to do with sex. It had been years since she'd had that kind of gift. She'd known that she couldn't expect it. It had to be given freely, like the fairy-tale kiss that woke Sleeping Beauty. She almost felt that way, as if the day before had woken a part of her that had long been sleeping and tucked away, insulated from pain. But in the waking there was much to fear. The note with his flowers had read only, "Warmly, Mike."

These thoughts ran through Ginny's head, blocking out most everything else. She had a hard time acting out her role, playing wanton when Mike was the only man on her mind. She tried to imagine that it was Mike she was with, when instead she was with a man who called himself Johnny Suds. He was a beer salesman, or at least that's what he'd told everyone. She'd seen him before and did not cherish the memory. Suds behaved like a gentleman with Miss Gertie and Kevin, but he had a very different reputation with the girls. He was rough and drunk.

Still, she did her best, moaning things that seemed like a bad jokes to her ears, but Suds didn't seem to notice. Speeding up, he tore at her already tender spots. She moaned again, but this time from pain. She did her best to get it over, using all the tricks she knew, but Suds was oblivious. His breath forced her to turn her face away. He kept hammering harder still, telling her she was a whore, a dirty little whore. He said other things too, things that Ginny had heard before, but never listened to. She tried to block them out and think of Mike, but she found she couldn't now. Her mind cried out for him to rescue her, but there was no rescue to be had. She began to listen then to the vile words growled in her ear and began to think again that those words were true.

She was crying when Suds collapsed on her, carelessly crushing the air from her lungs. She cried for herself and for what she had once again become. She was no lady, no girlfriend, nobody! She had no right to a man like Mike. She was dreaming if she imagined he could really want, much less love, a whore like her. How could she ever be with him again after an animal like Johnny Suds? Mike would always be beyond her if she stayed where she was, gasping beneath a stinking drunk.

She pushed Johnny's flaccid bulk off her, rolling him to one side, sobbing with the effort. Johnny stirred. "Like that, huh?" he mumbled. He sat up and grinned at her. "One o' them cryin' types, huh? Give you somethin' ta cry about, bitch." Suds pulled his hand back, an ugly glare flashing across his face.

Stamping feet echoed from the hall and Suds's eyes flickered toward the door. When he looked back, the heavy pitcher, filled with Mike's flowers, had found its way into Ginny's hand. It crashed against his head in a shower of jagged shards, old water, and happy colors. Kevin and Miss Gertie burst in, followed by a friend of Suds's that Ginny had seen downstairs. They arrived to see Suds as he hit the floor.

Ginny didn't feel much of anything. She should have been happy to have cracked Suds's head, but she couldn't stop sobbing. She wasn't even certain why she was. There didn't seem to be any emotion behind her cries, just a release, like steam from a kettle. Not even the blood that smeared her hands when she tried to cover herself from Kevin's eyes could bring forth a true emotion. The blood didn't seem to really be hers, though it stained the bed under her. The pain was hers, and the ache in her face where Suds hit her. She was sure of that, but it was somehow disconnected. She wondered at that as the shouting in her room boiled up. Suds was there, holding his bleeding head and pointing a finger at her. Kevin was there, one hand on Suds's chest, pushing him back, and Miss Gertie and Rachel and Eunice, too. They'd heard her cries and knew things had not been right and had fetched Kevin and Miss Gertie. They crowded around her bed, covering her, fetching sponges and towels. Ginny observed them all with a curious detachment.

"Hit me with that goddamn pitcher," Suds yelled. "Look at 'er. She still got the handle in her fuckin' hand."

"I am lookin' at her," Kevin shouted back, his slungshot ready in one hand. "I see blood."

"That ain't nothin'. She was lovin' it; all cryin' an' moaney," Suds spat. "I'll have the cops in here if you don't do what's right."

The balding, mustachioed man in the doorway buttoned up his trousers. He interrupted and said, "There'll be no cops, Miss Gertie, but there'll be other troubles if things don't go right. Johnny may not be a gentleman, but that's no cause to have pitchers broken on his skull."

Turning to Miss Gertie he said, "I know people. She's a whore for chrissake, she's gotta expect a little rough play. No real harm in it." With a gesture, the man herded Miss Gertie and Kevin into the hallway.

"Who . . . ?" Ginny asked. "He's got no right to."

Rachel shushed her. "He's got pull, Gin. He runs with Paul Kelly."

Ginny shivered. She knew that name and what it meant. She glanced at Suds, holding a towel to his head as he craned to see what was happening in the hall. Suds must be more than he appeared, she realized, and a part of her shriveled at the thought of what he might be capable of. They could hear the other man's voice from the hall, but not the words. His baritone vibrated the walls in tones that left no room for argument.

Kevin and Miss Gertie came back in a moment later. "You go now, Mister Suds," Gertie said as if it was in her power to make that happen. Kevin, who'd gathered up Suds's clothes, pushed them at his chest and moved him toward the door.

"What the—" Sud began to protest.

"*Ich*—" Miss Gertie caught herself. German always slipped out when she got angry. "I am doing right, sir. You get out now, please." She would have been pleased to set Kevin loose and watch him beat Johnny Suds to a pulp. There was no percentage in that though, no matter how glad she might be to see it. He'd hurt Ginny, an asset, a solid earner, and a favorite with many customers. But on the other hand, Ginny could be replaced. Any girl could be replaced. "Mister Suds, you vill please not come back. You are no longer velcome in this house."

The other man's voice rumbled from the hall, "It's settled, Johnny. Be a good sport and let it go."

Suds deflated visibly, but managed to rally as he left, grunting, "Fuckin' ain't heard the last o' this." Suds shoved his way past Kevin, who caressed his slungshot with longing. Miss Gertie put up a hand and shook her head. When Suds was out in the hallway, she whispered a few words in Kevin's ear. He nodded quickly and walked Johnny Suds out of the building.

It was perhaps two hours later that Ginny found herself standing in front of the house, looking left and right, trying to decide which way to go. She stood a long time, shifting from one foot to the other as if blown by a strong wind. A small carpetbag was in one hand. It held everything worth taking, which wasn't all that much. She had a splitting headache, which had made any kind of decision a painful process; her clothes and shoes the most painful of all. Most of her flashy things she'd given to the other girls, not caring how much they'd cost. They were worthless to her now. She'd even left her diary, a thing too much filled with her old life, and its sorry memories; although her recent entries about Mike had made her hesitate to put it aside. She had been cast into the street like a defrocked nun. The notion brought a faint smile to her lips. Despite her pain, her pounding head, her hatred of Johnny Suds, her indignation, Ginny Caldwell was happy.

Miss Gertie had told her she'd have to go. No hint of violence, at least on her girls' part, had ever been permitted to exist within her walls and could not be tolerated now. She didn't give a snap for Johnny Suds or his cracked head, but she couldn't be seen to let the matter slide. It wouldn't be good for the other girls, she explained, who might get ideas, and above all her business depended upon a clean reputation. Houses like hers were becoming a rarity now. Hers was no panel house, with thieves hiding behind the walls. Her customers paid handsomely for privacy, discretion, and security. They paid more than they had to so as to take their pleasures without fear.

Ginny didn't care, not about Miss Gertie's reasons, not about the proper behavior of whores, the reputation of the house, not even about the growing bruise on her face. She knew that it had been as much the work of Kelly's man as anything else. She was leaving, a thing that she'd learned was not easily done without Miss Gertie's consent, or the fear of being dragged back by Kevin. Ginny was leaving and the price of her ticket had been paid in full.

10

AN' HOW'S DA kids?" Connors asked as Big Tim Sullivan settled into his office chair. His headquarters were in the Occidental Hotel, a once fashionable affair, now in decline. It was in a good location though, in the heart of his empire, on the corner of Bowery and Broome.

"Ouch, growin' like weeds, Chuck. Eatin' me outa house an' home."

Connors laughed, though his own experience with children was of the bastard variety. He took a seat across the cluttered desk from Big Tim and got a cigar going. Though Big Tim wasn't a smoker or a drinker, he tolerated the habits in others. Connors looked about the office; a splendidly shabby affair with a window overlooking Bowery. He eyed the photos arranged on the walls. There were dozens; testaments to the warm and cordial relations Sullivan shared with the rich, the powerful, the political, the ecclesiastical, and the criminal elements of the city. McClellan was there, McKinley too, and, of course, Howe and Hummel, the best and certainly the most corrupt defense attorneys the city had ever seen. Even Roosevelt was captured shaking Big Tim's hand, though he appeared less than pleased to do so.

"Ah, if these walls could talk," Connors said. "You'se come a long ways, Dry Dollar," Connors said, calling him by his old nickname, from when he owned the Dry Dollar saloon on Chrystie Street, once the headquarters of the Whyos gang. Big Tim had six saloons now and many other interests beyond his nominal job; head of the Third Assembly District, which included the Bowery. Along with the famous gambler, Frank Farrell, and Big Bill Devery, possibly the most crooked cop in New York, Big Tim ran a protection racket for gambling joints throughout the city.

Sullivan smiled, but said, "It's just as well these walls stay silent."

"T'ings what get talked about here stays here. Always has always will," Connors said, bristling at a reminder that he of all people didn't need.

Sullivan was a powerful man, more powerful than even the framed photos might seem to indicate. All the ward healers, all the shoulder-hitters, gamblers, bartenders, gang bosses, cops, city inspectors, pimps, and banco men in the district owed their allegiance and, in many cases, their existence to him. There was hardly a job in any of the city's departments that he didn't have control of one way or another, at least when it came to his turf.

He'd started his career in his teens as a saloon keeper, but soon expanded that to controller of the Whyos' votes and was a repeat voter of great talent and creativity. He'd won his seat in 1892 with a vote of 395 to 4. He'd beaten poll-watchers in his younger days and was without doubt one of the best shoulder-hitters the city had ever seen. He was a master of the shakedown, regularly putting the arm on local merchants, saloon keepers, gamblers, whores, liquor vendors, and the like to buy tickets to his many clambakes, chowder suppers, and summer outings to College Point.

His generosity was every bit as outsized as his extralegal endeavors. It was widely agreed that he gave away something like $25,000 a year to the poor. He regularly went out at dawn with groups of the unemployed to secure jobs for them on the docks.

His Christmas dinners for the down-and-outers of the Bowery were legendary and it was not unusual for him to host well more than four thousand indigents. Thousands of pounds of turkey, hundreds of loaves of bread, thousands of pies, and at least a hundred kegs of beer would be consumed and every man left with a pipe, a bag of tobacco, new socks, and shoes.

"So, you got a problem," Sullivan said. He didn't ask. Nobody who visited his office came without a problem.

"Not my problem. A gentleman, name o' Saturn, got a gamblin' debt ta Kelly. Wants me ta meditate."

"Mediate," said Big Tim, crossing his hands over his stomach.

"Right," Connors agreed. "Anyway, I figured youse could help."

"How bad?" Sullivan asked, tapping a pencil to his lower lip in an attempt to hide a smile.

"Ten."

"Thousand?" Big Tim asked. He didn't raise an eyebrow or give any other sign of his astonishment. It wasn't that he was surprised at the number itself. Wealthy men sometimes lost that much and more. What was astonishing was that the debt was to Paul Kelly. Kelly wasn't one to let a debt grow to those proportions. He'd had men killed for much less. People who owed Kelly either paid up quick or got hurt, usually both.

"Who is this *gentleman*? Saturn, you said his name was?"

"Knickerbocker Steamship Company. He's da senior VP or somethin'. Kelly's puttin' da screws ta da guy."

"As only our Paul can do," said Tim thoughtfully. "Can Saturn pay?"

"Says he can. Needs time like they all do. Same ol' story."

"And why would I want to help?" Tim asked, narrowing one eye at Connors.

"Five percent. Five hundred fer a phone call or two." They both knew it wasn't quite as simple as that, but they nodded as though it was.

"What's your end?"

"Five fer me, too," Connors said. "Everybody wins."

"Except for this fellow Saturn."

"Well, o' course, not him. But what da fuck, he got himself in dis mess."

Sullivan chuckled. He was a notorious gambler himself, the only difference being that he could afford to be one. "What's his game?"

"Stuss," Connors said almost spitting the word with distaste. "Clever fella like him shoulda knew better."

"Funny what some men'll do, the risks they'll take for the thrill o' winning. Doesn't mean he's stupid, just that he loves the thrill, convinced himself he can beat the odds." Tim shook his head as Chuck let out a blue cloud of cigar smoke.

"Where'd he play? Not the Bottler's game, I hope?"

Connors shrugged. "Don' matter ta me. Could be, why?"

"Nothin' ," Big Tim said. He looked at his watch, then got up from his chair. "Take a walk with me, Chuck."

Connors stood. "Where youse goin'?" He'd just been getting comfortable in Big Tim's leather chair, feeling like a big shot, pulling strings.

"Out an' about, Chuck. Out an' about. A politician's no good to anybody if you can't see him."

As they left Big Tim's office, two men fell in behind them. One was Photo Dave Altman, his bodyguard, the other was called Sasparilla, though his real name was Thomas Reilly, Tim's sometime valet, factotum, and doer of things he preferred not to do himself. When they left the building they turned west on Broome. Photo Dave went two paces ahead, Sasparilla a pace behind. Connors had no doubt they were armed, but somehow that knowledge didn't make him feel safe.

Men on the street tipped their hats to Big Tim. Connors got his share of recognition as well, but it was nothing against the steady surf of greetings that followed Sullivan. A woman stopped them just a block from the park, stepping into their path suddenly and startling Photo Dave, who reached into his jacket. Tim just shook his head and Dave relaxed. The woman poured out a tale of woe, which Chuck only half heard. He watched with interest, though, as Big Tim listened carefully, questioning her in detail on one point or another. After a minute, he produced a wad of bills and peeled off a few into the woman's palm. Patting her on the shoulder and giving her a few soft words of encouragement, he sent her off. Sasparilla scribbled something in a notebook.

"Husband's sick an' the fookin' landlord's puttin' them out," Big Tim explained. "He's a good man, a good Democrat. Always good for two, three votes. We'll fix it with the damn landlord." He gave a slight nod to Sasparilla, who nodded back as he wrote.

They didn't talk about the Knickerbocker Steamship Company, stuss games, Kelly, or Saturn's debt, but Big Tim thought of those things constantly as they walked, rolling them around in his head, looking for the perfect angle, that delicate point at which the least leverage might be applied to the greatest advantage.

He had been in the habit of hiring a steamer for his day trips to the North Shore of Long Island in the summers; part reward for the party faithful, part extortion. They were splendid affairs, complete with massive barbeques, horseshoes, dancing, swimming, and fireworks. He always made sure that there was a solid sprinkling of families who needed a good meal and a day away from care. They were altogether satisfying endeavors and Big Tim took pride in them, always trying to make the next one a bit more fun than the last. And though they had always been moneymakers, he hadn't held them strictly for that. But this thing with the fool Saturn and his steamship company had the power to add another level of interest. Big Tim made a calculation and came up with a number. It was a good number, a number that put him in mind of how he might look in a captain's uniform. He imagined himself behind the wheel as the steamer churned the river, saw himself blowing the big steam whistle, and smiled at the notion of literally tooting his own horn.

"Somethin' funny?" Connors asked. Sullivan shook his head.

"Nothin', Chuck," Big Tim said, making a mental note to check his numbers before he made any moves. There was nothing funny about it, nothing funny at all.

11

MIKE HEARD THE Oldsmobile before he saw it. He was crossing at the corner of Spring and Crosby, not far from where the new police headquarters was being built, a grand beaux arts pile that was to replace the aging and unpretentious old building on Mulberry. The Olds's horn honked twice, like a goose made of brass and rubber. Tom was dressed in a white duster that enveloped him like an Arab. Long gloves in yellow kid covered his hands and little round goggles were strapped around his head just under his black bowler. He grinned incandescently and waved like a boy on his first bike ride, letting go of the tiller for an instant. The car weaved in response to the sudden lack of piloting, the white tires bouncing crazily, the tiller whipping about before Tom grabbed it again with a look somewhere between panic and foolishness. He brought the car to a stop beside Mike with a flurry of pulled levers and twisted controls. It stalled with an indignant chug and sputter, a puff of smoke shooting out the back.

"Damn spark," Tom said as he pulled the goggles down around his neck. "Haven't got the hang of it yet," he said with a wave at a brass lever. "Keep forgetting to retard the damn thing." In reality, Tom wasn't exactly sure why the Olds sputtered when he stopped but he was damn sure Mike knew even less about it than he did. "Heard about Mickey Todt," he added as he pulled off his gloves.

"Yeah. He's *todt* for sure now. We're back to square one. That's why I'm heading over to check the rogues' gallery, see if I come up with any aliases. Sure as hell the Bottler ain't his real name."

"Maybe Ma and Pa Bottler couldn't decide on a name for junior," Tom said with a glance back at the Olds. "So how's Primo working out?"

"Good. He's a wise guy, but he seems to have his head on straight. He knows what he's doing and he's careful. Did all right with the Mickey Todt thing. He'll be at headquarters in a minute," Mike said with a glance at his pocket watch. "So what're you doing here?"

"Meeting with the Chief. Going over budgets," Tom said with a grimace. "Spend more time looking at balance sheets and fuckin' reports than anything like real police work. It's all bullshit." He gave an audible sigh. "But necessary, I guess. Keeps us on the straight and narrow." Mayor McClellan, who'd only been on the job for a few months, was not toeing Tammany's line and had made a point of appointing Independents to his administration, which had not been lost on the higher echelons of the department.

"Heard you were out with Ginny the other day," Tom said, changing the subject abruptly. "I'm surprised they let you take her out of the house. Your mom almost never let that happen." He appeared to catch himself, then added, "But things were different then."

"Yeah, well, I paid for the favor," Mike said. He was uncomfortable with the subject as always with his father. "How'd you know, I mean about us going out?"

Tom just smiled and wiped his goggles on the hem of his duster. "Your mother got this outfit for me. Said it'll make me look sporty. I'm not so sure. Think maybe I just look stupid."

Mike grinned. "Maybe, but you know what they say, Stupid is as stupid does."

"Talking about yourself, Mike?" Primo said behind them. "Oldsmobile, huh." He said, looking longingly at the car. "It is good, the red. A very sexy color. The women they will chase you down Broadway like the bulls with the matador."

"Yeah, well, don't say that in front of my wife. I'd be driving a black one the next day," Tom said. "You boys open in an hour or two?"

"Maybe. Why?" Mike asked.

"Got an idea. Somebody you should maybe see."

"Who?"

"Tell you later. Meet me in say an hour an' fifteen."

It was closer to an hour and forty-five minutes later that they finally met again on the stairs.

"So who we seeing?" Primo asked.

"Marm Mandelbaum," Tom said.

"Who is this person with so silly a name?"

"The biggest fence in the city," Mike said. "Or at least she used to be. Never met her myself, but my dad knows her from way back. I thought she'd gone to Canada?"

"Trust me on this," Tom said. "Marm's in town though nobody knows it. She comes back every now and again."

Primo looked doubtfully at the seat as they approached the Olds. "They no make bigger ones? A second seat maybe?"

"Not Olds. Strictly runabouts right now," Tom said as he went through the starting procedure. He closed a small valve he told them was an air cock, depressed a button on the heel board, and moved the spark on the emergency brake lever all the way back. He then moved the electric switch lever forward, put his heel on something he called the relief lever, and told Mike to crank it over. "It should just need a couple turns, Mike. Fast as you can." The Olds started on the second turn, chugging to life like a tiny locomotive and puffing almost as much.

"Maybe running is no so bad idea," Primo joked as he climbed up onto the Olds's seat, shrugging his shoulders to squeeze between Tom and Mike. Tom threw the clutch lever into slow speed and stepped on the speeder. It was a strange sensation to be suddenly moving without any visible means of locomotion and both Mike and Primo found themselves smiling like fools. The Olds simply pulled away, gaining speed slowly, but steadily, until Tom moved the clutch lever to high speed. They were doing fifteen or twenty miles per hour in less than a minute and hanging on to the little rails at the sides of the seat. The engine chugged with the slow and steady stroke of a long-distance swimmer, not seeming to alter much even as they moved faster. Tom passed carriages and wagons, dodged a horsecar and generally terrorized pedestrians and horses alike, using the horn liberally. He wore a wicked grin all the while, his eyes big and excited behind his goggles. There was a constant sense of commotion, of people jumping out of the way and cursing in their wake.

In a remarkably short time they arrived at an ordinary four-story building on Orchard Street. Its only outward signs of prosperity were a bit of fresh paint on the windowsills and a handsome oak door of the very latest design, glossy with several coats of varnish. The first floor was occupied by a dry goods store and heavy drapes blocked the windows on the second and third floors, The fourth-floor windows were thrown open, however, and the drapes pulled back. Mike could see an intricately plastered ceiling, decorated with flowered moldings in a geometric pattern, clouds and cherubs chasing one another across the frames.

Tom twisted the bell in the center of the door, which was up a few steps from the level of the dry goods store. He was about to ring again when a young man opened it. He regarded them with unwavering eyes. They flicked from Tom to Primo and Mike, measuring and challenging. No words were spoken, except by Tom.

"I'm Captain Braddock," Tom said. "Your mom is expecting us. I called ahead."

The man gave a slight nod and stepped aside. Mike looked back at the Olds as the door closed behind them. A loose ring of people surrounded it.

"The Olds'll be okay there?"

A brief smirk crossed the young man's lips. "No one will touch your car," he said with certainty.

They climbed through the house on a broad staircase with a wide walnut rail and balusters. The lower floors were hidden behind tall pocket doors, but the stair was brightly lit by electric lights in sconces on the walls. As they turned onto the third-floor landing a woman's voice called from above, "Slowing down, Tommy? Used to climb them stairs a lot quicker in the old days."

Tom laughed and bounded up the last flight of stairs two at a time. Mike hurried behind, but stopped when he saw Tom at the top of the stairs lifting an immense old woman in a bear hug.

"Christ, you're a heavy old broad!" he cried and put her down with a thump that shook the floor.

"But you still picked me up, you old devil," the lady laughed. "I don't get hugs like that in Canada! I take it back, Tommy. You haven't slowed a bit. Maybe a little grayer though," she said, running a hand through his hair. "Definitely grayer."

"And you're definitely fatter," Tom said, rubbing his back. "How's Canada?

"Dull as the grave. Not like here. Goddamn Mounties don't know how to do business. Offer 'em a dollar an' they get all indignant. Imagine!"

Tom grunted. "I can't."

"The boys do most of the work now. I'm too old. Mostly I sit on my ass and get fatter every day goes by."

"Sure, Marm," Tom said with a twinkle in his eye. He knew she was a long sight from being retired, though she was careful to keep a much lower profile in New York than she did in the old days, when police, politicians, gangsters, and businessmen often mingled in her parlors and dining room. Marm had been famous for her dinners; as it turned out, a bit too famous. The papers had taken an interest in her social doings, and it had finally become politically expedient to bring her up on charges. Howe and Hummel had kept her out of jail long enough for her to flee north, much to everyone's relief.

"Marm, I'd like you to meet my boy, Mike," Tom said. "He's a detective now. And this is Primo Alfieri, his partner."

Marm looked them over. Though there was a smile on her face, her eyes were possibly even harder than her son's. She was an old woman with a huge beak of a nose, bulging cheeks, and a high, sloping forehead. She had a shrewd eye and a cast-iron will under her sagging flesh, a toughness that her over-rouged cheeks did nothing to disguise. Still, her voice was jolly when she said, "They're good boys, I can see," and extended a huge bejeweled hand to Mike, the hardness melting from her eyes. "But not too good, I hope, or you wouldn't have brought them."

Tom laughed. "Not too good, no. They've been around the block."

Marm ushered them into her apartment, offering them coffee and tea and seating them in an ornate parlor. Mike could hardly believe the opulence of the place. The carpets were Persian, of the finest silk woven in an intricate design. The furniture was an eclectic collection, crafted of rare woods and veneers, with deep tufted cushions in silks, damasks, and brocades, representing every style from Federal to Empire and Eastlake Victorian. Every piece was exquisite. Paintings hung on the walls in such profusion that it looked more like a gallery than a home. Mike tried not to gape.

"Marm," Tom said when they had settled, "ever hear of somebody goes by the name of the Bottler?"

"That's an odd one, Tommy," she said as she poured herself some tea. "What you want with him?"

Tom pressed Mike's foot under the table when he saw Mike was about to jump in.

"Not sure exactly, Marm. He might just be a link in a chain, so to speak. Maybe more, maybe less."

Marm chuckled. "Ain't we all just links in a chain, Tommy?"

"Of one kind or another," Tom agreed.

"And you come to me, which means you don't have more'n stink on shit," Marm said flatly. "Why ask me? Why not go to Big Bill?"

"You have to ask?" Tom said. He'd considered talking to Devery, who he knew well enough, but treated the idea as a last resort. Mike just frowned at the mention of Devery's name. He'd known better than to even broach the subject with his father until all else failed.

"There is always another way," Primo broke in. "A man can no hide forever."

Marm paid him no attention, putting a third lump of sugar in her tea with a silver spoon. "This is about that thing in the harbor the other night, right? You found some connection to this Bottler mug but not much more." Marm looked from one to the other. "And as you say, Detective Alfieri, you might find him eventually. But eventually ain't soon enough, is it?"

"Sooner would be more convenient," Tom said.

"Always is, ain't it?" Marm chuckled, passing around a cut crystal tray of pastries. "So what's this information worth, I'm wondering . . . information about a mug that might be a link in a chain? You're not a lad to come to me with nothin' to trade, Tommy. Always knew how to make a deal."

Tom just shrugged, but Primo said, "You are in no so good position to bargain, with all respect. The indictments, they are still open, no?"

"Technically," Marm grunted, her thin lips turning down in a snarl. A small blob of powdered sugar from one of the pastries hung at the edge of her mouth like a spot of foam.

"You have many things of beauty here," Primo said, looking around. "Why should we dangle the carrot when the stick is maybe better, eh?"

"You ain't got a stick big enough for me, Detective," Marm growled, all pretense of hospitality draining from her face. Her son appeared in the doorway to the next room like a dog sensing the tension in his master's voice.

"That's enough o' that shit," Tom said, his voice as final as a judge's gavel. "Marm, lets you an' me take a walk. Show me the rest of your place. I'm sure we can come to some kind of agreement. Always found a way before an' no unpleasantness needed." He stood, giving Primo a look only slightly less flinty than Marm's.

Marm hauled her bulk out of her chair with a grunt of effort. "Jus' like old times, eh, Tommy?"

It was some time before Tom and Marm returned, time enough for Mike to take a slow tour of the parlor to admire the paintings. He wondered whose walls they had hung on before finding their way here. There was a Bierstadt, a Tait, three Remingtons, a couple done by Dutchmen that had the look of real age to them, but the one that caught his eye and held it longer than the others was a colorful, exotic scene done by somebody signed Gauguin, a South Seas scene with palm trees and near-naked women with long black hair and nut-brown skin. Mike had never seen anything like them. He knew a little about art, enough to know that Marm's walls were covered with money. Primo, by contrast, spent more time examining the furniture.

"You see this marble? Italian Carrara, the best! There is only one place in the world with marble like this. And the wood; it is mahogany from Honduras. This chair it is French, maybe sixteenth century."

"Early seventeenth, actually," Marm said with a satisfied smile as she returned with Tom. Their conference seemed to have mellowed her, and any sense of tension had disappeared.

"You always had an eye for the best, Marm."

"I just keep what I like. Trouble is I like everything. It can be an ugly world outside, Tommy. I bring a little beauty into my place. I see it like I'm just taking care of them for a while. They're not mine in a way. The beautiful things, they outlast us all. They always do. I'm just enjoying them for my time until it's somebody else's turn."

"You've become a philosopher in your old age," Tom said in a way that was somewhere between a joke and a compliment. "But you still drive a hard bargain. Now you wanna tell the boys here what you told me?"

She took a deep breath and pursed her lips so the top one nearly touched her sagging nose. "First thing is *be careful*. I don't know him myself. Gambling never was my vice, but I heard of him and . . . things. He got his nickname from the old days when he started brewing his own stuff. Still does, some say. They say he cooks up everything from knockout drops to that swill they sell in the dives, them block-an'-fall places. Make ya go blind ya drink too much of it. Got benzene, cocaine, an' god-knows-what-else in it. Anyway, he's with the Five Pointers. Pays Kelly a healthy cut. He runs a stuss game. Not sure where exactly. Think it's somewhere around Suffolk Street. A real profitable game and as crooked as they come. What he mighta had to do with Smilin' Jack I couldn't say. Anybody's guess. Which brings me to the other thing."

"What other thing?" Mike asked, looking up from a little pad he was scribbling on.

"Kid Twist."

12

IT WAS A tiny room, dark and musty, but Ginny was glad to have it.

She'd searched all day, walking till her feet ached in her thin leather boots. With hopeful ignorance, Ginny worked her way through the places she couldn't afford, getting a quick and brutal lesson in Manhattan real estate. She'd lowered her sights as the day wore on, the neighborhoods growing less and less fashionable, the rooms smaller, the light nonexistent, the grime thicker.

Her emotions ran at random as if someone else was controlling them, pulling levers and flipping switches at an antic pace. But mostly she worried, worried that she wouldn't find a room at all, worried about Mike and if she would ever see him again, worried about how she'd support herself, find a job, buy clothes, eat. The thought of Mike left an empty, sinking feeling in her middle. She could only imagine what Miss Gertie might say about the circumstances of her leaving. What would Mike think if he knew she'd cracked a customer's head with a pitcher? She didn't like to imagine that. Her only chance was to somehow find him and tell him her side of the story. Maybe then she'd have a chance, maybe.

The shadows had crept across the avenues and were crawling up the west-facing walls when she had finally found rest. It was a room in a tenement apartment above a millinery shop. Ginny knew when she happened across the ROOM TO LET sign in the window that she'd find shelter there. Shops like that had a reputation; smoke shops, too. There were often willing girls working behind the counter, stacking shelves or making no pretense at all. Store owners often turned more profit on that than on their legitimate businesses. It wasn't that Ginny wanted to work that way again. She simply knew that it was at a place like this that she'd find a level of acceptance she wouldn't elsewhere, coupled with a veneer of respectability that suited her situation.

The woman who owned the shop knew she was a whore. Ginny could see it in her eyes when she walked through the door, felt their quick appraisal, running head to toe, and the way they'd narrowed until Ginny explained she was interested in renting the room. They exchanged pleasantries as if she was an ordinary working girl, dragging a pathetic carpetbag door to door before the terrors of the night closed in. They built up an illusion of respectability between them, Ginny with a story of coming to the city to find work, the shopkeeper with an air of knowing acceptance. The woman even went so far as to say she allowed no loose women to let her rooms above the shop, an assertion that Ginny said had her hearty approval.

Ginny paid what the woman asked, handing her the crisp bills she'd gotten at the bank that morning. A week's deposit and a week in advance; eight dollars in wide, green notes. When the door closed behind her new landlord, Ginny was consumed by darkness, relieved only by the transom window above the door. She lay on the iron bed, felt the springs digging into her back, heard them creak when she moved, and thought she'd never heard or felt anything so wonderful. Though her stomach echoed like an empty barrel, Ginny would not rise. She closed her eyes, erasing the walls that she could almost reach out and touch, the single dresser with the missing drawer knobs, the painted chair with the badly repaired leg and a cracking coat of paint, the wallpaper blackened by years of lamp wick, tobacco, and cooking smoke. Sleep crept into her room, lifting her like a feather.

13

"IF MANDELBAUM, SHE is right, Kid Twist will have men watching the game," Primo said after Tom had dropped them on the corner of Rivington and Ludlow.

"*If* we find the game and the Bottler," Mike added, "we're gonna have to be careful. But we're careful guys, right?"

"Right. Careful guys is what we are. But we maybe have stumbled into the nest of hornets, no? Kelly owns the Bottler, but Kid Twist is how you say, wanting to get his toe in the doorway. We are maybe putting ourselves between—"

"I know," Mike said. "If Marm is right, then the Twist has already started to make his move on the game. The Five Pointers on one side, the Eastmans on the other, and the Bottler is right in the middle of it."

"And us," Primo added.

"Yeah. We could find ourselves in a real sea of shit. They'll have Tammany backing them and guys like Devery and who knows how many others in the precincts who're on their payroll or too scared to help."

"We are not quitting, no?"

Mike looked at Primo. He wanted Primo's true feelings without any pressure one way or another. Mike wasn't even certain of what he wanted to do himself, how far he was willing to take this investigation. There was no point trying to pressure Primo into anything he wasn't sure of himself.

"We don't have to quit," Mike said at last, "not yet anyhow. Let's see how far it goes. Okay?"

"That is good. My mother, she told me she knew a woman once, in Sicily, I think, she was so frightened of snakes she would not go in the garden."

"Huh?"

"It is like a proverb, see," Primo said, "the woman, she let her fear keep her away from the beauty of the garden. It is how you say, ironic, no?"

They spent the better part of the day canvassing the neighborhood where Marm had said the Bottler ran his game. It was slow going. They tried posing as a couple of farm machinery salesmen, down from Albany on a business trip and looking for some sport. It didn't work very well.

They tried store owners first, stopping at random, talking to grocers, saloon keepers, haberdashers, shoe salesmen, vendors on the streets. The streets were lined with them, choking the pavement, one after the other, so that wagons could hardly squeeze by, spilling over the sidewalks too, pedestrians sometimes going single file to get around. Mostly they got suspicious looks and not much more. Only one or two admitted to even hearing of somebody called the Bottler. None would say where he was.

"This place, it stinks worse than the horseshit," Primo said.

"Yeah, and there's loads o' that," Mike grunted. Indeed, street cleaning in that neighborhood was a sometimes thing. "Listen, I don't think you should say anything to the next guy. It's the accent. Not too many Italian farm equipment salesmen from Albany, I guess."

"Maybe I can be somebody else. Like maybe I make the gelato and you are my partner."

"Gelato?"

"How you say . . ." Primo said, searching for the words, "ice creams."

"Right. We're a couple of ice cream guys." Mike smirked. "That'll fool 'em. What the hell, try it. We can't do any worse than we are now."

The next store they entered was a combination soda fountain, candy store, and tobacco shop, its narrow confines stacked to the ceiling with boxes of cigars and the new craze, cigarettes, while the little fountain was covered with bins and big glass jars of jawbreakers, licorice, jelly beans, rock candy, and chocolates. Leaning across the counter as they came in was a patrolman. He had the man behind the counter by the shirtfront and was talking to him in a low growl. Mike couldn't make out what the cop was saying, but the man clearly did. Whatever it was scared the hell out of him, judging by the sweat beading on his forehead.

The cop's head snapped around when Mike and Primo came in, his eyes narrowing. He let go of the man's shirt, but relaxed and gave them a knowing grin. "An' what're two boys from the detective bureau doin' on my beat, I'm wonderin'," he said, pushing his blue helmet back on his head. The man behind the counter took up a wet rag and began swabbing the red marble countertop.

"Detectives? We are no detectives." Primo said, smiling. "We are from Albany." He elbowed Mike in the ribs at his little joke.

The cop laughed, but he didn't look amused. "An' a fuckin' dago, greaseball detective at that," he said. "What the hell's the force comin' to?"

Without another word, Primo rushed the cop. The helmet went flying behind the counter as the cop stumbled backward against a stool.

"Primo!" Mike shouted. "What the hell?"

Primo landed two, three punches in quick succession. The cop's nose was bloodied in seconds. He flailed about, trying to ward off the blows and struggled to pull out his club. The store owner scurried into a back room. Mike managed to get a hand on Primo's shoulder and pull him off the man for just a second. Primo was cursing in Italian. The only word Mike understood was *greaseball*. The cop was tough though, and he took the opportunity to swing his club, clipping Primo across the forehead. His follow-through hit Mike's hand with a distinct crack. Mike shouted in pain. Primo stood holding his head with a stunned look on his face. The cop stopped and wiped his bloody nose on a sleeve. Mike's hand sent bolts of pain up his arm. He cursed and shook it as if he might somehow loosen the hurt. "Sonofabitch! You broke my hand!" Without thinking, Mike shot out a side kick, catching the cop hard in the middle, crumpling him like a rag doll against the counter. The man slumped to the floor, groaning weakly. One hand fumbled at his belt for his pistol. Primo saw and kicked the man again. Primo didn't stop until the cop rolled onto the floor and lay still.

"Primo, stop! Enough. For chrissake, don't kill the bastard!" Mike shouted.

Primo spat on the cop, but stopped the kicking.

"I no like that word *greaseball*," Primo said, huffing and out of breath.

"Jesus!" Mike said. "I'll remember that. You didn't kill him, did you?"

Primo checked the man's pulse. "No." Grinning in a guilty, almost apologetic way, he added, "It is his lucky day, no?"

They picked the cop up and propped him against the counter.

"He no look so good," Primo said. "Maybe we should get him to a hospital. What you think?"

"I think he's alive. Beyond that, I don't much give a shit," Mike said. His hand was already starting to swell and turning an angry shade of blue.

The cop was coming to. He groaned and suddenly vomited on himself.

"Maybe it is no so good if we stay," Primo said. Mike shrugged. "You might be right. He'll be okay. Hey!" he called toward the back of the store. "Hey, you got a phone here?"

"No," a voice said from the back.

"Listen, I'm leaving a dollar on the counter," Mike said. "Go to the nearest phone and call somebody for him. Okay?"

"Sure. I can do that," the owner said, sticking his head out of a doorway.

"Thanks. And you didn't get a look at either of us, did you," Mike added.

"Nope," the man said, not even looking at them directly. "Go on, get going."

"You need a doctor," Primo told Mike, looking at his hand as they walked down the street. "Get the bones how you say . . . set in a bandage."

"Yeah, a cast. Fuck!" Mike was reluctant to give it up for the day, but his hand was throbbing and it hurt like the devil just to move his fingers. Primo hadn't complained, but he had a knot on his head the size of an egg. "How's your head?"

"Feels like somebody does not like me so much," Primo said. "How you learn to kick like that? I never saw a man kick like that."

"My dad, he taught me. It's something he learned from the Chinese. He took lessons from an old guy in Chinatown years back. They call it kung fu." Mike hesitated a moment, then said, "The other day, when we met for the first time, I called you a wop." He looked closely at Primo. "You didn't kick the hell outa me. How come? I mean what's the difference? Wop, greaseball, dago, they're all the same."

Primo smiled. "The difference," he said, "is in the eye and the tongue. You say wop, but I see you no *mean* wop. That bastard, he say greaseball and he means it."

They were heading toward the nearest hospital when Mike said, "You know that cop might show up in the hospital pretty soon, too. Could get a little awkward."

"Awkward. Like he maybe shoots us, right?"

"Something like that. Let's find a doctor instead."

About two hours later Mike had a cast on his left hand. The doctor confirmed that at least one bone had been broken, but immobilized two fingers just to be certain. The cast felt heavy and huge, and the hand still throbbed despite a healthy dose of laudanum.

Mike called in from a nearby firehouse, the closest place that had a phone, reporting to his captain and coming up with a semiplausible tale of a suspect that got away. He was told to take the rest of the day, but to report in the morning. Primo headed back to the station house. A mere lump on the head wasn't going to buy him any time.

Mike was glad to take the afternoon off. The laudanum had him feeling fuzzy and tired. He threw himself on his bed when he got to his apartment near Madison Square Park. Not long after he was asleep, or more accurately in a drugged and hazy version of sleep where visions of Primo's stomping feet kept flickering through his head like a bad nickelodeon show. The afternoon faded into a gray evening as the sun sank into a pastel New Jersey sky, and real sleep took over.

When he woke it was to the sound of a bell. For a moment Mike imagined that it rang every time Primo kicked the cop. Mike shook the vision off as he staggered into the kitchen and lifted the telephone earpiece off its cradle.

"You okay?" Primo asked without saying hello.

"Yeah. You?"

"Going home now. I have no telephone there, so I call from here."

"Thanks. Get some rest. See you in the morning. Six?"

"Sure. There was a cop beat up bad by a couple gangsters they say, over on Grand. He is in hospital. They are looking for those guys."

"Uh-huh," Mike said, the sleep swept away like smoke in a high wind. "They're likely to talk to some of the same people we did."

"You mean those farm equipment salesmen from Albany?"

"Yeah, *those* guys," Mike agreed. "Some coincidence."

"Those guys might be in real trouble. That cop, he is hurt pretty bad," Primo said. "The captain says we should help, maybe go see this cop, get his story."

Mike grunted into the mouthpiece on the wall. He didn't know what to say to that idea. He was silent for some seconds. "We should talk about that in the morning I guess," he said eventually.

"Yes," Primo agreed. "We should sleep on it, like they say."

"Right. See you at six." Mike hung up the earpiece slowly. For a moment he considered calling Tom, but rejected the idea. He'd handle this with Primo. If their partnership had ever been in doubt before, it was no longer, at least not for Mike.

Thinking of partners reminded him of Ginny. Mike hadn't had a lot of time to really think through his feelings for her over the last couple of days. Things had been moving too fast for that. He was determined to stick to his decision and not let their day at Pastor's lead him deeper than he wanted to go. But he couldn't deny the thoughts that kept sneaking into his head. He'd see a pretty girl and think of Ginny, see a dress in a shop window and imagine how she'd look in it. And he could not stop thinking about her body; the flaring curve of her ass when she was on her knees, head buried in a pillow, the way her breasts swayed above him when she was on top, the way the soft down of tiny hairs on her belly glowed in the gaslight. And there was her way with him; the way she looked at him and wanted to know how he felt about things, the way she listened when he told her, the way she seemed to keep a special part of herself just for him.

He decided he should go to see her, and went down the hall to the bathroom, a luxury that had sealed his decision to rent the place. He got himself cleaned, shaved, combed, and out the door in twenty minutes with a fresh suit of clothes and spit-shined shoes, an amazing feat for a man with a cast on his hand. He found himself whistling as he walked uptown, the cares of gangs and bottlers, stomped cops and broken bones, fading to the corners of his consciousness like a twisted opium dream.

The first thing Mike noticed when he entered the brothel was the bouquet of flowers he'd sent Ginny. They were in a vase in the hallway by the front door. They were a little wilted, the vibrant colors faded and browning at the edges. The next thing he noticed was the way the girls in the parlor looked at him. He saw that Kevin, the bouncer, wore the same expression. None of them would meet his eye, yet they tried their best to make it appear that nothing was wrong.

"What happened? Where's Ginny?"

"She's not here," Miss Gertie said, coming up behind him. "I had to let her go. She stole from one of the customers."

"Stole? Money?" Mike could not believe what he was hearing though he knew it was certainly common enough in her trade. He'd had his wallet lightened a few times himself over the years. But Ginny? The possibility had never crossed his mind.

"*Ja*, Money. It happens," Miss Gertie said with a shrug of her ample shoulders, "but not here. I had to send her packing." She folded her arms over her fleshy cleavage, frowning for emphasis, but then smiled widely. "But we have many lovely girls here, girls that would be happy to entertain a gentleman like you.

Come," she said, putting an insistent arm through his and steering him to the back room. "I have a new girl just today. She is Creole, an octoroon of the finest color, very nice."

Mike pulled his arm away. "Where is she?" he said.

Miss Gertie pretended not to understand. "She's just back here, with all the—"

"You know who I'm talking about. You must have some idea where she's gone."

"You don't vant a girl like dat." Gertie clucked like a mother hen. "She stole! I saw the money."

Mike wasn't sure what to believe. The idea that he'd badly misjudged Ginny, seen her through a fun house mirror, twisted by sex, had him suddenly doubting all he thought he'd known about her.

Miss Gertie saw Mike's indecision. She hated to lose a good customer like him, especially one with his connections. A little lie was surely the right thing in this circumstance. "She wanted to leave this place too badly. She maybe wanted to use people to do it, take a man's money or maybe even his heart." Gertie was silent for a moment, watching Mike closely before going on. "Ginny would not be the first. I have seen it many times. I do my best to guard against such things, but it is not so easy." She sighed and shook her head with what appeared to be genuine regret.

Mike sighed. "And you don't know where she's gone?"

"I don't," Miss Gertie said. "I'm sorry. Maybe it's for the best, no? Maybe better to find out this way before . . ."

Mike said nothing, but a part of him began to think that Gertie might be right. It wasn't as if the idea had never crossed his mind. He too had seen it done and to men he'd thought to have better judgment on such things. Maybe Ginny *had* been playing him and he'd been too blinded by her attentions to see it.

"Come," Miss Gertie said in a reassuring, almost motherly tone, "come see my new girl. Her name is Chloe and she is well trained in all the ways of French love."

Mike allowed himself to be led, his head so muddled it hurt to think, his heart like lead in his chest. Chloe was indeed a gorgeous creature just as Miss Gertie had said. She was young and more than a bit exotic; skin like coffee with cream and eyes so wide and dark that a man could fall right into them and lose himself altogether. Mike allowed himself to be charmed into her bed, but he hadn't more than taken his shirt off when he stopped for a long moment and shook his head almost regretfully. "Chloe. You're a peach," Mike said with a sad smile, "but I have to go."

14

MIKE WAS STEPPING through the front door of Miss Gertie's when he felt a hand on his shoulder.

"Somethin' ta tell ya," Kevin said in a low voice, following Mike out onto the wide brownstone stoop. "Listen, Ginny, she didn' steal nothin'." He lit a cigarette and flicked the matchstick toward the curb. "Don' think she did anyhow."

"How you know that? I mean she didn't seem the type, but then . . ." Mike paused. "But who knows sometimes?"

"Yeah. Sometimes ya can't be sure o' t'ings, but I had a strong feelin', like. It's like ya said. She ain't da type. B'sides da prick she was wit, he was a right bastard. Roughed her up pretty good. I seen worse mind ya, but it went pretty hard wit Ginny. She clipped the mug wit' a pitcher though. Give 'er credit for that. Gertie got sore about it, can't have the girls bustin' heads. No good fer business, ya know."

"So Gertie's story was bullshit?"

Kevin gave a long pull on his cigarette and finally said, "Dat's right."

Mike thought for a moment as he leaned against the cast-iron railing at the top of the steps. A curtain moved in a front window, catching his eye. "We're being watched," he said with a nod toward the house.

"Miss Gertie," Kevin said dismissively. "She knows it wasn' right what she done; kicking Ginny out." He spat on the stoop. "Gertie's getting kinda skittish lately, I guess. Business ain't so good an' da precinct's always wantin' more money. She don' need da trouble."

"Who's the guy she was with, the one she brained?" Mike said.

"Johnny Suds, least dat's what everybody calls him. Don' know his real name."

"Where's the bastard live?" Mike asked.

Kevin grinned. "Now dat I can tell ya. Payin' him a visit?"

"Could be," Mike said. "And you don't know where she went, huh?"

"Wish I did. Got da feelin' youse'd pay good money ta know it."

Mike showed him a twisted grin while Kevin gave him the address, then started down the stoop. He stopped suddenly though, two steps from the bottom, turned and went back up. "I wanna take a look at her room."

A wave of guilt swept over Mike as he walked east toward Long-acre Square an hour later. It was an entirely new feeling and it surprised him. Guilt had never been something he'd associated with women. The allure of the sporting life had always meant the total absence of it. Maybe even more magnetic than the endless variety of women available in New York, the guiltlessness of it had always made his indulgences weightless, effortless, and all the more pleasurable. He'd never cheated on a loving wife or a doting girlfriend. He'd had no reason to take anyone's feelings into account save his own—no lies, no stories, no out-of-the-way assignations, no repercussions or disapproval—these were things no married man enjoyed. He had been free to whore to the depths of his wallet with no one to say a word to the contrary. Until now there had been nothing to stand in his way, least of all guilt.

But he'd found Ginny's diary when he searched her room, and though he hadn't read it all, he'd seen enough to make his temptation with Chloe feel like the deepest betrayal. He tried to shrug it off as he walked past the new Times Building at the triangle between Broadway and Seventh. But he could still feel its weight on his chest. The diary was damp in his sweaty right hand and his left ached under the plaster cast. Years of rationalizations, carefully constructed, layer upon layer, seemed suddenly transparent. It was true that his lifestyle had required no lies or excuses to others. But that freedom was a myth. He'd been lying to himself, believing he was hurting no one, that somehow the stones he'd cast into life's pond left no ripples. That lie now seemed infinitely more damning than those he'd avoided.

Mike stopped at the reservoir near the corner of Forty-second and Fifth, the weight of the diary more than he could carry any farther. He leaned against the towering stone wall of the reservoir, the huge blocks cool against his back. People passed in clusters, wagons and carriages rumbled, and hooves clopped on the hard pavement. A cop's whistle blared from the corner and brass horns honked like geese on migration. Surrounded by the din and clang, the endless tide of flowing humanity, Mike had never felt more alone. He opened Ginny's diary and began to read.

A heart is the heaviest of organs. Mike would never have believed that without reading Ginny's diary. As he read the words on those pages, writ with perfectly formed, rounded letters, their weight bent his back and bowed his head. Her heart was his to carry. That much was clear, even before he reached the last few pages, especially with the last entry. "Mike sent flowers today," it read, "his note broke my heart."

The apartment at Sixteenth and Second showed no signs of life. No light shone from under the door or through the transom window above. It was late, though Mike didn't realize it until he checked his watch.

Not thinking, Mike banged on the door with his cast, sending bolts of pain up his arm. "Sonofabitch," he muttered. It did nothing to improve his mood. He banged again with his good hand, shaking the door in its hinges, and rattling the transom glass. "Johnny! Johnny Suds? Open up!" No answer. He tried again, figuring Suds for a heavy sleeper, but got the same result.

He tried the knob, but it turned in his hand and Suds was suddenly in the open doorway, a nightstick in his hand. "Who the fuck're you? Gimme an answer you fucker 'fore I bash yer head in." Suds raised the stick and shook it under Mike's nose for effect.

Mike didn't hesitate. He swung around as he grabbed the arm, locking his own under it, and yanking up on the elbow until Suds gasped in pain and let the nightstick clatter to the floor. He put a finger at the base of Suds's neck and pushed Suds back into the room. "You should be more careful who you wave your fucking stick at." He gave a shove to the man's neck and Suds fell back, gasping against a table and holding his throat.

"Who the fuck're you? I don' owe you nothing. I paid the—" Suds started to say, but stopped himself in midsentence. "I know you," he said, frowning. "You was in the papers. You was that cop. Saw your picture."

"You were about to say something, Johnny? You paid the Bottler already?" He knew it was a long shot, but figured it was worth a try. "And you did pay him, didn't you?"

Suds gave Mike a disbelieving look. "Dunno what da fuck yer talkin' about," Suds said, standing up, still massaging his throat.

Mike's attention flickered for an instant as he considered what angle to take next with Suds. It was Suds who made up Mike's

113

mind, launching himself, hands grabbing for Mike's throat. Mike grabbed and twisted in one fluid motion, using Suds's momentum against him. He threw the man over his outthrust leg, catapulting him into the open door where he crashed in a heap. Mike didn't wait for him to get up. In the dim light he came down hard on the man's shin, feeling it break under his heel. Suds shouted out and grabbed for his leg, his breathing rapid and ragged. The automatic was in Mike's hands without his thinking about it.

"Lemme see your hands!" He kicked at the leg and got a high-pitched yelp. "Your hands. Now!"

A pair of hands shook in the light of the doorway, as pale as dead squid at the Fulton Market. "You were saying you'd paid the Bottler," Mike said calmly. Suds started to sob. "Fuckin' Bottler'll kill me," he said between gasps. "But you don' give a shit, do you?"

"Shut up or I'll kill you myself. The Bottler was behind that thing the other night," Mike said as if he was sure.

Suds nodded. "He's been shipping in the makins for his rotgut; cocaine, whiskey, the rest he gets legal. The stuff on that ship; that was Kid Twist's. The Bottler figured he was tired of the competition. But how the fuck you get on to me?" Suds said, shaking his head while he grasped his broken leg. "I'm just small potatas. Just sell the stuff around is all. Ain't no law against it."

Mike grunted. Suds was technically right. There wasn't, but Mike wasn't about to let that stop him. He kicked again at Suds's leg, wringing another wail out of him. "I want your complete attention, Suds." Mike crouched down and pulled out a leather sap from his back pocket. "Now you're going to be completely honest with me. And any time I think you're holding something back, I'm gonna make sure I have your attention. We understand each other?" Suds nodded and Mike stood to close the door, eyes never leaving Suds. "Now, you're going to tell me everything you know about the Bottler," Mike said as the door slammed shut.

It was at least an hour before Mike was satisfied that he'd gotten everything Suds had to spill. It wasn't a lot really, but it was enough. He'd only had to use the sap a couple of times, though in a way he'd hoped for more. "You know," he said as he stood, helping Suds into a chair. "I didn't really come here to find out about the Bottler."

"Huh?" Suds's brow knotted with confusion.

"That ain't what I came here for," Mike repeated.

"What da . . . ?"

"I came here because of Ginny, you pile o' shit."

"The little whore?" Suds asked, shaking his head in confusion. "That gash I fucked last night? Wha' da fuck? Who gives a shit about a twist like that?"

Mike was ready for it. He hit Suds in the nose, hit him so hard Suds shot backwards, the chair going out from under him, bouncing his head off the floor. "Little whore, huh," Mike growled. "You're lucky I don't kill you, you sack o' shit. You talking about Ginny? That girl?"

"I didn' do nothin'," Suds moaned through his hands, blood running between his fingers and down his cheeks to the floor. "She done it all and liked it. Hit me with a fuckin' pot, the bitch."

Mike's vision blurred, going red around the edges, his ears buzzing like a hive full of bees. He lashed out, kicking Suds again and again while the man screamed and blubbered. There was no kung fu in it, no trained precision, just a fury beyond his control. He didn't know how many times he kicked Suds or even where he hit him. He just kept at it until Suds cried like a baby, his screaming high-pitched and helpless.

Mike went down on one knee, thrusting his face close to Suds. He pushed the muzzle of the Colt into his gasping mouth. "How you like that? You want more? How you like I blow your fucking head off? You think you'd like that?"

Suds sobbed around the barrel of the Colt, his body shaking as if he was still being stomped.

"Where is she? You know? You got three seconds."

Suds shook his head, but couldn't manage anything more than sobbing moans. Mike thumbed back the hammer.

"No! No!" Suds managed, his eyes going wide. "No!"

It was all Mike could do not to pull the trigger. The thought of what the groveling piece of shit before him had done to Ginny had him as close to losing control as he'd ever been. The Colt shook in his hand. To stop it, he jammed it even farther down Suds's throat. Suds choked and drooled around the barrel.

"Who's there?" a voice called from down the hall. "I'm calling the police, damn it. I'm callin' the goddamn cops, see. See how ya like that." A door slammed.

Mike eased up on the pistol, the voice like ice water dashed in his face. "Where is she?" he hissed at Suds. "Tell me now or the cops'll be picking up your fuckin' corpse."

"Don' know. Don' know. Gertie's," Suds gurgled around the pistol. "Swear I dunno."

Mike waited a few moments before he took the pistol from his mouth and wiped off the spit on Suds's pant's leg. Without another word, Mike stepped to the door, the pistol staying on Suds like a compass needle.

"I need a doctor," Suds managed through swollen lips. Mike stopped. He almost pulled the trigger then, could feel his finger tightening of its own accord. There was no thought of consequences, no sense of right or wrong, just the blur again and the buzzing. He stood for a long time, almost a minute, not giving a shit if cops were called or not, holding the automatic on Suds's head, his nerves crackling, ragged and sparking beneath his skin in little jumps and starts.

Slowly he regained control. With great effort, the pistol lowered. Mike tucked the automatic into his shoulder holster and disappeared.

15

GINNY SLEPT LONGER than she could ever recall. She slept all through the next day, remembering it only because she had used the toilet down the hall. She had a foggy vision of shuffling bare feet on the cold hallway floor, and sometime later settling back into her creaking bed like an autumn leaf. She'd discovered the secret of plumping her single, thin pillow into something passably comfortable. It smelled faintly of old drool, but felt like heaven.

When she finally woke, she was hungry. The window above her door was the color of fireplace ash. She figured it was sometime around six. It was strange, yet somehow marvelous, to have lost a day like that. At Miss Gertie's she'd often worked until the iceman came knocking at the kitchen door in the morning. It had been a scrambled existence with sex the only real timepiece.

Ginny's stomach growled as she dropped her feet to the floor. She realized that she hadn't had a proper meal in nearly two days, not counting the apple she'd bought from a girl on the street while searching for a room. She splashed some water on her face and sprayed a little cologne behind her ears, hoping it would hide her unwashed condition. She smoothed the wrinkles from her clothes as best she could, realizing that she'd have to add an iron to the growing list of things she needed to buy. Her reflection in the small mirror screwed to the back of her door was indistinct and gray. She blinked and rubbed at the glass. She looked like a ghost, her skin pale and strands of hair straying off in a frazzled aura around her head. "You look a sight, girl," she said to her reflection. It was one of her mother's standards. She'd come back from playing with her brothers, or working with the cows or chickens and hear those words, colored with equal parts of disapproval, exasperation, and love.

She was changing, her old self dropping away. She was becoming something new, something entirely more ordinary, more regular, and respectable. Ginny brushed the errant hairs back and secured them in a neat bun. She smiled at her reflection. A factory girl smiled back, or a shop girl or maybe even an office girl, definitely not a whore.

She would set about making that transformation the next morning. She'd get herself a respectable job, new clothes with a bit less flash and with them a new way of thinking about herself. She'd put the old Ginny away. It would be the new Ginny who would find Mike. She wondered if he knew what had happened, if he was already looking for her. She hoped he was, but didn't want to be found, not just yet.

Ginny stepped into the street a few minutes later, her stomach growling, but her spirits high. She found a sandwich shop on Forsythe where she joined a small crowd of showgirls, whores, rubes, panhandlers, gamblers, and hawkers, sitting so close it looked as though they shared arms. The soup was hot and not as watery as she expected. She wolfed down a plate of boiled ham, slathered with mustard, and with burnt biscuits on the side. She just about cleaned the crumbs off the table, but still felt she could eat more. She thought about going back in line for more, but her purse wouldn't allow it. She had to watch her money until she got a job.

The whores at the next table were loud and Ginny couldn't

help but listen as she nursed her coffee. She imagined for a moment that she was back in Miss Gertie's kitchen with Eunice and Rachel and the other girls. She missed them in that moment though she hadn't really thought about them these last couple of days. She'd had companionship with them, if not much more, girls like her who knew how she felt and when to lend a sympathetic ear when things got bad. Ginny ached for that. She felt alone in that moment, so much that no amount of noise or laughter or elbows in her side could bridge the seas that surrounded her. She finished her coffee and fled.

Ginny left feeling better in body, though her spirit still lagged. The night had turned a little damp and there was a chill to the air. Ginny turned up her collar, feeling almost refreshed by the cold. The long rest and hot meal had taken the edge off her last night at Miss Gertie's, the blood and that animal Johnny Suds. Ginny smiled grimly and walked toward the Bowery.

She was wide-awake and couldn't think of going back to her room, so soon she found herself walking toward the Bowery a few blocks away. The lights from thousands of bulbs lit the night sky in that direction, sending up a glow that silhouetted the tops of the tenements for blocks. She could hear music too, faintly at first, a mix of instruments and styles that she mistook for the jangling of harness buckles and the bump and clop of wheels and hooves. As she got closer it was as if a dozen bands were parading in the distance, each playing a different tune. A constant hum came from everywhere and nowhere. She could see an organ-grinder working the block, hear a German band banging out a drinking song from somewhere around the corner and from a place Ginny couldn't identify there were strains of "My Pearl is a Bowery Girl," sung in a passable tenor. "She sets them all crazy, a spieler a daisy, my pearl is a Bowery girl."

Ginny had heard about the Bowery, of course, but had never actually been there. At Miss Gertie's none of the girls were allowed out much. The Bowery was never on the itinerary.

The crowds thickened as she drew closer to the cacophonous, glowing mecca of all things sinful. She noticed too that the vast majority around her were men, every one sporting a gray derby it seemed, with flashy clothes in bright colors. Plaids and stripes, the louder the better, were worn with flair and swagger as if every man carried a chip on his shoulder. What women she saw were of the low variety with gaudy makeup and trashy, close-fitting rags. They chewed gum, almost every one, making a show of the lips and mouth. They kissed their lovers openly, when and where they pleased.

The whores were little different, distinguished mainly by their clustering in little groups, trolling for customers, leading men into darkened doorways, fighting with their pimps. None of the girls at the house had ever walked the streets. That was where whores ended their careers. Ginny had always heard that such women were the most degraded, the most vile, their looks coarsened by alcohol or made lifeless by hop. She'd been told too that they bore the scars of angry pimps and rough customers and that the worst of them were walking disease factories. It went without saying that any man who'd lie with one was only slightly better.

Ginny watched them, taking a certain comfort in knowing that she had worked in the best of houses. Only the best and most beautiful girls would ever see the inside of a place like Miss Gertie's and she had been one of those. She felt superior to these tramps and with a small start thought that she had never felt superior to anyone before. But then the realization struck her that if she'd stayed at Miss Gertie's it would have been only a matter of time before another Johnny Suds scarred her, her beauty faded, and that she'd end her career here, whistling to Bowery boys.

Ginny came upon a small covey of whores just off the Bowery. They were clustered around a sandwich man. He had a wooden sign draped over his front and back, held up by straps over his shoulders. THE GRAND MUSEUM, it said on the back, HAS WONDERS FROM AROUND THE GLOBE, SEE MULITA THE SNAKE CHARMER, JO-JO THE DOG-FACED BOY, A PIECE OF THE TRUE HOLY CROSS, AND TORTURE IMPLEMENTS OF THE SPANISH! The girls were laughing and throwing their skirts up at the gaunt, hollow-eyed bummer. He grinned vacantly as he shuffled by them, but was stopped by one of the girls, who stepped in front of him, bent over, and threw her skirts over her back. She wasn't wearing panties and her pale ass stopped the sandwich man in mid-shuffle. He swayed before the sight as though he might fall over. The girls screamed with laughter. The sandwich man recovered from his shock though and lunged forward, both hands out like a child after a Christmas toy. The girl was too quick for him. She jumped out of his grasp with a laugh, turned, and slapped him hard across the face. He staggered to one side, where his ankle turned on the curb. He was pitched into the street, his sandwich boards clattering. Ginny stood still, fascinated and appalled as the man struggled to rise while men stepped around him and a wagon swerved. The signs were too much for him and at first he tried to roll like a turtle on its back. The whores shrieked and clapped their thighs as a loose circle of onlookers mocked the man's feeble attempts. No one helped. It was well known that sandwich men were the lowest of the low, so ruined by alcohol, syphilis, opium, or God knew what else, as to be barely human. Even ragpickers and night-soilers had higher status.

At last the man stopped struggling and lay there beneath his sign, the words THE ARMLESS WONDER, ONLY AT THE GRAND MUSEUM emblazoned in red letters across his front. The crowd didn't dissipate for some minutes though, seemingly unsatisfied with the show. There were taunts and someone threw a beer on him but he didn't move. At length a group of sailors picked him up and set him unsteadily on his feet. He stumbled forward like an automaton and soon melted into the crowd.

"Hey, sista, you workin'?" a man said to her a few steps further on. He wore a gray derby, tilted to one side, a bright white shirt with a Celluloid collar, a red plaid vest, and gray striped pants with shiny shoes peeking beneath the hems. The clothes were expensive, but the face had heavy, beaten brows, and a nose like a ripe strawberry. "Yer a beaut! What a bundle! C'mon, let's us have some fun, huh? I'll take ya spielin'."

Ginny didn't hear the rest. She walked faster, turned the corner heading south, and quickly lost herself in the crowd. The lights were almost blinding after the relative darkness of Forsythe Street. Dime museums, dance halls, pawnshops, bars, and cheap hotels lined the street. Hawkers shouted above the dance hall bands and street musicians. There were others whose sole job seemed to be to push as many people off the sidewalk and into doorways as possible. A man vomited at the curb just a few steps down the street and a woman was shoved into the back of a Black Maria, shouting curses at the cops who'd arrested her. A dance hall's open doorway gave a brief glimpse of a chorus line doing the cancan, legs kicking high, the audience cheering over the crashing of the band.

Ginny felt as if she'd been transported to another world where every base instinct was celebrated, raised on high and crowned with electricity. There was a free-for-all jump-and-crackle to the place, animating everything. The men had it in their faces, the women, too. It might have been from Edison's bulbs, but Ginny didn't think so. The crowds possessed the true fire. The bulbs were only the reflection.

The cops she saw seemed jaded and bored. They had the look of men who'd seen everything and strolled with what appeared to be relaxed indifference. Up close their eyes were hard and penetrating as they scanned the crowds, their helmets bobbing among the derbies, bowlers, boaters, and occasional top hats.

The cops eyed Ginny with interest and even curiosity. Most of the men she passed did. Though she knew she didn't look her best, she was still a very attractive woman. But that was not the only reason. She was unescorted. Unescorted women on the Bowery were either whores, showgirls, or out of their minds.

Further on, past a nickel shooting gallery, a wax museum, and a place that advertised TABLEAUX VIVANTS in lurid red letters, Ginny came upon a kinetoscope parlor. A crowd was just bursting from its doors, so she found her progress blocked just in front of the ticket booth. She had heard of kinetoscopes, of course, but had never actually seen one. Her parents had forbidden it, hinting that there was something unsavory or sordid about the places that showed them. The front of the building was all in lights and stills from the pictures were plastered like billboards on the walls, glued one on top of the other. A man shoved Ginny toward the ticket booth. "Just a dime! Just a dime fer a gran' ol' time!" he shouted, herding others after her. "Da wondas o' da woild faw yaw eyes unfoiled."

Ginny paid her dime and went inside the dimly lit hall. The fog and reek of cigarettes and the stink of unwashed bodies hit her like a wall, but a piano player in a straw boater by the screen tinkled out a quickstep that kept the crowd moving. The house filled and the lights went down. Suddenly, with the whir of unseen machinery, the screen came to life and the piano jangled dramatically. WHAT HAPPENED ON TWENTY-THIRD STREET, NEW YORK CITY flashed on the screen in black letters. They were gone in less than ten seconds, replaced by a view of the Flatiron Building, looking like the bow of a great ship plowing the concrete of Broadway. Carriages skittered by. Pedestrians walked with quick, jerky movements. A flag could be seen fluttering from atop one of the buildings on the Ladies' Mile. A horsecar came into view and one passenger jumped down at the corner of Twenty-third and Broadway. It took only a moment for Ginny to get used to the lack of color and only a moment more to feel as though she was actually there, standing by the park as the world put on a show just for her.

The whole thing lasted only half an hour. There were two more short films accompanied by the hardworking piano player. One was a boxing match, the other a rags-to-riches fable set in a Hester Street tenement. For thirty minutes, Ginny forgot about Johnny Suds, about Miss Gertie, her loneliness, and even about Mike. She remembered him when the lights came up and she saw couples sitting close. She wished he'd been there with her, holding her hand as they filed out into the electric night.

She was on the corner of Chrystie Street when a man stepped in front of her. "Hey, doll," he started, the rest she didn't catch. She'd already grown used to the propositions of strange men and had ceased to listen to their cajolings. Almost every man on the Bowery seemed to be either a pimp or a sport. She'd attracted a string of them, one more insistent than the last. This one was different though. He wouldn't step aside and wouldn't quit. He wasn't rude. In fact, he was almost well-mannered in a Bowery sort of way. She could not get a good look at his face though. She knew instinctively how dangerous it was to meet the eyes of a strange man here. He followed her for half a block, talking sweet, asking her where she lived and if she'd like to spiel, which she understood meant some kind of dancing. She shook her head at all of his efforts. He gave up at last but without the bitterness that some men showed at her rejection.

"Hope I'll see ya 'round, doll. Me heart's all but broke till I do," he said to her back, which drew a little smile across her lips. "I see ya smilin', doll," he called after her. "I'll be here t'morra. Come see me."

"Fuckin' bitch!" Ginny heard the shouting from nearly a block away and turned to see the commotion. The man who'd just been propositioning her was there with another woman, arguing as she gestured wildly, hands cast open.. He hit her with his fist and she fell like a rag doll. Ginny didn't look back, but she could hear shouted curses and the wailing of the woman. Instead she ran until she could hear the cries no longer.

16

PHOTO DAVE STOOD outside Barney's Old Treehouse Saloon, waiting for Chuck Connors to finish his bullshit. The man had made a career of it, spending half his day conducting tours of the Five Points and Chinatown, the rest spent lubricating his prodigious vocal cords. He was finishing up with some slumming uptown types and a couple of foreigners, giving them one last grisly tale of the Old Brewery and its cellar full of graves. The place had been the most notorious hellhole in the city, disease and murder taking its residents in equal measure. When the place had been torn down, dozens of bodies were found buried under its earthen floor . . .

"A word," Dave said when Connors had finally gotten rid of his tour and approached the door to Barney's.

"Huh?" Connors grunted without really looking at Dave.

"Big Tim," Dave said, "I got a message from 'im."

Connors looked then, looked closely. "Well, Dave, damned if it ain't yerself. C'mon in." He led the way to his back table where Chinatown Nellie waited over a nearly empty bottle of gin. "Hey, sweetie, get us a new bottle like a good molly, eh?"

"Fuck you, Chuckie," she said, but she got up to do it with a devilish grin nonetheless.

"Great ass on 'er," Chuck said, watching her walk to the bar. "That woman gonna kill me wit that ass."

"Worse ways to go," Dave said, though he didn't look.

"Yeah," Chuck said. "So how's it Tim didn' come 'imself?"

"Busy," Dave said. "He says to tell ya he'll . . . he's gonna . . . what the hell was that word he used? Tim's got some words you never did hear of. It was like inter . . . something." Dave fished about and a moment later came up with it. "Intercede! That's it. Tim's gonna intercede on behalf of your client. Those were his exact words."

"Okay," Chuck said. "Glad to hear it. "He didn' say when it's gonna get fixed?"

"Didn't say."

"What'll I tell my . . . ah . . . friend?" Chuck said. "I mean he's in a hell of a bind." Chuck didn't want to say more to Photo Dave. He wasn't sure how much Big Tim might or might not have told him about Lionel Saturn or the Knickerbocker Steamship Company.

"Don't know. Tell him Big Tim's gonna intercede. That should fuckin' well be enough."

" 'Course it is. 'Course it is." Chuck said, seeing that Photo Dave had developed a sour frown. "Damned if you ain't right, an fuck 'im if it ain't good enough."

"Right," Dave said with one raised eyebrow. He got up to go.

"Leavin' without a drink?" Chuck asked. A breach of etiquette in his book.

"Things to do," Dave said. "Tim keeps a full schedule doin' the people's work. Another time."

Chuck waved him off. "Me regards ta Big Tim," he said so the rest of the bar could hear, before turning toward his girl. "Nellie, you sweet little bundle, sit that bottom on me lap like a good molly an' we'll see if we can find the bottom o' this bottle."

17

"HOW IS THE hand?" Primo asked when he met Mike at the station house the next morning. "The pain, it is keeping you up?"

"Pain?" Mike said, seeming confused. He knew he wasn't looking so good. He hadn't shaved and there were deep circles under his eyes. "Oh, yeah, the hand. Hurts some."

"Uh-huh," Primo said. "You no look so good. Maybe you need a day off."

"Ginny," Mike mumbled as if he hadn't heard. "She had a . . . problem at the place an' they . . . well. She left."

"The girl? The one you sent the flowers?"

"Yeah."

"Mamma mia. You are in love! Look at you. You are like shit from the goat. We will find this girl, no?" Primo said, as if that were a matter of course.

"And there's another thing," Mike added with a weary but satisfied tone. "I learned a little something about the Bottler."

"How, the hell did . . . ?"

"I went after a guy, a guy that Ginny was with . . . at the house. He needed some straightening out, so . . ."

"So you straightened him," Primo said with a little grin. "But why do I think he is not so straight really."

"Yeah, well," Mike said. "Truth is I nearly killed the bastard. Came that close."

"And? What does that have to do with this Bottler?"

"Everything," Mike said, then took a deep breath and told Primo what he'd learned from Johnny Suds.

"Okay, so we find the girl—" Primo started to say once Mike had finished.

"Maybe," Mike said as he dropped into his chair.

"What is this maybe? We will find her. That is all there is to that."

"I talked with the captain," Mike replied. He stopped to check on who was within earshot. "He wants us to see that cop; the one that got stomped by those two guys."

"Shit! I was hoping maybe we could get out of that." Primo threw up his hands "When it rains it comes in the cats and dogs."

"You mean it pours," Mike said. "Suppose you're right about that."

"Right. It pours in cats and dogs."

Mike gave a slight shake of his head. "So whadya mean by that anyway? What else is going on?"

Primo handed him a note. It was written in Italian. The letters were big and jagged like stabs at the page. Whatever it said, it was no love letter. "What's it say?" Mike asked, turning it over to check the other side. "How'd you get it?"

Primo pulled a knife from his pocket. It was a stiletto, with a long, thin blade and an ebony handle. Primo raised it and jabbed it down into Mike's desk, where it quivered dramatically, which seemed to please him somehow. "The note, it was stuck to my door with that. To make a long tale a short story, it says they will cut me up into little pieces and feed me to pigs." Primo shrugged. "The usual thing."

"Pigs?" Mike said, not entirely sure that Primo wasn't making one of his jokes.

"Pigs. Sure. They eat anything, bones, shoes, brains. They are not so picky eaters."

Mike grimaced. "Nasty. The Black Hand?"

"Of course. They no forgive so easy. For them it is vendetta."

Mike grinned at that, which drew a puzzled frown across Primo's brow. "What is so funny? They want to turn me into pig shit and you think that is funny?"

"Exactly! That's what's funny, partner. You're pig shit already." Mike pulled the knife from his desk and examined the hole it left with a frown. He fingered the needle-sharp point of the blade. "I suppose you thought about fingerprints?"

"I put the talcum powder on it when it was still in the door. No prints. They are angry, but not so stupid."

"Listen," Mike said, turning serious. "You can stay with me if you want. I got room. Probably be a lot safer."

"With you?" Primo shook his head and said with a smile, "You draw trouble like flies on the shit. I would be a safer man in the Tombs."

"Could be, but don't say no. Say maybe at least. Think about it."

"Maybe then."

"Good. The door's always open, partner."

Primo didn't say anything. He just stuck his hand out to shake. Mike took it, standing as he did.

"Now what," Primo said after an overlong silence.

"Now we solve the case, find the girl, put a muzzle on that stupid cop, and try to keep you from getting fed to the pigs."

Primo laughed. "Easy. What are we doing after lunch?"

They headed toward the hospital, but made a detour to the shop where they'd beaten the cop, whose name they had learned was

Bascomb. The shop owner was happy to see them. "The cops was just here," he said with a glance out the window. "No more'n two minutes ago. Listen, I told 'em all about the two gangsters beat that cop in here. Eastmans they were; one tall an' dark with a scar on 'is cheek, the other shorter an' heavier with bandy legs an' a tooth missin'."

"Very convincing," Mike said with a somewhat relieved grin. "Anything else?"

The storekeeper told them everything he'd told the cops, pretty much a straight description of what had actually happened while leaving out any references to him and Primo. There was no need to embellish that really. They thanked the man and Mike made an effort to give him ten dollars, a week's wage for a man like him, but he refused. "Worth ten bucks just to see that bastard get a good beatin'," he told them almost wistfully. "You boys go on an' don't worry 'bout me."

They started toward the hospital, but stopped after a couple of blocks. Mike looked at Primo, who seemed to know what he was about to say. "What the hell are we going to see that bastard for?"

"You are saying what I'm thinking," Primo said, nodding. "We tell the captain Bascomb was sleeping when we went."

"Sleeping. Yeah, he was sleeping an' the doctor said not to disturb him."

"Sleeping, yes. So what now?"

"I was thinking we should stop back at that store," Mike said once they were outside the hospital. "We forgot to ask him about the Bottler."

"The clerk? Why bother?" Primo said. "I thought you got everything from that Suds guy."

"Ya don't ask you don't get any answers, right? Besides we did him a favor, maybe he'll help."

The shopkeeper was surprised to see them again. He was still friendly, if a bit puzzled. "You boys forget somethin'?"

"We have returned to ask the thing we wanted yesterday," Primo said, which brought a wary cloud to the shopkeeper's face. "We are looking for a man. He is called the Bottler, a strange name I know, but maybe you have heard it?"

The shopkeeper looked from Primo to Mike as if measuring them before he replied. They caught his look, but said nothing, watching as the man made his decision. Mike could almost see the gears turning in his head. He'd helped them out with the Bascomb situation. He might figure they were even. So they waited, hoping that the weight of silence might do what words could not. The shopkeeper took a swipe at the marble counter-top with a damp rag he'd been holding, rubbing at a stain on the stone. He looked up from his countertop after a moment and took a deep breath as if he was about to plunge into icy waters. He smiled then in a resigned sort of way and said, "Ain't you boys had enough trouble?"

18

MIKE SALTER'S BAR on Pell Street was as good a place as any to meet without causing too much of a stir. Big Tim sat in the back, facing the door. Photo Dave was to one side, Sasparilla on the other. They were both well armed, a wise precaution given the situation. Big Tim's brother Dennis, known as Flat-nose Dinny, and his half brother, Larry Mulligan, stood at the bar as close to the door as possible. Between them all they had six pistols, three dirks, four pairs of brass knuckles, and three blackjacks. Big Tim wasn't armed. He considered it beneath a man of politics to carry weapons.

Flat-nose Dinny nodded to Big Tim shortly after they had settled in and a moment later Eat-'em-up Jack McManus was framed in the doorway. McManus had a reputation out of all proportion to his stature. He had a compact physique, all chest and shoulders with only the hint of a neck sprouting from his Celluloid collar. He wasn't more than five foot eight, but for him that was an advantage. Low to the ground, and heavy as he was, he didn't go down easy. Many a larger man had found himself looking up at Jack. He'd been the bouncer at the New Brighton Dance Hall, Kelly's place from years back, a place where wild nights and wilder characters were commonplace. Jack had handled them all, gangsters, drunks, bricklayers with hands like stone, upstate farmers hard as the earth. They got out of hand at the New Brighton and Jack had shown them the door. It was not his size or strength that had made his reputation, but his absolute unwillingness to ever give up, and to use whatever tools necessary to win. Brass knuckles, a knife, and at least one lead-filled sap were his standard equipage, though he was known to resort to teeth, beer bottles, chairs, and anything else that came to hand with equal aplomb. He was still head bouncer, but had left the daily bone-breaking to lesser men and was now said to be one of Kelly's top lieutenants. He was at ease today and when he entered he stepped to one side and quickly surveyed the room, which at that time of the afternoon was hardly filled. He eyed Dinny and Larry, but gave no sign he recognized either, though he knew them both well enough. Slowly he moved down the bar and positioned himself near the back. He looked at Big Tim and touched the rim of his bowler before he ordered a beer. The door opened again and Johnny Spanish stepped in, followed closely by Paul Kelly, sporting a snappy homburg and dressed in a tailored suit over a plaid vest. Pearl buttons and cuff links gleamed and a gold watch chain hung at his waist. A diamond stick pin secured his cravat and gleaming white spats framed his black leather shoes. The man ran the largest criminal empire in the city. He strode into Salter's like he owned the place even though Pell Street had become neutral territory just the year before.

Kelly looked neither left nor right, seeming not to care who might be in some dark corner, a measure of his confidence in Jack and Johnny. He'd left Kid Dropper at the door outside to head off any last-minute interruptions. Kelly walked over to Big Tim's table, a warm smile lighting his handsome features. Tim hauled his bulk from his chair as he approached and stretched out a massive paw. "Ach, you're lookin' like a new penny, Paul. Good ta see ya."

"You too, Dry Dollar. Always a pleasure. It's a shame our commitments keep us so busy. It's been too long."

It had been about a year since they'd seen each other, when Big Tim had presided over a gangland sit-down in a dive called the Palm Café on Chrystie Street, the goal being to settle a turf battle between the Five Pointers and the Eastmans. Minor skirmishes had occurred with increasing frequency in 1903 to the point where the newspapers were starting to call for a crackdown on gang activities. But the skirmishes erupted into an all-out gun battle when a group of Five Pointers raided a stuss game run by the Eastmans. They shot it out under the Second Avenue El at the arch at Rivington and Allen. More than a hundred gangsters had blazed away, including Monk Eastman, arrested when a company of police charged into the melee, killing three and wounding seven. Nobody knew how many had really died. The gangs were known to bury their own in cellars throughout the East Side.

Big Tim and a Tammany fixer named Tom Foley had arranged a truce and set up the meeting at the Palm, which had for a while ended the war. But renewed skirmishes had required another summit later in 1903 where the famous boxing match between Monk and Paul had been arranged to settle gang boundaries. The dapper Kelly had fought the apish Monk Eastman for hours, bare-knuckled in a neutral spot in the Bronx, both men collapsing in a draw. Some said the draw was a fix, but Eat-'em-up Jack could attest that Kelly had pissed blood for a week after, a fact that had only heightened Jack's respect for the man. Since that battle, things had remained relatively calm, which pleased Big Tim greatly. Murder and mayhem were bad business and he absolutely prohibited such foolishness around election time.

Tim sat back down and waved a hand at a chair for Kelly, who settled in after a warm greeting to Photo Dave and Sasparilla. Big Tim had always liked Kelly's manners. The man had polish, he had to give him that. Kelly could have gone far in the Wigwam if he'd chosen politics, despite being Italian. Kelly's real name was Vacarelli, a fact not generally known by his gangster associates. He'd named himself Kelly to better fit in with the Irish gangs when he'd started his criminal career in the eighties.

"Things are going well I hear," Big Tim said.

"Well enough, Dry Dollar. The Tiger prospers too I trust." The Tammany machine was often referred to as the Tiger, in political terms all too fitting.

"May it ever be so, Paul," he said with an adjustment on the hard chair. "Is there anything the Wigwam can do for you?"

Kelly raised an eyebrow. He was unused to offers of assistance from Tammany Hall, especially the unsolicited sort. "Nothing comes to mind," he said.

Big Tim nodded as if these were words of deep import. "Kid Twist keeping to his own?" he asked.

"Twist is Twist," Kelly said with a shrug. "He'll try some things now that Monk's away for good, but it's gonna take more than a flashy suit to fill Monk's shoes. For now my boys are minding our own business."

"Wise," Big Tim said. "Give Twist enough rope and he'll end up with it around his neck, eh? Might actually work out that way. The Kid was always a bit too bold for his own good, too impetuous. Not that Monk was a model of decorum," he added, laughing. Kelly grinned, but said nothing. In a way he had been sad to see Monk get sent up. But Monk wasn't the reason Big Tim had called for this meeting and he was getting tired of the chitchat.

"So, Dry Dollar, you didn't ask to see me to talk about old times, as enjoyable as that might be."

Big Tim smiled sadly and shook his head. He steepled his fingers in front of him and appeared to consider something before he spoke. Finally he said, "There's a gentleman by the name of Saturn."

"Saturn? Like the planet?" Kelly said.

"Like the planet," Tim replied. "He owes the Bottler something around ten thousand. I'm presuming you're aware of that."

Kelly nodded, his mind racing, but his face a mask. "A lot of money," he said. He made a show of plucking a bit of lint from his lapel, seeming quite unconcerned. "The Bottler must be getting lax with his accounts. I'll have to have a chat with him, remind him of proper procedures."

"Really?" Big Tim absorbed Kelly's words slowly like a man tasting a new wine. This particular vintage was all vinegar. Tim knew he had the upper hand, but it wasn't wise to show it. A man like Kelly needed his dignity, especially in front of his lieutenants.

"So, the Bottler hadn't told you," Tim said without inflection.

"The Bottler doesn't tell me everything, Dry Dollar. In fact, I leave him pretty much to himself, so long as he's on time with payments," Kelly said evenly. The fact that he actually was ignorant grated on him.

"That's a big number, Paul. Maybe you should ask him about it," Tim said.

Kelly shrugged and said. "So what's this Saturn mug to you?"

"A friend," Big Tim said. "A friend of a friend actually."

"Nobody's got more friends than you, Dry Dollar," Kelly said with a grin that had no mirth in it.

Big Tim couldn't help but grunt a laugh. It was nice to see a man like Kelly squirm a bit. As much as he enjoyed his job, enjoyed helping his constituents, it was the exercise of power, the subtle bending of wills that he truly reveled in. "The curse of the political man, Paul," he said with some theatricality. "And so long as I can keep 'em contented they'll stay my friends, and voting Democratic." He reached into an inside jacket pocket, a move that he noticed made Eat-'em-up Jack and Johnny Spanish tense up like dogs at the end of their chains. He brought out an overstuffed brown envelope and put it softly on the table. He slid it toward Kelly with one big finger. "This is to pay off Mister Saturn's debt to the Bottler, with my compliments. And there's something extra in there for your trouble," Big Tim said. "A couple hundred to keep the peace so to speak."

Kelly didn't touch it. "I can't speak for the Bottler, Dry Dollar, not without knowing the particulars."

Big Tim waved a hand at the envelope. "If it ain't enough, come see me. If it's too much then keep the difference with my thanks, eh?" He knew Kelly had no real choice. He and the former Chief Devery had been taking protection from the Bottler for some time. They could yank that protection and let him twist in the breeze or shut him down outright. The Bottler's game was the most profitable on the East Side. Nobody wanted anything unfortunate to happen, least of all Paul Kelly.

Kelly seemed to read his thoughts. "Why not go to the Bottler yourself? Devery knows where to find him."

Tim smiled broadly. "Because Paul, like so many others in this great metropolis of ours—*you* are a friend of *mine*."

19

THE ENVELOPE FELT like a lump of lead in Kelly's pocket. Normally he'd be pleased to feel that thickness and weight there in his jacket. But this was no normal wad and there was no comfort in it. If anything it was a reminder of how easily he'd been trumped. Worse still there didn't seem to be a damn thing he could do about it. Kelly ground his teeth as he stomped down Pell Street. McManus, Spanish, and Kid Dropper followed with glum resignation, walking fast to keep up. When the boss was like this it was best not to follow too closely.

They climbed the stairs to the station of the Second Avenue El a few blocks away with Kelly still in a brooding silence. Jack mused on them taking the El like common citizens. The boss could afford a chauffeured barouche if he wanted, or one of the new automobiles, but those things meant nothing to him. Despite his sophistication, the boss still had the common touch.

"Jack," Kelly said with a twist of his head to indicate he'd like to talk to him alone, "I have a job for you." He trusted McManus about as much as he trusted any man alive. He was a reliable, if somewhat unimaginative, lieutenant, not a bad combination to Kelly's way of thinking.

"Yeah, Paul. What youse want?" Jack said as he followed

Kelly to a deserted portion of the platform. "Youse want me ta pay dat mug Saturn a visit?"

Kelly let a smile creep across his lips. "You see, Jack, that's why you and me get along so well."

Jack nodded as if that were true. "Youse want 'im hurt but not dead, right? Teach 'im a lesson in how t'ings is?"

Kelly hesitated a moment before answering, considering again the implications of what he was about to order. Kelly had to assume that Big Tim did, in fact, have designs on Saturn's Knickerbocker Steamship Company. The Tammany boss was not a man to make a ten-thousand-dollar investment for the sake of goodwill and a few votes. Sending a message to Saturn was therefore a dangerous business. If Saturn wound up dead, he could lose Big Tim's protection. At the very least, the cops would be all over his operations. It would be open season on the Five Pointers and everything he had built.

"This has to be handled neat, Jack. Nobody pointing fingers back at me. Recruit somebody through one of your guys, a low-level guy, but somebody smart, who can do what he's told. Got it?"

"Sure, Paul, sure. I'll fix it so's nobody'll know 'cept Saturn. He's gonna know, I guarantee!"

Kelly shook his head and stared hard at Jack, his eyes as black as a grave in a cellar. "No! Not even that! I don't want him to know. Just make it look like a regular mugging or something. Maybe get it done on the street near the Bottler's if that damn fool is still gambling. But remember, he's gotta live."

"Sure sure. Livin' an' breathin'. I got it."

"And Jack, once that job's done, I want to see the Bottler."

"Sure, boss, but youse could just go an'—"

"No! Bring him to me! You got that? I want him where I can . . ." Kelly hesitated. The El train rumbled toward them, vibrating the steel beneath their feet. There really wasn't a need to say more. "Just get him."

20

MIKE AND PRIMO stuck to the shadows of Suffolk Street as much as possible. They'd been watching the tenement where the Bottler ran his game for almost four hours. The shopkeeper had confirmed the address Mike had gotten from Johnny Suds and they'd set up near each end of the block where they could observe men going in and out. It was like watching the tide and about as interesting. With the exception of a small-time gangster or two, most of the men they didn't recognize. The only thing of interest was a carriage that had sat at the curb the entire time they'd been there, its driver dozing most of the time, getting down only once to tie feed bags to each of the horses.

They had decided to just watch the place for a few days, see who went in and out, maybe match someone up with Smilin' Jack's gang of river thieves. Suds's admissions weren't enough to arrest a protected man like the Bottler. They'd need more for that. Though Mike would have liked to go in hard, wring the Bottler for his connection to the Hookers and cocaine smuggling, he knew that a more patient approach was likely to yield the better result.

They'd spent some time that morning trying to track Ginny, managing to find the bank branch she used, simply by canvassing the ones closest to Miss Gertie's. Unfortunately, the only address on file was for the brothel. They got a promise from the manager to call if he saw her. Mike figured that couldn't be long. With no source of income, she'd need money soon. It was a small step, but a hopeful one. As the day wore on he wondered where she was, how she was and whether she was thinking of him. The words from her diary entries repeated in his head.

It was getting late, somewhere near midnight when Mike and Primo rendezvoused at the corner of Suffolk and Rivington to compare notes.

"I'm seeing double," Mike said, rubbing his eyes. "What about you?"

"Triple," Primo said groggily. "I fell asleep on a stoop up the block. The Pope could have gone to play stuss and I wouldn't have seen him."

Mike looked at his watch. "Eighteen-hour day. Roll call at six A.M."

"Do not remind me," Primo replied.

"What'd that driver say?" Mike asked as he tucked his watch back into a pocket. Primo had come down the block to meet Mike and had engaged the driver of the parked carriage in a brief conversation.

"Not much. Said his boss likes to gamble."

"That's a surprise," Mike grumbled. "He didn't say who his boss is, did he?"

"I did not ask. I thought it might be too nosey for just then."

"Nosey," Mike said. "You're supposed to be fuckin' nosey. You're a cop."

"Exactly," Primo replied with his hands in the air. "But I don' want him to know that!"

Mike shook his head and ran a hand through his hair. "Fuck it, we're both so tired neither of us is thinking straight. Sorry."

"Maybe I should ask that question, but I did not say I no have the answer."

"Huh," Mike said, unsure of what Primo had said.

"We talked about the carriage; a fine one. Good horses. The driver, he said his boss works for the Knickerbocker Steamship Company."

"Never heard of 'em," Mike said, sounding confused. "But did you just say you got his name, the boss I mean?"

"Sure I got his name."

"But you just said you didn't ask. What the hell were we just talking about?"

"I no ask," Primo said with a little grin. "That does not mean he didn't tell me."

Mike gave Primo a shove. "You dumb wop. It's too late to be playin' games. You got the guy's name?"

"Sure, but it is a strange name. Saturn, like the planet."

"Saturn. You sure?"

"Sure I'm sure."

Mike looked back at the Bottler's doorway. "I'm tired of waiting. I'm going to go play a little stuss before the night's over, get a look at the Bottler in the flesh, and see if this steamship guy is cozy with him. Awful coincidence a boat captain or whatever he is being here."

"A coincidence, yes, but I go gamble, not you." Primo said. When Mike started to object, he said, "I am easy mark. I do not speak so good English. They think they can take my money easy, not suspect I'm a cop, eh?" Primo said. Mike considered this for a minute and had to agree, though he hated to admit it. Primo was through the Bottler's door a few minutes afterwards.

An hour later Primo emerged and met Mike in a darkened basement doorway down the street. "He is a big man around the waist," Primo said when Mike asked for a description of the Bottler. "But he has the big shoulders and hands, like a stevedore. Nice satin vest in yellow, very good material. A big mustache and red cheeks like Saint Nick."

"A right jolly old elf, huh?"

"Not exactly. He has the eyes of the hunter. Very hard eyes, but he tries to hide them with a smile."

"And that guy Saturn? "

"He was winning when I left, but I think he was still down for the night. He sweats a lot."

"Knickerbocker Steamship Company," Mike mused a few minutes later after they'd decided to quit for the night and were heading back to headquarters. "It's definitely a connection to the waterfront but . . . ."

"They run those cruises or something?"

"Yeah. I think they do those trips out to the North Shore of Long Island, the picnic grounds out there and such. Can't see what an operation like that might have to do with the Hookers or the Bottler."

"Who knows, they . . ." They heard shouting two blocks behind them. Mike and Primo both turned to look, but neither could see the cause. Saturn's carriage passed as it made the turn off Suffolk onto Stanton and disappeared from sight. It was moving fast.

Mike looked at Primo. "What the hell was that?"

Primo threw up his hands. Neither really wanted to go back and find out, but the shouting continued. Then they saw someone in the middle of the street.

"Ah, shit," Mike said. "Let's go."

The shouting got louder as they walked back and they clearly heard the name Bottler. They sped up then, their weariness draining away.

"C'mon out, ya bastard! Youse owe me, Bottler. Hear me in there? C'mon out so's I can pop yer fat ass!"

144

The man doing the shouting was still in the street and now that they were near they could see he was waving a pistol.

"Bottler, goddamn it come outa there and get what's comin' ta ya! Twist says ya pays me an' youse betta fuckin' pay!"

The man paced under a streetlight and for a moment turned in their direction.

"Shit! That's Kid Dahl," Mike said, reaching for his Colt.

"He's an Eastman, right? So, he's with Kid Twist."

"Yeah. I've pinched 'im twice the last couple years. Dangerous little bastard."

"Youse got ten seconds, Bottler! I'm comin' in!" Dahl shouted from the curb, hopping like a spoiled child. Mike and Primo were on him before he knew they were there. "Wha da fuck?" he managed before the butt of Mike's Colt cracked his skull. Primo kicked Dahl's gun away when he fell and they had him in cuffs a second later, cursing and kicking, his head bleeding a little river into his collar.

As if this were a perfectly reasonable excuse for waving a pistol in the street, Dahl said, "Twist gave me a piece. That fucker thinks he can hold out on me. Braddock:, that you? Shit, you busted my head for the last time, damn, it. When I get out youse betta watch yer back."

"Tough talk for a mug rolling in horseshit," Mike said. He put a foot on Dahl's chest and pushed him backwards onto the street. "So how's it Kid Twist's got claim to the Bottler's game? That don't figure."

"How da fuck should I know?" Dahl groaned into the cobbles as he tried to roll over. "Twist don' need Kelly's permission. He takes what 'e fuckin' wants."

Mike and Primo yanked Dahl to his feet, trying not to get blood and shit on themselves.

"Twist makin' a move on Kelly's territory?" Mike said, holding the Kid's arms up painfully high behind his back. Dahl didn't answer. Perhaps he'd finally realized that he'd said too much already.

"Screw this," Mike said after trying a few more questions with no success. "Let's get him over to the Thirteenth." The Thirteenth precinct station house was just a few blocks away at the corner of Delancey and Clinton.

He and Primo had just started Dahl on his way when a patrolman came around the corner. After a brief conference, they gave Kid Dahl into his custody.

"Disturbing the peace, public drunkenness, and whatever else pops into your head, patrolman," Mike told him. "I'll be by in the morning. I want to talk to him, got it?"

The cop marched Dahl off to jail and Mike looked around. "Not gonna be so easy to carry out surveillance now, damn it."

"Not now," Primo agreed.

"Maybe shoulda thought o' that before, but what the hell. We know somethin' we didn't know before. May as well take a look," he said. The Colt came out again. Primo followed.

They entered through a heavy wood door, at least three inches thick, with steel straps and a tiny window with a steel cover. A second, interior door had been left open in an apparent hurry to leave. It opened on a parlor. The gaming room was behind that. There was no sign of the Bottler or anyone else in the back room of the tenement basement. A large, green felt-topped table stood at one end of the room. A number of chairs sat empty as did the bar. Cigars burned in ashtrays and seat cushions still bore the imprint of gamblers' hindquarters, but there was not so much as a deck of cards left to prove that this was much more than a social club.

"Fuck this," Mike said after a quick search and a look out the back door. "Start fresh tomorrow?"

Primo gave an audible sigh. "I am not so fresh now," he said. "Maybe some rest is a good thing." He nodded back toward the Bottler's card table. "Leave it alone?"

"Yeah. Besides, I wouldn't bust the place up without clearing it with the Thirteenth first."

Primo grinned. "See? You are not so stupid. I do not care what they are saying."

"Go fuck yourself, partner," Mike grumbled. He was too tired to kibitz.

21

GINNY HADN'T SLEPT well. She forced herself out of her bed, its springs squealing, and blinked like an owl at the thin light through her transom window. She forced herself to get moving quickly though, washing up and doing the best she could with her hair in what for her was record time; though still close to an hour. At the house she'd had hours to get ready for the evening's customers, often taking long baths with one of the other girls to save hot water. Miss Gertie had insisted on cleanliness, a tradition held over from the great madam Mary, whom Ginny had only heard about in legend. The girls had all enjoyed that indulgence. They'd do hair and makeup for one another, often experimenting with exotic looks. At times they'd dress up, picking clothes from Miss Gertie's extensive collection. There were always those customers who liked a girl dressed as a nun, a teacher, a schoolgirl, or a maid.

Ginny thought of Mike as she put her hair up. He'd never asked her to try on any of the costumes. He'd liked her the way she was. She'd given him that, whether he'd realized it or not, given him her true self. Ginny smiled wickedly as she recalled his one weakness, a fondness for white corsets, with matching garters and black stockings. She'd taken them when she left Gertie's. It was tempting to put them on and imagine he was there. Her hand stole down her belly and she closed her eyes, imagining it was Mike's.

But the image of Johnny Suds came flashing behind her eyes. Ginny took a deep breath and did her best to banish Suds to some particularly hellish corner of her brain. The urge to write in her diary about her experience brought the sudden realization that she'd left it behind at Gertie's.

The loss hurt for only a moment, when she remembered that this was a new life she was embarked on and that it was only right to put aside the things of the past. Mike was the only thing worth saving from those days, but even that reunion would have to wait a little longer. Ginny had a full day before her, so with a final check in her flaking mirror she set out to find a job.

She had been a competent seamstress by her mother's standards and like most girls had learned to sew as soon as she could handle a needle and thread. When she'd left home she'd taken her sewing kit with her—a small pair of scissors, two thimbles, and a few needles of various sizes folded into a leather case with a corduroy lining and a brass catch. Ginny tucked it into her handbag before closing the door behind her.

Her breakfast was a roll she'd saved from dinner. It was a little hard now, but still soft in the center. She nibbled at it as she walked west and north, not knowing where she was headed precisely, only that she didn't care to work on the East Side in what she'd heard were the most horrible sweatshops—cramped, dark, and smelling of unwashed bodies. She was determined to find work in one of the new, tall loft buildings she'd heard about, where they had windows and air and elevators, a modern place where a girl could feel like a human being. She knew such places existed, but wasn't sure exactly where, only that somewhere around Washington Square there were a few.

Ginny kept her eyes open, searching for *HELP WANTED* signs. Walking west on Washington Place, heading toward the leafy cool of Washington Square Park, Ginny was lost in thought

149

when a girl, no more than a teenager, burst from a doorway and ran into her. Ginny had a brief impression of red eyes, cheeks damp with tears, of a hurried apology, and heels clicking on the flagstones as she ran off. Ginny stood as if woken from a dream, watching the girl disappear around the corner of Greene Street. Looking back at the doorway, Ginny could see no cause for such an hysterical exit. It was an ordinary New York doorway although to a hulking, modern loft building that bellied up to the sidewalk, climbing skyward with stony indifference. Ginny felt curiously drawn to the place, the mystery of the crying girl like a magnet, pulling her hand to the brass latch, and guiding her into the lobby.

She looked about, seeing nothing out of the ordinary, a pair of men waiting at the doors to two narrow elevators and a sign for something called the Triangle Shirtwaist Company. What caught her attention were the words above the elevators: IF YOU DON'T COME IN ON SUNDAY, YOU NEEDN'T COME IN ON MONDAY. Ginny thought it a perfectly sensible sign, if a bit sinister. She hadn't experienced a Sunday with no work for her entire adult life. Even at home, there had always been chores after church. It was a day like any other to her and so long as she was paid for it, a day not wasted.

The elevators hissed and groaned until the doors of one opened, disgorging a dapper salesman with a bulging valise, two yarmulked tradesmen in black vests and white shirts, their sleeves rolled up on hairy arms, and a boy pushing a handcart stacked with boxes towering so high over his head that he had to peer around as he wheeled it out. Ginny stepped to one side to let the boy pass and was bumped from behind by a distracted-looking tradesman rushing for the elevator. They did a shuffling dance of mumbled apologies, which somehow carried Ginny into the elevator where a second later the door was yanked closed and the brass gate clattered shut.

"Floor," the operator said without looking at any of his

passengers. He threw over a lever at his right hand and they began to rise. The man who'd bumped her mumbled, "Nine," to the operator and Ginny decided in that instant that that's where she'd go. The Triangle Shirtwaist Company was listed as occupying three floors; eight, nine, and ten on the elevator directory, so nine seemed as good as any.

Ginny counted the floors as they slid by the gate, trying to remember if she'd ever been so high and deciding by the fourth that she hadn't.

"Nine," the operator intoned as the car bounced to a stop. The tradesman pushed out first and disappeared through a door to what appeared to be an office, leaving her standing beside an open barrel of machine oil, the hard, maple floor around it black with drippings.

Like a mechanical hive, the place hummed to the beat of hundreds of machines. Rows of them receeded into the unnatural gloom of the factory floor, clattering and whirring in staccato bursts. The whole place vibrated; the floor beneath her feet and the oil in the barrel. A curtain of lint danced in the air to their incessant beat. Women were hunched over them, heads held low, feet pumping pedals, hands feeding fabric under blurring needles. Walls of windows let in light and air, but the billows of lint were not to be overcome. The machines farthest from the windows were in perpetual gloom. Gas jets burned halos in the clouds and Ginny could feel their heat even though the nearest was several feet away.

"C'mon," a man's voice said beside her, startling her. He turned and walked to an empty machine near the end of a row. A pile of material sat stacked next to it.

"I am seeking employment," Ginny said to his back as she followed. The man turned and looked at her as if she might be insane. Ginny smiled, trying to appear firm yet affable, professional and pretty all at once. She wasn't sure if she pulled it off.

"Yeah," the man said.

"You have work, I take it," Ginny said. She was doing her best to sound like a woman of some education might, a woman of experience and worth. The man looked her over and turned back to the pile of fabric with a slight shake of his head. "We got woik, an' ya don' gotta put on airs ta get it. Youse wanna woik; ya shows me what ya can do," he said over his shoulder. "Sew dese up," he told her, separating some fabric and tossing it on the chair in front of the empty machine. "Lemme see what ya can do, den we'll talk about it."

Ginny got herself settled in. She got the feel of the machine, working the pedal to get some sense of its speed, the way the thread fed from the bobbin and checking if the needle was true. The man watched her for a moment, then stalked off down the row of machines, hands behind his back, bending now and again to examine a shirtwaist with a critical eye. Ginny set to work, trying her best to sew like the others, head down, feet and hands moving with practiced economy. She felt slow and awkward and was sure the women around her noticed, their sideway glances giving them away. Toward the bottom of her little pile though, she started to develop a rhythm and for a few rows of stitches felt she actually deserved to be there.

The shop foreman returned before she was done and hovered for a minute or so, watching silently. He picked through the shirtwaists she had finished, pulling at the seams and turning them inside-out to examine the work. "Six a week. Not a penny maw," he said before she'd finished the last piece. "Dis heya's yaw machine. Youse get heya at seven, woik ta seven." He looked at his watch. "Half a day's gone awready. Fawty cents fer t'day."

Ginny said nothing. Six a week was what she'd hoped to make even though it was laughably less than she'd been accustomed to at Miss Gertie's, where she'd easily make double that in an evening.

"Youse make a mistake, ya get docked," he went on. "Youse ruin a piece, youse pay fer it."

152

Ginny nodded. It was no worse than she would have expected. She thought of the crying girl who'd run into her on the street and wondered as she settled in to her work if the girl she'd run into had come from here, from this factory floor and this very machine. She couldn't imagine what might have driven her off. To Ginny this was a great and exciting opportunity, the start of her new life, the beginning of her new self. The noise and dust and bent backs of the factory were just part of the path that would take her away from her old life and, with a little luck, into Mike's.

He'd set her on this course. She'd been primed like an anarchist's bomb and Suds had set her off. She shuddered in disgust at the thought, but had to admit a certain debt to the man. Though Ginny had wished it would be Mike who would take her away, she was now at least free, at the beginning of a new life. All that remained would be to work hard and find Mike. As Ginny guided shirtwaists through her machine, those things seemed virtually accomplished.

22

L ISTEN, WHADYA SAY after we stop at the Thirteenth, we try to find Ginny?" Mike said to Primo as they walked out of police headquarters. Mike had been reluctant to press Primo into helping find Ginny, even though he'd seemed willing enough. It was a personal thing to him and nothing Primo should get involved in.

"You don' have to ask, Mike. The Bottler, he will be there later," Primo said. "Where we start?"

"Back at the house," Mike said. "Maybe some of the other girls know something. She might have gone home, or sent a message back to one of the girls. Who knows."

"Where is home?"

"From the way she talked I think she might be from New Jersey or Long Island, maybe up in Westchester. Ginny never talked about that, at least not to me. She'd always change the subject if I asked. Guess there were some hard times she'd just as soon forget."

It didn't take long to get to the Thirteenth Precinct station house and even less time to get the bad news about Kid Dahl.

"Fined 'im five dollars," the desk sergeant told them when they asked what cell the Kid was in. "Let 'im go last night."

"Shit! I wanted him held, goddamn it. Who the fuck let him go?"

The sergeant gave Mike a look that spoke volumes about his opinion of detectives in general and demanding ones in particular. He closed the log book with a snap and shrugged. "Wasn't on duty last night," he said.

"Listen, I gave that patrolman explicit instructions. I told him I wanted him fucking booked, not fined for chrissake."

"Explicit," the sergeant said. "How you spell that? I wanna write that one down. Got a fine sound to it."

"You fucking—"

"Mike! What're you doing here?" Tom's voice called behind them as he descended the stairs from the second floor.

"Hey, Tom," Mike said, turning. They'd agreed when Mike had entered the force that he shouldn't refer to Tom as Dad in front of other cops. "What the hell are you doing here? I didn't see your car out front."

" 'Cause it's in the back," Tom said, shaking hands with him and Primo. "So how's it going?" he asked in a way that told them he already knew the answer.

"Not so good at the moment," Mike said with an evil look at the desk sergeant, who had started scribbling dutifully in some report or other.

Mike explained the problem, but Tom hardly seemed to listen. "Come on outside," he said. Once they were on the sidewalk he told them, "Listen, I was just upstairs with the captain. We go way back. We had some, ah, you know, business to talk about. You know how the damn phones are; fine for official stuff, but there's always another pair of ears or two might be listening in."

Mike nodded. He'd used operators himself to help get

information, a tactic the force was only beginning to develop, let alone perfect.

"We've got some mutual business; stuff that cuts across a couple of precincts," Tom went on. "Anyway, he told me they let Kid Dahl go."

"But—"

"Listen, Mike, he's in up to his fucking neck with the Eastmans, okay?" Tom said in a low voice. "He lets certain things go by so long as they don't get outa line, start poppin' civilians, that sort of thing. You know how it works."

"Yeah, sure but I—"

"But nothing. You should've taken Dahl somewhere and gotten what you needed from him right then, broke his fucking fingers or something. Bringing him here was a mistake."

"It was late," Primo said in a way that indicated he knew it was no excuse. "We were tired."

Tom gave Primo an admonitory smirk, which slowly turned into a grin. "Fourteen-hour day? I guess I know how that can be. He was making a fuss outside the Bottler's, huh?"

"The captain told you? He knew?"

"Yeah, he knew. That was one of the reasons I drove over to see him. Once we knew what precinct the Bottler was in, I figured he'd know about it."

"I could've asked," Mike said.

"You could have, but he wouldn't have told you shit," Tom said. "I wasn't even sure he'd tell me. That's why I didn't mention it to you before."

Mike took a deep breath. "So what did you find out?"

"Where you two headed now?"

A couple of minutes later, Tom was at the tiller of the Olds, goggles down and duster flying as Mike and Primo held on to the seat as best they could. He was driving noticeably faster than just a couple of days before, surer with the controls, his shifts smoother and his use of the speeder and spark advance now much more confident.

"It's pretty much the way we'd heard it," Tom said over the noise of the engine and the whine of the gears and drive chain. "The Bottler pays Kelly. He's not exactly a Five Pointer, but he's aligned with them and Kelly gets a percentage. Dahl was waving his fucking gun because Twist's been trying to put the squeeze on the Bottler. Word is he told the Bottler he's paying Dahl now. Twist owed Dahl some favor or other, so he gave him the Bottler's game as a reward."

"But it isn't his to give," Mike said. "Not if the Bottler's paying Kelly."

"Right, but that don't mean shit to him. Twist wants something, he takes it."

"Kelly's not gonna like that," Mike said. "Shit like that's started wars."

"Hell, I've seen gang wars start over who's moll danced with who. This could get out of hand in a big way unless one of the Tammany fixers gets involved."

"What about the Hookers?" Mike said. Gang shenanigans and turf battles were not his primary focus. "The captain know about anything to do with . . . whoa! Watch it!"

Tom swerved around a carriage that had pulled out from the curb into their path. He seemed unperturbed, giving a couple of blasts on the horn and barreling by without slowing. Mike figured he had to be doing at least fifteen miles an hour, a breakneck pace for city traffic.

"He didn't know anything about them. The Hookers usually operate outside his precinct, so his men rarely cross paths with them," Tom said.

"You believe him?"

"Don't have any reason not to. Hold on!" He flew through the intersection of Houston and Broadway, forcing a man to jump out of the way and a delivery wagon to stop short, horses snorting in fright. "Damn, I love this car!"

"Gotta be a connection," Mike said, as they turned north on University Place. "Whether they know about it or not."

"You believe Smilin' Jack? He wasn't exactly known for his honesty."

"Smilin' Jack was about as close to death as a man can come. No need for him to lie." He looked at Primo, who was hanging on at the edge of the seat. "Guess maybe we'll watch and see what we can see for another week or so. Don't think my captain will let it go much beyond that anyway, not unless we turn something up."

Tom nodded. "Sounds about right. But no arresting the Bottler without a damn good reason, not just because he's running a stuss game, got it?"

"That coming from the captain of the Thirteenth?" Mike said.

"That's coming from everybody, me included. There's a lot involved here and . . . how should I put this . . . some outside interests that have to be considered, deals that have to be honored."

"Yeah, I guess Paul Kelly's not the only one the Bottler's paying. Devery, too?"

Tom didn't answer directly. "Listen, I'm not saying that if you can prove he's somehow running a river piracy operation you shouldn't nail him. He ain't paying protection for that. But you have to be able to prove it, understand?"

They didn't respond right away, so he went on. "You act too soon you'll just fuck it up, maybe fuck yourselves up too, end up walking a beat in the Bronx. Maybe worse. Your best bet is you find something, you clear it with me or your captain. Got it?"

Mike nodded. Primo grinned. "Got it."

Tom just rolled his eyes behind his goggles. He shook his head and hunkered down as they neared the intersection of Fourteenth.

The southwest corner of Union Square Park, where University Place and Fourteenth met, was as busy a corner as the city had, with horsecars, stages, pedestrians, hacks, carriages, and wagons making the crossing tricky at best and downright dangerous the rest of the time. Tom passed a horsecar, bumping over the rails, but not slowing much as a delivery wagon and a pair of carriages scissored in front of him on Fourteenth. Seeing an opening, he steered for the gap that he anticipated would open between them and powered through with no more than a foot to spare on either side.

They all heard the whistle, but at first didn't pay any attention, figuring it was just a cop they hadn't noticed. But oddly the whistle seemed to follow them and if anything grow closer. Tom didn't bother to look about until they were nearly past Tiffany's at the corner of Fifteenth. But Mike saw him; a bicycle cop, pedaling furiously to overtake them, tooting his whistle like a little steam engine. He'd never have believed a bike could go that fast if he hadn't seen it himself.

"Pull over!" the cop yelled once he spit his whistle out to flop on its lanyard. "Pull over!"

Tom applied the hand brake, pulling hard, retarded the spark and let up on the speeder. He put the tiller over and bumped to a halt at the curb, stopping so quickly that the bike cop had to swerve to avoid him. The cop hit the curb too hard, dumping the bike and sending him hopping and flailing in a most undignified manner.

"Who the fuck're you," he shouted at them, "going through an intersection like that? You coulda killed somebody! Ya got a dandy new rig here, but goddamn it, you're gonna get a dandy new fine to go with it!"

Tom, his uniform hidden under his duster, and Mike and Primo, in plainclothes, appeared to be ordinary citizens, a fact they didn't really appreciate until just then. Tom opened his duster as the cop put one foot on the spokes of the front wheel.

"I'm on official business, officer," Tom said. "Sorry if I was speeding. I'm Captain Braddock. These are Detectives Alfieri and Braddock." Tom elbowed Mike to show his badge, which was under his jacket. Primo flashed his, too.

The cop looked up, seeing the captain's badge and uniform under the duster. "Oh, for the love o' . . ." he said, half in apology and half in disgust.

"Officer, that's okay," Tom said. "Damn fine job of running us down, too. Fucked if I knew a man could pedal that fast."

The man grinned as a trickle of sweat ran from under his helmet.

"Who's your captain? You're out of the Fifteenth, right? So it's McConnell then? I'm sending him a commendation this afternoon, Officer . . ."

"Barber. Richard Barber," the man said, touching the brim of his helmet in something between a salute and a thank you.

"Good man," Tom said. "It'll go in your record, Barber. Ever try bicycle racing? You'd be a natural."

"Once or twice," Barber replied. "I do all right."

"Bet you do at that." Tom put the Olds in gear and one gloved hand on the spark. "Gotta get moving, Barber," he said, returning the officer's salute as they motored away.

By the time they reached Miss Gertie's, Mike had told Tom all he knew about Ginny and her disappearance. Tom mostly listened and Mike held nothing back, including the details of his visit with Johnny Suds. That story seemed to bring a nod of satisfaction from Tom, though it could have been the result of a bump in the road, Mike couldn't be sure which.

"So the Bottler was smuggling in cocaine," Tom said, seeming to ignore the information about Ginny. "No idea where he cooks his little brew, huh?"

160

"Not yet," Mike allowed. "But I have an idea how we might find out. That joint down on Park Row, you know the one?"

"Know it? They used to let the poor bastards lay in the street, but now they bring 'em a block from the precinct after they pass out." Tom shook his head with a rueful grin. "Better for the public image."

Tom brought the Olds to a stop in front of the townhouse about ten minutes later. "Okay, listen, I'm going to make some phone calls when I get back to my office. Your Ginny might have gone to one of the other houses, most of which I'm sure you know," he said with an attempt at a disapproving frown. "It'll save you the time checking them out. There's some places they only know about at the precinct level, real local stuff. I'll have them checked too. Lotta girls just work out of their own rooms now. Get a phone line put in and run ads in *The Rake* or something. Anyway, I'll put the word out she's wanted for some damn thing or other, not that any of the other captains give a shit. By tomorrow night there'll be a visit paid to every damn, ah . . . house in the lower half of the city. If she's working, we'll know it."

"Thanks. I'll let you know if I find out anything here," Mike said with a nod toward Miss Gertie's door. "One way or another, I'll call you later."

"Good," Tom said. "You should call your mother more often anyway. By the way, how's the hand?"

"Not bad," Mike said. He flexed his fingers, trying not to grimace. "Still aches a bit, but it'll be okay."

"Bascomb had a pretty hard head, huh?"

"Bascomb?" Mike said, stealing a look at Primo.

"Yeah, Bascomb. You remember Officer Bascomb, don't you boys? Kicked the shit out of him a couple of days ago?"

"Oh, that Officer Bascomb," Primo said, a little sheepishly.

"Yeah, that one," Tom said. "He was a useless fuck. Had him in my command a few years back. Couldn't stand him."

"How'd you know?" Mike said.

"Shit, I was a detective before I was an old fuck riding a desk. Besides everybody knows. Well, maybe not everybody, but nobody gives a shit. Hell, his captain's happy to be rid of him for a while."

Tom gave Mike a shove. "Anyway, get your sorry asses moving. I got places to go."

Mike and Primo watched as Tom pulled away from the curb, grinning under his goggles. A puffy cloud of exhaust lapped at their knees.

"How the hell did he know that?" Primo said.

"Been asking myself the same thing for the last twenty years," Mike replied. "He'll never tell you either, damn it!"

They left Miss Gertie's place about an hour later not knowing much more than they had before, aside from the fact that Ginny was originally from someplace on Long Island's North Shore. Mike figured he'd try the telephone directory back at the precinct later, but didn't have much hope. The city was sprouting new phones by the hundreds, but they were still a rarity outside the boroughs.

"So, we check that block-and-fall joint on Park Row?" Primo said.

"Guess so," Mike answered, still thinking of how he might locate Ginny's family.

"I know this place," Primo said as they headed for the El at Forty-second Street. "How they stay open so close to City Hall I don' know."

Mike looked at him with a disbelieving frown. "Don't know, huh? Not much of a detective, are you?"

They rumbled south on the next train, bouncing on the oversprung cane seats and fifteen minutes later were getting off at Chambers Street. A short walk across the park at City Hall had them at the front door. They pushed by a huge boulder of flesh at the front door, with a too-small bowler atop a head the size of a watermelon and a jacket large enough to hide an entire arsenal. The bar was sparsely attended this time of day, hard-drinking newspapermen, a smattering of down-on-their-luck Wall Streeters, clerks, and laborers making up the clientele, with the occasional hard case slouched on the bar or in a corner. Mike and Primo went up to the bar and Mike rapped on the mahogany to get the bartender's attention.

"Oh, Christ. Get the fuck outa here!" the man said as soon as he set eyes on Mike.

"Good to see you too, Bobby," Mike answered. Before he said anything more, he felt rather than heard the rumble of the bouncer behind him. He saw Primo reach into his jacket and turned to find the man two paces away.

Stepping forward almost casually, Mike shot out a hand, his fingers together like a knife. They buried themselves for just a moment in the base of the bouncer's neck, just above the collarbone, and came away before the giant could grasp them in his puffy paws. He emitted a gasping gurgle, doubling over and hands going to his throat as he wheezed. Mike grabbed the back of his head with both hands, pulling him down as he brought his right knee hard into his face. The giant went down like a deflated balloon, shaking the floorboards as he settled in a heap. "Now, Bob, let's us have a little chat, eh?" Mike said, crooking a finger at the bartender and pointing to the back as patrons drifted toward the doors.

The bartender put a hand under the bar and Primo whipped his pistol out. "Your hand, it better have a dishrag in it," he said and waved with the barrel for him to step away from the bar. With a grumbled curse and an unidentified thud behind the bar, Bob stepped back and followed Mike to a rear storage room,

Primo bringing up the rear, watching their backs. Mike sat him down at a battered table.

"I'm not gonna dance around this, Bob. Where do ya get your concoctions, the ones with the cocaine, benzene, camphor, that shit?"

"Fuck. I dunno. A mug delivers me a couple cases a week."

Mike clucked at him with a disappointed frown. "For chrissake, Bobby, nobody's gonna know unless I tell 'em. We understand each other? We can do a lot o' damage here if we want or it can go real easy."

"I got protection, Braddock. You can't fuck wit' me like dat."

"I ain't talkin' about your place, Bobby. I'm talkin' about you." Mike brought his short daystick down hard on Bobby's fingers on the table.

"Motherfucker!" Bobby shouted, almost crashing his chair backwards. "Goddamn it, Braddock. Wha da fuck you do dat for? Sonofabitch!" He shook the hand out as if it was on fire.

"Don' be a fucking whiner, Bobby. I din' hit you hard enough to break anything. Just getting' your attention. "

"Fuck you!"

"Right, well we'll see who gets fucked here, won't we?"

"The big one, he is groaning, Mike. I think he is waking up," Primo said from the doorway. "Maybe I go tune him up."

"Suit yourself, partner, but he's probably not gonna cause us any more trouble." His voice lowered. "So, Bobby, where were we? Oh, yeah, we were right about the place where I tell you I'm gonna spread the word on you. Word is you're a snitch for Devery. You get a kickback on every fuckin' lead you give 'im. Bunco men, stock swindlers, confidence men, pickpockets, the whole bunch."

"But I ain't done—"

"Oh, I know, I know, Bobby, but you know how the word on the street can be. Somethin' gets said an' before ya know it, yer havin' a chat with a couple o' Kelly's mugs an' a swim in the river. So, we understand each other?"

A sheen of sweat lit up Bobby's receding hairline. He managed to stifle a groan, but just barely.

"I'll take that as a yes," Mike said. "Now, where you get that stuff from again?"

Bobby sighed as the bouncer gurgled accompaniment from the barroom floor.

23

THE OLD BRICK warehouse they watched was near the corner of Mangin and Corlears. The streets were heavy with drays and Clydesdales. Packing crates and great rolls of rope stood at the curb before the chandlery next door. A constant fury of laborers and teamsters hummed about the streets, cursing, shouting, and sweating as they loaded and unloaded a stream of wagons.

The warehouse was a smallish, one-story affair, with a single, windowless door, three inches thick, leading to the office and a large double door, into the storage area. The big doors, painted a fading red, were thrown open and a wagon had been backed halfway in since they first arrived at around two.

"You know what's on the back side?" Primo asked. "I don't know this place well."

"I think it's a coal yard," Mike said. "Not sure though. Best to check. Might want to get in later and those doors look pretty damn solid."

"I will take a walk," Primo said. "Maybe see if I can get a look at the roof. Might be a how you call-it . . . a skylight." Primo walked off, lost in the street traffic in seconds, while Mike tried to stay out of the way.

Bobby had given them this address once he understood the way things were. Mike really had no intention of spreading the word he was a snitch. It would've been more trouble than it was worth, but the bartender didn't know that, and couldn't afford to bet otherwise. He got a shipment of the ingredients on a regular basis, at least every ten days, and often sooner, he'd said. Of course, there was nothing illegal about the benzene and such, so long as taxes were paid on them, but there was definitely something illegal about the cocaine, as any number of inmates of the Tombs could attest. Mike hadn't noticed any recognizable criminal faces going in or out of the warehouse, but he hoped patience would pay out in the form of the Bottler himself, or at least someone they could tie to him. So, he picked his teeth and cleaned under his nails with a little gold fob knife and waited.

Primo was back maybe a half hour later. "A coal yard is behind, but one building over," he said. "We could get in, I think. There is an alley behind these buildings and the coal yard. Just a fence to get over."

"Okay," Mike said. "Might be we'll have to check it out later." He glanced again at the warehouse. "Hey, I know that face."

"Huh?"

"That guy getting on the wagon," he said, nodding toward the wagon in the warehouse door. "Where the hell do I know him from?" Mike scratched his head as the man clicked at his single horse and edged out into the street traffic. "C'mon, let's walk."

They started after the wagon, which moved at a slow pace, due to the street traffic.

"Shit, I know him from somewhere," Mike said again.

"Somebody you arrest maybe years ago?" Primo guessed.

"Nah, I don't think so." They'd come to a corner and the wagon slowed a little in front of them. They slowed with it, but were still close behind. The driver looked left and right and then looked right again.

"I think he spotted us," Mike said, looking down. The driver clicked at his horse and snapped the reins in a hurry, hunching a little as he did.

"C'mon." Mike ran and hopped up on the tailgate of the empty wagon. Primo was just behind.

The driver heard them and turned to look. "Hey, what the—"

"You're the guy from the boat," Mike blurted out, suddenly recognizing him. "The guy I found on the deck. How ya doin'?" He said it in a friendly way, but it wasn't at all convincing.

"Okay," the driver said, although Mike could see he had bruises and cuts around his eye and over his forehead.

"Listen," Mike said in a voice just loud enough to be heard over the rumble of the wagon, "we need to talk. Pull over."

The driver let out a sigh and nosed into the curb. "How'd ya find me?"

"Not that hard," Mike lied. "What'd you drop off there?"

"You should know," he replied, "you bein' so smart." The man seemed to regret his answer though and said, "Listen, I'm grateful for what you done last week. Them mugs'd probably have cooked my bacon, but you gotta know I ain't all mixed up in this like it seems."

"The cocaine, you mean," Mike said, knowing he'd hit the mark. The man flinched visibly.

"Yeah, that, sure. Those guys were sent by the Bottler. We was shipping for Kid Twist see, well, my captain was anyway; takin' a little extra cargo, a little somethin' more to make the trip worthwhile so to speak. An' some of us got a little cut, too. It was a sweet deal. But the fuckin' Bottler got wind of it an' told the cap he wanted the stuff, an how he better deliver to him instead o' that fucker Twist."

"So that shit the other night was about the white stuff, huh?"

"Hell, yeah. Now we deliver to the fuckin' Bottler, an' me, I don' sleep on the ship no more. Won't be long before Twist sends his fuckin' goons to even the score."

They let the man go a short time later. There seemed no reason to bother with him. Mike and Primo watched the wagon roll off into the traffic.

"You think Kelly is in on this?" Primo asked.

"Good question," Mike said. "If he isn't, he'd be real interested to know, don't you think?"

"He might tell," Primo said, nodding at the disappearing wagon. Mike said nothing. The man was small potatoes, and had helped as much as he could, seemingly holding nothing back. Mike got an address for him and other information in the event he was needed in court, but figured that was enough for now.

"You thinking we might sell that to Kelly? It is maybe something he would pay nice money to know."

"Maybe," Mike agreed without considering the idea seriously, although the lure of a fat payoff had its pull on both of them.

Mike thought on that as they turned away and started back toward the Bottler's place, many blocks inland. Mike and Primo had considered raiding the warehouse because Barrows told them he'd just dropped a sizeable shipment of cocaine among other things. But they decided against it, figuring it might be better to wait and see who came and went and establish a connection to the Bottler that way. Without a clear link, the Bottler would skate easily on the evidence they had so far. According to Barrows, the Bottler never set foot in the place. He had flunkies for that stuff; mixing his booze and moving it to the dives that sold it. Sometimes they sold it mixed, sometimes they just sold the ingredients, some dives preferring their own recipe. Even at ten cents a drink, the profit was huge.

The carriage was there again, sitting at the curb in front of the Bottler's gambling house since about six thirty. It was now ten fifteen by Mike's watch, which tended to be a bit slow. He and Primo had spent the evening attempting to look inconspicuous, moving now and again from one concealed vantage point to another, and taking notes on everyone who went in or out. They'd tried to rent a room overlooking the street, where they could watch with better concealment and a lot more comfort, but there were none to be had anywhere on the block. Mike had taken a turn at stuss, wanting to get a close look at the man himself. He played cautiously, but still lost money at an alarming rate, while the Bottler dealt the cards with the ease and flash of long practice. He was a charming yet unyielding character, with the face of a favorite uncle and the eyes of a snake. Win or lose, he was unreadable, yet somehow encouraging and almost jovial, his red cheeks and satin-vested belly shining to match his balding head. He was not a soft man though. His forearms, which were bare and wore a mat of thick, black hair, were thick and scarred in places. Mike could well imagine that he'd spent many an earlier year in heavy labor, though on close inspection, his hands lacked the calluses of recent work. His eyes were sharp under clouded, bushy brows and they belied his almost folksy manner. Mike did his best to lose quietly and deflect unwanted attention. He left with a lighter pocket and as firm an image of the Bottler as he could form, tucked away for future reference.

Mike and Primo met a few minutes later, against the dark side of a high stoop, the shadow just enough to wipe them from the casual eye. They shared a growler of beer that Mike had fetched from a bar down the block. It was none too cold and noticeably watered, but it went down well enough at the end of a long day. Mike liked his pints and rarely let more than a couple of days pass without their happy effect.

"Shame the girls were little helping," Primo said, referring to their morning's stop at Miss Gertie's.

Mike grinned. Primo's English tended to slide toward the end of the day, but he said nothing about it, just nodded over his beer. They'd interviewed almost every one of them, Gertie and Kevin, too. Although some of them had known Ginny for nearly two years, their knowledge of her life outside the house was remarkably limited. Ginny had kept that part of her life behind a veil, not lifting it even for the other girls. Mike wondered if it wasn't like that for many of them; the outside world put away, its hurtful reminders tucked in memory's drawer. It was his experience that everyone had those little drawers, repositories of guilt or regret or pain. Mike had one of his own, but he kept it unlocked. It was healthier that way, he thought, to acknowledge the mistakes, accept the losses, come to terms with failures. But if Ginny had faced her own failings and losses, she hadn't shared it with the others.

Ginny was there in Mike's drawer of regrets. He hadn't thought of her in that way before. Her diary had changed that, an acknowledgment made clearer by the effects of the beer, which brought to mind one of Tom's truisms. "I ever tell you what my dad says about beer?" he asked Primo.

"No, what is that?" Primo said, taking the growler from Mike's hand.

"There's truth in one pint, bullshit in two, and confession in three."

Primo laughed. "That is a good one, eh? Your father, he is a wise man, but what that have to do with the girls at that Gertie place?"

Mike shook his head. "Nothing, just a random observation. I—" Mike's attention was plucked away by someone leaving the Bottler's. "Speaking of observation, looks like our Mr. Saturn's had enough for the night," he said as a figure hopped into the carriage.

Mike looked down to scribble in his pad as the carriage got rolling at a smart pace, the horses seemingly happy to be on the move. He didn't see where the three men came from. He heard the shouts though and felt Primo stiffen at his side.

"What the fuck!" Primo said, pointing at the carriage.

Mike looked up to see the carriage stopped a half block away. A man had a hold on the harness on the right horse, which snorted and stamped, trying to shake him loose. Mike couldn't see what was going on at the other side of the carriage, but he did see a pair of legs, joined a moment later by another. There was more shouting and a body landed among the legs, curled in a defensive ball. Mike had his pad tucked away and his slungshot in his right hand without realizing he'd reached for it. He and Primo didn't exchange a word. They took off at a run, angling to keep the carriage between them and the attackers. Primo had a short, hickory daystick in one hand. A pair of brass knuckles decorated the other.

It took no more than thirty seconds to cover the distance, but in that short time the body on the street had absorbed at least a dozen kicks and blows. Mike's last impression before he lost sight of him was that the body on the ground was going limp.

". . . goin' ta da fuckin' Wigwam, you asshole!" Mike heard, as he and Primo rounded the back of the carriage. One of the men had his back to them and was a little closer to Primo. Mike went for the other, just as he saw them coming.

Jack McManus didn't have time to do much more than duck. Something hard clipped the top of his head, but didn't do any harm aside from maybe making him take the situation a bit more seriously, stompings being such common work they hardly got his blood going anymore. It was the fist in his ear that really got his attention, making the street jump sideways and setting his head ringing like church bells. But he'd had worse and was still on his feet, so he swung back with his brass-knuckled hands, both of them, charging forward, growling like a rabid dog. Bones was down and enjoying a hickory head-bashing, so he knew it was up to him to establish proper order. But the bastard who'd hit him, a detective most likely, was damnably hard to hit. The best Jack managed in the first minute was a couple of grazing blows and a half-blocked shot that bounced harmlessly off the tip of the bastard's chin. Jack wondered where the hell Billy Shingles had disappeared to, hoping that the fucking half-wit had figured out that now was the time to let go of the horses and start some serious business. Jack wished he had his cannon too. He'd have popped this shifty bastard a dozen times already if he hadn't left it back at Paresis Hall with his squeeze, Ellie. He regretted that now. But the boss had been so determined that Saturn not get dead that he'd insisted Bones and Billy leave their pistols too, popping victims being so much less work than a traditional stomping. Jack tried to duck again, but lost his balance and tripped over Saturn's legs. The slungshot glanced off his shoulder and into his jaw and he found himself kneeling against a carriage wheel, not sure how he got there. Jack put his hand down to get back up, but the carriage rolled forward, the wheel crunching over his fingers with a sound like popping corn. Jack howled and in that instant knew he had to run.

Mike felt he'd been lucky to that point. He'd withstood the man's attack though it had taken all his skill to do it. Whoever it was who'd just gotten his hand run over was an animal, ferocious and elemental in his attack, a storm of fists and feet and unexpected angles. Mike wasn't about to let him get up. He didn't give a shit how many fingers the wheel had broken. His slungshot was raised. A clean blow would put an end to any further resistance. But the man's fist, the one that still had all its fingers in one piece, was brought up smartly against Mike's balls, enough to crumple his knees and weaken the strongest arm. The slungshot dropped harmlessly.

Mike watched as the man dove under the carriage, rolling as he did, scrambling out on the other side. He sprinted across the street and into an alley. From there Mike knew he could pop out at a half dozen points in a two block area or lay a trap for anyone foolish enough to follow.

"Mike, you okay?" Primo was saying. "You are no stabbed?"

Mike shook his head. He could hardly speak, but finally said, "Balls."

Primo couldn't restrain a smirk. "You sing like the choirboy now."

"Oh, you fucking bastard!" Mike groaned as he started to get up. "I'm gonna kick your wop ass when I get up."

"Take you time," Primo chuckled. "My wop ass is not going anywhere." He hauled his prisoner to his feet. The man's head was running red, his hair clotted with blood. Mike got both feet under him, but remained with his hands on his knees as he waited for the pain and nausea to subside.

Neither he nor Primo paid much attention to the man on the ground until he groaned and rolled over. His driver, who'd been cowering on his high perch had finally descended, a small flask in hand. "Here, take some of this, sir," he said, kneeling and putting the flask to his master's lips. "Who were those men, Mister Saturn? My God, I thought they were about to kill you until these gentlemen arrived."

Lionel Saturn, who'd been sucking at the flask as if he'd spent the last week in a desert, seemed to notice Mike and Primo for the first time. The flask lowered and he looked from one to the other with a mixture of gratitude and wariness.

"Detective Alfieri," Primo said. "And that's Detective Braddock. We were . . . we witnessed the men attack you."

Mike went to Saturn. "How are you, sir? Is anything broken?"

Saturn looked at him as if he were speaking a foreign language, but said at last, "I am bruised about my entire body, Detective, but I am amazed to say I appear to be in one piece." He recognized Mike from the Bottler's, though he'd paid him little mind at the time. The realization that Mike was a cop put him immediately on alert.

"Can you get up?" Mike said, putting out his hand. Saturn took it and between Mike and his driver they hauled him to his feet. He swayed like a palm in a hurricane, took another pull at the flask, and shuffled toward his carriage, sitting heavily in the open doorway. "They might have killed me," he mumbled as if trying to convince himself of what had happened. "I was blacking out. I don't know where . . ." He shook his head, which was bleeding a small trickle into his high, starched collar. He looked up at Mike and Primo. "I am grateful to you, gentlemen, both of you."

"Did you know those men, sir?" Mike asked.

"No. I've never seen them before. I assume they were trying to rob me."

Mike noticed the tone of Saturn's voice, the doubt in his eye. He stole a glance at Primo, who twitched an eyebrow.

"I ask because it seemed to me as if one man—"

"The one that got away," Primo interjected with a smirk.

"Yes, the one that got away," Mike said, "appeared is if he were . . . I don't know . . . as if he was delivering a message or a warning."

Saturn looked at Mike with a guarded expression, but said nothing at first, preferring to let the distraction of his driver dabbing at his bloodied head cover his lack of an immediate explanation. "I'm afraid my brain is rather frazzled. The one man was saying some things, but none of it made any sense to me. I think he must have been mad. Or"—Saturn looked up with an almost hopeful look in his blackening eyes—"a case of mistaken identity. I don't know. This is all such madness."

Mike and Primo cast a glance at Primo's prisoner, who had been unable to stay on his feet and now sat handcuffed at the curb.

"I'm sure you'll press charges?" Mike said.

"Yes, by all means," Saturn said a bit too quickly.

Mike nodded and told him where to go in the morning to file

his charge. Saturn made a great show of writing it down in a little notebook taken from a vest pocket.

"Do you need medical assistance?" Mike asked.

Saturn stood, albeit a bit unsteadily, and started to brush himself off. "Thank you, no, Detective. And if I do find my injuries involve more than I suspect, I have an excellent physician to call upon."

"I'm sure," Mike said.

Saturn extended a hand to Mike and Primo in turn, thanking them again. Clearly he meant it. Mike mumbled something about just doing his job, which reminded him to take down Saturn's addresses, both home and work, telephone numbers, too. Saturn turned to climb back into his carriage when Mike added, "I'm sure you're aware of more respectable places to gamble than the Bottler's."

Saturn stopped and looked back at Mike. In that instant, the man appeared to actually shrink. It was a momentary thing, as illusory as it was brief.

"It's not safe for a man like you here," Mike said almost solicitously. "The Bottler's a Five Pointer. You understand what that means, don't you?"

Saturn only nodded.

"I suggest you don't return, sir."

Mike and Primo watched the carriage drive south.

"You think this has something to do with our, ah . . ." Primo started, not wanting to say too much in front of their prisoner.

"Probably, but no point squeezing a gentleman like that when we got this miserable piece o' shit sitting here in handcuffs."

"Fuck youse guys," the miserable piece of shit said.

Primo put a foot to the man's chest and pushed him backward, his head bouncing off the sidewalk. "You don' wanna get on my bad side, bub," he said as if giving advice to a friend. "An' my partner, he is in not so good mood, with his balls in a knot."

"Fuck you, Primo," Mike said.

Primo just smiled. "Sure, but when *you* say it I know you no *mean* it."

24

GINNY HAD RELUCTANTLY taken the new sub-
way uptown the last two mornings. Spending the little
money she had on hand seemed to hurt almost as much as her
back and her legs. She'd even taken a horsecar across town so as
not to have to walk the few blocks to Washington Square. It was
her right calf that hurt the worst, though her back was almost as
bad. She walked like a cripple, hobbling and bent after only two
days of work, not even two days, she reminded herself, because
her first day hadn't started until almost noon.

As she joined the crowd of women and men pressing into the
Triangle Shirtwaist Factory Building on her third day, she tried
to figure how long she'd have to work to earn back the subway
and horsecar fares. It was a depressing calculation, made more
difficult by the close-packed bodies funneling into the lobby.
Lots of them took the stairs, unwilling to wait the long minutes
for the elevators, which seemed to run slower the closer the
clock approached seven A.M. Ginny could not imagine climbing
nine floors the way she felt and could only wonder at the
strength and determination of those who did, a steady stream of
them trudging cheek to bum up the ringing metal staircase. But
she knew it wasn't all strength and heart that drove them. If they
weren't at their stations on the hour they'd be docked. Losing

even a nickel or a dime was far too heavy a price, which re-minded Ginny again of the cost of her commute. She reckoned finally as the elevator gate closed behind her at 6:46 that she'd have to work until nearly eight to earn back those fares.

Returning to work, it hardly seemed she'd left at all. Her trip home last night, the hurried meal, the collapse into her sheets were blurred events, as if they'd been dreamed between trips in the elevator. For an instant she even doubted she'd left the thing at all, had ridden it up and down all night, the clatterings of the gate marking the minutes of her captivity.

"C'mon, miss, I ain't got all day," the operator said, yanking her out of her stupor. She was the last one off on her floor, the steel gate crashing behind.

The broad factory floor was buzzing, not with machines, but with feminine chatter. The low hum and the occasional laugh-ter were like the dripping of water over polished stone compared to the cold voices of the machines once they got going, drown-ing everything when the clock struck seven. The machines would do the talking then. That was the sound the foremen loved. Chatter was discouraged. It caused mistakes and mistakes came right out of a girl's pocket. Of course, mistakes were in-evitable, chatter or no. Each mistake meant a nickel or a dime or even a quarter less at the end of the day. It was as if the Tri-angle Company had cut a hole in Ginny's purse, in all their purses. Foremen paced the aisles, watching like birds of prey for any reason to pluck another nickel through the holes. Only the very best, the most skilled, the most determined, and dexterous women could reach the end of a week with a full week's pay.

The pieceworkers were the best. Ginny wished she'd known that before she started. The good ones could make seven or even eight dollars a week and in less time than it took her. They'd start trooping out at six while the salaried girls were still hunched over their machines. The foremen regularly kept the girls past seven too, working them hard for a few more shirtwaists a day.

Ginny had been forced to stay late the last two nights fixing "mistakes" she'd made so she could make up for what she'd been docked. Her right leg ached from pedaling her machine, especially the muscles in the lower leg, whatever they were called.

"How ya doin', hun?" the woman at the next machine said. "The leg; ya soak it like I said?"

"No, Esther," Ginny said, knowing she'd get more advice for admitting it. Esther seemed to have an unending store of advice on almost any topic or complaint and wasn't shy about sharing any of it. "I was so tired last night I had only enough energy to eat."

"Poowa thing," Esther said. "I know how it is. Since I was twelve I been workin', sewin' hems, sleeves, collas, everything. See these fingas," she said, holding up her hands with the fingers splayed. "I run a needle through every one 'cept this little one on my right hand. So sore, but not so bad right away."

Ginny had seen a girl do it yesterday, punching the needle right through the nail, ruining two shirtwaists with her blood. The foremen were furious and she'd stayed later than Ginny trying to make it up.

"That leg, you soak it good like I tol' ya, sweetie. Some nice bath salts you get an' hot, hot wawta, maybe a must'd plasta ovanight; you'll be fine."

"I will, Esther," Ginny said as she readied her work. "I'm limping like a cripple all morning."

"You'll feel betta afta a good soak."

At a few minutes before seven the machines whirred to life. Slowly the lint billowed, rising like fog from the swampy floor. The foremen paced and Ginny's leg cried out at the indignities heaped upon it with each revolution of the pedal. She ground her teeth through the pain and within a few minutes found that it had eased to a dull ache. She began to imagine she could make it through another day, a thing she hadn't counted on just a half hour earlier. It pleased her to think she might. She'd hated the notion that she might not last the day, be forced to quit before she'd fairly started. There was no such thing as a day off for a new girl like her. If she left her machine there'd be another girl operating it within an hour.

She hadn't learned yet that leaving, even if she were quite ill, was no simple thing. Once work commenced nearly all the doors were closed and locked, with the exception of the elevator. Women worked through all manner of illness and injury and Ginny had begun to notice a few on her floor who were so pale and drawn they could not possibly be well. The foremen ran the place like a prison, with every door locked except the stairs and elevator, "for security" they were told if they even dared to ask. Bathroom breaks were counted by the second. Permission to leave a machine was given grudgingly at best and always with the implication that a girl was somehow stealing from the foreman's own pocket. It didn't matter if it was a pieceworker or not. A minute lost was not recoverable, literally money down the drain.

Although all the girls at first seemed to work for the Triangle Shirtwaist Company, Ginny soon learned that was not the case. Talking to the other girls during their half hour lunch break, she discovered that perhaps more than a quarter of them worked for subcontractors.

"Six, maybe six-fifty a week, you could get if you worked faw the company," Esther said over a mouthful of herring sandwich. "The fawmen they get so much a goil, or so much a shirtwaist. Maybe fifteen, twenty dollas a week they make if they got enough goils."

"But I didn't know," Ginny said. "How can they do that? It sounds illegal or something."

"Ya don' know till ya get paid. They don' want ya ta know anyways. You get a check from the company, you work faw the company. You get cash, you work faw one o' them." She jerked her head toward a small knot of derbied men in the far corner.

181

They were eating fast just like the girls, but washing it down with beer. They were not a particularly dapper lot, Ginny noticed, especially when seen as a group. Shirttails dangled, buttons were undone or missing. Not more than one in three had a fresh shave.

"You'd think they'd be a bit better dressed."

Esther laughed. "I'd be a sight prettier than them slobs on twenty a week."

"They can't help it," a girl they called Em said with a shrug. "They come from nothin' like the rest of us."

Esther nudged Ginny with an elbow and gave her a wink that Em couldn't see. Ginny almost said something, but a stern look from Esther told her to keep her mouth shut. She looked out the window to hide her confusion.

The trees of Washington Square Park looked like puffy green clouds below her feet. She wondered what it might be like to float at their billowy tops and let the leaves tickle her feet. The idea fled quickly when she looked down at the unforgiving street farther below. It was so far down it nearly took her breath away. Though she'd had a chance to look out these windows the day before she still hadn't gotten over her alarm at how far from the earth they were. Still the windows were wonderful, drawing her to their unfamiliar and dangerously thrilling vistas. Looking down, her nose almost pressed to the glass, she could see the traffic on the street, garment workers pushing carts and racks of clothes, vendors selling ice cream, a pair of street musicians, strollers in the park. She yearned to be down there or anywhere the air didn't smell like lint.

Watching the people far below, her eye was caught by a man. He stood out, for despite the comings and goings of the street and park he remained almost motionless. She could not see his face from that height, especially since a straw boater covered much of it. She didn't think it was Mike, but she felt a surge run through her at the thought it might be. Ginny strained for a better look, pressing her hands against the glass, which gave way with a sudden screech of hinges, pitching her forward, hands flying into space. She gave an involuntary shout, but caught herself on the window frame, her heart galloping like a racehorse. She hadn't really been in danger of falling, she told herself, but she had to sit down to hide her shaking knees. The foremen's heads turned as one.

"Careful wit da windows, huh," one of them called. "Ya break da glass youse pay for it."

"Cocksucker," Esther said, but not so loud as to carry. "Flat as a latke you could be on the street an' him worried about the glass."

"They're not all like that," Em said.

"You were lookin' at somethin', sweetie?" Esther looked down with a hand against something solid.

"A man," Ginny said, "in a straw hat."

"Ooh, a man looks nice in a boater; like a sailor, sexy." Esther craned to look. Em did, too. Ginny was reluctant to look again, but she did, putting a hand on Esther's shoulder. "He was right down . . . oh, I don't see him now. He was standing just there by that big tree." She said. "He looked so familiar."

"An old customer?" Esther said this with a wink and a nudge at Ginny's ribs. It took a moment before Ginny realized what Esther was implying. When she did her face went red.

"A customer?" she said in what came out in a particularly unconvincing tone. She scowled as best she could, but Esther paid her no mind.

"You wouldn't be the first, sister. Lots of us done it for money."

Ginny looked at her with more than a little shock.

"To make the ends meet, kinda," Esther added. "You know. When it's a new dress you need or shoes you can't afford. Or when the damn landlord needs the rent you ain't got. Whatcha gonna do?"

Ginny looked at Em, who was younger than Esther, younger even than herself. Em wouldn't meet her eye.

"The single girls, they can't really make a living this way. Most got families," Esther went on with a nod to the rest of the room. "Fathas, brothas, they make enough for food on the table and a roof ova the head. Those goils woik for the extras, clothes faw the kids, a better cut o' meat once in a while, a nice dresser for the bedroom, like me now that I got a husband. But single?" She gave a wicked little laugh.

"But what makes you think—" Ginny was interrupted by the harsh clamor of the bell that marked the end of the lunch break. Esther just shrugged and went to her machine with a cryptic smile, her attitude saying it was of no more consequence than if she'd had eggs or toast for breakfast.

The warm chatter of the women was gone, replaced by the true conversation of the factory floor, the talking of needles and thread, fabric, gears, pulleys, and pounding treadles. It would continue unbroken for another six hours. In Ginny's case, as it was for many of the others, she worked well past the official end of the day. Though she'd tried her best to stitch with impossible perfection, the long hours and inexperience took their toll. By six, she'd been docked a total of fifteen cents for various errors, real or imagined. Her foreman, a taciturn Polish Jew, was inventing and sometimes even creating imperfections in her work. He'd pull at seams and grumble over the slightest gathering of fabric, deducting nickels for work that was perfectly acceptable and daring her to protest. Rarely did any of it actually get resewn. The shirtwaists went into the pile for the pressers upstairs, rolled into the elevators in big carts by small boys.

Ginny did not complain. It wasn't because she was too timid, rather it was the weight of silence around her. None of the other girls complained, though each was as badly used as she. They seemed to take it as a matter of course that they'd be treated as such and set about their extra work with no more than a sigh.

At eight, as she took the elevator down, Ginny said to Esther, "How do you stand it? You know he's just milking us for extra pieces for no good reason. It's like blackmail."

"You thought something different," Esther said with a grim laugh. "Listen, sweetie, he's no worse, that Polack shuffler than the rest of them. Till ten o'clock I used to woik sometimes," Esther said, "making up mistakes only a magnifying glass could see. At least that Polack don't grope me or nothin'." There was a general murmur of agreement as the gate clanged open. "Anyway, heaven this ain't," Esther said as they stepped out into the graying street, "but I been to hell, sweetie, an' you got it better here, lemme tell ya."

Ginny said her good-byes and headed for the subway on leaden feet. She stopped after just a few steps, turning to look back at the park and the tree where the man in the straw boater had stood. He was not there, but she'd felt as though she had to look. What if it had been Mike and he'd been looking for her, she wondered, a pang of guilt running through her. She had not been looking for him. That uncomfortable truth weighed on her more heavily than her aching back and sore leg. He'd be looking for *her* by now, searching the city, turning every brothel upside down, every hat shop, tobacco store, dance hall and dive, or so she imagined, so she hoped.

Ginny wanted to be found. But she was so weary, with barely the strength to drag herself to her machine in the morning and her bed at night. She'd told herself she'd get used to it, that her muscles would cease their stabbing pains and that her energy would return. None of those things had happened yet, which only made her guilt grow deeper. She should have contacted him by now, should have at least tried. He'd have been to Miss Gertie's. He'd have heard the story or rather Gertie's version. Ginny could only speculate on what he'd heard, but she knew her disappearance and her silence could only be seen as signs of guilt. She wondered then if Mike was really looking for her at all. The thought alone added weight to her feet and a slump to her shoulders. She'd thought that once she had a job, had shed the oily skin of her old profession, that then she'd let Mike find her, let him see the woman she'd become. But the Triangle Shirtwaist Company was peeling not just skin from her back, but muscle from the bone.

Nearing Astor Place, Ginny saw a boy selling apples and bananas out of an old packing crate. Her growling stomach commanded her to stop and reach into her purse for a penny. The fruit was mostly bad, the apples bruised, the bananas black, but it made no difference. She ate a banana, bruises and all, and before she even thought about it, handed over another penny for a second. She ate that one only a bit slower than the first. Within minutes she felt a surge of energy run through her and she realized that perhaps part of her weariness was due to her simply not eating enough. She'd never had to worry about food before, nor the money to pay for it, not at Miss Gertie's and certainly not at home. But feeling the amount of energy a couple of pennies worth of bananas produced, she knew she hadn't been doing a very good job at keeping her strength up.

Ginny lingered at the top step of the new subway entrance, weighing her guilty thoughts of Mike, the lateness of the hour, the ache in her back, and the stab in her calf against the glow of two overripe bananas. Making her decision, she headed down, using the handrail to ease her way. She took the train to Spring Street. Police headquarters was just a couple of blocks north and east, looming shabbily over the surrounding neighborhood. It stood in stark, self-conscious contrast to the tenements with clothes fluttering on fire escapes and the cast-iron façades of the loft buildings on Spring. Ginny walked the short distance, feeling better than she had in many days, aching but resolute. She had no idea if Mike was stationed there. He'd never said exactly. The stories he'd told her about cases he'd worked, things he'd seen and criminals he'd known, seemed to have taken him all over the city. If she was to find him she had to start somewhere and she was certain they would know at police headquarters where any one of their detectives were stationed.

"What's your business, ma'am?" a desk sergeant inquired after she'd stood in the echoing lobby for an uncomfortably long minute. The place wasn't set up like a traditional precinct house. Instead of the high main desk and railing that loomed like a rampart in most police stations, here there was a single desk, of more or less regular dimensions, where a sergeant passed his hours in institutional boredom.

"I was looking for Michael Braddock," Ginny said.

"And who would he be, miss?" he said, managing to ask the question without a hint of curiosity.

"He's a detective, I think."

"You think?"

"Yes, a detective," she said with more certainty.

"But you're not sure."

"No, I'm sure." She tried to get more conviction into her voice and thought she managed it, but the sergeant didn't appear convinced.

"Okay, now you're sure," he said, "and this detective that you're sure of; you think he's stationed here at the detective bureau? You know there's detectives in all the precincts, don't you?"

Ginny nodded as though she did, but thought it might be better to say as little as possible on the topic.

"You think he's here, but you aren't sure, are you?"

"Not exactly," she admitted. "It seemed like the best place to start."

"You wouldn't be in the family way, would you, miss? That wouldn't be the reason you're trying to find Braddock? You know there's homes for women in your condition, places where you could go and quietly—"

"No! No! That's not it at all!" The color was rising above

Ginny's tight collar and her eyes were flashing daggers. "I just need to find him. We're . . ." Ginny searched for the perfect definition of what she and Mike were to each other. "We're very close," she said, knowing it wouldn't do. "But we haven't seen each other for some time. I've been away at Albany with my sister and I'm back now and thought I'd surprise him."

The desk sergeant looked at his watch. "At eight thirty," he said, looking up at her only a bit less skeptically. Ginny kept quiet. "So you want to surprise Mike Braddock, who might be a detective and might be stationed here, because you and him are very close. Am I getting this right?"

Ginny gave the sergeant as innocent and winning a smile as she could muster. "I suppose when you say it like that it sounds a little silly, Officer, but I confess that is my dilemma, which is why I would be so very grateful for your help."

The sergeant seemed to soften a bit, though he didn't go so far as to return her smile. "Ma'am, I know Mike Braddock pretty well, see him most every day. Used to work with him at the Fourth."

Ginny's heart began to race, so she barely heard what the man said next.

"What did you say your name was?"

"Virginia Caldwell."

"Well, Virginia Caldwell, in all my years I've known Mike Braddock, never once did I hear him mention your name. Pretty odd you being very close like you say."

"Are you going to let me at least go up to the detective bureau?" Ginny said, her voice flat with defeat. "Please?"

"Listen, I can't let you up unless it's on police business and clearly this ain't that. Only thing I can tell you is come back tomorrow, sometime around four. I think his shift starts then."

Ginny was grateful for the information, but knew she couldn't take advantage of it. Leaving her job in the middle of the day wasn't possible, not if she wanted to return. She sighed. "Can I leave him a note?"

188

The sergeant hesitated and for a moment Ginny was sure he'd say no. She waited, determined not to speak until he gave her an answer. He opened a drawer, took out a pad and pencil. "This is no message service," he said, "but I'll put it on his desk before I leave tonight. How's that?"

Ginny wrote as fast as her mind and hand could work, afraid that at any instant the sergeant might reconsider. Walking out a few minutes later she turned north, covering almost two blocks before she realized that her leg had stopped cramping. She looked down at it with a puzzled frown, stopping to flex her foot. She bent to feel the calf and was surprised when she poked herself with something sharp. The pencil was still gripped tightly in her hand. She put it in her small handbag with a shake of her head.

25

"CHUCK! IT'S FOR you," the bartender called to the back. He'd had a phone installed primarily for Connors's calls and was used to acting as an informal answering service. "You comin'?"

Connors snatched the mouthpiece after a slow shamble to the bar. "Yeah?"

"Mister Connors? Are you there?"

"Who da fuck else'd be here?"

"My God! I've been trying to reach you since early this morning. This is Lionel Saturn."

Connors didn't see any reason to comment on the first bit of information and certainly not on the second. He knew who it was.

"Mister Connors. I say I've been trying to reach you. This is an emergency, man!"

"Yeah, well, I don' keep reg'lar hours, Lionel."

"But I've been assaulted. They were Paul Kelly's men. They almost killed me!"

It was Connors's turn to digest things. "But you ain't dead now I take it?"

"No, no, of course not. I was rescued by two detectives. Listen, Connors; you have to do something. They said Kelly didn't like me going to Big Tim. Told me to keep him out of it or they'd kill me. You have to get Big Tim to back off or I'm a dead man."

"Can't do it."

"What?"

"Kelly's been paid off. Big Tim done what youse wanted an' now by da way youse owe me a grand."

"But for God's sake, there has to be some way to reverse this, something you can do."

Connors thought for a moment. "Listen," he said "Big Tim's out maybe eleven grand on dis. Youse gotta pay 'im back, an' quick. What youse owe me, too," he added.

"God!" There was a long pause. "I suppose. There's stock, I suppose, stock in the steamship company. Would he take that?"

"Stock?"

"Yes, you know, shares in the company. They're worth quite a bit actually," Saturn said with an air of resigned sadness.

"Don' know what Tim'd do wit dose," Connors said, though he knew quite well. "How much youse got?"

"Never mind how much, Mister Connors. Suffice it to say it's enough to pay Big Tim several times over."

Connors waited for what he thought was an appropriate time before saying, "I could call Tim, I guess."

"Good, good," Saturn's voice sparked through the earpiece. "And what about Kelly?"

"Fucked if I know. What about 'im?"

"Well, damn it, man, that's what this is all about. Can't Big Tim talk to him or something? I mean with Sullivan out of the picture, maybe Kelly would be more amenable."

"Paul Kelly's a lotta t'ings Lionel. Fucked if 'meanable is one o' dose."

"But he has his money, you say. What more can he want?"

"Listen, I ain't gonna talk for Kelly. What 'e wants is what 'e wants, get me? My advice is you wanna stay breathin', youse play along, see?"

"All right, Connors. What choice do I have?"

Connors smiled into the mouthpiece. "Youse could go ta da cops."

"Don't patronize me, Connors." The line went dead and Connors chuckled. He had the bartender flick the cradle for the operator and a few moments later had Big Tim on the line. "Tim? Looks like Kelly done youse a favor," Connors said into the phone. He gave Sullivan the short version of his conversation with Saturn. He heard a chair creak and pictured Sullivan's bulk leaning back in victory.

"Easier than I thought, Chuck. But then Kelly is nothing if not predictable, eh?"

26

MIKE AND PRIMO took the thug they'd caught for an intimate conversation in an outhouse behind a decaying tenement on Ludlow Street. There they persuaded him to tell them all he knew about the attack on Saturn. His name was Joe Martin, but he went by the moniker Bones. He was uncooperative at first, but came around once they shoved him halfway into the pit. With him suspended by his feet, they promised to drop him in if his attitude didn't improve.

Martin was a low-level bone-breaker for the Gophers, a gang that controlled a large portion of the West Side. He'd been recruited by Jack McManus for this job in return for a favor Jack had recently done him. He said he didn't know who Saturn was nor why he'd merited a special visit from Eat-'em-up Jack and his pals. When Mike and Primo were convinced they were getting the whole truth and nothing but, they went on to ask about the Bottler. In this area he was of less assistance. He knew of the Bottler and freely admitted to gambling there, a risky thing to do for a Gopher, but his knowledge of any other activities, smuggling, or river piracy was nonexistent.

The interview came to a sudden and unpleasant end when Primo lost his grip on the leg he was holding and Mike was forced to let go or fall into the cesspool himself.

"Damn," Primo said, seeming more surprised than upset.

"It's okay. It's not that deep, I think," Mike observed as the man thrashed about to right himself.

"No. It is my handcuffs. He still has them on. What am I gonna do?"

"Hey, I wasn't the one who let go first."

Primo grumbled under his breath. He paused when the thrashing in the cesspool stopped. "Bones, you okay down there?" he called.

"Fuck you, you motherless cocksuckers," echoed out of the hole.

"May as well leave him the key," Mike said. "You won't be needing it."

They split up when they reached the El at Houston. They'd phoned in from the precinct, reporting on the evening's events and clocking out of their shifts. Technically they were supposed to physically report when their shifts were done, but in their case Mike's captain had allowed a wider degree of flexibility.

"Can't figure what McManus would be up to unless it involves Kelly," Mike said as they lingered at the stairs to the El. "From what I hear, he's Kelly's bulldog. Don't take a shit unless Kelly says so."

"So, Kelly, he has the Bottler's game," Primo said, "but why have his good customer beat like that? Maybe he is no so good customer, eh?"

"It's the only thing that makes sense. We've seen that carriage at the Bottler's at least what, three times now? You'd think they'd be kissing Saturn's ass to keep him coming back."

"He owes too much," Primo guessed.

Mike appeared skeptical. "Places like that you don't walk out of if you can't pay up. But what about this, we know Kid Twist wants to muscle in on the Bottler's game? Suppose Saturn's got a line of credit from the Bottler?"

"Kelly, he'd have to approve such a thing."

194

"Sure, but suppose he did? And suppose Saturn's run up some debts. Suppose Twist knows and wants him to keep losing."

"Why? Why a guy like Saturn would do such a thing, put himself in the middle, it is not so smart."

"No, it's not, but maybe Twist has something on him, something to blackmail him with?"

"The frying pan is not so hot as the fire, eh," Primo said.

"Exactly and maybe that's where the Wigwam comes in. I could swear I heard McManus say something about the Wigwam. He was delivering a warning."

"So you say Saturn he does not like the frying pan so much and he goes to somebody at Tammany Hall maybe, to help turn the heat down?"

"Right, and it gets back to Kelly. And by now Kelly knows that Twist is putting the screws to the Bottler. Twist's got Dahl, that punk waving guns in the street, and in his back pocket he's got a big gambling debt that he knows Saturn got trouble paying. Gives him leverage."

"Twist is not so stupid, I think," Primo said. "He tells Kelly we can do this with the gun or with the dollar. Either way, Twist he gets the Bottler's game."

"Good theory," Mike said. "But not a hell of a lot of proof for any of it."

"In the old country that is proof enough. Here you Irish heads-of-shit need things nice and neat for the courts. Sometimes the old ways are better."

"Sometimes," Mike agreed, "but for this head-of-shit it's the way it has to be for now." He trudged up the iron stairs of the El with a parting wave to Primo.

Twenty minutes later, Primo opened the front door to his building on Prince Street. He'd been careful since he'd started receiving threats from the Black Hand. Before entering, he'd circled

195

the block and observed the building from both ends of the street, watching for unusual activity, loitering strangers, anything out of the ordinary. There were times when he'd enter by the rear of the building just to be safe, cutting through the tenement on the next block and vaulting the crude fence between, feeling foolish, but knowing he wasn't. He wondered what the neighbors made of his nighttime fence-hopping. He was sure he'd been seen from time to time, but wasn't so concerned with what they might think, rather who they might tell. Primo knew the risks he was taking staying in his apartment, but to him moving out would have been a retreat, a thing he was determined not to do. Still, he wondered if he'd ever feel safe walking in his front door. The lights were on in the lower hallway, single bulbs swinging on their cords from the ceiling. He could see clear to the back door, which for once was closed. It was probably Mrs. Peccia and her proper ways. She was the only tenant he'd ever seen, aside from his wife, who swept the halls or cleaned the toilet on their floor. It would be like her to notice an open door.

Primo started up the stairs, but not before he craned his neck to peer up. The stairs in his building were not the sort with an open, central well, but were built with one staircase atop the other, so as not to waste the least possible rentable space. He couldn't see beyond the next floor, but that appeared well lit and quiet except for the usual sounds from the apartments. He went up softly, skipping one stair tread that he knew had a terrible squeak to it and pausing when his head cleared the level of the floor to survey the hall before exposing himself completely. He wanted nothing more than to drag his weary body directly to his empty bed, but if he was to die for his stubbornness he was determined it wouldn't also be through thoughtlessness or inattention.

He followed the same routine with the third staircase, but this time saw that the hallway light was out on the floor above.

That wasn't at all unusual. The landlord never kept up with changing the bulbs. Again he went up the stairs with a careful tread, peering down the darkened hall, still dimly lit by slivers of light from under doorways and through uncovered transoms. Nothing moved save for a shadow under the toilet door. Primo slid his revolver from under his jacket. It was probably old man O'Neill from down the hall whose irritable bowels were the scourge of the building, but he could not assume that. He moved to his door as lightly as he could over the floorboards, which gave off a comfortable series of muffled creaks and groans. The key clicked as the bolt pulled back and the latch receded. He started to push the door in, but noticed his bit of string was no longer stuck in the jamb. He left it that way whenever he left, an early warning sign of tampering. He pointed the revolver at the door as he jerked back his hand from the knob. Nothing happened. There was no sound from within, no attackers springing from darkened corners. The toilet flushed down the hall and Primo calmed and took a second look, thinking the string may have shifted or that perhaps he hadn't left it exactly where he'd thought. He bent in toward the door, searching the jamb, feeling his way, crouching to grope along the floor.

The door exploded above his head, blowing outward, something hitting the top of his head and knocking him backward to the floor. A second explosion tore through a little lower than the first and the door flew open. A dark form filled it and Primo fired three times, amazed that the revolver was still in his hand.

"Merde!" the shooter cried, dropping a sawed-off shotgun and staggering into the hall. Primo watched from his knees, uncertain if he should fire again. The toilet door opened behind him and he started to turn, but the crashing of the man's body snapped his head back. He heard steps behind him and turned too late. He was struck on the arm and shoulder and side. Twisting away, he fell on his back again and kicked at a pair of legs,

197

giving him the time to raise the revolver and fire. In the muzzle flash, Primo had a brief impression of an open-mouthed snarl and bad teeth, framed by a thick, black mustache. Primo fired again and the man toppled upon him, the knife blade glinting in the dim light.

27

THE TELEPHONE WAS ringing and wouldn't stop. Its raucous bell sounded as if it were miles away though it was just down the hall in the kitchen. It barely broke through Mike's sleep-fogged brain at first and for some time it seemed the ringing was only a dream. It could have been ringing for ten minutes or ten seconds, he couldn't say which. It stopped finally and he rolled over, rubbing his eyes and fumbling for his pocket watch on the table beside the bed. "Four thirty, for chrissake!" Mike rose and stumbled to the kitchen, figuring he'd try the operator and see if she could tell him who might have called. His hand was reaching for the earpiece when the brass bell started clattering again, making him jump. He grabbed the earpiece and put his mouth to the speaker.

"Detective Braddock," a tinny voice said in his ear. "I have—" His front door shook on its hinges as someone hammered on the other side. Mike took a couple of steps away from the door as his sleep-muddled brain tried to focus. He dropped the phone and ran back to his bedroom, fumbling for his automatic hanging from the bedpost in his shoulder holster. The banging got louder, shaking the walls and vibrating through his naked feet. "Mike! Mike!" he heard outside as he jacked a bullet into the chamber. "Mike, open up!"

He went back to the kitchen, keeping the pistol ready. "Who's there?"

"Mike, it's me. Open up!"

The voice sounded strange, yet he knew who it was.

"Dad?"

"Yeah. Open up for chrissake."

Mike unbolted the door and Tom pushed his way in.

"You all right?"

"Yeah, of course. What the hell's going on?"

"You're sure? What's the gun for?"

"For the asshole who was knocking my door down at four thirty in the fucking morning."

Tom looked about the kitchen as if needing confirmation.

"Get dressed. It's Primo."

The Oldsmobile raced across town, not even slowing at intersections. There was no traffic save for delivery wagons. The streets glistened with the early morning damp. Tom had the speeder pressed as far as it would go and the little single cylinder engine thumped with an urgency Mike had never thought possible. The wind in his face was like a gallon of coffee, though it was what Tom was telling him that had his nerves jangling.

"They found him about one o'clock!" Tom shouted over the rush of the wind. "A dead guy right on top of him, bullets through the neck and sternum, another dead on the stairs."

"What do the doctors say?"

"Not sure. A shotgun blast grazed his head."

"Jesus!"

"Yeah, he was lucky. Should've cut him in half. Stabbed four times, too. The dead guy who fell on him pinned his arm to the floor. A fucking bloodbath."

"Anybody call his wife? Damn it! I forgot. He said she doesn't have a telephone wherever she is," Mike said, "and I don't know where she's in hiding except somewhere north of the city."

"Yeah, well, he had his reasons for being careful."

"He hardly talked about it," Mike said. "It was almost like a joke."

"No joke now," Tom said as the tires bounced over some rough pavement. The Olds whipped back and forth like a Coney Island ride as Tom fought to steady it, the oversprung suspension bucking and the tiller whipping side-to-side. He let up on the speeder and brought it under control, giving Mike a guilty grin. "She likes to wag her tail now and again."

"Let's just try to make it to the hospital in one piece, okay?"

There were cops everywhere when they arrived—by the front door smoking cigarettes, in the lobby trading war stories, and in the hall outside Primo's room, talking in whispers. Mike had been prepared for them. What he wasn't prepared for was the priest.

"*In Nomini Patros et Fili et Spiritos Sancti,*" the clergyman droned as he touched Primo's bandaged forehead with a drop of holy water. They stood quietly as the priest finished the last rites.

"He's not . . ." Mike said to the priest when he was done.

"No, no, son. Just a precaution," he said in a most unreassuring murmur. Mike mumbled his thanks before shuffling to Primo's bedside.

"I don't know, Dad. He looks bad. Primo, buddy, squeeze my hand if you can hear me, okay? Mike leaned close and almost growled in Primo's ear. "C'mon, you wop bastard, squeeze my hand."

Primo opened his eyes just enough to see Mike's face and gripped him back as hard as he could. "Irish shit," he croaked.

Mike and Tom sat by the bed as the dawn filtered in. They talked in low tones. They spoke of Primo's family and how to find them if he didn't live. The cops disappeared a little before six A.M. They had to report back to their precincts for their shift change. Tom and Mike said their good-byes one by one until they were the last left and the hall outside was no longer filled with murmured conversation and shuffling feet. Finally they too got up to leave, pressing Primo's hand and speaking to him as if he were deaf. He didn't open his eyes this time, just raised a finger.

"He'll be okay," Tom said as they brushed past a white-coated orderly, wheeling a cart.

"Hope so. I was just getting used to his shitty sense of humor," Mike replied. "Gonna be hard without him."

"Yeah. You'll need another partner," Tom said. "Maybe—" He stopped before finishing his thought. He was looking at the polished floor in an odd way. Mike followed his gaze. A pair of dirty footprints ran past. He turned to look back, following the tracks to the orderly's feet. The man was almost at Primo's door and cast a dark glance over his shoulder. He hesitated when he saw they were watching, stopping his hand as it reached for the doorknob.

"Hey, buddy," Mike called, starting back down the hall. "Can I talk to you a minute?" The man turned his back on them, wheeling his cart with a quickened step. "Hey! Hold up! I wanna talk to you!" Mike shouted. A second face peered around the far corner, where it met another hallway. A hand seemed to signal to the orderly and the face disappeared. Mike put a hand on the butt of his Colt. Tom did the same. They both walked faster. "Stay right there! Keep your hands where I can see them!" Mike thundered as he thumbed the safety on the Colt.

But the man turned fast and something sparkled in his hand, like a Fourth of July firecracker yet twenty times the size.

A pistol cracked in Mike's ear. The orderly doubled over. Tom fired again. A tremendous explosion erased the man from

202

sight, enveloping him in a ball of fire. Tom and Mike dropped to the floor as a jagged hail of glass and tile spattered around them.

"Jesus Christ! You okay?" Mike called out as the air cleared.

"Yeah, I guess," Tom said as he rolled to his knees. He was bleeding from a half dozen cuts to his head and hands. "Hell, I don't know." He sounded dazed and far away.

Mike realized that his ears were ringing like sirens. He looked at the smoking ruin down the hall, the walls and ceiling so splashed with blood it appeared they'd been painted, the man's shoes, yards away, with his feet still in them, and again, this time through the haze, he saw the face peering around the corner. It disappeared and was followed by the sound of running feet.

"Stop!" Mike shouted.

Tom was on his feet, hands on his knees. "You see that guy?" he said as he started forward.

"Yeah," Mike said, breaking into an uncertain run. "We're gonna lose him, we don't get moving." They passed Primo's door, hanging on one hinge, the glass jagged and gaping like the mouth of a shark. "Primo, you okay?" He got a lifted hand in reply. "We'll be back," he called as he ran after Tom, sprinting against a tide of nurses, doctors, patients, and orderlies, shouting, "Police! Out of the way!" Mike followed Tom to the stairs, which they took in leaps and tumbles. Bursting into the early morning sun, they squinted up and down First Avenue, but saw no one.

"You sure he came this way?" Mike asked between breaths. He wiped his forehead at what he thought was sweat, but the hand came away bloody.

"I saw him duck into that stair," Tom said, looking back at the hospital. "I was sure he was below us." They were near the front gate. "You check up the block, I'll go down."

He turned, but Mike stopped him. There was a man walking toward them with both hands on his middle. Even at a half block away they could see him stagger. He croaked something at them and they ran to him.

"Ice wagon," he said in a reedy voice, his hands red at his belly. "Got my horse."

Tom spotted a white-coated doctor and shouted for help, waving his arms. "What wagon? Where?" Mike asked. Looking up the block, he saw a man on a horse with no saddle, the remains of a harness dangling. An ice wagon sat at the curb nearby. "There he is!"

He started to run, but Tom stopped him. "Never catch him on foot. C'mon." He ran in the opposite direction, all the while shouting for the doctor. Mike took off after him with a last worried look at the blood pooling at the iceman's feet.

The Oldsmobile started with a quick turn of the crank and Tom was behind the tiller before Mike could climb aboard. The horse and rider were three blocks ahead, disappearing around the corner of Thirty-fourth Street by the time the Olds got moving, the single cylinder hammering hard. They passed wagons and carriages at an alarming rate and the turn was coming up fast. Tom braced himself, leaning into it, one hand on the tiller, the other on the seat rail. He looked wild and ragged, hair flying, blood running from his cuts and into his paper collar. They skittered through the turn, the thin tires screeching and slipping. Tom stayed at full throttle and when they were through and running straight again, he was grinning like a crocodile. He and Mike exchanged a look. He hunkered forward, willing the little car on.

The rider was closer now. His horse, not accustomed to anything beyond a trot would not stay at a gallop for more than a short distance despite the man's flogging.

"We got this bastard" Mike shouted as they started to climb toward Fourth Avenue. Slowly they closed the gap, whittling it to no more than a hundred yards as they neared Lexington. The rider hadn't looked back, probably figuring it unlikely he was even followed, much less caught at the rate he was moving. The horse had slowed to a jog as it climbed the hill, passing the corner, going straight on toward Fourth. The Olds slowed too, but not as much, its momentum carrying it forward. Mike had his Colt out, though the distance was still too great for it to be of any use. The rider saw them then, glancing over his shoulder almost casually before booting the animal into a run. Still the Olds closed, the engine grinding away the distance with each thump of its cylinder. Mike shouted for the rider to stop as the gap narrowed to fifty yards. He threw a wide-eyed glare over his shoulder as he bent low over the nag's mane. Mike tried holding the pistol on him, but the bouncing of the Olds had the sights waving like a kite in a storm. "Not yet!" Tom shouted. There were pedestrians at the corner of Fourth, businessmen off to work, a woman pushing a pram. Some were crossing the street, unaware of the horse and automobile bearing down on them. The horseman didn't slow, riding as if to continue straight on Thirty-fourth, but at the last instant with people shouting and running for safety, he turned south, hooves flailing at the pavement, slipping, clattering, but somehow keeping horse and rider aloft. Tom and Mike braced for the turn a moment later, leaning to the left like sailors in a racing yacht, hanging over the side. Tom put the tiller over, fighting it as the tires screamed and hopped sideways. Faces in the crowd flew by, mouths open, cursing, shouting.

The road was not wide enough. They were going sideways into the curb. Tom yanked the tiller the other way and took the curb at an angle, bounding onto the sidewalk and so close to the side of a building that Mike could not understand how they didn't hit it.

The rider was now more than a block ahead, running hard downhill toward Thirty-second, widening the gap. The Olds careened back onto the pavement. Tom pressed the speeder hard, trying to regain their lost momentum. The rider was almost at

Thirty-second Street and rode into the turn as hard as his ice wagon horse would go. Again Tom and Mike braced for the turn. But they were going downhill and had gained at least another five miles an hour by the time they hit the corner. Tom fought to slow the Olds, hands and feet dancing at the controls, one hand hard on the brake handle. They slowed, but not enough. The Olds tilted as it reached the apex of the turn, rising up on two wheels before hitting the curb.

Mike felt them going over, the sidewalk hitting his shoulder and head and knees, felt Tom crash on top of him. They rolled into a wall in a tangle of arms and legs. Mike was on his feet before he knew it or even considered what his injuries might be. He tried to focus on the rider, now nearly two blocks away and disappearing fast, but his head was spinning and he fell against the wall and slipped to the sidewalk. Tom groaned at his side, holding one arm and bleeding from somewhere.

"You okay?" was all Mike could manage.

"I look okay?"

"No."

"Fuck it," Tom said and got up, wincing as he set his feet under him. "C'mon, let's get this car up." A crowd had gathered, angry shouts and curses ringing them. "Police," Tom growled at them. "Out of the way!" He grabbed a crumpled fender at the front and Mike the one at the rear, his head still wobbling about on his shoulders in a most unsettling manner. "On three," Tom said.

It took two tries to get the Olds on her wheels, but then it became clear that the little red car would go no farther. Two flat tires spread like pancake batter under her.

"Shit!" Tom kicked at a fender and leaned heavily against the car, then turned and slid to the sidewalk.

"Dad?"

"A little light-headed is all. I'll be okay" Tom said in a fuzzy voice. "Where's all this blood coming from?" He wiped at his eyes and smeared his face with it.

"Your head's bleeding. Hand too, I think." Mike was leaning on the fender now himself, trying to sort out where he hurt the most. No one in the crowd offered to help, though most had at least stopped cursing them. There were distant shouts and heads turning. Mike couldn't see what the commotion was. He climbed unsteadily atop the Olds, standing on the seat. "Something's happened. There's a crowd over by Broadway."

Tom got to his feet, gritting his teeth. "Let's go."

He and Mike hobbled west. Tom found a handkerchief and wiped at his face.

"Sorry about the Oldsmobile," Mike said, doing his best not to grimace as he walked.

"Me too, but I'll be damned if that wasn't fun!"

"Oh, Christ, if that's your idea of fun—"

He didn't finish. The crowd ahead had grown and high-pitched screams echoed down the block at them.

"Let's get moving," Tom said, breaking into a jog. They ran the last two blocks, parting the crowd, and shouting, "Police!" There was a patrolman on the scene already, but there wasn't much he could do. A woman was screaming repeatedly, the cries ripping from her throat with steam-whistle intensity. Others tried to calm her with no success. The ice horse was down, struggling and screaming, two legs broken, bones protruding, a deep gash in its side. A streetcar was stopped, blood pooling in its wake, bits of flesh and clothes in a short trail to the body. Behind the streetcar lay the man they'd chased, cut diagonally in half from crotch to shoulder.

28

Y OU'RE SURE THEY were cops," Paul Kelly said, looking closely at McManus. They were in a back room at the New Brighton Dance Hall, Kelly's headquarters.

"Saw a badge on one of 'em."

"Badges aren't that hard to come by. Could be they were Pinkertons or something like that."

Jack held up his left hand, wrapped in a fresh cast. "T'ings was dicey, Paul. Could'n be sure, not a hun'ed percent." Kelly sat back, considering the situation. He was not a believer in chance or coincidence. For a man like Kelly such inconveniences as coincidence or lack of information could not be allowed to get in the way.

"Truth is, Jack, that Big Tim had some protection arranged for our friend, Mister Saturn. No matter if it was Pinkertons or detectives or goddamn Daybreak Boys."

"Daybreak Boys? Paul, them mugs been gone fer years. I don'—"

"I was making a fucking point, Jack. Anyway, the point is that Big Tim is protecting that fuck Saturn. He's the ticket into the goddamn steamship racket, so naturally he'd want to protect his stupid ass." Kelly wanted to find out what the Bottler had going that he hadn't told him about. Kelly figured it for smuggling.

He knew the Bottler's style and that would fit him like an old suit. What bothered him was the Bottler's trying to keep it quiet. That wasn't to be tolerated. He'd have to be confronted and he'd have to cut Kelly in if he wanted to stay healthy. But Kelly wanted that boat for his own reasons now that he knew there was a possibility of getting a piece of it. There was gambling, prizefighting outside the three-mile limit, and smuggling of his own to be done. "You say you stomped him pretty good before the cavalry arrived, right?"

"Sure, Paul. Kicked his ass proper."

"Okay, that's good. The message got sent. You told him to stay away from the Wigwam?"

"Sure, jus' like youse said."

"Wish you'd had the chance to bring me the Bottler. Between this and that fucker Twist we got an interesting situation."

Kelly sighed. "So, first things first. We have to protect the Bottler, but I need him here as soon as you can haul his fat ass. You got that? Anything happens to him, it's gonna be me makin' it happen. We gotta keep Kid Twist off him, and get his ass back in line, so we're in on this *Slocum* thing. Let Twist get his flippers on the Bottler's game and before you fuckin' turn around, we'd have every fucking up-and-comer on the East Side trying to eat our lunch." Kelly looked McManus in the eye. "You make sure nothing happens to the Bottler. Not until I say so, got it?"

"Sure, Paul. I got some mugs we can count on if t'ings get noisy."

"Good. Make it happen. Now as to Big Tim." Paul steepled his fingers and took a deep breath. "The man will not get what's rightfully mine. I don't give a shit about the money or whether we're palsy-walsy come election time, nobody pushes me like that. But whatever gets done, Tim can't know who did it. That's more important than anything. I fucking hate what Tim did, but we can't do business on the East Side without him. Simple as that."

"He could have a accident. Every mug has accidents."

"No! Only make things worse," Kelly said. "Forget it."

"He's gonna hear about Saturn."

"Yeah, but he won't be sure who did it, will he?"

"No way, Paul. Da mugs I used don' know nothin'."

"Good. That's exactly how it's got to stay. Now listen, I want you to go back and keep an eye on the *Slocum*. There's a couple of things I want you to look into."

29

ALL THROUGH THE day Ginny dreamed. Her hands and feet worked on their own. She'd made two mistakes already and it wasn't even one o'clock. Nickels and dimes had lost their significance. They were hardly worth worrying over. Esther was beginning to look at her strangely. Ginny didn't care. Each time the elevator door rumbled open her heart danced in her chest. When Mike came she'd leave with him and never look back.

Her lunch was eaten in big tasteless lumps, hardly chewed, washed down with a bottle of Moxie. Esther and the other women chattered and gossiped as usual, but Ginny didn't join in.

"Your head's someplace in the clouds today," Esther said. Ginny shrugged as if she had no idea what Esther was talking about.

"A man's in your head, maybe under your skirt too from the look of you." Ginny blushed. "He's good to you, too?"

Could Ginny say Mike had been good to her, or nice in a conventional way? They'd had only one afternoon together, one afternoon without sex and money to tip the scales. But Mike had been good to her and kind in almost every way, so for now that had to be enough. Ginny smiled.

"And he's nice between his legs, too," Esther said, holding

her hands six or so inches apart then slowly widening the gap till they both broke into gales of laughter. The bell rang, ending the lunch break and they went quickly back to their machines, the shop whirring to life again and the lint billowing like mist.

As the day wore on Ginny's mood turned. With each opening of the elevator doors her hope dwindled. She tried not to think that Mike had gotten her message and ignored it. She imagined the sort of stories he might have heard about her at the house, from Gertie, or some of the other girls. Had he believed them?

The sun sank slowly in the western windows and still Mike did not come. One by one the machines stopped and the women went home, until there were only a few, making up for the day's mistakes. Ginny couldn't continue past eight. Her heart wasn't in it. Even her foreman could see that. "Go home, girlie. Come back ready to do a day's woik. No more days like today, eh," he grumbled, holding a perfectly good shirtwaist. Ginny just nodded and left her machine without a word. He watched her go with a shake of his head.

The elevator sank to the lobby with Ginny wondering how it could be that Mike hadn't come. It was possible he'd never received the message, that somehow it had gotten lost or placed on the wrong desk or even that Mike had not been back to his office. It was all possible and she clung to the possibilities, fearing she'd drown if she didn't. As Ginny stepped into the street, she resolved to leave another message for him.

"Pardon, miss," a man's voice said softly by her ear. The voice startled and thrilled her beyond anything she could have imagined. She turned wide-eyed, her breath catching in her throat, but realized before she'd even seen the man that it had not been Mike.

"Sorry ta bother ya, miss," the man said when she'd turned, "but these streets ain't safe after dark, specially not for a lady as pretty as yerself."

Ginny saw a solid, honest-looking face under a raked straw boater, a full mustache above a gentle mouth. The eyes were wide and hazel brown, the brows high, lending the face a hint of refinement. He wore a well-cut suit and a silk bow tie. White spats topped his polished shoes.

"I could walk wit you a ways, keep da lowlifes from gettin' too fresh," he offered. He was almost charming when he smiled, not that she was interested.

"Suit yourself, I suppose," she said and continued on her way.

"I'm Carl Woertz," he said, catching up to walk at her side.

"Ginny." She didn't want to give her last name, but extended a tentative hand.

Carl took it with surprising gentility. "Pleased," he said.

They walked to Broadway, then south toward Houston. Ginny usually rode the El, but decided against it. The cramps that had crippled her the first few days at the job had eased, the evening was fine and cool, and the man at her shoulder was not unpleasant to look at, so she walked.

Carl gabbed almost nonstop. Ginny didn't feel much like talking and was content to have the company of a man even if it wasn't Mike. She had always enjoyed men's company and thought nothing of allowing Carl to rattle on at her side. She began to realize after a few blocks that she'd needed the companionship and was surprised to find herself smiling at Carl's observations.

They strolled on, past Houston with its dangerous traffic, past organ-grinders, a German street band, kids selling stolen fruit, newsboys with late editions, vendors of apple cider, ice cream, and confections, all trying for the last few customers of the night. Ginny was surprised to find herself responding to her newfound friend, and when he insisted they stop for ice cream in a waffle cone, she began to really look at Carl, to take inventory in a way.

Perhaps it was the disappointment of the day, the many small stabs at her heart with each opening of the elevator doors, but when Carl Woertz handed Ginny her vanilla cone, she took it with just a tiny bit more on her lips than a mere "Thank you." Carl noticed and caught her eye to be certain, a rakish grin canting his mouth at the angle of his boater. "My pleasure," he said, touching the brim. She thought at that moment she'd seen him somewhere before. She was almost certain he hadn't been a customer. But there was something illusively familiar about him that she just could not place. She thought it might be the boater, which reminded her of the man she'd nearly fallen out of the window looking at the day before. But she hadn't seen that man's face, so it couldn't be that. She strained to remember, eating her ice cream too fast and freezing the roof of her mouth. She forgot her doubts in her huffing attempts at thawing herself out.

"I have a cure for that, but I ain't so bold to do it," Carl said.

"What, what?"

Carl leaned toward her and kissed her on the mouth. Ginny pulled back, but he said in almost a whisper, "Trust me," and she let herself be kissed, feeling his warm breath melt the glacier she'd formed. It was not a kiss to stir the passions or quicken the blood, just a breath exchanged, as if she'd been drowning. Still, it had been a kiss and could not be called anything else.

"You mustn't do that again, Carl," Ginny said, not certain that she meant it, but feeling that a good girl should say it, a factory girl, a girl whom a man like Mike might some day come for should say it.

"Of course not. Only when yer tonsils are froze."

Ginny smiled back and licked at a dribble of ice cream escaping her cone. "It did work though," she admitted. "I'm all thawed out. Thanks."

Ginny let Carl walk her all the way to her door, a thing she'd not have done if she'd taken the time to consider it. After they'd said their good-byes, Ginny went up the dark stairs to her room, but hesitated before opening the door. She tiptoed back down

214

and opened the door a crack, peeking out at the dark street. The road and sidewalks were almost deserted, save for the glow of a cigarette in a doorway on the other side. Ginny closed the door and locked it.

30

MIKE ACHED IN every place that had feeling, but he'd refused to be admitted. Tom had been, and the doctors insisted he should stay. He had sustained a concussive shock to the brain as the doctors put it, accounting for the dizziness and vomiting that had overcome him shortly after their accident. They'd been going through the assassin's pockets when Tom had gone to his knees, retching into the street. He'd been embarrassed. He hadn't been subject to a weak stomach since his early years on the force and was certain that not even the sight of a man cut in half could upset him. But when he'd been too dizzy to stand, Mike knew it was due to more than the blood and guts, no matter what the volume.

Bandaged and aching, Mike walked the halls of Bellevue from Primo's room to Tom's, chatting with cops and slouching on hard, battered chairs through the morning, dozing now and again, his eyes fluttering closed of their own accord.

It was late afternoon by the time Mike made it back to his apartment. He opened the door and almost stepped on the envelope laying on the floor just inside. It had KNICKERBOCKER STEAMSHIP COMPANY in fine Gothic print in one corner, with a little picture of a steamship below and his name in fine script across the crisp off-white paper. Mike opened it to find a note and a pair of passes from the Knickerbocker Steamship Company. They appeared to be season passes, with no particular cruise date. Mike put them on the small table by his front door and read the note.

I am in your debt, Detective, and though this small gesture is hardly compensation for the great service you have done me, I pray that it may give some recompense for a job very well done. Use them in the best of health.

Your servant,
Respectfully,
Lionel Saturn

"Pretty damned civilized," Mike muttered, imagining how Ginny might look with the wind in her hair, the sun glinting off it in streaks of gold. He sighed and lost himself in the daydream for a moment longer. He stumbled to his bed, a wave of fatigue knocking him onto the rumpled sheets. He was unconscious in seconds, fully clothed.

He awoke hours later, feeling guilty for sleeping the afternoon away. The sun had disappeared, leaving only the streetlamps behind, throwing their watery light through his windows. Mike rolled his feet to the floor and sat up groaning. He didn't think he could have ached any more than he already had, but he was wrong. He was bandaged in half a dozen places, scrapes and cuts from the explosion and the accident. He seemed to be bruised everywhere and his hand ached beneath the cast. He gave his rumpled clothes a look in the mirror and finally said, "Fuck it," to his reflection. It wasn't worth the aches and pains just to clean up, so he left for the hospital.

Tom was roomed just down the hall from Primo, who had been moved after the bombing. He was sitting up in bed while Mary spooned hospital soup into him.

"The soup's godawful," Tom said when he saw Mike, "but the service is great." He extended a bandaged hand.

Mike took it and then gave Mary a long hug. He knew this was far from the first time she had come to the hospital to spoon-feed her husband. Over the years he'd been a regular visitor, the doctors slowly turning him into a kind of patchwork quilt, stitches running this way and that about his body. Tom didn't seem to mind much, but Mary did, though she was doing her best to pretend otherwise.

Though Tom's handshake was still strong, he appeared older than he had that morning. A number of small bandages covered his larger cuts and scrapes and Mike could see the pain in his eyes. But the usual light was there too and Mike knew he'd be back at work before he really should.

They sat for a while and talked, Tom propped at the head of the bed, Mike and Mary on either side. They didn't speak about what had happened that morning. Instead they talked about Rebecca and the new play she was in, what her role was, about her director and his old-fashioned ways, the leading lady and her affair with the set designer, the costumes and how the producer had them made so cheaply they were falling apart at dress rehearsal, anything but how close he and Tom had come to killing themselves. Mike got up to leave and could see from the brief look in Tom's eye that he wished he could go, too.

"Oh, Mike," Mary said when he was halfway to the door. She got off the bed and came to speak with him in low tones. "I've been calling everyone I know and sending notes to the ones that still don't have a telephone." By "everyone" she meant all the madams she still knew. Mike was pretty sure it was an impressive list. She gave an apologetic sigh. "Nothing so far. Ginny hasn't turned up anywhere. But don't worry, there's a few more I haven't heard back from and everybody promised to call if she turns up, so . . ."

"Thanks, Mom," Mike said. "But don't bother doing anything more. With everything that's been going on, I just can't." He hesitated. "I mean, why hasn't she tracked me down after all? She wants to put it all behind her, I think. Everything. Can't say I blame her."

Mary just nodded, though she could not hide her disappointment.

Primo wasn't conscious when Mike stopped by, but he talked anyway, hoping his partner would rouse and open an eye. His breathing was steady though, and when Mike felt his pulse it was strong and regular. A nurse told him that there'd been a procedure a few hours before to stop some bleeding in one of Primo's wounds. He'd been given more laudanum and he'd be out for another hour or more. Mike left with a nod to the patrolman stationed at the door and without giving it much thought walked to the Second Avenue El and rode downtown.

It was force of habit that had him observing the Bottler's game that night. He and Primo had spent so many hours on that street that it seemed natural to return. He was wide-awake and knew that going home wasn't going to accomplish anything, so even though it was past ten o'clock when he got there, he settled in to watch for a few hours.

In an earlier life, maybe a month or two ago, he'd have gone whoring on a night like this. He'd have enjoyed them and gone home feeling tired but empty. That had been the difference with Ginny, the emptiness had been of a different sort, the kind that had kept him coming back. He'd recognized it too late. Ginny had known before him. The way she'd looked on the day they'd gone to the show; it was clear she'd meant to bind him with the kindest cords. It had been his reluctance to change that had kept him from taking her away from Miss Gertie's. Cowardice was another word for it, though Mike winced at the thought. In honesty

219

that's what it had been, the fear of abandoning his old ways and carefree pleasures for something deeper, more demanding.

Mike looked at his watch, extending a hand from the shadow that hid him to catch the light of a streetlamp. It was near twelve and he'd made no more than a passing note of who'd been in and out of the Bottler's. He sighed and glanced up and down the street before stepping into the light. Turning toward Delancey, he walked away from the game. He'd only gone a little more than three blocks, his thoughts far from the streets around him when he became aware of another presence on the street; a dark form approaching from across the road, angling to cut him off. Mike slowed and reached into his jacket, thumbing the safety on the Colt. There were footsteps behind and a glance showed a second man closing in on him fast. There were no words exchanged, no demands for money, no threats. A dark hand reached into a waistband and that was enough.

Mike's Colt wasn't the first to fire. One of the other men did that, Mike wasn't sure which. The bullet seemed so distinct, so impossibly slow, he almost doubted what it was. It skimmed off the bricks behind him and into the night. Without hesitation, he fired two rounds at the first man, and turned to fire at the second, as more bullets pelted around him, his target crouching. He fired twice, then turned back to the first gunman, and saw the man rolling on the street. The second man was down too, arms spread wide, motionless. A footstep sounded to his left a moment before an explosive impact brought the sidewalk up to meet his face, his head ringing in one continuous, deafening tone. A shoe appeared before his face, then melted into blackness.

31

CYCLONE LOUIE NEVER had liked the Bottler, so it was of little concern to him when he'd gotten the job to plug the fucker. He was a part-time Coney Island strongman, able to bend steel bars and wrap tenpenny nails around his fingers. Breaking bones was easy work and he'd hardly have broken a sweat. He would have preferred to beat the Bottler into oblivion, but the contract was clear on one point; the man had to be dead beyond any hope of resurrection and an extra two in the head was the order. Louie had gotten the word from Kid Twist, but suspected something more than the Kid putting pressure on Kelly's operation, though he didn't really give a shit one way or another. Twist was a friend from way back, and a source of regular work, so the whys and wherefores of the job were not even a source of curiosity.

Louie checked his pistol before turning the corner onto the Bottler's street. He walked slowly, watching for anything unusual. He stopped a moment when he heard gunshots coming from a few blocks away. It was clear after a moment's pause that they weren't directed at him. A few gunshots on the Lower East Side at night were nothing to raise much of a hubbub. In fact, when he thought about it, he figured they'd be a nice distraction for the cops, all the better for a clean exit.

He strode in to the Bottler's place, nodding to the man at the door, who he knew in passing. Standing just inside the stuss parlor, he let his eyes get accustomed to the smoky light and swept the room for any danger. There was the usual crowd; rubes, losers, gangsters, and degenerates, maybe twenty in all surrounded the green felt, some sitting, some drinking at the bar. The Bottler held court in the middle on the opposite side. Louie walked to the table, pulled out his pistol and shot the Bottler in the chest. The bullet made a little red puff in his vest, bouncing him back against his chair. The Bottler tore at the satin as if it was on fire, before pitching forward over the table. The room, which had been loud with the voices and curses of the losers, went silent and emptied immediately with a single crash of an overturned chair. One enterprising gambler scooped as much cash as he could and ran out the back. Louie didn't give a shit. He walked around the table, listening to the Bottler wheeze as a red stain spread out on the green felt. He turned a wide eye toward Louie, but couldn't seem to raise his head. He croaked out something incoherent before Louie shot him in the face. The last two in the back of the head were mere formalities, the bullets crashing through his skull and into the table.

32

JACK MCMANUS CHECKED his men. One was dead, the other dying. He put a bullet through the man's head just to be certain and took his wallet as he had the other's. It took him no more than twenty seconds. He left their cannons, neither of which were any damn good. He did grab the Colt automatic though, as neat a piece of iron as he'd ever seen. He looked closely at Mike's body, making sure.

"Din' think youse was so stupid ta come back alone," Jack said. "Big mistake, palsey." He put the automatic to Mike's head. Mike didn't appear to be breathing, but Jack liked to be certain. A police whistle stopped him. It might have been just a block away, hard to be sure in city streets but it was surely time to go. He ran into the night.

Once he turned the next corner, he settled into a fast walk, not wanting to draw attention. He wished he'd had time to pop his mark again, but if the pool of blood under his head was any indicator, it would've been a waste of lead. He headed back toward the Bottler's, where he'd have plenty of intimidated witnesses to swear he'd been there all night. He tried to move the fingers on his broken hand, itching in its new plaster. "Damned if it don' feel betta aweady," he said with a grin.

The grin left his face quickly. In fact, the jovial mood the killing had put him in vanished altogether when he neared the Bottler's to see cops out front.

Jack ducked behind a front stoop and stashed his pistols, brass knuckles, blackjack, and knives in a trash can. More whistles sounded and he realized that the one before had probably not been on account of him and his mugs, but had something to do with the scene unfolding before him. The Bottler paid protection to everyone, the precinct captain, Kelly, Devery, and that gang of thieves led by Big Tim, they all got their cut. Paul was going to be like a terrier in a rat pit when he heard about this. He'd want answers, he'd want someone to pay, and he'd want to know why the fuck he and his goons hadn't been there when it happened, a detail that bothered Jack considerably. Of course, Jack had known all that when he made his deal with the Bottler, but it was still a chancey thing to risk Paul Kelly's anger.

He decided on the direct approach when he spotted a couple of cops he'd done business with in the past guarding the front door.

"Well, well, Jack. What a coincidence you being here. Just passin' by?" The cops laughed at him, a thing he'd normally have put a stop to in a hurry, but with an effort he managed to control his disposition. "Sure, Jimmy," Jack said with a dismissive wave of his hand. "What da fuck's goin' on? Da Bottler don' pay youse piggies enough awready?"

"Now, now, Jack. No sense getting testy," Jimmy said, pointing his nightstick at Jack's chest. "Won't do you any good and it damn sure won't do the Bottler any good, either." The cops laughed as if this were high humor.

"Da hell it won't. Paul'l have Howe an' Hummell break 'im out by fuckin' mornin'."

"Won't do the Bottler any good if he has an army of Howes and Hummells, not where he's going."

Jack looked at the cops closely then, his brow knitting. "Wha da fuck, Jimmy? Wha's dis all about? He jus' runs a game's all."

The cops looked at each other. "C'mon, Jack, see for yourself." He ushered McManus into the Bottler's stuss parlor. A couple of detectives were pocketing the last few dollars lying about as they came in. Chairs were overturned, drinks spilled, cigars were burning holes in carpet and felt, and the Bottler was leaking blood like a tin roof in a thunderstorm. He was slumped in the dealer's chair, his blood puddling in chunks of his own brains, arms dangling nearly to the floor.

The detectives saw Jack and ordered him out and he went without any trouble. "Wha da fuck happened?" he said to no one in particular, more concerned with how he was going to explain to Paul how he'd gotten two of his mugs dead and the Bottler left defenseless and full of holes.

"Cyclone Louie," Jimmy said. "At least that's what one of the witnesses said. He's down at the station house."

"Cyclone Louie? Da fuckin' strongman? You caught 'im?"

"No, the witness. He says Cyclone walked in, didn't say a word, just shot the Bottler where he sat. Twenty guys in the joint. Nobody else got a scratch."

McManus picked up his weapons and walked off without a word. Paul was going to want to hear about this double-quick and he'd want to hear it in person. He had another stop to make after that, but Paul would have to come first. It was only fair.

33

PAUL WAS ANGRY. His neck was red above his high, starched collar and a vein stood out on it like a blue rope. "Didn't I tell you to watch the Bottler? That's what I said to do, right? Keep an eye on him, so fucking Twist don't get his mitts on him."

"Sure, Paul but—"

"Do I look stupid to you?"

"No, but—"

"No. That's good because I was beginning to think you thought I was fucking stupid, that telling you to watch the fucking Bottler was stupid."

"Nah, Paul. Dat wasn't stupid. But—"

Paul Kelly held up what could have been the manicured hand of a railroad baron or a Wall Street tycoon, but that Jack had seen beat the life from a man's body, cut another's throat, and pull the trigger on many more. "But you saw this fucking guy and you had to go kill him."

"Dat's right! Da fuck needed killin', Paul."

"A natural instinct, Jack, I don't doubt that. But what happens?" He spread the contents of Mike's wallet on the table and tapped it with a shiny fingernail. "Who is it you fucking killed, but Mike Braddock."

"So, what's dat ta me? He had it comin'."

"No doubt," Kelly said. "But for chris sake, he's a fucking detective, you half-wit!"

Jack shrugged his shoulders as if being called a half-wit wasn't boiling his blood up to his eyeballs. He put his good hand in his lap. He had a .32 Smith & Wesson in his waistband. Any other man on the planet would have been dead already, but he managed to control his instincts.

Kelly sat back and watched McManus stew, smiling slowly. "You thinking about shooting me, Jack? You wouldn't be the first, but you're not *that* fucking stupid are you?"

Jack managed to sneer in return. "Just scratchin' my balls."

"Ah," Kelly said with a solicitous nod.

"Half-wit?"

"If the fucking shoe fits," Kelly said in a low growl.

Jack twitched one shoulder and after a long pause put his hand back on the table.

"Good." Kelly gave a slight nod to his bodyguard, who was standing behind Jack, then frowned and leaned forward. "Getting back to our problem, the fucking detective you killed; you know who that was?"

"Braddock? No. Why should I?"

"Because it's Tom Braddock's son, you fuck!"

"Da Captain Braddock, from da Toid Precinct? Holy shit!" Jack's face cracked open in a delighted grin. "Da boys're gonna *love* dis!"

Kelly's fist slammed down on the table, making his drink jump and heads turn in the bar. "We do business with Tom Braddock, you asshole," he hissed. "He might be a pain in the ass, but you have no fucking idea what's going to happen if he finds out you did this. You got me? All the protection is off, not just in his precinct, but all over the fucking city, and he is going to come after your ass like there's no fuckin' tomorrow."

"I ain't scared o' no mug wit a badge, captain or not."

"Sweet Jesus! I don't give a shit who you're scared of, though if you had any sense you'd be fucking scared of Braddock! If the gloves come off, we're done, all of us. Something like this they don't forget and don't forgive."

"So, we lays low for a while. Da Tammany crowd'll smooth t'ings ova like always."

Kelly shook his head. "Not gonna happen. Big Tim and all the rest, they just want things to go their way. They do not give a shit who runs the gangs, the whores, the cons, the rackets, the swindles, any of it. They just want it run and run quiet. And I fucking guarantee you that killing cops is not their definition of quiet. Now tell me again what happened."

It was curious to Jack how Paul was more concerned with Braddock than the Bottler. He'd have bet it would be the other way around, so in a way he was not all that unhappy with how things were going and he was glad to reassure Paul on the details of the Braddock killing. "Nobody seen it. Nobody on da street but us. My two boys they could identify maybe, but I took their stuff."

"Mickey Thumbs and that mug Bones?"

"Yeah, good mugs. Bones was mad as hell at what they done to 'im, droppin' 'im into a shithole. But he was a good leg-breaker an' knew how to keep his pie-hole shut. Braddock plugged 'im foist."

"Maybe if we're lucky they'll figure it was just them that shot Braddock."

Jack hadn't thought of that, but he brightened at the idea. "I left their cannons, but da vultures prob'ly got dat stuff. Took Braddock's iron, too. Nice new Colt automatic. You shoulda seen it shoot! He plugged da boys so fast youse wouldn' believe it."

"Jesus Christ, Jack! Are you out of your fucking mind? Get rid of it! Today! Go throw it in a sewer somewhere."

"Yeah, but, Paul, it's a sweet cannon. You shoulda seen—"

Kelly reached into his pocket, and Jack stiffened in midsentence.

Kelly pulled out a wad of bills, peeled a few off, and slapped them on the table. Leaning forward, he said in an almost pleasant tone, "Go buy a new one."

Later, after he and Paul Kelly had gone over their stories for the police, Jack had to ask, "What about da Bottler?"

"We'll send flowers, especially you. Come to think of it, did he have a widow, kids, or anything?"

"Dunno."

"Well, find out. If he's got any, you take care of them, all right?"

"But the Bottler's game I meant; what're we doin' 'bout dat?" Jack said. "Twist'll move in. Youse know it was him behind fuckin' Cyclone Louie. Gotta be."

Kelly said nothing for a while. "Kid Twist," he finally spat out. "I knew that punk coming up; holding up tourists and poisoning horses. You know his real name's Max Zweiback? His parents were nice people; quiet, hardworking, went to temple every week. But he was always a punk." He sighed. "I'm going to let it go for now."

"But, Paul, what'll da boys t'ink? Dey gonna be lookin' for a war."

Kelly shook his head and said in a low voice, "I have bigger fish to fry, Jack. The Bottler's game will have a spotlight on it now. The take'll go down because those kind of gamblers don't like the spotlight. Besides I'll talk to Big Tim, he'll see they get raided a few times, and then he'll squeeze Twist for twice the protection the Bottler ever paid him. Fuck Twist. He'll be left holding an empty bag. So tell our minions to be quiet. Their time will come. But you I want on that boat, Jack."

Jack nodded. "Da *Slocum?*"

"Right. Stay there. Do some real work for a change. I want to know what's going on with Big Tim. That's the thing that rankles me more than anything else. If there's a war starting, it's over that."

34

MIKE COULD NOT stop the ringing. The side of his head resonated with a single high-pitched tone. It was as if billions of tiny cries had merged into one deafening scream that he could not stop. He felt cold, too. He couldn't understand how the weather had changed so quickly. He imagined that maybe he'd been lying there like Rip Van Winkle, sleeping away twenty years, facedown on the street. He tried to focus, to move his frozen feet and break the crust of ice that encased them. He tried his fingers, wiggling them in their gloves of permafrost. It was incredibly tiring and he had to take a deep, bubbling breath before he tried to do more. There was something in his mouth. He realized a moment later that it was his tongue, now swollen to double its size, as if a balloon had replaced it. He groaned and tried to spit. There were jagged things that dug into his cheeks, and bright circles of pain on either side of his face. He coughed and spit again and pushed the bits of teeth out to dribble down his chin. He breathed a little easier then and decided to try and open his eyes.

It seemed like a day before Mike was able to get to his feet. He stood with his hands on his knees, wondering where his clothes had gone. Shoes, pants, jacket, vest, shirt, everything but his shorts was missing. He'd seen murder victims stripped like that, anything of value taken before the body had even gone cold. He couldn't understand how it had happened to him though, thinking that perhaps he'd just managed to wander out like this. It made no sense, but he couldn't deny that he was on a city street in this condition. Wiping blood from his eyes, he saw the bodies, lumps of flesh appearing oddly flattened, most of their clothes missing too. He had a vague recollection, a flash card image of shooting at them, of it happening so fast that it was more feeling than vision, bursts of sound and light that repeated somewhere in his ringing skull. He shook his head. He almost fell over, staggered sideways and caught himself, realizing someone was on the street coming toward him. The figure loomed in the darkness, his head appearing unnaturally huge until he stepped into the glow of a streetlight and Mike saw that it was a helmet the man was wearing. It was a cop. He realized at that instant that he was a cop too and that despite this man's huge head he might be able to help. Mike began to stagger forward, hands outstretched, a liquid croaking coming from his mouth that he meant to sound like "Help," but was really nothing like it. He tried to say, "Detective Braddock," but should have known better. His balloon tongue couldn't get around it. He sounded like a lunatic even to himself. The cop with the huge head must have thought so too, expressing his opinion with a sharp rap of his nightstick on Mike's temple. The street came up to meet him again. A part of him was grateful for the rest.

35

THE TRIANGLE SHIRTWAIST Factory Building didn't appear quite as grim this morning, the press of workers just a bit more tolerable, the stack of material by Ginny's machine slightly less intimidating. She'd walked all the way from her apartment, which she began to realize toward the end had been a mistake. But it seemed such an auspicious day, a flower bud of a day, ready to burst open with possibilities that she really had no choice. Mike was sure to come, and even if he didn't, she was determined to leave another note and another again until he did. She *would* see him. She couldn't be more sure of it.

She supposed that she had Carl to thank for the way she felt. Their walk home the night before had had an effect, though surely not the one he'd intended. It wasn't that she hadn't found him interesting. She supposed he was, on some less polished level than Mike. He was funny and attentive and comfortably fixed, if his expensive clothes were any indication. But it was just being with him, walking with an attractive man and enjoying his company that had stirred her yearning for Mike. She had to make that yearning stop. It was not a thing that could be lived with. It was a flame that had to either be fed or extinguished, not left to smolder. She *would* see Mike and tell him the things she needed to and then it would be his choice.

She'd survived so much already, risen above obstacle, hurt, and hardship. Surely if it came to that, she could endure Mike's loss, too. It wasn't something that she liked to think about. Even thinking it caused an ache to grow in her middle and a weakness to run through her limbs. But she would live. This was a new notion for her, the idea that she could go on, take the blows, and move forward.

She hadn't realized that her fear of fending for herself had kept her at Miss Gertie's. It seemed the simplest of things now and obvious. But it had not been obvious then. The change amazed her. Her confidence amazed her. The winds that had tossed her about, buffeted the breath from her body, and the strength from her bones had deposited her on another shore.

The day, all twelve hours of it, passed in a blur. The elevator opened countless times, but she wasn't disappointed when Mike didn't emerge. She was determined not to be and after a while didn't even look up when the gates clanged open. If he didn't come that day, it was of no real consequence. She'd planned on going to headquarters tonight and had already written another note, a message she felt sure he'd respond to. It had been written last night by candlelight and was now tucked in her purse, a sprig of lavender pressed in its folds. Day passed into evening and for the first time, Ginny left the Triangle Shirtwaist Factory Building feeling that the day had just begun.

Carl was waiting for her. He'd asked the night before if she'd mind seeing him again. She'd liked that he asked and said she wouldn't mind the company. Tonight he was as dapper as before, but with a bit more flash and color than appropriate for a true gentleman. Ginny had known a number of those. The best of them were always understated in their dress and accessories, more elegant and confident of their position in life. Carl seemed a paste diamond by comparison.

He had brought her a gardenia for her hair and helped her

clip it so it stayed just above her left ear. He said it made her look Hawaiian, especially when she smiled. Ginny tried not to smile too much. She liked Carl and didn't want to hurt him if her designs on Mike came to pass. At the same time, she was beginning to realize that if Mike was not to be in her future, then Carl was not an altogether unattractive alternative.

As they walked south, Ginny began to comprehend the delicacy of the situation and quickly tried to think of some plausible excuse for going to police headquarters. They turned onto Broadway when they got to Houston and angled over to Crosby then Mulberry, with Ginny increasingly distracted.

"You awright, Ginny? Somethin' on yer mind?" Carl finally asked. "You ain't laughin' at my jokes like last night. An' where we goin' if ya don mind me askin'? Not that I mind da walk wit' a pretty girl like you."

Ginny smiled an apology. "No, no, Carl. It's just that I'm a little distracted. There's something I have to see to." Her mind whirred about like a carousel, stopping at what she thought was a suitable story. "You see I got a letter from my mother yesterday. My brother's gone. He came to the city a week ago, they live on Long Island you see, and she hasn't heard from him since, so I'm going to have to stop at police headquarters down here and tell them he's missing."

Carl stiffened. "Whoa! Dat's no good. Disappeared you say?"

"Well, that's what my mother says, but I don't know whether to believe it or not. Knowing my brother, he's off on a bender somewhere," Ginny said, realizing that she hadn't been acting quite as upset for her dear lost brother as she might have. Carl stopped walking though and she wasn't sure if he was more upset about the prospects for her brother or of having to go to the police. They were within sight of the building and Carl was looking at it as if it were an oncoming train. He must have realized it be-cause he gave a thin smile and said, "I don' like da cops so much. Had my disagreements over da years."

Ginny nodded as if she understood. "You don't have to go, silly. Besides, they don't bite."

Carl gave her a frown in return. "Youse don' know da cops I know."

Ginny went in, feeling a little guilty for lying to Carl. But if she'd told him the truth about Mike, she'd probably never see him again. She realized then that she really had been thinking of Carl as a replacement for Mike, a fish she might throw back if a bigger one came along. She climbed the steps of headquarters feeling confused. She didn't like to think of herself as a liar. But then, despite her efforts to get Mike back, the truth was she couldn't be sure it would ever happen. She sighed as she fished for the note.

There was a different desk sergeant that night, a man not so inclined toward uncomfortable questions. She handed him the note and asked that it be left for Detective Braddock. An un-usual look crossed the man's face, a look that Ginny couldn't ex-actly identify, something between sorrow and pride she might have said.

"Sure, ma'am, lots of messages for Braddock this evening." He said it as if she would know why. She left, feeling puz-zled and uneasy. She didn't see Carl at first when she came out and thought with a sinking feeling that he'd gone, that he'd seen through her story. But Carl was just up the block, his face buried in a newspaper, his lips moving slightly as he read. "That was fast," he said with a quizzical frown. "What happened?"

"Oh, they, ah, said I should come back tomorrow. The detec-tive who handles missing persons has gone home for the night."

Carl nodded as if that made sense. Ginny was about to embellish the lie when she noticed the headline on the newspaper. HERO COP LIES NEAR DEATH, the headline read, then in smaller type beneath GUNS DOWN TWO GANGSTERS IN DEADLY SHOOT-OUT. But what caught Ginny's eye was a photograph of Mike just below, a picture of him as a patrolman, a helmet on his head that he seemed uncomfortable in. Ginny grabbed the paper from Carl's hands.

"Hey, what's up?"

Ginny didn't answer. She had to know what hospital he was in and scanned the article twice before she found it. "Carl, I have to go. I'm sorry, so sorry. I . . . I just have to go."

"Ginny?" Carl started after her as she practically ran down the street. "Ginny!"

36

MIKE WAS SURE it was a dream. He felt a hand in his, and he'd opened his eyes just a crack. They didn't seem to open much more than that. His face felt as if it had been inflated to twice its size, even his eyelids felt bloated. But when he focused he saw Ginny, bending low. He blinked to clear the milky paste from his vision. She was still there, whispering his name and telling him her name. She looked impossibly beautiful, so far beyond even his fondest recollection of her that he had to doubt his sight. She had changed somehow, in ways he could not put into words. She was plainer without the makeup and finery, but her beauty seemed to shine like an Edison bulb.

She was saying something. It was hard to understand. The ringing in his head made her urgent whisperings blend—syllables ran in unnatural ways, and sentences had no start or end. But he could see the feeling in her eyes and the care carved across her brow. He knew that what she was telling him was true. He didn't need words to know that.

Mike wished he could talk. He tried, but when he moved his tongue and jaw, he was paralyzed with pain. The lower half of his face was swaddled in bandages and his tongue was a dead thing in his mouth. Everything hurt with a throbbing ache that went deep into the bone. He wanted to tell Ginny how sorry he was and how guilty he felt for not finding her. He'd tried, though his efforts seemed puny and halfhearted now. It had been his job to find her and he hadn't done it. He understood as he watched her face that everything else should have come second to that. All that had happened in the last weeks, everything that had seemed so all-consuming, he knew to be almost trivial by comparison. He made a silent promise to himself and to Ginny that if he survived she would never come second again. He gripped her hand, and looked in her eyes, tears running into his bandages, hoping she knew.

With a sudden surge of energy, he realized what he had to do while he still held consciousness. He signed for a pen and paper, and Ginny, understanding almost immediately, produced both after a brief absence. It took nearly every ounce of his energy and focus and will, but Mike brought the paper close and with a dead hand wrote, "Read your diary. I love you, too!"

Ginny took it from his trembling hand, now so weak it fell to the sheet, laudanum and shock leaving him limp after so small an effort. She read it and even as he slipped into unconsciousness he heard a sound escape her lips, the wordless sound of love.

"You'll have to leave now, miss," a voice said from the door. Ginny squeezed Mike's hand and kissed his forehead. "I'll see you tomorrow," she said, holding back her tears until she turned away.

Ginny went out into the hallway, not certain what she should feel. Half of her was elated that Mike was even alive. Half was so deeply uneasy about his condition that her fears nearly overcame her hope. The sight of Mike's head, shrouded in bandages, his eyes swollen nearly shut, his shaking hands, had nearly unnerved her. Still, she held tight to his note, a life raft in the storm.

An arm went round Ginny's shoulder and she started. "You'll come home with us." Mary said in a gentle yet unyielding voice, a tone that left no room for debate. She noticed the paper Ginny held. Mary didn't ask what it held. Ginny felt she knew.

Mary and Ginny walked down the echoing tiled hallway, the hospital lights like halos at intervals in each direction. Tom waited at the end, giving them the space Mary had asked for. "I'll have someone fetch your clothes," she said. "You can get settled in the spare room. It's really quite nice." She somehow felt it necessary to reassure Ginny on that point, though she needn't have bothered.

Mary took Ginny's silence for trepidation, but it wasn't that at all. It was closer to bewilderment, the feeling that her world had shifted and would not shift back, that everything she'd known had gone under the waves and she'd been deposited on some distant shore. She'd been washed up sputtering, exhausted, and gritty with the sand of her past.

"Thank you, Miss Mary," was all she could muster.

Neither Mary nor Ginny noticed the figure across the street from the hospital entrance when they climbed into Mary's carriage, but Tom let his eye linger on the dark silhouette, while his hand rested on the butt of his revolver. He thought about Mike for an instant, but there was a police guard on his door, so he forced himself to relax.

Carl lounged against the back of a coal wagon, watching them leave. He blew a last smoke ring and ground his cigarette against the back of the wagon with something between a sigh and a growl. Even he could not have said which.

37

BIG TIM SULLIVAN stuck out a meaty hand, giving Tom a heartfelt smile. Tom took his hand. He was impressed that Tim had taken the time to come, but it was the sort of gesture Sullivan was known for.

"Thanks for coming, Tim, and for the flowers," Tom said as they shook. They'd known each other since Sullivan's early days at the bar on Chrystie Street, where the Whyos held court and Tim had made his start in politics, but they were acquaintances, more than friends, their paths intersecting over the years whenever their shared interest met.

"Och, it's nothin', Tommy. How's the boy? Hell of a thing he got into."

"A little rough right now," Tom said with a look over his shoulder at Mike. "He's lucky though. Bullet went right through his mouth. An inch or so higher and he'd probably be dead, a little lower and the jaw would've been shattered. As it is, he's lost a few teeth and they had to stitch a gash in his tongue. They say he's got a hairline fracture of the jaw, but it's not too bad. His brain's shaken up pretty good. A patrolman cracked his head with a nightstick, if you can believe that."

"What for?"

"I'm going to find out what for," Tom said. "That guy better have a fucking good excuse. My temper's on a short fuse, and I'm in no mood for bullshit." Though Tom's head was aching and his balance wasn't right, he was mad enough to go after that cop and ask questions later. Technically he wasn't even supposed to be out of his bed, but he wasn't about to let a doctor tell him what he could or couldn't do.

Big Tim put a hand on his arm. He knew how impulsive Tom could be from the old days. "Better let that cool for a bit, Tommy. How's Mary holding up? All right, I hope?"

"Thanks for asking. She didn't sleep all night. Hell, neither of us did. But she's strong, stronger than me in some ways. She'll be okay. She'll be here later. She's setting up a room at home for Mike to stay with us when he gets out."

"They'll not be releasing him so soon though, right?"

"No, not for a few days at least, but you know Mary; lots of nervous energy."

Tim pursed his lips. "Understandable." He looked again at Mike, who could barely be seen for all the flowers that had sprouted around him. They'd been arriving all morning; big bunches in wicker baskets, roses, carnations, ferns, and baby's breath.

"Hope the flowers aren't too much. I asked for somethin' nice and cheery."

"No, they're fine, Tim. It's the bunch on the other side of the bed." Tom pointed to a huge basket, the flowers bursting out in a riot of color, a large, golden ribbon with *Get Well Soon* in red script draped around them.

Tim nodded. "Who the hell was it, Tom? They know yet?"

"One's a Five Pointer, the other's with the Gophers from what I hear. Not sure how it happened. Mike hasn't been able to tell us."

"A Pointer and a Gopher," Tim said. "An odd combination."

"Yeah, you could say that. Makes you wonder."

"Anything to do with what happened at that stuss game?"

"Not sure." Tom had no intention of telling Tim anything about Mike's suspicions of the Bottler. He didn't think Tim would consciously do anything to hurt Mike, but he wouldn't doubt that he might put his interests ahead of Mike's. On the other hand, Tom didn't have a problem with asking a few questions. "You ever hear of a gentleman by the name of Saturn? He's a vice-president at the Knickerbocker Steamship Company."

"I've heard of him," Tim said. "Chartered one of his boats last year for my annual picnic. Great fun. I keep asking you to come. You really should."

"Never met him though, huh?"

Tim turned his palms up. "I meet so many damn people, Tommy. Can't remember 'em all. Probably did, but I don't remember. Why do you ask?"

Tom was pretty sure he wasn't getting the whole truth. Big Tim had more secrets than the U.S. Mint. "Anyway, he got jumped, this fellow Saturn that is, a couple nights ago, just after coming out of the Bottler's. Three guys."

"The same who attacked Mike?" Tim was as interested in that point as Tom. He and Connors had been almost certain it had been Kelly's doing, but there was no real proof beyond Saturn's hysterics.

"Not sure, but Mike and his partner, Primo, broke it up. Two attempts on Primo's life and this thing with Mike in the last two days; an awful lot of coincidence."

"You think there were three? But you said he shot two, right?"

"Yeah, but there might have been a third."

"But Mike hasn't said." Tim pursed his lips in thought.

"Nope."

"So let me understand this, Tommy, you learned about the attack on that Saturn fellow because Mike and his partner were

243

there, is that right?" Tim hadn't decided what to do about Saturn yet, only that Paul Kelly was going to have to learn his place in the pecking order before he got his beak clipped. This new information about Mike's attackers was starting to give him an idea.

"Yeah, Mike and Primo pretty much saved his skin," Tom said, watching Tim's face for a reaction.

"But the suspects got away, I assume, or this would not be a mystery."

"They had caught one, but let him go after questioning. Mike's partner was able to tell me that." Primo had begun to speak that morning and was now conscious and relatively lucid. Tom didn't mention to Tim that he was going to bring Saturn in to help identify the bodies if he could.

Big Tim scratched his nose and thought how this information might be of use. There was certainly a nugget of something there. He decided to phone Saturn later that morning. The man might prove more useful than he'd imagined. "You tie these crimes together and who knows where it may lead, eh?" he said. "Maybe the whole is more than the sum of its parts, or something like that?"

Tom looked at Mike, the bandages on his head so white among the riot of flowers. "That's what I'm hoping to find out."

Mary and Ginny, who arrived just after Big Tim left, sat with Tom and Mike all morning. Ginny felt herself to be little more than a bystander. A procession of cops and friends paraded by, sometimes crowding the room to the point where it seemed more like a bar than a hospital, and there was no time to speak to Mike in the way she wanted. Mike felt like a cigar store Indian, unable to talk and barely able to move. He saw how Mary and Ginny had come in together, and was amazed by it, but relieved, too. He smiled inside, knowing how his mother had undoubtedly taken charge and found himself more appreciative of her than he could possibly express, even if he could have opened his mouth to speak. His jaw hurt like nothing he'd ever known, so the best he could manage were grunts and hoarse whispers. He tired fast and though he tried to put up a strong front, Mary could see his exhaustion and shooed everyone out by noon.

He'd been put on a liquid diet, which he didn't mind. He could hardly open his mouth and the thought of chewing made him cringe. He was hungry though and sipped all the broth Ginny fed him. Mary had started to do so herself, but stopped after taking the tray of food from the nurse, and turned it over to Ginny instead. She watched with a secret smile. Mike gulped gratefully, feeling the strength flow back into him with each spoonful.

Tom went to speak with the doctor. He needed a headache powder. The morning's activity had given him a real pounder. The doctors had released him only after Tom threatened to walk out, permission or not. The way his head felt, he figured maybe the doctors knew what they were talking about after all. Mike's doctor, a rumpled, balding gentleman named Alpert, who wore a ready smile under his bushy mustache, told him that Mike would require some follow-up surgery to repair his face. There was a doctor on staff who specialized in such things.

"Makes the tiniest stitches on staff. He makes the finest seamstress jealous," Doctor Alpert told him. "He'll always have scars, of course, but hopefully they can be minimized."

"And what about his teeth? He's lost how many?"

"Five."

"Ugh." Tom's jaw hurt just thinking about that. "He's got to have one hell of a toothache."

"I'm afraid so. We've given him something for the pain, but there's a limit to how much we can do with something that severe. We don't want to send him home a laudanum addict."

"Understood," Tom said. "So what'll happen with the teeth?"

"Denture plates," he answered, "but that's not my specialty.

The oral surgeon took out the roots when we had your son in surgery. When the gums heal he'll be able to fit him with new teeth."

Tom thanked the doctor, who said he'd be in to check on Mike during the afternoon rounds. Then Tom stopped in to see Primo, who was conscious, but in a lot of pain, his whispered words sometimes not making complete sense. A nurse said his appetite was good though and that was always a hopeful sign. Tom decided not to tell Primo about Mike. He seemed too weak to take that sort of news just then. Primo gave Tom's hand a hard squeeze when he bent to tell him he'd be back later.

Ginny had finished spooning broth into the narrow opening of Mike's mouth, when Mike signaled that he wanted a pencil and paper. Mary found them in his nightstand drawer and gave them to Mike, who took the pencil and wrote quickly, "You're amazing." Ginny watched as he wrote and said, "I'm not the one who's amazing." Mike hoped they could see him smile through the bandages.

Ginny took his hand. "Your mother has been so kind to me, Mike. I can never repay such kindness. She took me in. I'm staying in the guest room upstairs." She didn't tell Mike how magnificent the room was to her, or how she'd sunken into the huge, white bathtub down the hall, letting the steam take her away with a sigh. She didn't say how unworthy she felt at such treatment, or how she'd tried to protest when Mary insisted they go shopping for new clothes the next morning. Those things were almost unreal and she experienced them in a near dreamlike state, certain that they'd slip away when she awoke.

"You're beautiful," Mike wrote next, giving the note to Ginny. She put the note to her breast, and with a sigh lowered her head to his chest. Mike's hand went to stroke her hair.

Mary coughed. "I'll just go talk to the nurse for a moment."

38

THE BOTTLER WAS pretty happy for a man who'd had his brains blown all over his stuss table. Jack McManus couldn't remember when he'd seen the man more relaxed. The Bottler could be a regular fidgety bastard most times, worrying over this or that, and giving the boss headaches over his fucking stuss game.

But the stuss game was over now. Kelly would let Kid Twist have the dregs of it. The Bottler didn't care, not anymore.

"Fuck, I would've given anything to see it; watch myself get shot to hell," He said. "Can't anybody say they saw themselves get their fucking face shot off," he said.

McManus just grinned. "An' live to tell it, least not da ones I done."

They were in the cellar of a Pitt Street dive, one of the hell-holes the Bottler had bought with the profits from his brew. It smelled of fresh concrete and wood, but it was finished as finely as any parlor on Gramercy Park, with a rich Persian carpet, mahogany paneling, and deeply tufted leather chairs. There were at least three ways in or out of the place that Jack knew of and probably at least one more he didn't. Small doorways cut through the brick foundations of the adjoining row houses, leading to others Jack had to presume. He'd entered through the tenement next door, admitted by a boy of sixteen, a hard-looking lad with the dead eyes of a killer. The Bottler had himself a fortress here; a little kingdom that Kelly didn't even know existed. Jack's grin widened. There was a lot Kelly didn't know.

"Christ, he must have been one surprised sonofabitch. Damn, wish I could'a seen his face." He laughed as Jack did a pantomime, mouth open in a big O, eyes wide as headlamps.

"Where'd ya find 'im?" Jack asked. "'E was a pretty good fuckin' match; did his hair da same an' everyt'ing."

"'Course he did! I been trainin' him for weeks. Had to know how to deal stuss first off, but I got 'im set up right; clothes, haircut, mustache, the works. Even had him talking like me."

"An' he didn' s'pect nothin'? Jus' went along wit it?"

"Sure, why not? I was paying him good to keep his pie-hole shut. Best damn money I ever spent."

"Where'd youse find 'im?" Jack asked again.

"Had some of my guys on the lookout for a mug who could play me," the Bottler answered. "I think they found him blacking boots somewhere on the Bowery." The Bottler had known as soon as he'd decided to go against Kelly, keeping his hold on Saturn and the steamship line secret, that a double would be a useful thing to have. His odds of living had gone way up when he'd found the right man. They'd gone through the roof when he'd heard that Saturn had fucked things up by going to Big Tim. He had McManus to thank for that bit of information. He didn't need to tell Jack that having his double killed by Cyclone Louie, a known confederate of Kid Twist, was about as certain a thing to start a gang war as anything he could ever have devised. It had cost him five hundred, but was worth every cent. He'd been disappointed when Jack told him that Kelly had decided not to retaliate, at least not yet. Kelly was smart, too smart to be drawn into a war when there was nothing to be gained. The stuss game was worthless now, and the Bottler's hopes of watching from the shadows while Kid's and Kelly's gangs shot each other to pieces were going to have to wait. But there were other ways to get that done.

The idea of devising a strategy like the Bottler had made Jack's head swim, but he knew he'd made the right decision to go with the Bottler on the sly. He was a thinker like Kelly, but he could be a sharer, too. Jack had another thousand-dollar wad in his pocket to remind him of just how generous the Bottler could be. Kelly had never been that generous, not in all the years they'd known each other. He'd always kept the prime rib and left the soup bone for everybody else.

"Paul musta been pissing nails when he heard I was dead," the Bottler said. "And you let it happen."

"Had to tell 'im," McManus growled. "If I didn', 'e woulda known somethin' was up. Dis way, it was just a fuckup, nothin' more to it. He was not fuckin' happy though, I can tell ya dat."

"Paul can be a bastard, but still, you've been together so long, I was surprised you came to me. Not that you haven't had your reasons," he added a little hastily when he saw McManus tense. "Believe me, I know."

Jack had become restless under Paul's thumb, and less willing to put up with errand-boy shit like watching the boat. "Yeah, Kelly, he wants ta run da whole damn show, an' he don't share wit da mugs like me what does da woik."

"I know it," the Bottler agreed.

"Always liked da way youse ran da game, too. An lemme be honest, youse ain't got a problem wit spreadin' da dough aroun'. Paul jus trows us da crumbs." Jack raised a glass in his direction.

But mostly Jack liked the Bottler's angles, the money from the coca smuggling, and the bottling of the concoctions he sold to the block-and-fall joints were pure genius. There was a bigger future to be had too once the *Slocum* thing got moving at full throttle. Just like Kelly, the Bottler had plans for gambling, prizefights, and whoring, too. And he was much more willing to share.

"Kelly didn't wonder why you went after Braddock?" the Bottler asked.

"Nah, t'ought it was just a grudge, which it fuckin' was anyway."

"The nerve of him!" the Bottler said, "And that fucking dago partner of his, sitting in on my game, like I'd never figure out who they were. That cop who booked Kid Dahl came the next day and gave me the whole story, Saturn, too. They know I pay good for information. That's how I've stayed in business so long. You gotta spread the money around."

"A t'ing Kelly could loin about."

"Exactly! A shame Braddock ain't dead," the Bottler said. "Not your fault though. Put one right through his fucking kisser. Musta looked dead enough."

"In a fuckin' puddle o' blood last time I saw 'im," Jack said regretfully.

The Bottler thought for a moment and said, "Well, he'll be out of commission for a while and no bother to us anyway. You sent him those tickets, right?"

"Sure, made it look like that Saturn shithead sent 'em."

"Good. We'll have another opportunity then. And the girl?"

McManus barked a low laugh. "Johnny Suds! Jesus, was he fucked-up! Couldn't wait to give me every goddamn thing he knew about that bitch. Hell, I almost thought he was gonna pay me to take care o' Braddock. Anyways, I got a mug on it; keepin' an eye on 'er."

"Good," the Bottler said with a grin. "She might be useful somewhere down the road. If nothin' else we can put her to work on the ship once we've got things in hand."

"Wouldn't mind a piece o' dat twist," Jack said. "Saw 'er da otha night wit' Carl. Nice little bustle on 'er."

The Bottler laughed. "You'll get your chance, Jack. I guarantee it."

39

"THAT'S ONE OF the men who attacked me," Saturn said, his voice muffled by the handkerchief held over his mouth and nose. They were in the city morgue at Bellevue. The cold and damp had him and Tom shoving their hands in their pockets and despite the constant mist of cold water sprayed over the bodies to slow decay, the room had the stink of death and disinfectant. "I'm sure of that one. The other I've never seen before. Sorry."

"Don't be," Tom said. "This is a help. I don't imagine you caught his name?" Tom knew he could probably identify the man by going through the rogues' gallery, but the file of police photographs was becoming so large that he knew it might take hours.

"I'm afraid not, Captain. This gentleman didn't bother with formal introductions."

"Of course," Tom said. "Anything else you can tell me? Did they refer to each other by nicknames?"

"Let me think," Saturn said. "You know I've been reliving that entire episode over and over these last few days. Mostly I imagine the things I should have done differently."

"I understand completely. And sometimes things come back, things you hadn't thought about before," Tom said.

"Yes. I have to tell you that I think the third man was named

Jack. This one here," he said, pointing to one of the bodies, "called him Jack. I'm fairly sure."

"How sure?"

"Well, it was hardly a clear recollection as I said. I just recall hearing the name Jack. He seemed to be the one in charge." Tom already had a description from Mike, who'd been able to write it out this morning, but he asked Saturn as well. "I'm afraid I didn't get a very good look at him. I saw more of his shoe leather than his face, although I can give you a general description. He was about one hundred and eighty pounds and around five foot eight. and maybe somewhere around thirty-five years of age. I must tell you too," Saturn added, "he was a singularly ferocious character, and quite powerful for his size."

Although it fit about a quarter of the male population of the city, the description was useful. Saturn had corroborated Mike's description and given Tom a name, which was even more critical. Tom had an impressive list of criminal names and aliases stored in his battered brain, a lifetime of acquaintance with the shadier elements of society. A number of Jacks came immediately to mind.

After he'd thanked Saturn and they'd each gone their own way, Tom had gone over that list and come up with at least five Jacks who were not either dead or in jail, one of which was a pickpocket, hardly the sort to go in for stompings-for-hire. At least three could be said to fit the general description Saturn and Mike gave and all of them had connections in one way or another to the Five Pointers or the Bottler. Tom looked at his watch. He'd have to be back at the station house for the start of the next shift and didn't have much time for anything more.

Still, he took a few minutes after saying his good-bye to Saturn to look at the body of the Bottler, who'd been laid on a steel slab in the next room. The coroner's assistant was working on him. "Can't tell much from the face," he said, nodding toward the mass of gore on the table. "Plenty of witnesses though."

Tom nodded. The body certainly fit the Bottler's description and the captain of the Thirteenth had come down earlier to identify the body as best he could while they looked for next of kin. Still, Tom looked closely. "These his clothes?" he asked, pointing to a bag on a nearby counter. He went through them, examining the pockets, looking at labels, then he noticed the shoes. "New soles. Mind if I take one of these?"

"Nope. Just fill out the form if you don't mind. The coroner hates it when things go unaccounted for."

He walked to the horse he'd been able to secure for his use, a fine, chestnut mare, at least sixteen hands tall. She was a solid mount, but he longed for his Oldsmobile. He resolved to pay a visit soon to the mechanic's shop he'd had it brought to in Brooklyn, a place recommended by the factory. He mounted his horse and flicked the reins, guiding her into the light traffic of First Avenue. He hadn't gone more than a block when a big Marmon touring car barreled past with a blast of its claxon horn. His horse pranced sideways and shook its head with fear, making Tom work to control her. "Asshole!" he shouted, half in anger, half in envy.

"I gave him the name, Mister Sullivan," Saturn said into the mouthpiece.

"Good. But not too quickly, I hope," Big Tim said. "Cops are naturally suspicious of information that comes too easily."

"No, it was sufficiently difficult to recall."

"That's fine," the scratchy voice replied from the earpiece. "This will work to both our advantages. One less fly in the ointment so to speak."

"And five hundred off what I owe you," Saturn reminded him. "Not that I'd mind if that particular fly finds himself food for the spider. Tell me though, who is this Jack fellow?"

Big Tim harrumphed into the phone. "No need to concern yourself on that score, Mister Saturn," Tim's voice said with tinny finality. Setting Braddock sniffing after McManus would be just the sort of payback Paul Kelly deserved. "Now as to our other business."

40

GINNY HADN'T SLEPT more than a few hours, tossing through the night. She couldn't get Mike's bandaged face out of her mind. It was only with great effort that she'd managed to keep her head and not let Mike see how upset she'd been that first night. She couldn't see his wounds, but she could imagine what lay beneath the bandages, the torn flesh, the stitches. It hurt her to think of it, but she couldn't stop. She found herself wondering how badly scarred he'd be, if he'd appear hideous when the bandages came off. She'd had frightening visions of him as a freak that children pointed at as he passed.

But her feelings for Mike were even more intense. She longed to be with him all through the morning, during her shopping trip with Mary. Picking through the dress racks at Stewarts Department Store, a saleswoman at their sides, she could hardly focus on the cut or color, the cinched waists, or lace detailing. They were her true feelings, she told herself. But driven by her doubts, the images of Mike's face waited for her moments of weakness. It was not horror those thoughts conjured. It was the weakness in herself. Could she love a man deformed? She was determined to try.

Mary had seemed to sense Ginny's mood, not rushing her decisions or asking too many questions as they picked out new outfits.

She did her best to distract Ginny with their mission, immersing her in a world of endless choices, each more attractive than the last. "I'll pay you for all of this, I promise," Ginny said at one point, realizing suddenly how much they were likely to spend.

Mary smiled. "Of course you will. I have no doubt. But it's not your money I want," she said with a squeeze of Ginny's arm. "In fact, you've earned this much and more already."

"But I haven't done anything."

Mary held up a hand. "You've been there for Mike," she said, her dark eyes glittering. "It's not you who owe me, it's I who owe you."

Late that morning, after they'd finished their shopping and Ginny had three new outfits, with all that went with them, she asked Mary if she'd mind taking her back to the Triangle factory.

"You don't have to work there anymore, you understand, Ginny. Not unless you want to," Mary said, though it was obvious which she'd have chosen for her. There was a part of Ginny that wanted the independence and worth that a job carried with it, even one that left her so tired she could barely shuffle to her bed at night. But for now her employer owed her for more than two days' wages and she was determined to have it. She'd worked hard for those few dollars and she'd be damned if she'd let them go.

Her machine was occupied when she got up to her floor of the factory, Mary following her off the elevator with a sour look at the open barrel of oil beside the elevator door. Her shuffling Polish boss sneered at her as she approached. "And now it's your job you want back, heh? You don' show up for woik, you don' have a job to come to," he said, turning his back on her.

Ginny wanted nothing more than to slap him, but she held one hand in the other and gritted her teeth. "I have wages coming, sir"—raising her voice above the clatter of the machines—"you owe me for almost three days."

The Polack waved a dismissive hand at her and shuffled down his row. A porter, who Ginny knew doubled as an enforcer on her floor, put down a stack of cloth and watched with a leering grin. Esther looked on, not missing a stitch.

Ginny's face went red, the color rising up from her bodice like a tide. "You will kindly address me like a gentleman!" Ginny almost shouted in as commanding a voice as she could muster. "I will have my money, mister."

The man turned, an amused look on his face. He shuffled back toward her, not stopping until she could smell him. His breath reeked of onion, cabbage, and stale coffee as he said, "Youse got some noive, you little twist, coming in here like—"

Mary stepped between them suddenly, gripping the man's arm. "May I have a word?" she said with a brittle edge to her voice. She steered the man a few feet away and spoke to him in a low tone. The sneer left his lips as he listened and he seemed to shrink as Mary spoke, his shoulders drooping and a hint of an obsequious smile crept across his mouth. He started nodding and a moment later, he returned to Ginny, holding out a handful of coins, a pair of silver dollars and assorted change. Ginny took it and Mary started toward the elevator. He hissed a stream of curses then, too low for Mary to hear above the machines. Ginny grabbed his hand, his fingers slipping away except his pinky. She held onto that and twisted as hard as she could, feeling it pop. He cried out just as the lunch break bell rang, the girls all rising, chairs scraping, the women gathering quickly around, forcing him back, holding his broken finger.

She told Esther everything a few minutes later. Mary left them, after Ginny had introduced her, saying she'd wait for Ginny in the carriage.

"I knew it had to be a man," she said. "A blind woman I'm not. Don't worry, sweetie, your Mike'll be fine. He's gonna have scars? Sure, but those we all got. You listen to me, there's all kinds of scars. On the outside and inside, too. The scars inside, they're the ones run deepest. But take it from me"—Esther lowered her voice then as if sharing some long-held secret—"they don't gotta be there forever."

For some reason, Ginny hadn't expected to see Carl that evening. She'd parted with Esther, promising she'd come to see her on the weekend and took the elevator to the lobby. She realized as soon as Carl appeared at her side in the Triangle Shirtwaist Company Building lobby that she hadn't thought about him at all that day.

"Hey, Ginny! I was worried about you," he said with what appeared to be genuine concern. "Youse ran off so fast, like you seen a ghost or somethin'."

"I'm sorry, Carl," Ginny said. He was actually a sweet man, Ginny thought, feeling guilty for wronging him. "Someone very dear to me was in the hospital. I had to see him." She realized as soon as she'd said it that she hadn't told him that Mike was her boyfriend or lover. She wondered at herself, feeling guilty for the deceptive understatement. Still, she told herself she was shielding Carl with her little lie.

Carl just nodded. "Youse have to take care o' da ones important in yer life. Ya don't an' it'll eat ya up."

"Exactly," Ginny said, surprised at Carl's understanding.

"I hope da guy wasn't too dear to you," Carl said. "I mean I suppose you know I got feelings for ya."

Ginny looked at Carl with a mixture of dread and affection, not knowing exactly what to say. "I know," she said finally, looking quickly out the door for the Braddock carriage, then adding, "I'm flattered, Carl."

He smiled, but it was a wistful grin. "That's good. It's a start anyways," he said, taking hold of her hand. She let him hold it for a couple of seconds, torn for allowing even this small sign of affection.

"Ya know, Ginny," Carl said after a long silence, "I'd do any-thing fer you. Yer a peach, an' I'd be proud to have ya on me arm at any racket in town."

"That's nice of you, Carl," she replied, though going to one of the rackets was something that never appealed to her.

Ginny took her hand back. "You know it's really not right to be talking about things like that."

"Yeah, but a girl like you don' come along every day. A mug like me can't let that go, not if he's got any brains in his bucket." Carl had noticed her glance out the doors and had positioned himself in front of them, blocking her view.

Ginny laughed, but she couldn't hide the edge to it, becom-ing more uncomfortable by the second. "Carl, I have to go to the hospital this evening, so I guess I'll just say good-bye here," she said, thinking of the safety of the Braddock carriage.

"It's da cop, right? I seen it in da papers. I can put two and two togetha."

"Yes, Carl," Ginny said. "I really have to go."

"What's he to you, Ginny? Just how dear is dis guy?" The way he said *dear* made her skin crawl, for it was mocking and derisive.

"Carl, I don't know what to say," she started. "Yes, it is Mike Braddock, the one you saw in the paper. I'm very concerned about him."

"So, he's yer long-lost brotha?" he said mockingly.

"I'm sorry about that, Carl. I didn't want to—"

"To what? To tell me you been humpin' dis mug an' I ain't nothin' but a waste o' time," he said, his voice rising.

"No, Carl." Ginny didn't look at him directly. She didn't see the door opening behind Carl. "But Carl, the way you've been acting tonight—"

Carl grabbed her arm, pulling her closer, his face just above hers. "Youse like me," he said. "All my girls do. Dis mug, you go see 'im if you like it, but youse come back to me, see 'cause if you don't I'll come an' find ya." Carl's tone was light and earnest, as if he hadn't just threatened her. "'Cause I like you, Ginny, I really do."

"Carl, I—" Ginny was about to say she loved Mike, but she never got the chance.

"Is this man bothering you, Miss Ginny?" she heard a voice say behind Carl. It was the Braddocks' driver, Riordan, an ex-cop with hard eyes, but a gentle hand when he helped the ladies. He pulled his jacket away from his side for just an instant, exposing the pistol he carried in a shoulder holster. Ginny didn't see it, but Carl saw it well enough.

"No, Peter," Ginny answered. "He was just saying good-bye."

41

TOM HAD MIXED feelings about what he was about to do. He knew it might be smarter to take a more prudent course, but just then he didn't give a shit for prudence. He got off the police wagon in front of the New Brighton, and six officers with shotguns got down after him, fanning out and covering the entrances and exits. Two followed him when he entered the dance hall. He hoped to find McManus there, but suspected he wouldn't. Jack was stupid, but not so foolish as to keep to his usual haunts now.

Though there was little actual proof that he'd had anything to do with Mike's shooting, Tom wasn't waiting for proof. Saturn's vague recollection and the coincidence of the two assaults were enough for him. If he had any luck, he'd sort it out with McManus cuffed to a chair in the precinct basement. Otherwise, he'd at least send a message that would be heard loud and clear across the Lower East Side. Within a day all of gangland would know that Captain Braddock was on the warpath. McManus would have a price on his head, officially or not, and be as likely to fall victim to one of his own as to Braddock himself. Tom felt it was a no-lose situation, though venturing into a place like the New Brighton the way he did had more than its share of risks.

He stood at the door for a moment, the two officers at his

back, shotguns held conspicuously. The toughs and bouncers gave way and Tom walked through the raucous crowd of gangsters and their molls. The band continued playing, the piano tinkling gaily, the dancers prancing about with abandon, the smoke from a hundred cigarettes swirling like cream in coffee. Tom went to the back, where Paul always sat, a couple of fireplugs with bowlers glowering on either side.

"A dramatic entrance, Tommy," Kelly said. "Surely old friends can dispense with such histrionics."

Tom pulled out a chair and sat across from Paul. They didn't meet more than once or twice a year and then only on sensitive business, usually as much political as it was financial. They never met openly like this either, a definite departure from protocol.

"Good to see you, Paul," Tom said. He motioned to the bodyguards, who disappeared with a confirming nod from Kelly. "I want McManus."

"Just like that?" Kelly would have been shocked if he'd said anything else. Still he was amazed at how Braddock had put the pieces together and come up with Jack, wondering how he could have done so that quickly without some inside help.

"Just like that, Paul. I'm asking you to give him up," Tom said, not patient enough to tiptoe around the subject.

"With shotguns? Here? You insult me in my own place, Tommy. This could have been handled another way."

"Bullshit," Tom said in a low growl. "You know my son's been shot. McManus had something to do with it. You don't know how fucking insulting I can be. I haven't even started."

"My sympathies, Tommy," Paul said, meaning it. Having no personal or business reason to see Mike hurt, he could afford sympathy.

"Thanks. Looks like he'll be okay," Tom said. "I have no reason to believe you had anything to do with it, so I'm asking nice. McManus has to come in. He doesn't, then the next time I ask, it won't be so nice."

"All stick and no carrot, Tommy? Not really your style."

"Yeah, well I lost all my style when Mike got shot."

"I understand. But you may get farther with a reward. The men he associates with are all too often motivated by money, Tommy, or the lack of it. I honestly don't know where the fuck McManus is. He hasn't shown in two days. A wad of green might pry up the rock he's under."

"A grand," Tom answered. "And another if I find out he was the shooter."

Kelly looked at his fingernails. "I'll spread the word, Tommy. No guarantees though."

"Didn't expect any. Sorry to disturb the festivities," he said and strode back out through the parting sea. The heavies with the shotguns followed him out, one backing through the door, the other checking the street before they walked to the wagon. They climbed aboard and rolled away slowly, shotguns sticking out at the sides like cannons on a battleship. Jeers followed at a safe distance and a bottle broke on the cobbles behind, but they left without firing a shot.

Kelly sat sipping scotch and thinking for some time after Tom left. He was not about to give up McManus, not alive at least. Jack had to render a service first and it would be useful to let him think that that would be his redemption for the mess he'd made. He would have to alert Jack to Tom's suspicions though and warn him to keep well out of sight. Having him dragged in now would not do at all. He decided to keep McManus happy and well financed until he took care of his plan for the *Slocum*. He could not stand to have Big Tim steal the ship out from under his nose. The *Slocum* would have to be made worthless to him. Once Jack accomplished that, Braddock could have him, or what would be left of him.

42

MIKE COULDN'T STAY in bed. After just two days his back ached and he was restless and bored. His face hurt like hell, but he could still walk. The nurses tried to put him back in bed, but he wasn't having any of it. The doctor clucked at him from the foot of the bed, "Don't be stupid. If you feel dizzy, sit down. We've got better things to do than pick you off the floor." Mike nodded and that was that.

He was dizzy, of course, and his head still rang, although not as bad as in the beginning. As he walked to his window, Mike started to wonder if it would ever stop or if it would just keep going, a continuous, high-pitched tone that could never be escaped. He stood, holding onto the windowsill until the dizziness and nausea subsided. They told him he'd had a bad shock to the brain and was likely to experience these things, but he was far too concerned with getting on his feet to let that worry him. Ginny would be back this evening. He wanted to surprise her. Looking out on the city in the sooty afternoon light, chimneys belching, streetcars clanging, factories humming, telephones ringing; he knew that somewhere in all that noise and stink and frantic activity a heart beat for him.

Mike turned too quickly and had to steady himself, grabbing onto the bed until the room stopped moving. With a deep breath he tried walking a straight line to the door, which he managed with only minor deviations. Hitching up his baggy hospital pajamas, he opened it and stepped into the hallway. He could smell fresh plaster and paint and the faint, sweet-sour smell of cut wood overpowering the usual hospital smells. Down the hall, workmen were expunging the last traces of the bomber's work, though for a moment, Mike thought he saw a shoe with a piece of leg they'd somehow overlooked. He held onto the doorjamb until the vision disappeared.

Primo didn't recognize Mike at first. He was propped up in bed, a nearly empty food tray in front of him. His eyes were closed when Mike came in. They fluttered open and Mike was relieved to see that they were clear, though pain and weariness circled them. "You got wrong room, buddy," he said in a surprisingly strong voice. "But you wanna get blown up, come on in."

Mike chuckled without moving his face. It hurt too much to smile. "Doctor told me you were here," Mike said through a burst of pain. His swollen tongue and aching face making it come out like, "Ocho 'ol me oo wa ere."

Primo looked at him with a concerned frown, but said, "You look like stupid Irish bastard I work with except you are more handsome than that asshole."

"Ach," Mike cried. "Urts oo laf."

"But it is good to laugh, no? I have no laughing for days. The doctors, they are not so funny guys," Primo said. "I see you have not been laughing, too. What the hell happened?" He took Mike's outstretched hand and held it as he looked into his eyes.

Mike tried to fill him in on what had happened, but had to stop after a few garbled sentences, the pain too great to continue. He spat a bright gout of blood into Primo's bedpan and sat on the edge of the bed, taking out the pad and pencil he'd remembered to bring.

"Great. Now the nurse will think I piss the blood. They will start looking up my ass or something."

"Good," Mike wrote. "Maybe they'll find your head."

They laughed then, each wincing with pain.

"You have not done so good without me" Primo said when he'd caught his breath. Mike scribbled, "Should see the other guys," but neither of them laughed at that.

Mike told Primo about his visits from Ginny, written simply, with a thousand words in between.

"That is good," Primo said, smiling. "I am happy for you, my friend."

Mike saw the sadness in Primo's face and knew that he missed his wife and kids more than he would ever say, even to him. "You gonna send for family?" he wrote.

Primo shook his head. "I will wait," was all he said.

Mike figured it was for two reasons. Primo couldn't be certain he had eliminated the threat from the Black Hand, so in his mind it was still unsafe to bring his family home. Mike was also sure that as much as Primo would like to see his wife, he didn't want her to see him in this condition. He put a hand on Primo's shoulder and said nothing.

After a long silence, Mike wrote, "How's the wounds?"

"Better, a little," Primo answered. "The one on my head hurts like a devil. Shotgun took my hair off. They sew the skin back together. It is tight like a drum."

"When you get out?" Mike asked before spitting more blood into Primo's pan.

"Who knows, week or two, I guess."

Mike could see Primo was tiring and he could feel his own head becoming light. He pushed himself carefully off Primo's bed and said, "Ee oo 'ater, okay?"

Primo raised a hand in good-bye. His eyes were closed when Mike looked back from the door.

Mike eased himself back into bed a few minutes later. A bowl of tepid broth waited for him but he managed only a few spoonfuls before his eyes closed. He didn't wake until he heard Mary's voice above him. Tom was with her, Ginny too, talking in hushed tones. Mike opened his eyes and said, "H'low," which was far more painful than it should have been. His mouth and tongue were so sore from his few words with Primo that now he found he could hardly speak. After a hug from Ginny, Tom did most of the talking and Mike stuck to the pad and pencil.

Tom told him about his meeting with Saturn at the morgue and his recollection of the name Jack. "I know there were two guys you killed, but could there have been a third? A real coincidence you shooting one of the same guys who had attacked Saturn."

Mike had been trying to remember every detail of the shooting. He recalled the Colt going off in his hand and the dark forms firing back, but that was all. He felt sure he'd hit them, but never saw a third man. He knew there could have been a third but he was not sure. He just shook his head. "No 'memba," he said, pointing to his head and swirling his finger.

"That's okay, Mike," Ginny said. "How are you feeling? The nurses said you were up and walking this afternoon," she added brightly.

Mike noticed that there was no longer any sunlight coming through his windows and realized he must have slept for hours. "Ugh," he said.

"Hurts?" Mary asked with a frown. "I'll fetch a nurse to get you something." Mike tried to stop her, but she wouldn't be deterred.

"You know your mom," Tom said when she'd gone. "She'd move this whole damn hospital for you if she had to. Listen, I paid a visit to Paul Kelly today. Told him to give me McManus. He's most likely the Jack that Saturn described, which makes him suspect number one in your shooting." He stopped for a moment and ran a hand through his hair. "Damn! And I forgot the most important part, the Bottler's dead! They say it was Cyclone Louie, came in and shot him in front of everybody, but so far we can't find a soul who'll talk about it."

"Shit!" Mike wrote. "No war?"

"Not yet, but you know how Kelly is; waiting for the right time."

They went over what Mike had found out about the Bottler's activities, Mike writing furiously. Despite the Bottler's death, it was still clear that McManus and maybe Kelly were involved to some degree. What wasn't clear is how much they may have known about the Bottler's activities. The one connection was Saturn and the steamship company. "McManus and his goons wouldn't waste a beating on Saturn if there wasn't a damn good reason. It wasn't just a robbery. It was a message, a warning from Kelly or the Bottler or both."

"You think Saturn had something to do with the smuggling?" Mike wrote.

"Who knows," Tom said. "It's clear that the Bottler was smuggling coca by boat from somewhere. Saturn is vice-president of a steamship line, and he's been a target of intimidation. Seems like something's up to me. Anyway, I figured I'd rattle Kelly's chain a little and put the word out on McManus. Kelly didn't like me doing it like that. Pissed him off, but it'll make him think too."

"Shake the tree and see what falls out," he wrote.

Tom nodded. "Listen, we'll find out who did this to you and we'll go put some fucking holes in him, right?" He stuck his hand out and they shook as if it were a business deal.

Mike got something for his pain and some broth for dinner, which Ginny insisted on spooning into him. He tried to tell her he still had two good hands, but it wasn't worth the effort, and he liked the attention anyway.

"You're getting thinner already," she said. "And you need to get every bit of this into you. I talked to the nurse and tomorrow they're going to try giving you some mashed vegetables." Although the prospect of baby food wasn't too appealing, Mike's stomach had spent most of the last couple days growling at him.

He was sure that anything more substantial than broth would be welcome. "Inny," he said between spoonfuls.

"What?"

Mike wiped a dribble of soup from his bandaged chin. "Thank you." Mike put his legs over the side of the bed and stood. Ginny moved back, surprised. He wasn't as dizzy as he'd been in the afternoon. Mary had a hand out, ready to catch him, but Tom said from the foot of the bed "He's okay. You still got two good legs, right, Mikey?"

Mike put a thumb up and walked to Ginny, who stood amazed, the soup bowl forgotten in her hands. He took it from her and placed it on the nightstand, turned back, and without a word encircled her in his arms and pulled her close. Ginny held him and her tears started to soak the bandages on his face. Tom and Mary smiled and started for the door. "The best medicine he's ever had," Mike heard Tom say in the hallway.

Mike caught a glimpse of himself in a mirror over the washstand. He frowned at his reflection. "Omb?" He pantomimed combing his hair and Ginny produced one. His hair hadn't been washed in days and still had some dried blood in it. Frustrated with raking his head with little result, he took the pitcher from the washstand, bent over the bowl, and poured some water over his head. Ginny dried Mike off and slicked his hair back, parting it carefully. A minute later they emerged from his room, walking slowly down the hall. Mike had his pad with him. On it he'd written, "Someone I want you to meet."

"So, this is the famous Ginny," Primo said, putting out his good hand. "Now I can see why you search for her." Ginny blushed and Mike did too under his bandages.

After a few minutes spent getting acquainted, Ginny busied herself in rearranging the masses of flowers in Primo's room, pulling the wilted ones and checking water. Mike and Primo began to speak of the possible third man and if it was Jack McManus or one of the many other Jacks they could think of. They talked about getting out of the hospital. Ginny told Mike that his room at his parents' house was all ready. But he shook his head. "My home." He held out a hand. "With you."

Ginny's breath was taken away. She had never imagined that possibility, not so soon. But there it was, the culmination of everything she'd wished for, sitting on the side of a hospital bed. She dropped the wilted flowers and came to him. They clung to each other for a long time. Primo swiped at his eyes and nodded his approval.

Dinner came and Mike and Ginny went back to his room with a promise to return. When Tom and Mary returned they found Mike and Primo arm in arm, walking in the hall with Ginny a step behind. "Well, look at you two," Mary said, hugging them both. "This is a sight for sore eyes."

"We have lots of sore between us," Primo said, "but my eyes are fine."

43

LATER THAT EVENING, Tom was banging on a door in a fleabag hotel just off the Bowery, where the rumble of the El was enough to stir a cup of coffee and the two-legged tenants were badly outnumbered by the four-and six-legged varieties. His driver, Pete Riordan, had told him about the man he'd seen with Ginny at the Triangle factory, a man he recognized from his days on the force, a pimp he'd arrested years before and whose name finally came to him.

"Go away," a man's voice called from somewhere inside.

"Police, Carl. Open up! I need to ask you a couple questions!" Tom shouted through the door.

"Fer da love o' Christ, I answered all da goddamn questions—" Carl opened the door at midsentence and never got to finish. The heel of Tom's hand shot through the gap and broke his nose. He stumbled back and fell at the foot of the bed, where one of his whores lay. She sat up when Tom came in. She was naked, but made no attempt to cover up and she didn't shout like Carl, who was holding his nose as if it might fall off.

"Hands where I can see 'em if you don't mind, ma'am."

The whore gave a little smile and put her hands on her breasts, massaging the nipples. "This okay?"

Tom grinned. "Just fine. Keep 'em there." Carl tried to get up, but Tom stomped on one leg and he stayed put.

"You broke my fucking nose!"

"Could be worse, Carl," Tom said. "Hell, I ain't even mad at you yet." He glanced at the whore, who hadn't stopped kneading her breasts and seemed to be enjoying the show. "You listening?" he asked Carl, who'd started moaning. "Virginia Caldwell, was she working for you?"

"No! Okay? She wasn't workin' fer me. Would've if I had more time ta work on 'er. But I ain't no grabber, see, no white slaver or nothin'. My girls love me. I don' need ta work 'em over or nothin."

"Okay. I get the picture. Where'd you meet Miss Caldwell?"

"Triangle factory," Carl said. "Place is full o' girls workin' like dogs. Lots o' mugs work da place, steerers, grabbers, you name it. Me, I like da easy way. Everybody happy, makin' money."

"Yeah, you're a real prince, Carl," Tom said, making the woman giggle. "You okay, ma'am?" he said to her in such a way as to make it clear that she could leave with him and escape Carl if she chose.

Her eyes clouded for an instant before she picked up her chin and said, "Carl's good to me."

Ginny visited Esther that evening after leaving Mike. She'd promised to visit as soon as she left Mike. Esther had talked about her children so often that Ginny almost felt she knew them. They were every bit as endearing as Esther's words had made them out to be. Esther's children, Emily and Josh, came running into the room and hugged her. They'd been playing and doing homework in their bedroom. Emily was a bright and cheerful child of eleven. Josh, who was just finishing kindergarten, seemed to spend most of his time knocking things over and running into walls.

"How you feelin,' Ginny," Esther said. "You look like a million bucks! Toin aroun' fer me," she commanded, admiring her new dress. Esther clucked her admiration, but noticed something off in Ginny. Maybe it was her smile or perhaps the way she'd held her hand to her waist as she turned. "But you're down a bit honey, right? Somethin' not right?"

Ginny shrugged off Esther's question and launched into how Mike was making amazing progress, how he'd started walking stairs, and by that night had actually run up a flight just to show her he could. But Esther could see there was worry in Ginny's voice.

"Ain't that something?" she said. "Ain't it wonderful what that modern medicine can do? But you gotta not worry so," Esther said with a look of concern. Esther bustled about the kitchen, lighting the stove and putting a kettle of water on top. Ginny let her buzz without moving. An inexplicable worry had crept into her consciousness earlier in the day and would not let her go. Like a leech, it sucked at her happiness, feeding her doubts. Ginny was so consumed by it that she could hardly put her fears into words, but Esther had no such trouble.

"This thing, it's about the best thing ever ain't it, sweetie? I mean dreamin' about this is all you've been doin' an' now when you got it, it's like maybe it's too real to last, huh?" Ginny shrugged. That was close to how she felt, but not quite it. "Afraid of losin' him? Afraid when he's better he won't need ya?"

"Maybe," Ginny allowed. Everything had been so good, so perfect these last days; Mike recovering so quickly, Mary treating her like a daughter. It couldn't last she reasoned. Nothing that good could.

"Maybe," Esther said with a cluck of her tongue. "Da woild is full o' maybes, sweetie. Every day ya got a ton of 'em, an' ya neva know which way they'll go. Your Mike, I got a feelin' he's no maybe."

44

MIKE WAS MOVED out of his private room and into a ward where beds lined the walls and men with every kind of malady except the contagious sorts were laid out in white like so many headstones in a cemetery. The place stank of unwashed chamber pots. Medicines, elixirs, tonics, and poultices competed with the aroma of general human decay. It was supposed to be a ward for those on the mend, but it doubled as a place for the dying, and it did nothing to heal Mike. Ginny's visits seemed to strengthen him more than any amount of food, rest, or medical prodding.

Tom stopped by that morning. He didn't tell Mike what he'd found out about Ginny and Carl Woertz. He doubted he'd ever have to. It was enough that he knew and could help Ginny if the subject of Carl ever came up. She was almost part of the family now, although it amazed Tom that he'd begun to think of her that way. But he could see how Mike was when she was there, how she cared for him, and how Mary felt about her. It was enough.

"You know, when I was at the morgue with Saturn, I took one of the Bottler's shoes, and—" Tom started to tell Mike, putting his thoughts about Ginny to the back of his mind.

"His shoes?"

"Yeah, shoes. They were old ones that had been resoled. I thought I'd ask around and see if I could find out where they'd been done."

"Why bother?" Mike wrote. "He's dead as last year's herring, right?"

"Oh, sure, dead as dead can be, but I wanted to check because his face was all shot to hell; hard to identify him." Tom held up a hand, stopping Mike from interrupting. "I know, I know, there were witnesses. But it never hurts to be certain. Anyway, I went to a couple of shoemakers in the neighborhood, and I came across the one who did the repair. Now here's the interesting thing. He said it was for a guy named Mahoney; Dabney Mahoney."

"Huh? That's not the Bottler's real name, right?"

"Nope."

"Mahoney was an errand boy for the Bottler maybe?"

"Possible, sure."

"But the other possibility is . . ."

"I know, I know . . . highly unlikely. Just odd is all," Tom said.

Mike improved remarkably over the next couple of days. His wounds were healing well and he was told he should try to speak a little at least three times a day. He had been doing that and more with Ginny. In fact they spoke constantly, though often not in words.

One day, when they'd gone outside to sit on a bench at the back of the hospital overlooking the river, Mike remembered about the *Slocum* tickets. "You know, I have these passes for a day cruise."

"A steamship? Where does it go?"

"Not sure really," he answered. "Who cares? It'd just be wonderful to spend a day with you. Would you like that?"

"That's funny because Esther, my friend from the factory, she told me yesterday that she was going on a cruise. Some ship called the *Slocum*. It was arranged by her church, an outing to Long Island."

"When?" Mike asked. "My passes, are for any time I want this season, so we could go if you'd like?"

"Of course, I'd like that, silly. I think it's for the fifteenth, just a few days from now. But will you be well enough by then?"

"I think I'll manage," Mike said. He was really starting to chafe at being cooped up in the hospital anyway.

"Would you buy me an ice cream? I'll do anything for an ice cream you know," she said this with more than a suggestion of her old self and worried immediately that she'd seemed too wanton, so she added with a whisper, "but only for you, Mike."

Mike said nothing for a handful of heartbeats, then turned to her and said, "You are who you are, Gin. I loved you then and I love you now. There's no burying of the old you, not between us." He laughed and added, "I can't have you getting too proper now, can I?"

Ginny squeezed his hand and breathed in the salty river breeze. She looked back at the hospital. "You don't suppose there's an empty room in there somewhere?"

Mike smiled wickedly under his bandages. "I do suppose you're right. Shall we find one?"

Primo arrived on the ward the following day. "So, this is what we get for feeling better, eh? They throw us in this shithole," Primo said as a nurse wheeled him in. He was well enough to walk, but they didn't want him to tax himself. Mike chuckled. "Welcome to your new shithole, partner."

"Makes me want to get stabbed again," Primo said, looking around the room with a sour face.

"Makes me want to get the fuck outa here," Mike shot back,

finding he could now pronounce the letters with hard sounds like *t* and *k* more easily, though there was still pain in doing it. "At least you look better," Mike said, for the first time noticing that Primo, once he'd been deposited by the nurse, was walking without holding on to things.

"Better than a couple days ago, not so good as I wanna be."

"Yeah," Mike agreed. "Not that good." His tongue hurt, even though he was taking his time and pronouncing slowly like the doctor told him.

"You look better, too," Primo told him. "Your Ginny, eh? She is your medicine."

Another day crept by, the sun crawling across the floor of the ward with mind-numbing slowness, the moon stealing between the beds at night like a ghostly nurse. The next morning, Mike was doing push-ups beside his bed and running the stairs. Primo too was healing well, but more slowly. The wound in his back had gone deep and still felt like it might tear if he tried to do too much. Still, he was able to walk the corridors and climb the stairs with relative ease.

"You'll go home tomorrow," Primo said. "I heard a nurse talking. She said it sad, like she did not want to see you go."

"Sure," Mike said, knowing Primo's bullshit when he heard it. "You going to see your wife when you get out?"

"I have been thinking a lot about that and I think maybe I will take the chance," Primo said softly. "The Black Hand, they work in the small groups. The ones I killed, the ones you killed, that is most of them. There are others yes, but they are not together. They will not be so bold now. They go crawl back under the rock," he said with a snaky motion of the hand.

Mike nodded. "That's good because you need a woman bad." He grinned. "God, your wife is in trouble! You'll have her belly out to here in no time."

"That would not be so bad a thing, I think, and if the Virgin Mother is good to us, it will be Micaele if it is a boy and Margherita if it is a girl child."

"Michael, huh?"

"Sì, Micaele, after the best man I know."

Mike didn't know what to say. His tongue seemed to have swollen again so that it filled his mouth completely. "That might be the greatest honor I ever had," Mike said. "I mean it."

"What?" Primo said, raising his eyebrows.

"I mean, that's really wonderful, you know, having a child named after me, it's . . ."

"It is my father I'm talk about, you asshole," Primo said. "You think I name my child after Irish shitheads?"

"Okay, okay, You don't have to be nasty about it. After I saved your wop ass I just thought . . ."

"What? What you think?" Primo said, but he could not hide the sparkle in his eye.

Mike caught it and stopped to think. "Hey! Your father's name is Paolo. You told me that yourself."

Primo started to chuckle, then burst out laughing. "Maybe you are not such a shithead after all. Micaele is a good name I think, no?"

The first thing Mike did when he left the hospital the next afternoon was go to the firearms district on Chambers, west of Broadway, where giant, wooden pistols and rifles hung over shop windows and gunsmiths catered to wealthy sporting clients, for whom $500 was a trifling price for a good bird gun. Tom had given Mike one of his old pistols, a .32 Smith & Wesson with a two-inch barrel, a "belly gun," suitable for distances of an arm's length and not much more. It made a bulge in Mike's pocket as he shopped for a new Colt. He eventually found an automatic in a shop that also had an entirely new kind of pistol, imported from Germany, a Luger. It was a thoroughly modern weapon and very tempting to Mike even though the price was greater than for the Colt. But he put it down after he'd tried its feel, remembering how well the Colt had served him.

"You're that detective," the store clerk said, looking at the now small bandages on either side of Mike's face. "You killed those two men." Mike didn't know what to say, so he said nothing at all. "I understand Roosevelt himself sent you a bully telegram."

"Yeah," Mike said. "He shares my views on getting shot at." Mike had the telegram in his back pocket, having almost left it at the hospital in his haste to get gone. Though it had been just more than two weeks, it had seemed like forever.

"I'll give you ten percent off on that Colt," the clerk said, "if you don't mind me using your name in my next ad. The automatics are catching on. They're the next big thing in pistols and as far as I know, you're the first to use one on anything but a target. Come to think of it, you're the same detective from that shoot-out in the harbor back a month or two, right?"

Mike bought a new leather shoulder holster too and put the Colt in it before he left, its bulk feeling odd under his arm.

"Thanks for shopping with us," the clerk chirped as he left.

"Oh, yeah. I shoot any more bad guys and I'll expect twenty percent off."

Though he wasn't expected at headquarters, he went anyway, sitting at his desk and feeling like a phantom once the tide of backslapping and handshaking had ebbed. He started to pick through the mess that blotted out the top, reports, file folders, envelopes. They seemed to have lost their meaning in the last two weeks and he read the words on them as if they were in some foreign language.

Mike was flipping through the pile when his captain's voice boomed from the office. "Braddock, do I have to tell you again to get the hell out of here? Take this and go home," he said, pushing a new badge across the desk.

Having his old shield stripped from him had been almost as painful to Mike as being shot. In his world it was an even greater disgrace than losing his gun. The fact that he'd managed to do both in one night didn't go against him though. A lot could be forgiven a "hero," especially one with notches on his belt and bullet holes in his face.

"Now go home! You're on leave until next week for chris-sake. Take a trip, read a fucking book or something, just don't let me see you till next week. Got it?" Mike assured him he did and thanked him for the badge, pinning it to his jacket lining before he left.

Mike took a deep breath when he got outside police head-quarters. He floated for a minute of two, imagining the coming week with Ginny. He'd remembered the tickets he'd gotten stuffed under his door. The next few days were his to live how-ever he liked and he liked the idea of a day cruise a lot, imagin-ing the sun lighting Ginny's face, ice creams, cold beer, and an evening full of stars. But thinking about the *Slocum* put him in mind of the Bottler. What if Tom's guess was right and the Bot-tler wasn't dead? What if Eat-'em-up Jack was still out to kill him? Jack had every reason to want to finish the job he'd started. But it was likely that the Bottler was exactly as dead as everyone said he was, and that McManus was hiding under a rock some-where. Weighed against the certainty of a week with Ginny, these seemed like trivial concerns.

Still, Mike thought it best to have a plan. He started off to see his sister. She'd visited twice while he was in the hospital, but she was in a play now with a major role and two shows a day. It ate up every free minute, but she'd have to spare a few minutes for him. Rebecca had something he needed, and he wouldn't board the ship without it.

45

"CHARLIE, WHAT'RE YOU doing here?" Mike said when he recognized Charles Kelk of the harbor squad, standing near the gangway to the *Slocum*.

Kelk squinted at him hard. "And who would you be?" he asked with suspicion, "And how would you be knowing me?"

"Oh. Sorry," Mike said, taking off the fake glasses and slightly pulling aside the beard Rebecca had given him from the theater's prop room. "It's Mike. Mike Braddock. And this is Ginny Caldwell," he said turning to Ginny, with a smile. She'd thought it silly of him to wear a disguise, and gave him a dubious, amused look, although once he'd explained his reasons, it had seemed prudent enough.

"Mike! What the hell?" Kelk said, then lowered his voice even though they were still far from the ship. "Why the disguise? Oh, and pleased to make your acquaintance, I'm sure, ma'am," he added, giving Ginny his hand.

"Just a precaution, Charlie. The mug who shot me is still out there, and he might have reason to be on this boat."

Kelk gave a frown in the direction of the gleaming vessel. "Who the fuck is it? I'll give Van Tassel the word to keep an eye out. He's working this cruise with me."

"How's that?"

"Pastor Haas asked the captain if he could hire a couple of men to keep an eye on things," Kelk told him. "He's the pastor at St. Mark's Lutheran, over on Sixth. They do this big outing every year. The parish, which is most of the neighborhood, goes on these things."

"Sounds like easy duty," Mike said. "Plenty of sauerkraut and knockwurst, maybe a little beer?"

"Maybe more than a little."

"Yeah, well, I hope that's all we'll have to worry about. You know a mug named McManus, Jack McManus? He's the guy."

"I know about him, but I don't know his face," Kelk said. "Maybe Al might know." Mike gave him McManus's description and he promised to keep an eye out.

"How you doing?" Charlie asked. "Feelin' better?" Mike gave him an abridged version, which amounted to, "Not bad if you don't count the holes in my face." They laughed and commiserated for a few minutes. It had been almost six weeks since the harbor shoot-out and they had some catching up to do. "That Reverend Haas?" Mike asked, pointing to a bearded and bespectacled gentleman of middle years whose mission it seemed to shake the hand of every passenger as they boarded.

"Yeah, that's him. C'mon, I'll introduce you. You have a ticket, right?"

"Sure, compliments of the steamship company. Worked out nice with me just getting out of the hospital. Ginny said it'd be good for my recovery, and my doctor agreed."

Mike readjusted his beard and glasses and set his straw boater low over his eyes before Kelk introduced him to Reverend Haas, who welcomed him and thanked him for supporting the church with the purchase of a ticket. He urged Mike to enjoy the day to the fullest, as there was to be a fine band and plenty of food, beer, and games once they got to the beach at Locust Grove.

Mike and Ginny joined the crowd filing into the *General Slocum*, making their way up to the promenade deck, dodging

282

children, who, once on board, were cast loose from their mothers' grip to run with their friends while the adults claimed the best seats. He and Ginny leaned against the rail, watching the ship load, Mike scanning the crowd. Ginny sensed his tension, but felt it best to let him be cautious. He had every right to be. She didn't really appreciate how much more he worried with her at his side. The idea of something happening to her because of him pebbled his skin with fear and turned his knees to water.

There was a dizzying number of families, groups of adults surrounded by swirling, eddying tides of children. Some were clearly extended families—cousins, aunts, grandparents, and the like. But there were relatively few men. It was a hard thing to get a day off from work and few seemed to have managed it, a fact that had Mike feeling suddenly self-conscious. He could feel the eyes of the adults around him on the promenade deck, wondering at the man with the beard and the beautiful girl on his arm.

"C'mon, Mommy, we'll miss the boat!" Josh cried, pulling at Esther's arm and leaning to his task like he was pulling a lifeline. "C'mon!" Ginny heard him and looked down to find them climbing the gangway. She waved, but Esther didn't see her. Josh did though, and he tugged Esther's arm again and pointed. "I'll be right up, sweetie!" Esther shouted, trying to keep up with Josh. They disappeared into the side of the ship a deck below.

"Gin, can you wait here a few minutes?" Mike asked when they'd settled on a piece of a bench at the rail. "I want to take a quick look over the boat. Just a precaution," he added lightly. He pulled his eyes from her as if she were the sun and he a planet in her orbit. They'd have all day after all.

Mike walked the decks one by one from the bow to the stern,

doing a full turn of each before climbing the stairs to the next. He checked the saloon in the interior, he looked into the engine room, he walked the hurricane deck, the kitchen, the dining room, and the promenade deck. He saw children, hundreds of them, mothers looking harried but sunny, grandparents, aunts and uncles, a German band tuning up in the stern, and a wiry stoker with a coal-blackened shirt. But he didn't see the Bottler or Jack McManus.

He'd made his way back to the bow on the promenade deck, coming back down from the topmost hurricane deck when he saw Ginny again, standing against the rail, a woman at her side and two children close by. He picked his way through the crowd, dodging a boy running after a ball and tipping his hat to a distinguished-looking lady with a parasol.

"Ginny," Mike said behind her. "Ginny?" The way he said it was like nothing she'd ever heard. There was longing in his voice, a desperate tightening of the throat as he stepped off into the space of her name. His relief at finding no one lurking in dark corners flooded through him when he saw her and realized as if for the first time that he'd have her all to himself for the entire day. It seemed almost too perfect to bear.

"Hello, Mike," she whispered, "Everything okay?"

Esther watched spellbound, her children tugging to go for ice cream.

"Yeah. Looks that way," he said, staring at her in the morning light.

"What?" she asked, looking at him with a curious frown.

"Nothing," Mike answered. "I'm just so damn lucky, that's all."

"I guess," she said with a little smile. "Oh, I'm sorry, this is Esther and her children, Emily and Josh. I told you they were coming."

Mike took Esther's hand. "And I'm glad you did," he said.

———

The *Slocum's* steam whistle blew twice, signaling for the last of the stragglers while Reverend Haas waited, suddenly alone at the top of the gangway.

"Esther, Ginny tells me you work at the factory. How is it? I heard it was the most modern of its type when it was built."

Esther looked at the children and whispered "It's a little piece o' hell if you gotta know. But there's worse lemme tell ya. I do okay," she said with a shrug. "Helps put bread on the table."

"Oh, maybe I should take this beard off," Mike said. "I don't think I'll need it now." He got it off quickly, to the stares of some, and stuffed it and the glasses into a pocket. Ginny reached out to touch his face. It was better, but the scars hadn't healed entirely. A small, angry, red pucker was on one side, a larger one on the other. "Do they hurt?"

"Not now," he answered. "Everything's perfect."

He kissed her then under the brim of her snow-white hat, and she was helpless not to kiss him back. She pulled away for a moment, digging in her bag. "I have something to show you," she said. It was the note he'd scrawled the first night at the hospital, folded into a lacquered snuffbox. "I kept it."

Mike buried his face in her neck and pulled her close. "I know all your secrets," he said into the hollow of her neck, the words vibrating into her like ripples on a pond.

"It's not fair," she whispered back. "Now you have to tell me yours."

Esther's kids were tugging and whining for ice cream and she finally had to give in. "I'll meet ya later back by the band," Esther said over her shoulder as Emily and Josh pulled her away. "Have fun you two."

46

S EE HIM YET?" the Bottler asked McManus. They had
placed themselves in a lower compartment with a porthole
overlooking the dock. "You asked Carl if they left together?"
Woertz had followed Ginny and Mary home from the hospital
days before, had been watching the Braddock place once Mike
had been released. He'd called that morning with the news that
Ginny and Mike were on their way.

"'Course I did. 'E just got out of the fucking hospital, so it
makes sense he'd come. Carl said Braddock's got a beard an'
glasses."

"Maybe he grew it in the hospital to hide the scars. Could be
the shot to the head scrambled his eyesight, too."

Jack shrugged. "I hope. Anyhow, wha' da fuck, if he don't
show, there's always anudder way. We can get 'im any time now
he's out an' about. I done it before an' I can do it again."

The Bottler frowned. "Like the last time?"

The *General Slocum* pulled out to midchannel and shuddered as
the huge engine was brought up to three-quarter speed, the massive piston thumping in the bowels of the ship, the sidewheels
churning the green water into foam, where seagulls dove for fish

and flotsam. A cool breeze developed as the ship started to move upstream, smoke belching from its tall twin stacks. Esther and the children had disappeared into the crowd. The city began to slip by, the Williamsburg Bridge appearing ribbonlike as it curved over the river in their wake. The breeze ruffled Ginny's hair and pulled at the broad brim of her hat, which she tied down again for fear it might fly off. Children shrieked and ran, their feet stampeding across the three decks in playful thunder as bartenders started to pull beers. Cooks began preparing a huge kettle of chowder for the picnic and stokers shoveled coal into the boiler. The city, which for many had never been seen from this perspective, seemed oddly quiet, the horsecars, the police whistles, the hammering of never-ending construction, the rumble of freight wagons, the shriek of steam engines, the honking of automobile horns all silent in the distance. Tenements, mansions, warehouses, office buildings, monuments, and sky-scrapers shouldered one another for every square inch, were seemingly built one atop the other, and there was hardly a tree to be seen. A gray-brown pall of coal smoke hung over all, a choking blanket of progress taken in with every breath. In the middle of the river the air seemed cleaner, the breeze bracing. The lungs of the *Slocum*'s 1,300 passengers breathed a little easier. Fourteenth Street passed, then Twenty-third and Thirty-fourth and the cares of the city were slowly left behind while Professor George Maurer's German Band played songs that set toes tapping and young girls dancing.

They were watching the city pass by, leaning on the rail in a moment of silence, when Ginny looked to her left. A man was there by the rail, a man she recognized, but she could not say from where and couldn't put a name to the face. Still, it didn't seem to be a pleasant memory. Mike noticed the man just beyond Ginny's shoulder a moment later as Ginny turned her back to the stranger. It was the Bottler, and at the same instant Mike felt something hard in the small of his back.

"Got my tickets, huh?" a voice said in his ear. "Don' do nothin' stupid an' da twist don't get hurt. We's gonna take a walk, see."

Mike was about to move when he saw the muzzle of a pistol peeking from under a folded newspaper pointed at Ginny's back. He stopped and said, "I'll do what you want, Jack. But—"

"But nothin'. Da twist comes along, see. Too bad fer her, but good fer us, hey?"

The Bottler, who had his pistol on Ginny's back, nudged her in the right direction with a warning. "Nothin' funny now, miss. We don' want to hurt you. You're going to be just fine," he said it low, but loud enough for Mike to hear, and that at least was some slight comfort.

They descended two levels to the lamp room, unnoticed amid the crush of revelers and their children. Mike's mind frantically searched for options. He'd have taken his chances if he'd been alone, would have gone for his gun, probably once they were on the stairs, where he'd have had a slight advantage. But with Ginny in the equation, he could think of nothing that wouldn't put her life in danger.

"So you're playing both sides, huh, Jack," he said. "How long you think it'll take Paul Kelly to figure this out?"

"What Paul don' know could fill a fuckin' book. Da Bottler's got a sweet operation goin'. Dis boat's gonna put us where not even Paul can touch us. Smugglin', gamblin', whorin,' and a little bare-knuckle now an' again, an' we all make money like we're printin' da stuff."

"Jack—" the Bottler started to say, but McManus shrugged off the caution.

"Don' worry. Dis mug ain't tellin' nobody nothin'. An' da twist'll be fucking fer Carl tomorra."

"Carl Woertz?" The name burst from Ginny's throat. Mike almost stopped in his tracks, but got a jab in the ribs with the muzzle of Jack's gun that kept him moving.

Once down below the main deck, there were no passengers to be seen and it was easy to disarm Mike without attracting any attention.

"Youse got a cannon? Hand it over," Jack said. "Slow! Wit' two fingas." Mike did as he was told, handing over the new Colt gingerly, grinding his teeth. "Youse got a new one," Jack said with delight. "You got a bad habit o' losin' yer popper, donchya?"

He chuckled as the Bottler opened a door and backed inside, keeping his gun on Ginny.

Mike followed with Jack behind. "So what poor slob got killed in your place, Bottler?" Mike asked as he went in. A kerosene lamp was the only light in the cluttered lamp room. Mike didn't see all of it and never got an answer to his question. Jack brought the butt of his pistol down hard on the back of his head and the light went out.

Mike regained consciousness as Jack was tying his feet together. There was blood in his eye and a wad of rag in his mouth tied with a gag. He was back-to-back with Ginny, hands tied tight. Ginny was calling him, as best she could, wiggling against him and poking him with her fingers. "Ugh," he managed as the room spun. His doctor had warned him about undue exertions and further traumas to the head, and he supposed this would qualify. Colors swam and McManus went in and out of focus.

"Got yer attention, you fuckin' piece o' shit? Now, youse're gonna stay in a nice little bundle fer a while," he said as he stood. "We'll be back in a bit, so you sit tight now."

Mike remembered his backup pistol, strapped to his ankle. There was at least some hope he'd be able to get to it and surprise Jack and the Bottler when they got back. His hopes rose until Jack turned around and Mike saw the butt of his .32 poking from Jack's jacket pocket. The door closed and the lock clicked into place.

It seemed as though hours passed as Mike and Ginny worked at their bonds with little result. Jack apparently had some experience with tying his victims and they made no progress until Mike spotted a nail protruding from a packing crate on the other side of the room. They had to get up, but it was no easy task to get their feet under them and push themselves erect back-to-back. It took at least five tries, punctuated by slips, falls, and bruises, but at last they were standing. They shuffled to the nail and began to rub the ropes that bound their hands, picking them apart one strand at a time. It was awkward and they had to hold their arms at a painful angle, but they made progress. Mike lost count of the times he stabbed himself or Ginny with that nail. Their wrists were bloody in minutes. With each footstep in the corridor, with every bump and noise, they expected to see McManus burst through the door and their only chance evaporate. Finally, one of the ropes was cut and they struggled almost frantically to be free of them, writhing together and working hard while the bonds fought their every effort, clinging to their wrists.

When at last their hands were free, and their gags off, they clung to each other, trembling with the effort. Sweating and shaking, Ginny gasped, "Oh, my God, Mike. They're going to kill us when they come back. What're we going to do?"

Mike saw a crowbar on a shelf that had probably been used to open the packing crates and he reached for it. They both heard a key in the lock, saw the knob turn as Mike got his hand on the cold steel. But their ankles were still tied and they were too far from the door. It opened and Jack stepped in. All Mike could do was lunge. It was more of a jump actually, and he propelled himself across the room with all the energy that was in him, swinging the crowbar as he did. Startled, Jack raised his injured hand. The crowbar crunched into it and a howl of pain was ripped from Jack's throat as Mike tumbled into his legs, knocking Jack off his feet and smashing him into the wall. He rolled and scrambled to his feet, Mike swinging wildly. But Jack's back was now turned to Ginny and she threw a can of linseed oil at him, a full gallon can that must have weighed at least ten pounds. It hit him in the back, knocking him off balance and bursting open, soaking his back. Mike had rolled to his knees and swung at Jack's leg, seeing it buckle under his blow. Eat-'em-up Jack McManus collapsed against the crate where the kerosene lamp sat. It crashed against the wall, spilling kerosene across the floor, soaking the straw packing that littered the floor.

The straw burst into flame, lighting the hem of Ginny's dress. She swatted at it as Mike flailed again at Jack, hitting something soft, getting a kick in return. He had time to aim his next blow and it smashed Jack's shin like dried cordwood. McManus rolled with a deep grunt of pain, almost a moan. He somehow got to his knees, reaching for his pistol, when the crowbar came down again with a sickening crunch, breaking his arm and setting Jack to shrieking. Another blow put an end to his noise. Mike hit him twice more in the ribs for good measure as Ginny tried to extinguish her dress.

Mike fell panting and exhausted across Jack's body, almost losing consciousness until Ginny cried out. The fire was spreading, fueled by the lamp oil and straw. Smoke billowed and started to cloud the room. Mike worked at the ropes on his feet, his fear growing as smoke bloomed at the ceiling. He could feel the heat on his cheek, his scar burning as if on fire itself. Mike got himself free, and worked on her ropes, freeing her a moment later. Mike retrieved his and Jack's pistols, and they staggered out the door and closed it behind them. Mike had thought for a moment about pulling Jack out into the hallway, but instead ran for a fire hose, Ginny behind him. It was a small fire at that point and he had no doubt it could be extinguished in short order. With Jack in custody and with Kelk and Van Tassel to back him up, he'd find the Bottler and put an end to everything.

A boy on the deck above saw a puff of smoke escaping the

stairs and alerted a deckhand. The deckhand descended to the level of the lamp room just moments after Mike and Ginny ran to find a fire hose. Seeing the smoke seeping from under the lamp room door, he opened it wide. The sudden burst of air fanned the small fire like a giant bellows and it exploded toward the door and the flood of oxygen. He didn't have time to see McManus. Horrified, he ran to alert the first mate, but didn't close the door.

The deckhand and the first mate rushed to the hose a moment after Mike and Ginny got there. A deckhand pulled the hose toward the fire, unwittingly kinking it in a dozen places. Mike watched as they turned the valve and the hose writhed and filled. But at every kink, the hose became bloated, the water pressure so strong it created an instant series of choke points, while the nozzle at the other end dribbled uselessly.

Mike and the others tried to straighten the hose, but the dried-out linen burst in a half dozen places, spraying water everywhere. A second later, the hose burst from the coupling to the valve. The fire had now started to burst out the lamp room door and flames could be seen flashing in the acrid smoke.

"Get to the boats!" the first mate shouted, all attempts at fire fighting abandoned. Mike stood, drenched by the burst hoses, the men around him running. Mike was no mariner, but he'd seen the condition of the lifeboats. Countless coats of paint had all but glued them in place. He stood with Ginny, trying to decide what to do when the screaming commenced.

Up on the hurricane deck, just below the pilothouse, far above the fire, a boy came running up the stairs from the decks below, and yelled up to the captain, "Hey, mister! The ship's on fire!" The stairway nearest the lamp room acted like a chimney, drawing the smoke and fire up from below, but there was not yet any sign of smoke on the upper decks.

Unfortunately, this wasn't the first time the captain had heard words like those. Excursion cruises were often full of mischievous boys willing to try anything on a dare. Not once had such a warning proven real and he was sure that this time was no exception. "Get the hell out of here and mind your own business," he growled.

Jack regained consciousness with a searing pain in his legs. His pants were on fire and he rolled and swatted at them amid the burning straw, grunting and cursing in panic. Frantic, he struggled to his feet despite his broken leg. The temperature at the ceiling was by then well more than 1,500 degrees and his hair burst into flame, followed an instant later by his clothes. He staggered toward the door, fire in his eyes. They shriveled in their sockets and his lungs cooked with his last breaths, seared from the inside out. He screamed and staggered—a human torch—no longer seeing where he was going. He ran into a wall, knocking himself unconscious—a small blessing as his flesh bubbled under the flames.

Ice cream was being served on the main deck, one level above the lamp room. Children from all over the boat were converging on the refreshment stand when a sudden eruption of flame caught a group of mothers and children, who had been watching the huge Fletcher engine thunder and thump. Clothes ablaze, they ran out of the engine room and into the area where the ice cream was being served, fire following them in hungry gulps, swallowing those who had fallen and panicking the rest.

Mike and Ginny had taken the stairs to the promenade deck two levels above the fire. They tried not to feed the panic of the growing catastrophe below, the sounds of the commotion and the shouting drowned out by the rushing wind and the intervening decks. They held each other silently, side by side, as they passed Wards Island. "They'll ground the ship, maybe after we pass Hell's Gate," Mike said, pointing to the channel they were passing through, where the East River and the Long Island Sound met. "We'll be safe. We'll get off. Don't worry."

"But, Mike, the fire spread so fast!"

A black billow of smoke caught Mike's attention, an ugly cloud rising from the forward stair. "They're burning the chowder again," someone joked in the crowd, prompting a round of nervous laughter.

"Ginny, come with me, hurry," he said, moving forward on the promenade deck as far toward the bow as they could get. The dread in his eyes was as horrifying to Ginny as any amount of smoke.

A piercing shriek, carrying up from somewhere below, cut through the crowd's denial, a hot knife of terror, severing all attempts at calm. The crowd erupted, mothers scrambling, shouting the names of their children and relatives. There was no order, no direction from the crew, nothing to stem the tide of panic that suddenly gripped the passengers. Infants screamed, old people and young were knocked to the deck, everyone was running in different directions.

The smoke had started to obscure the deck and people seemed to materialize from the swirling haze only to disappear again. It was clear though that the forward momentum of the ship was pushing the smoke toward the stern.

"The children!" Ginny shouted to Mike above the clamor of hundreds of running feet, shouts, and screams.

Mike stood, uncertain what to do. The idea of joining the panicked mob sent a chill through him. And leaving Ginny with the Bottler still somewhere on the ship was a terrible risk. All around people who had been laughing, chatting, and playing in the sunshine moments before were now fighting over life vests, pulling them from overhead racks, snatching them from outstretched hands, tying them on children. "Gin, they could be anywhere."

"But, Mike."

"Ginny, I don't want to lose you again!" Mike shouted. "I won't. Understand? No matter what happens, we go together. We'll need to get down to the main deck, where we can jump off easier. Come on!"

Ginny nodded, wide-eyed, but resolute.

They fought their way down the stairs to the main deck while everyone was scrambling to go up, Mike elbowing his way through the knots of frantic passengers. The heat on the stairs was building, the smoke so thick and choking they had to feel their way, holding their breath. At the bottom they saw the flames, leaping from the stairs at the opposite side of the ship, mushrooming to the ceiling and spreading in waves, an inverted ocean of fire. A woman, her hair and dress engulfed in flame, ran past them with a screaming infant in her arms and disappeared over the side. They tripped over prostrate forms on the deck, people trampled in the panic, some moaning and incoherent, some silent. They hesitated, wanting to help, but a glance at the raging beast at their backs pushed them forward. Mike felt the *Slocum* shudder, the engine advancing into a full gallop, vibrating the deck beneath their feet.

"C'mon, the captain's gonna beach her!"

They ran forward, but were stopped by a huge knot of people trying to pull life vests from a storage area in the ceiling. Held up by strong wire mesh and painted countless times, the wires would not budge. Mike let go of Ginny's hand and jumped up, catching hold of the wire. He hung, kicking and jerking, until his fingers bled and his arms felt like they'd pull from their sockets. Finally the wire ripped away, dumping a heap of life vests on the floor. The mob fell on them with a ferocity unlike anything he had ever seen. Women gouged and tore at each other, men punched and kicked and literally threw women and children aside. Mike saw a woman tear a life vest off a child to put it on her own. A man, flailing wildly, grabbed an armful before disappearing into the smoke. But one thing was immediately clear— the vests were mostly useless, the fabric moldy and rotten. Often the vests tore open or the belts and buckles pulled away. Clouds of cork dust spilled from them, powdering the deck. Mike grabbed one anyway and managed to get it on Ginny as they moved forward to the bow, where the wind whipped the smoke away.

"Ginny, we might have to swim!" he shouted over the tumult. "Can you swim? Ginny?"

She was almost unable to respond. The horrors they'd witnessed in the space of just a few minutes left her numb, speechless. She knew that if Mike had not been there, she'd have gone mad like the rest and even now in the relative shelter of the bow, she felt like screaming. "A little," she said at last before covering her eyes. Looking back over Mike's shoulder she could see the flames like a wall now from one side of the boat to the other. She watched as a woman, frantic and screaming for her children, dashed into the flames and disappeared, while others, sometimes alone, sometimes in groups, began to jump over the side to the cold death offered by the river.

A keening wail rose from the *Slocum*, the pain and despair of 1,300 souls. It went out over the water to either shore. They could see tugs, launches, rowboats, and pleasure craft racing toward them, but the *Slocum* did not slow. The increased speed fanned the flames, pushing them back toward the stern. The cries from the back of the vessel cut through the veil of fire.

"Esther and the kids!" Ginny shouted.

Ginny almost started to run off, but Mike stopped her. "Gin, you have to stay here! Please, you have to! I'll never find you otherwise." He looked at the wall of smoke and fire, knowing that there was no possibility of getting through it. There were well more than a hundred people around them, all in frantic motion, searching for loved ones and children, fighting over useless life vests, some jumping overboard or hanging from the railings over the side of the ship. Esther and her children could have been within feet of them and not be seen. Nevertheless they searched through the crowd, meeting within a minute at the bow with no results. "Ginny, stay here! Promise me you'll stay. It's the safest place. When the captain grounds the boat it'll probably be bow in, so the water'll be shallow. Just hang on. I'll be back."

But Mike couldn't leave. The terror in Ginny's eyes had him holding her tight and he couldn't let go. She was shaking, her whole body trembling. He encircled her in the muscled cocoon of his arms, but he knew in his heart there was little he could do to keep her safe. He felt the best he could do was to share her fate, and hope. "I can't leave you, Gin. I'm sorry, but I just can't."

She pulled back a little. "Mike," she said in as calm a voice as she could muster, "I'll be all right. I'll stay right here. I know you'll come back for me, so I won't move. Okay? But those kids and Esther, they have nobody here, Mike, nobody to save them, not like I have you. So you go, but make sure you come back. No matter what. And here I'll be."

Mike didn't believe her, but he felt he had to try. What good would it do if he saved her only to lose her to regret and recrimination, to subject their bonds to a slow, acidic erosion of guilt? He'd rather die than risk that. He broke their embrace and kissed her, saying, "Promise me you'll be here. Promise me!"

"I do. I promise."

Mike turned, unable to look at her longer. Climbing on the railing, he reached up and pulled himself up one of the many posts that supported the promenade deck above. With a heave and a kick of his feet, he disappeared.

The scene on the promenade deck was every bit as nightmarish as below, the passengers berserk with fear, the crew nowhere in sight. Life vests lay shredded on the deck, powdered cork blowing with the heat waves. He watched as mothers threw their children overboard, vests strapped tight. Hardly any of them came back to the surface.

Swimming, especially for women, was a rare skill. The waters of the East River were no sanctuary, life vests or no. But the river offered a less excruciating way to die, and the hope, however faint, was that someone might pluck them out of the water. Whole groups clung to the rails, the wind whipping their hair and clothes, waiting until the heat forced them to let go. Mike couldn't see the back of the boat, but knew it had to be bad, the wind blowing the flames back. He looked down the ship's side and saw dozens clinging to the side, more thrashing the water, and bodies just floating in their wake.

Mike scrambled about the deck as fast as he could, trying his best to find Esther or her children, but they were not among that mob. It seemed as though he might be able to make his way to the stern on the starboard side, where just then the smoke seemed less dense. He started in that direction, trying to blot out the scenes around him, the small knot of women and children praying on their knees, the child with her hair singed to the scalp, the people trampled underfoot, the young girl he saw standing paralyzed as a yellow eruption of flame overtook her.

But in the minute or so that had passed, the fire had broken through the deck and ate its way toward him at an alarming speed. The heat was almost unbearable. Covering his face, he was forced back, smelling his hair singe. A fresh chorus of screams erupted from the crowd. A whole section of the deck gave way and for an instant Mike could see down the gaping maw of the beast, a shimmering, writhing thing with yellow fangs and a thousand red tongues. He fell back, beating his jacket and head where he smoldered, his face felt like it was on fire, his eyebrows burned off completely.

He stumbled back toward the bow, doubting if he'd even get back to Ginny. The *Slocum* was still running at full throttle, the shoreline on either side streaking by. It was as if the captain had lost his mind, dooming them all instead of beaching the boat. Mike made his way toward the rail near the bow, looking for a way to climb back down to Ginny. But the rails were packed four and five deep and he could not bring himself to punch his way through the terrified wall of women and children as he'd seen another man do. Searching for any way down, he turned back, going to the other side and closer to the fire where the mob was thinning, the heat blistering, passengers going over the rail almost continuously. Looking back, Mike was brought up short. Little Emily was standing with her brother Josh in hand, their clothes singed, hair wild and burnt.

Mike ran to them. "Kids, where's your mom?" They couldn't answer, they just shook their heads and stared back at the advancing flames, mesmerized, in shock. "Come on," he said and lifted them both, shoving his way toward the rail.

The mob around Ginny was beyond all control and reason, pressing against the railing, climbing over one another to throw themselves or their children into the river. Ginny couldn't breathe. A mass of humanity pressed her against the rail. She grew faint, the crushing weight reducing her to painful gasps as the rail bit into her ribs. Losing consciousness, her knees began to buckle, but she could not fall, held up by the screaming mass. Then with the groan of splintering wood and tearing metal, the railing gave way and she tumbled into space. She had a brief impression of the impact, thinking she'd fallen on land, the water hitting her head with surprising force. There was a moment of muffled, liquid suspension and a half lungful of water before she bobbed up, shocked and choking. She didn't see the *Slocum*'s paddlewheel bear down on her, didn't feel the flaming monster strike her and drag her under.

Mike, on the deck above, was now in an even greater crush. The fire had gone up through the boat, then spread fore and aft. The space left to the passengers was diminishing by the second, the fire advancing in leaps, sending a lick of flame through the deck, followed a few seconds later by a volcanic eruption. Driven mad by the heat and fear, some actually ran into the fire or cow-ered before it, letting it consume them. The stench of burning flesh, the terror and madness had some vomiting uncontrollably. Mike did what he could, trying to pass children to the front, fas-ten life vests, though he knew they were of little use. He found a few that seemed to be in slightly better condition, making sure that Josh and Emily got those. But the fire came on and the space left was becoming too hot to bear, forcing more over the side. He didn't notice the island they were headed toward until they hit it with a grinding crunch.

Within seconds there were boats of every description ringing the *Slocum*. Tugs, launches, a rowboat with a cop in it, a fireboat and pleasure craft from the Bronx Yacht Club all converged on her, some nosing against her side to take people off. But the fire still forced many to jump. A group of mothers and children went over the rail and Mike found himself pressed against it by the crowd behind. He saw that the bow was only twenty feet from the shore and was preparing to somehow climb down to Ginny, feeling sure that they'd finally find safety. Leaning out, he could see people on the deck below tumbling overboard through the broken railing where Ginny had been and was al-most hit by someone jumping from the hurricane deck above. He tried to climb down, but with the children in his arms it was impossible.

He was forced over, hitting the water headfirst, striking more than one person who'd jumped before. The children slipped from his grasp. He surfaced, fighting his way through arms and legs, thrashing, grappling, punching. He was immediately pulled under by two women, who fought over him, dragging them all down in their hysteria.

Choking, he thrashed to the surface only to have a leg crash across his shoulder, driving him under again and nearly knock-ing him unconscious. But that jumper had fallen on one of the women and when Mike came up, he was able to wrestle the other one off. He had to practically beat her into submission to stop her frantic struggling, pulling her toward shore.

Then he saw Josh and Emily clinging to a woman, a body really, for she was just floating motionless. He swam to them and they tried to climb on his back, carrying him under again, small arms wrapped around his neck. Mike very nearly gave up then and sank under their weight, floating down to the river bottom. He was surprised to feel rocks beneath his feet, surprised that it was not as deep down as he'd thought. With a wrenching struggle and a push off from the bottom, he used the last of his strength to gain the surface, two pairs of arms and legs clinging to his back. Choking, he realized the woman had disappeared and struggled toward the shore with the children.

Mike found after a few strokes that he could stand and he let the children loose to scramble toward the rocky beach. Exhausted and spitting up water, he stood, hands on his knees, trying to regain his strength. He looked back at the *Slocum* and the surrounding river. The surface boiled, thrashed into foam by the drowning mass. The *Slocum* towered above, flames shooting skyward with volcanic intensity. Ginny was out there. He tried to call her name, but retched up a quantity of water instead. He dove back in and stroked out into the river. Almost immediately he had no choice, but to rescue the closest child, who lunged at him with a last desperate effort and grabbed his jacket, not letting go.

He dragged the child to shore and plunged back in again, his strength waning, but the drive to find Ginny overcoming his weakness. He pulled a woman in next but was forced to rest, so exhausted he could barely stand. He dove in once more, tortured by the screams of the drowning.

Countless times, Mike called Ginny's name, losing count of the lifeless bodies he swam past, sometimes turning them over to see their faces, in terror that it might be her. But there was no reply to his calls and no sign of her anywhere. Mike almost gave up while pulling a girl to shore who'd sunk her teeth into his collar and wrapped her arms so tightly around his neck that he could barely breathe. He was beginning to thrash, unable to stay afloat any longer, when his foot touched bottom and with a final surge he dragged the girl to the beach, collapsing on the rocks.

Slowly, the *General Slocum*'s decks started to collapse one on the other, trapping or crushing those still on board. Many were pulled from the water, or had jumped onto one of the tugs that braved the flames to get close enough. The thrashing of the waters faded and all who could be saved were either ashore or on the boats. An unreal stillness settled over the scene, the screams and cries dying away and only the roar of the fire left.

Mike vomited up water until his gut ached. He crouched on the rocky beach, his head in his hands. He heard a shout and looked up. There on the top deck, a boy of no more than six or seven could be seen climbing the flag pole, chased by the flames. Inching up, he managed to escape his fate for a few moments as the flagpole wavered and swayed. Mike watched in horror as people on the beach called for him to hold on though there was no possible means of rescue. With a groan from the survivors on the beach, the flagpole finally fell, pitching the *General Slocum*'s last passenger into the heart of the furnace.

47

WHITE SHOES. THEY were the first thing that registered in Mike's exhausted brain when he came to. He hadn't realized that he'd collapsed again, lying facedown on the rocky shore, his feet in the surf. The white shoes said, "Here! This one's alive!" and they were joined by another pair and another. They turned him over and pushed on his chest and put something under his nose that had him coughing and spitting up more water than he'd have thought possible.

"Where is this?" he managed to ask.

"North Brother Island," the white shoes said. "Are you burned?"

"Maybe." Mike couldn't actually tell. No part of him felt as it should. "Ginny!" The name burst out of him, a spasmodic reflex of despair and hope.

With help, he got to his feet, where he swayed and looked about at the shore. Dozens of nurses tended to the survivors or labored over the dying. Rows of bodies lined the beach in the surf. Doctors in white coats bent over the worst cases. Rescuers helped put people ashore, but more often carried bodies up the beach and over the seawall.

"Who are you? How'd you get here so fast? Where's Ginny? I had two children, Emily and Josh. Have you seen them?"

"We're from Riverside Hospital, sir, it's on the island here. Come, you've been burned." They helped him up the shore and sat him on the grass with a crowd of other passengers, some wide-eyed with shock, some with blistered hands and blackened faces, some who just appeared wet. There were infants and children, mothers stiff with shock, grandparents lying exhausted, parents wandering, calling the same names over and over, but whatever their state or condition, their eyes told the same story. Mike didn't take the time to think what his eyes looked like, or if they'd ever stop reflecting the horrors he'd witnessed.

"Ginny," he called and hauled himself to his feet. "Ginny!" He began the dreadful search, stumbling from one body to the next, one stunned passenger to another. He stopped for a moment behind a priest giving last rites to a dead girl of no more than four or five, her face composed as if asleep on the grass. A nurse nearby was covering the body of a woman with an infant clutched to her breast. Mike looked away and started to sob, the cries wracking his body, doubling him over with uncontrollable spasms. He stumbled away, unable to call Ginny's name any longer.

All over the lawn at North Brother Island, cries of joy at a relative found alive mixed with sobs of anguish over the dead. There was no sign of Josh or Emily, so Mike moved through the bodies, looking at each as they were brought in, sometimes jostled by desperate passengers, frantic for even the worst of news. It was clear that Ginny was not among the survivors there, but he clung to the hope that she'd been rescued by a boat and had found her way to another shore, another hospital. Doctors and nurses from Lincoln and Lebanon hospitals, from Harlem Hospital and Bellevue, hundreds of them had arrived within an hour. Countless vessels had plucked survivors from the *Slocum* or out of the river. Mike knew that Ginny could be almost anywhere. Still, he searched among the dwindling number of bodies being brought to shore and each time it proved to be someone else his heart gave a guilty leap of hope.

After many long, fruitless hours, Mike left the island with a group of other survivors aboard a tug named the *Massasoit* and was deposited at a pier at 138th Street, where a police wagon drove some to the nearest train station. Mike rode the train south, figuring he'd start at Bellevue, where the city morgue was located. Other passengers on the El cast uneasy glances at him, but he saw nothing, felt nothing. Not even the insistent throb of his burns broke through his fixated mind. He had to find Ginny, wherever she was and bring her home. Mike shuffled through Bellevue, checking the wards and morgue, then continued on, working his way uptown, hour after hour, checking hospital after hospital, to Harlem and to the police station at Alexander Avenue, where another man searching for his family told him a temporary morgue had been set up, then to Lebanon and Lincoln hospitals, where again he walked the wards and viewed the dead.

Everywhere he went he saw a steady stream of men searching for lost wives, children, mothers, relatives. They collected at hospital doorways, police stations, and piers, a desperate band combing the city for what they hoped they would not find. It was at the police station that Mike realized there was another yet to be found—the Bottler. He wasn't concerned with McManus. He'd heard the man's final scream, had seen the flames roar sideways out the lamp room door. No man could have lived through that.

Hours crawled by, Mike's remaining energy trickling away, drained by alternating hope and despair. He collapsed at Lincoln Hospital. It was well past eight, nearly ten hours after the first cries of "Fire!" A nurse revived him, rebandaged his burned hands, and put a salve of some sort on his face. She gave him a cup of strong, black coffee and a sandwich, which he gulped down, suddenly realizing he hadn't eaten in more than twelve hours. He resumed his trek, almost immediately running into a man searching for his family, who told him that a temporary morgue had been set up at the Charities Pier at Twenty-sixth Street, not far from Bellevue. Mike headed south again, riding the El, feeling like he was lost in a Coney Island house of horrors, unable to escape.

The Charities Pier was a cavernous, enclosed space, with a high, vaulted ceiling supported by spidery steel trusses. It was mobbed by upwards of ten thousand people. The line to view the dead stretched for blocks, but Mike didn't wait. He flashed his badge at one of the dozens of officers forming a blue wall around the pier and was admitted with a nod. The bodies were laid out in plain, wooden coffins, and elevated somewhat at the head for viewing. Two long rows stretched down the pier into the distance. Mike joined a group of fifty, the number admitted at any one time. Some visitors were nearly out of their minds. Women sobbed and fainted, one man went to three different coffins, sobbing uncontrollably, claiming they were each his wife. Mike had witnessed the police restrain two men who were driven mad with grief, watched woodenly as they were stopped from jumping into the river, one silent, the other screaming that he wanted to die and join his family.

Numb, Mike walked the long rows, his shoes splashing in water from the melting ice, that each body was packed in up to the chin, like fish at the Fulton Market. He saw Ginny in each dead face, sensed her presence among the hopeless searchers. He felt a strange, awful kinship with the people around him, like a family; a common thread binding them all in a bloodline of pain and loss.

Mike went through the line again. After a while the faces started looking the same, even the small girl who'd drowned clutching a kitten. Ginny was not there. But as he talked to other searchers he found his predicament was horribly common. Hundreds were still missing. Many men had been searching all evening, going to the same hospitals, police stations, and morgues he had, and like him still had not found their loved ones. And the Bottler was still out there; Mike hadn't seen his face among the dead. And if he was alive, the Bottler was probably looking for him as well. He'd have a score to settle if he still lived. Mike resolved to be more cautious than he'd been so far, hardly even noticing those around him. Mike stopped at the tables set up for the coroner's office, where death certificates were being filled out as fast as they could be written and bodies released to anxious relatives and harried undertakers. There were more than five hundred still unaccounted for he was told, but the search had been called off for the night. There would be no more recovered until morning. Mike went to Bellevue and slept in a chair for a few torturous hours. He could not imagine going home to his bed. It seemed a violation, a betrayal of trust. He had no right to be in a bed while Ginny was out there. Alone.

He was up again at five A.M. and ate a quick, bleary breakfast at a local shop that catered to nurses and orderlies. The *Slocum* was on everyone's lips, and in every headline. It was for Mike a continuing and inescapable nightmare. He hurried his meal and stopped in a store to buy a bowler. He still had the glasses he'd worn yesterday and although his fake beard was lost, his own had grown to a rich brown stubble in the last two days. If the Bottler was alive, he'd be searching for Mike and for McManus, too. Mike was determined not to be surprised again.

It was early morning and the temporary morgue was set to open in ten minutes. Mike walked past the lengthening line of searchers, bowler low over his eyes. He was about to use his badge to get in like he had before, when a hand shot out of the crowd and clutched at his sleeve. He whirled about, one hand on the butt of the Colt.

"Mike?"

It was Ginny. Mike felt as though he'd been hit in the gut and almost collapsed. The blood drained from his head like a waterfall, crashing to a pool of oblivion. "Is it you? Is it really you, Gin? I've looked for hours and hours. I thought you were dead." Stumbling, he led Ginny away from the crowd and to a nearby oyster shop, all the while whispering. But he didn't hug her until they were inside, away from prying eyes.

"It's me, Mike," Ginny said over and over, her head buried against his neck. Mike stroked her hair with trembling hands, hardly believing his own senses. "It's me," she said again. "I'm sorry I broke my promise. I'll never leave you again. Never! I can't believe I found you. We're alive. My God, we're alive."

Mike stepped back to look at her again. She had a nasty bruise on her head, running across the right side of her forehead, and blackening her eye. He put a gentle hand to it. "What happened? I saw that the rail you were at collapsed, then I got pushed over, too."

Ginny told him all she knew, which was really very little. She'd gone over when the rail gave way and didn't remember more than that, except waking up in the bottom of a small boat. Two men in a rowboat had plucked her from the water and after she'd regained consciousness she'd been taken to Lebanon Hospital, but they'd released her after just a couple of hours, as they were overwhelmed with far worse cases than hers. Like Mike, she'd spent the hours after searching for him as well as Esther and the children.

"I saved the children," Mike told her. "I carried them to shore, but I lost them in the crowd when I went back out to find you. You haven't seen them?"

"No, I even went to Esther's apartment, but nobody was there. Her husband is probably out looking like everyone else. Maybe they got returned to him and they're with their grandparents or something. Thank God they're safe though." Ginny hugged Mike again as if to reassure herself that he was real. "I thought I'd never see you again." Tears streaked her dirty cheeks. She kissed him as they waited for coffee. "What about the Bottler?"

"The Bottler's not accounted for."

"I recognized him," Ginny said. "Just before they surprised us, I saw him beside me, but couldn't remember who he was. I do now. He was with Johnny Suds that day at Miss Gertie's."

"And that Carl; the guy they mentioned. You knew him?" Mike said.

"Not really. He was hanging around the Triangle factory, trying to sweet-talk me. I met him two days before you got shot."

Mike absorbed this and didn't ask for more. Instead he said, "You need to go someplace safe. You can't be seen with me around here. They may be watching. That guy Carl is still alive and if the Bottler is too, you're in danger. Unless they can confirm that I'm dead and you too, they'll know they're still in trouble. I want you to go to my father's house. My God! My parents! I haven't telephoned them. They must be going crazy. You haven't seen them, have you?"

"No."

"Okay. I'm going to telephone them. They'll expect you." Ginny started to protest, but Mike stopped her. "You have to go, Gin. We barely got away with our lives before. I will not let that happen again."

"I don't want to leave you, Mike. Not now, not ever again."

"God, I don't want you to go either, but it seems like the only way to be sure you're safe, and I won't have it any other way." He hugged her hard as their coffees arrived. Mike looked over her shoulder and saw the long line stretching from the morgue.

48

ANOTHER DAY PASSED, twenty-four hours of frozen faces and dwindling hopes. Hearses shuttled continuously to the Charities Pier, sometimes taking away four caskets at a time. Embalmers worked around the clock to handle the crisis. Mike slept on benches and doorsteps and ate only when he could no longer ignore his growling stomach. He had at last been forced to do what he'd dreaded deep in his bones. There were thirty bodies held at the city morgue proper, victims burned beyond recognition, bodies deemed too gruesome for public viewing. He met Tom there and they walked through like dead men, Mike still wearing the clothes he'd worn on the *Slocum*, his bandages dirty and tattered. He saw all thirty, saw what a blast furnace could do to a human body. He forced himself to look more closely, to examine the blackened flesh, the teeth for any clue. One was surely Jack McManus, but the body was burned so badly he could never be positive.

There was one he lingered over, a woman according to the coroner. It could have been Esther, but there wasn't enough left of her to be certain. He'd promised Ginny he'd keep up the search, but he'd seen Esther for only a few minutes and among all the many dead faces he'd already viewed, there was no way he could have been certain, even if he saw her. A part of him wished for it to be her if only to end her family's torment.

It was late that evening, around nine, when Mike decided to go through the dead at the Charities Pier again. He had heard there were another couple of bodies brought in while he was at the Bellevue morgue and he hoped one of them was the Bottler. Tom had returned to his station house a couple of hours before to send out a description of the Bottler to the other precincts, describing him as a dangerous fugitive. He also sent two cops to Carl Woertz's fleabag hotel, with orders to pick him up, too.

Again, Mike was admitted to the Charities Pier at the flash of his badge and began to shuffle down the dwindling aisles of dead. The same frozen faces swam before his eyes. He wondered if those faces would ever leave him. He feared that they'd always haunt his dreams, floating up from the depths of the river, or materializing through a veil of fire. He shuddered and forced himself to look harder. He'd spoken with Ginny after Tom had left, and assured her that he was still looking for Esther. He tried to persuade Mary that he was fine, which, of course, he was not. She told him to come home with Tom. He'd pick him up and she'd prepare him a good meal. Mike's stomach churned at the thought.

Tom arrived back at the Charities Pier while Mike shuffled past the remaining bodies. Primo was with him, and they hugged with reddened eyes to see each other again.

"I am so happy you are okay, you bastard. And your Ginny, too. You are a lucky Irishman, no?"

"I don't feel so lucky," Mike said. He resolved at last to go, and turned toward the door. It was far off, at the end of the pier, but the bright lights inside cast enough brilliance to make it appear as bright as day. The Bottler was in that doorway, mixed with the crowd of searchers. Their eyes locked, and then he was gone.

Mike's feet splashed in the water on the pier's floor as he sprinted toward the door, men and women calling to him to slow down, have some respect, cops thinking he was about to leap into the river. Tom and Primo were left far behind, shouting for him to stop. Two cops wrestled him to the floor, rolling about until Tom and Primo managed to convince them of who he was, Mike pushing his badge in their faces, cursing in frustration. Precious minutes were lost, and Mike was soaked by the time they hit the street.

He stopped, looking north, then south, water raining off his hair, seeing nothing of the Bottler, only a long line of the hopeless, seeking to confirm what they already knew. A few reporters still buzzed like flies, harrying the weary, the childless, the motherless for quotes for tomorrow's headlines. Mike went to one who was closest to the door.

"Hey, you see a guy just leave here, seemed like he was in a hurry? Mustache? Heavy fella with hairy arms?"

"Sure," the reporter said. "Went south a minute ago."

Mike started to run, not knowing where exactly, but he was brought up short by the blast of a horn. It was Tom at the tiller of his Olds, now repaired and shining in the lamplight. He and Primo had run to get it without Mike even noticing.

Mike ran toward the Olds. "The Bottler, he's headed south, let's go!" He hopped up on the engine box behind the seat, shouting, "Go! Go!" and holding on to the seat rail as they picked up speed, the Olds moving slower than he hoped it would.

"It is good again, no?" Primo shouted over the chugging engine. Mike grabbed his head in both hands and kissed him on the cheek. They laughed into the wind. Mike pulled the Colt and chambered a round, barely managing to hold on as the Olds bucked over the cobbles.

"Where the hell is he?" Tom shouted. "Is he on foot or what?"

"Don't know. I only saw him inside for a second," Mike answered. "A guy said he'd gone this way." Tom drove on, looking for anything suspicious.

"There!" Mike cried a few moments later, pointing with the Colt. Up ahead, about two blocks, a horse-drawn ambulance rumbled at an unusually fast clip and a face appeared at the edge of the wagon body, peering back. The ambulance picked up speed, the horse whipped to a gallop. Tom pressed the speeder as far as it would go, Mike now kneeling on the engine box, holding on to their shoulders for support.

They'd already gone ten blocks down South Street, and Fourteenth Street went by a moment later, the ships and docks thickening as they went. There was little traffic and they were able to fly southward, closing the gap with each block they passed, weaving to avoid the occasional wagon, carriage or pedestrian. They passed Houston, Stanton, Rivington, and Delancey, narrowing the distance to less than a block. Mike extended the Colt, but Tom said, "Not yet. You won't get a good shot."

"Fuck it." Mike fired, the blasts ringing their ears, splinters flying off the back doors of the wagon. He emptied the Colt in one long burst of bullets, the hot casings flying into the night, tinkling off the cobbles. Before the last bullet flew, the wagon began to veer left then right and an instant later, a body slipped off one side and under the rear wheels, kicking the rear up as the wagon turned and spilling it forward, the horse screaming and flailing with its hooves, falling sideways. The wagon and horse crashed, sliding across the cobbles, the horse kicking, sparks flying from the hubs as they ground across the stone.

The Bottler was up an instant later from the overturned wagon, running toward the docks. Mike's Colt was empty. Primo and Tom both fired after him, but he ran on without slowing as Tom brought the Olds to a stop.

"Who the hell is that?" Mike said as they got out near the

body. Tom ran over, holding his pistol on the unmoving form. "It's Carl Woertz, that pimp," Tom said, and with a kick, added, "I think he's dead."

Mike slipped another clip of ammunition into the Colt and started after the Bottler, who had disappeared among the densely packed shoreline—canal barges, schooners, steamers, fishing boats, oyster barges, dry docks, and piers forming an almost unbroken maze south to the tip of Manhattan. He saw a figure in the moonlight scurry across the deck of a low oyster boat, jumping across a narrow gap to another. Mike followed with Tom, while Primo covered the shoreline. Primo was still in no shape to be jumping and clamoring from ship to ship. Still, with gun drawn, he was able to block an escape back into the streets of the city. A patrolman, drawn by the shooting, joined Primo a moment later and after a brief conversation, they spread out, forming an even greater barrier.

Mike made the leap onto the oyster boat with Tom fast behind. They had lost sight of the Bottler and went forward warily, one covering the other as they leapt to the next boat. A dry dock was ahead and a fishing schooner was in it, looming above the other ships, well out of the water. As Mike leapt to the next boat, shots rang out from the edge of the dry dock, flashes of light momentarily illuminating the Bottler. The bullets whizzed by, close enough to drop him and Tom to the deck. When they got up, cautiously peering over the bulwark, the Bottler was gone.

"That was fucking close," Tom said. "Nearly parted my goddamn hair."

"Yeah," Mike said, unconcerned. He was more worried about losing the Bottler in this maze of ships. He ran forward and, using a rope, swung across to the dry dock's edge, where he clung for a dangerous moment until he got his feet under him. He crouched low, looking under the hull of the schooner, the huge

314

ship, towering above, was held there by massive blocks of oak. It was as black as coal under the ship and the creeping, wet hand of fear slid down Mike's spine as he held the Colt in shaking hands.

Tom joined him a moment later. "I ain't goin' in there," he said sensibly. "And you ain't either. It's a dead end. Only way out is up onto the ship. Let's check the other side."

They could hear the roar of a steam screw tug coming up-river against the tide as they rounded the other side of the dry dock and looked south. A floating grain elevator loomed next to a row of canal barges, full of grain from Buffalo and Syracuse, sent down the Erie Canal for shipment to Europe.

"There!" Tom said while the roar of the tug grew louder.

A flitting shadow moved across from one barge to the next. They jumped again to the deck of a barge, rolling as they fell. Another shot cracked the night and pinged against something metallic, but neither Tom nor Mike shot back. They positioned themselves behind the rear of a small cabin at the back of the barge.

"Hold on," Mike whispered. "See that grain elevator?" It loomed maybe three or four stories high, a big, rectangular building on a barge. "He's got to jump to that or he's trapped."

The roar of the tug receded upriver as Mike and Tom held their positions, guns ready. The barges began to rock, riding the swells of the tug, the river lapping and splashing against their hulls, pilings grinding, wood-on-wood, an eerie creaking and moaning of unseen origins went up.

The shadow moved again, and made its leap for the grain elevator. Mike and Tom fired two, three, four times, and the shadow fell short. Mike had a last glimpse as he ran to the canal barge alongside the grain elevator. He saw the Bottler hanging to the edge of the hull, struggling to pull himself up. But the adjoining canal barge swung back against it with irresistible, grinding force, rocked by the oily swell. The Bottler didn't move fast enough. There was a single, gurgling scream and he disappeared between them. When they again separated, the Bottler was gone under the black surface of the river.

Mike woke on the floor of his parlor, his head on his arm, a blanket across him. He had no recollection of how he got home that night. He looked at his clock. It was nearly ten A.M. Slowly, painfully, he rolled to his knees and stumbled to his feet, where he swayed as if in a strong wind. He stank of smoke and sweat, burnt hair and vomit. For the first time he was actually conscious of it, and revolted by his condition. He looked at his sofa and was amazed to see Ginny under one of his mother's handmade blankets, sleeping peacefully. Mike had to rub his eyes to be sure of what he was seeing, but he did not wake her. There was a part of him that feared she might disappear.

Shuffling into the bathroom, he looked at himself in the mirror and recoiled from his reflection. His face was a mottled red, his eyebrows were gone and his hair was wild and burnt nearly to the scalp in places. Soot and dirt streaked his cheeks and brow. Oddly, the wounds on his cheeks seemed almost to blend in. He shook his head and began to cry over the sink, holding the white porcelain in his blistered hands so that he wouldn't fall. He didn't actually know why, a combination of relief, weariness, and enough pain to last a lifetime, he supposed.

But Mike had few tears left in him and things to do before the day was done. It was already late. He called to Ginny and went to her side at the sofa, kneeling to hold her as she woke, and telling her again that he'd never let go as she laid a warm cheek against his.

They left his apartment an hour later, Ginny at his side, wearing a black dress Mary had given her. He'd had a hot bath and Ginny had cut his hair so it was almost even, and shaved him over a steaming bowl. He hailed a cab and they got in. "Lutheran Cemetery, Queens," he told the driver.

The line of hearses and carriages stretched to the horizon. Impatient, and in pain from his burns, Mike ordered the driver to take alternate routes, but time after time their progress was slowed by the tide of grief breaking over Queens. They had already missed a number of funerals and Mike felt that failing acutely. He could not have put into words his need to attend them. It was almost a compulsion, a driving force that would not let him rest, a longing for some kind of an end to this nightmare. He felt that if he let these rites slip by unobserved, that they might never have the opportunity to stand over a grave, cast flowers on a casket, and hear the graveside reassurance of resurrection. They'd agreed on the need to go, to say a prayer, and to offer their hidden, guilty thanks that it had not been their day to die.

He supposed that in some way he held himself accountable for the *General Slocum* fire. Ginny felt it, too. "We didn't start the fire, Mike, but I still feel like there had to be something we could have done, something different." Her voice trailed off and Mike knew the depth of her doubts. "I don't even know anyone except Esther," Ginny said, "and little Josh and Emily, of course. I haven't any idea where they might be. I just know that Esther was listed among the dead."

They arrived at the Lutheran Cemetery at last and followed the first funeral they saw to the grave, where a small, white casket and two larger black ones sat side by side. The service was dignified and short, the minister undoubtedly had others to lay to rest. The mourners slowly scattered, disappearing into draped carriages for the silent ride back to the city.

Mike and Ginny slipped away to attend another, hands held tight. It was madness really, a form of it to be sure, but they

317

repeated the ritual again and again as the day wore on, the stink of lilies imprinting itself so deeply in Mike's brain that he felt sure he would never be able to stand their scent again.

After standing beside an uncounted number of graves, listening to priestly dronings for some hint of solace, Mike and Ginny found themselves standing at the fringe of yet another burial, hardly seeing the black casket, the mourners, the weary priest with the sweat-stained collar. They heard the same words of comfort they'd heard before, but the name of the deceased cut through Ginny's clouded mind, jolting her out of her trance. Esther Claymaan. She looked at the small crowd, many of whom were women, and she suddenly recognized some from the factory.

Mike recognized the change in Ginny, and squeezed her hand tighter, craning over the crowd to see if Josh and Emily were there. At the front there was a man. Mike could only see his back. His hat was in his hand and his head was bowed, shoulders shaking. A few minutes later, when the funeral was at an end, and the mourners began to melt away, Mike and Ginny stepped forward and came near to the man they assumed to be Esther's husband.

"You're Esther's husband? I'm so sorry for your loss," Ginny said, getting a grateful, but somewhat puzzled, look from the man in return. The children stood silently behind their father, their eyes still wide and blank.

"I tried to find Esther," he said wearily, "but I never saw her, until days later at the morgue."

"I'm so sorry," Mike said, not letting go of Ginny's hand, and holding out his other, which was gripped firmly enough to make his burns turn again to fire. "Ginny wanted me to help them so badly, and I . . ." He could not go on, the memories came crashing over him, weakening his knees.

"He saved them," Ginny said. "He saved both of them, pulled them from the burning ship and swam them to shore."

"My God!" He took hold of Mike's hand in both of his, tears starting down his cheeks. "I have you to thank for my children. I . . ." Words left him and he began to sob, collapsing onto Mike's shoulder. Mike held him up and Ginny put a reassuring hand on his shoulder. Finally he raised his head, a bit embarrassed, and asked for Mike's name.

"This is Mike Braddock. Esther may have mentioned him. He's my beau." Ginny said, the phrase sending an unexpected thrill through her. Mike squeezed her hand in return.

"You're Braddock! I'm Frank Claymaan." He started pumping Mike's hand, a strange, sad smile coming over his face. "Esther talked about you and Ginny going on the cruise. She was looking forward to meeting you. She said Ginny was head-over-heels for you. I had the operator try your telephone these last days but I got no answer."

Mike's smile was fleeting. "I haven't been home."

"Emily, sweetie, see who it is?" Frank said.

Emily stepped from behind Frank's legs and looked up at Mike. "Hello, Mister Braddock" she said, a shy smile creeping across her face. Mike was speechless. He started to bend down, but fell to his knees, Frank holding out a hand to steady him. He took Emily in his arms. "I'm so happy to see you," he sputtered, embarrassed by his own weakness. "I was so worried. I couldn't find you."

"I'm sorry you couldn't find me. I wasn't hiding. The nurses took me and Josh."

"No, no, don't be sorry," Mike whispered. "It's not your fault, not your fault." He held her tight with Frank's hand trembling on his shoulder, while Josh started to cry and rub his eyes.

Some way off, out of sight on the other side of a rolling hill, thousands of mourners had gathered for the burial of the unknowns and had commenced to sing "Nearer My God to Thee." The voices swelled, rising up as if from the earth, piercing the hearts of all who heard them.

Postscript

A N IN-DEPTH INVESTIGATION, prompted by public outrage and a campaign by the press to punish those responsible for the *General Slocum* disaster, resulted in a number of indictments, most notably of Captain Van Schaick and Frank Barnaby, president of the Knickerbocker Steamship Company, among others. The subsequent trials revealed a litany of neglect, falsified records, bogus safety inspections, unsafe fire hoses, untrained crewmen, rotting life vests, and inoperable lifeboats. Ultimately, the only person to serve any jail time was Captain Van Schaick. He was sentenced to serve ten years at Sing Sing prison, but was paroled after three. Upon his conviction, Van Schaick said, "The United States Government made me a scapegoat." He died in 1927 at the age of ninety.

The *General Slocum* fire claimed more lives than any other civilian maritime disaster in U. S. history. Eclipsed in the public mind by the sinking of the *Titanic* in 1912, and most recently by the attack on the World Trade Center, the *General Slocum* fire stands alone in the loss of multiple family members, and its devastation of an entire community. The disaster claimed 1,021 lives. Hundreds of the victims were children.

Adella Liebenow Wotherspoon, the last living survivor of the *General Slocum* disaster, died on January 26, 2004, at the age of one hundred. Her two sisters perished on the *General Slocum*, as did two cousins and two aunts. Her mother survived, but was badly burned. She was both the youngest and last living survivor.

A memorial monument was erected over the graves of the sixty-one unknown victims of the *General Slocum* fire in the Lutheran Cemetery in Middle Village, Queens. It stands to this day.